There are none so blind as those who
will not...trust their hearts

Blind to Love

They faced the biggest challenge of their
lives. Could they find the courage to
overcome all barriers and accept what their
hearts were telling them?

Blind to Love

Relive the romance...

*Three emotionally compelling novels by
three of your favorite authors*

About the Authors

EMMA GOLDRICK

was born and raised in Puerto Rico, where she met and married her husband, Bob, a career military man. Thirty years and four children later, they retired and took up nursing and teaching. In 1980 they turned to collaborative writing. They have written over forty books, using Emma's name as their pseudonym. Goldrick hobbies include grandchildren, gardening, reading and travel.

Sadly, in 1996 Bob Goldrick passed away. Emma continues to write in his memory.

CONNIE BENNETT

is a multipublished author. In addition to her twelve Harlequin Superromance novels, this Missouri author has written for Harlequin Intrigue and American Romance. She's also written historical fiction. Connie's books have been critically acclaimed. In 1990 she won the *Romantic Times* Lifetime Achievement Award for Best Romantic Mystery. She's also been nominated for the *Romantic Times* Reviewer's Choice awards, and in 1995 she was a finalist for RWA's RITA Award.

REBECCA WINTERS

is well-known to Harlequin Romance readers. Since 1990 she's written more than twenty titles for the line. In addition, she's now also writing for Superromance. Her third title will be out later this year. Rebecca has been widely recognized for her dramatic, highly emotional and often unusual stories. Honors include a *Romantic Times* award and a Readers' Choice award. In 1995 she was named Utah Writer of the Year.

Blind to Love

EMMA GOLDRICK

CONNIE BENNETT

REBECCA WINTERS

Harlequin Books

TORONTO • NEW YORK • LONDON
AMSTERDAM • PARIS • SYDNEY • HAMBURG
STOCKHOLM • ATHENS • TOKYO • MILAN
MADRID • WARSAW • BUDAPEST • AUCKLAND

HARLEQUIN BOOKS

by Request—BLIND TO LOVE

Copyright © 1997 by Harlequin Books S.A.

ISBN 0-373-20131-1

The publisher acknowledges the copyright holders of the individual works as follows:

IF LOVE BE BLIND
Copyright © 1987 by Emma Goldrick

WHEN I SEE YOUR FACE
Copyright © 1989 by Connie Bennett

BLIND TO LOVE
Copyright © 1989 by Rebecca Winters

CONTENTS

IF LOVE BE BLIND   9
Emma Goldrick

WHEN I SEE YOUR FACE   185
Connie Bennett

BLIND TO LOVE   471
Rebecca Winters

It was a marriage of convenience.
Until he saw his attractive, twenty-seven-year-old
wife...for the first time.

IF LOVE BE BLIND

Emma Goldrick

CHAPTER ONE

PHILOMENA helped the two little girls into their coats and hurried them to the door. The bride and groom had left an hour ago. Little Sally, barely eighteen, going off bravely, her heart in the hands of the boy next door. Samantha, twenty, and her doctor-husband, Albert had been called away long since. Deborah, twenty-one, was waiting on the porch for her two little twins, while husband John brought the car around. The rest of the guests had filtered away into the late afternoon sunshine. That leaves one little Indian, Phil told herself as she leaned tiredly against the door-jamb and waved.

Stillness settled over the house like a shroud. It had never been this quiet before. Never. She smiled at her daydreams, seldom allowed. Miss Practical Pill, the younger girls had often said of her. That was before they could form the 'ph' sound, of course. Later too, when they were feeling just a little bit saucy. Phil smiled at the reminiscence. She brushed her shoulder-length straw-coloured curls away from her neck and walked slowly back into the house.

There was a musty smell about everything. The living-room was crowded with dirty dishes and glasses. The kitchen was awash with clutter. Neither of her younger sisters had thought to stay and help with the clearing-up. They had been conditioned by years of, 'Oh, Phil will do that'. And so she would. But not just yet.

She wandered back into the living-room, fingering the furniture as she went, feeling the metes and bounds of her world with tactile hands. The old armchair sagged to one side, but it was comfortable. She sank into it, and the stillness surrounded her again. *They were all married.* She relaxed against the back of the chair, and the load placed on her shoulders by her mother on her deathbed slipped away. Phil had been seventeen that year. 'Take care of the girls, Phil.' And with that faint whisper her mother had gone.

The wind rattled at a loose shutter. It seemed as if the house were trying to defy her. 'Mother,' she called as loudly as she could, 'have I done well?' Her voice echoed up the old staircase, bounced off the empty upstairs hall, and returned without answer. She hadn't expected any. Philomena Peabody shrugged her shoulders and went to face the cleaning.

She was up at her habitual hour of six the next morning, and it was not until she fumbled her way downstairs that she remembered. There was no school lunch to be made. No early breakfast for the three of them. No laundry to sort and start. Nothing. Her pattern of life had come unstuck. She went out into the warmth slowly. It was mid-February, and the fog clung to the valley as usual. Fog and low clouds were forecast in the local newspaper, the *Sacramento Bee.* Light northerly winds. High in the 50s, low in the 30s. High for the Sacramento River, 5.3 feet at I Street Bridge.

Her elderly Subaru stood bravely beside the house, in the shadow of a few scrawny old olive and almond trees. It was a family joke of sorts. Her grandfather had farmed one hundred and sixty acres. Now it was all reduced to the old house and a half-acre of regrets. Urban sprawl had conquered the rest. Sacramento was expanding beyond its boundaries, and here in Rancho Cordova the future of farming was written plain on the wall.

Phil shook her head. The regrets were all hers. She would have given anything to keep the farm—but bringing up three sisters was expensive, and her talents never had leaned towards farming. She shrugged her shoulders and put it behind her. The treasured old vehicle started at the first touch. She drove slowly over to Folsom Road, and then on to Route Fifty for the long commute. 'Maybe I could get a flat in town,' she mused as she wheeled through the typical California traffic jam. 'Maybe.'

She was still pondering when she came to the turn-off, jockeyed her way over to Fifteenth Street, and made it safely up to P Street. The small modern building that housed Pacific Mines and Metals was just a couple of blocks south of the golden dome of the State capitol building, and parking was always a problem. Which explained why she arrived at her office an hour late to find that the world of work had come unstuck also!

Betty Pervis, young, moderately attractive, and a newcomer to the typing pool, was standing by Phil's supervisory desk, shaking. All the other eight girls in the office were bent over their word-processors, but the tag-ends of wild conversation hung in the air. Phil put an arm around the young girl's shoulders, and laughed wryly at herself as she did so. Here I am, the Spinster Aunt, she thought. Twenty-seven years old, and over the hill!

'I'm never going back up there again,' Betty whimpered. 'Never!'

'Of course not,' Phil encouraged. 'Where?'

'His office,' she hiccupped. 'Mr Wilderman. Never!'

'Of course not. Here, use my chair. Harriet, could you bring Betty a cup of coffee?' Phil bustled aimlessly, knowing that the weeping woman needed time. When the paper coffee-cup arrived she pressed it into the twisting hands.

'Mr Wilderman isn't usually an—an ogre, Betty. He's too old for that. Was he ill, or something?'

'Ill? Foul-mouthed, abusive—and I don't know why you say old. He's—'

The internal telephone rang. Harriet answered it, blushed, and set it down. 'He says—he wants somebody else,' she reported grimly. 'And he's—wow.'

Phil patted Betty's shoulder and looked around the room for volunteers. Every head ducked. 'So all right,' she sighed. 'I'll go myself.' She nodded to Harriet, gesturing in Betty's direction, then picked up a notebook and a handful of pencils. It had been some months since she had taken direct dictation. Just to be on the safe side she reached into her desk drawer for her micro-recorder, and slipped it into the upper pocket of her blazer.

The lift was the only fast-moving thing in the building. It chuckled to a stop on the ninth floor and seemed to spit her out on to the gold carpet. Which reinforced one of Phil's long-held beliefs. *Anybody who was not an engineer rated as nothing in this business, and even the lift knew it!*

It was quiet up here. Even the air-conditioning equipment only dared to whisper. Six widely spaced office doors, all closed, glared at her. 'You can't intimidate me,' she murmured at them as she went down the corridor. An adjacent door opened and two men came out. They stared at her as if they had heard.

The door at the end of the corridor was half open. Phil smoothed down her navy skirt, checked the recorder in the pocket of her jacket, and pushed into the room. She knew the outer office, having visited with Mrs Simmons a time or two, and once had actually substituted for the regular secretary for a couple of days.

The outer office was empty. Mrs Simmons favoured an electronic typewriter. It stood mute, covered, and her desk was bare. So Mrs Simmons was out today. Phil shrugged her shoulders. One piece of the puzzle had just fallen in place. Now, to beard the lion. She moved resolutely forward, taking deep breaths, building confidence. She rubbed the perspiration off her hand before she turned the door knob to the inner office.

The room was dim, with curtains pulled across the four wide windows. A man was slumped in the swivel chair behind the highly polished desk, with his back to her. She took two or three hesitant steps across the thick-pile rug, and stopped. The man, whoever he was, was not Mr Roger Wilderman. *That* worthy was sixty-five, bald on top, slightly rotund. The present occupant of the executive chair sported a full head of raven-black hair. The rest of him was huddled out of sight in the gloom. Phil cleared her throat as loudly as she could manage.

'Well, it's about time.' A deep voice, vibrating off the beige walls. A voice that brooked no arguments. 'Lost your tongue? Dear God, what do we hire these days, a bunch of rabbits? Sit down.'

Bully, Phil commented under her breath. Just the sort of man who required a little trimming. She settled herself into the chair beside his desk. He must have heard the rustle of her skirts, but he did not turn around.

'Letter to McPherson,' he began, and the words flowed. Phil had ten years of practice behind her pencil-point. It skated across the paper just a trifle ahead of his comments, pausing on occasion to let him catch up. Three letters in a row, right off the top of his head. She acknowledged the expertise with a wry grin. With his back turned it was hard to see what notes he was using. He stopped. 'You've got all that?' The tone doubted it.

'Yes,' she said quietly. His chair half-turned, as if he could not believe it, and then returned to its former position.

'A memorandum to the entire staff,' he began. This time he spoke sharply, moving along faster. And at the end of each of the following memoranda, he increased his speed. Phil smiled again, grimly this time. He was waging war, and she had no intention of losing the battle. He stopped to organise his thoughts. Phil tucked her pencils neatly into her pocket, turned on the tape recorder, and settled back. After another ten minutes of racing, he stopped. 'You've got all that?'

'Yes,' she acknowledged. This time the chair turned around all the way, and he sat up out of his slouch.

'You're sure you have all that?'

'Positive.'

'Read me back that last paragraph.'

There was a moment to look him over. There was nothing in him of the Mr Wilderman she knew. Husky, in his early thirties, she thought. A mass of black hair that kept falling down over his right eye. A stern sort of face, that would have been more at home in a Western movie than in a boardroom. And wearing dark glasses!

'Well?' She snapped back to attention. One finger fumbled for the replay button on the recorder in her pocket, and his words rolled off the tape effortlessly. His head came up as he listened, and a smile played at the corners of his mouth. 'Smart,' he commented as the tape came to a hissing end. 'I don't know you, miss?'

'Peabody.' She gave it the New England pronunciation of her ancestors—Pee-buddy. It drew a chuckle.

'Miss Peabody,' he mused. 'You're a long way from New England. An immigrant?'

'Isn't everyone in California?' She was using her most prim voice, a soft contralto. He nodded as if acknowledging the comment.

'And what do you do for me, Miss Peabody?'

'I'm the supervisor of the typing pool,' she returned. 'But I don't do it for you. I do it for Mr Wilderman. I don't know who you are.'

'And that bothers you?'

'Among other things.' The words snapped out as if she were biting their tails off.

'Do I detect a little censure there?' His laughter was a low rumble. Pleasant, but also threatening. Philomena squared her shoulders and plunged into battle almost happily.

'You certainly do hear censure,' she snapped. 'I don't allow anyone in this corporation to yell and curse and storm at my girls!'

'Ah!' That chuckle again. 'Protecting your little lambs, are you, Miss—Peabody?'

'Very definitely,' she returned primly. 'Betty Pervis is downstairs crying. I'll have to send her home. We have a large workload. Failures of this kind by the executive staff cost the corporation money. It's something that's just not done, Mr—whoever you are. In addition, our union contract prohibits this sort of thing, Betty could file a grievance.'

'Ah!' It was almost as if he were licking his lips, relishing the fight to come. 'I do believe you're threatening me, Miss—Peabody. What the devil is your first name? I can't spend all day calling you Miss Peabody.'

'I—I don't think you really want to know,' she murmured.

'That bad, is it? Well, Peabody, I don't take well to threats. Maybe you should have your shop steward contact me.'

'Maybe I should,' she returned bluntly. 'Here I am.'

'Here you am what?' Was there a little laughter behind the words? Phil strained to think, to measure.

'Here I am, the shop steward,' she announced. 'I represent all the clerical and staff employees of this headquarters.'

'And?'

'And I think you owe Betty—Miss Pervis—an apology.'

'Or else? Lay it on the line, lady. I can hear the "or else" hanging in the air.'

'All right, if that's what you want to hear.' She squirmed in her chair. One does not throw lightning bolts casually, but having been cast they must be followed up. 'Ninety per cent of the people in this building are union members,' she said very coldly. 'It's conceivable that the union could strike over an issue like this. We had a strike three years ago, and—'

He waved it all aside with a casual hand. 'I've heard,' he said. 'Man, have I heard. So OK, lady—' He fumbled across the desk searching for something. 'Where the hell is that telephone—' Phil slid the internal telephone over beneath his hand. He grunted an acknowledgement. 'What's the number in your lion's den?'

'Lioness,' she muttered as she dialled the number and handed the telephone back to him.

His gruff character disappeared the moment he started talking on the telephone. Warmth and charm flowed down the wires. Apologies were offered, spirits were soothed, and he hung up. 'There,' he groused. 'I hope that satisfies?'

'Yes,' she acknowledged grimly.

'That's all—just yes?'

'Yes.'

'You are without a doubt the least talkative woman I've met in ten years or more,' he returned. 'My grandmother was like that. To the point. I like that.'

Well, I don't particularly like you, she told herself. And restraining comments were pure torture. Luckily her ten years as a substitute mother had taught her to guard her tongue. She cleared her throat again. 'Will that be all, Mr—?'

The question hung in the air between them until he laughed again. 'I wish I could see what you look like,' he pondered. 'This damn eye problem—well. For your information, Peabody, my name is Wilderman. Penn Wilderman. I suppose you know my father?'

'I—' He had caught her off guard, almost to the point where her real personality was showing. She struggled to suppress it. 'I don't really know him,' she said, truthful to the detail. 'I did substitute for Mrs Simmons twice in the past five years, but I don't really know him. I'm not an executive, or anything like that.'

'So you'll have a chance to know me,' he snapped. 'My father has been overworking. My mother laid down the law to him last Friday. They've gone on a three-month cruise. So I flew home to take charge.'

'I'm sorry to hear that.'

'Sorry that I flew home?'

'No,' she snarled, 'don't twist my words. I'm sorry that your father isn't well. He is well liked.'

'Now what do you know?' he chuckled. 'A kind word from the guardian dragon. You must be years older than those light-brains I've seen. What do they call you down at the typing pool? Battleaxe?'

'Something like that,' she admitted. 'What's the trouble with your eyes?' she offered as a tangential thought.

'Snow blindness,' he returned. For a moment she was afraid he would refuse the bait, but he relaxed again and settled back into the deep swivel chair. 'I was doing some advisory work down at Little America, the South Polar station. We were caught in a blizzard, and a stupid female technician lost her protective glasses. I gave her mine—and before we could make it back to the base camp I got burned for it.' He fiddled at the frame of the dark glasses over his eyes, and then removed them. Both eyes were covered by small medical pads, taped in place across the bridge of his nose.

Phil would normally have reacted with sympathy. One thing held her back. That phrase, stupid *female* technician. With the emphasis on *female*. As if, had the technician been male, no catastrophe could possibly have occurred. She offered a non-committal 'Oh'.

'Don't be too enthusiastic,' he grated, replacing the glasses. 'It's not permanent. Three or four weeks more, perhaps, and then maybe I can figure out the horrible mess the corporation is in. How soon will you have that material ready?'

Phil looked down at her notes and considered. 'Perhaps two or three hours,' she offered.

'Perhaps? Is that the best you can do?'

'Yes,' she snapped. He leaned forward over the desk as if he were about to argue—or demand—or order. And then he thought better of it.

There's something funny going on here, Philomena told herself. Not with or about him, but with me. Why do I have this crazy itch when I look at him. He's a strange sort of executive, but I've seen stranger. What's wrong? Her logical mind could find no answer. She stood up, brushed down her clinging skirt, and started for the door.

'Peabody,' he called. She froze, with one hand already on the door knob. 'Come back here.' This wasn't his real voice. It was the smooth charmer of the telephone call. It doesn't really affect me, she told herself quickly. I'm not little Betty Pervis, to be soothed by a telephone call. But her feet carried her back to the side of the desk. She stood there, silently.

'Peabody?'

'Yes?'

'I couldn't even hear you breathe!' Which is not surprising, Phil told herself. I haven't been breathing since he called me back! The imprisoned air boiled out of her in a long deep sigh.

'Peabody. Ever done any nursing work?'

'Me? Of course not.'

'Funny. You sound like somebody's mother—'

'Oh, that sort of thing? Band-aids and Solarcaine? I've brought up three—'

'Just what I meant,' he chuckled. 'I need some drops in my eyes. Would you?' He gestured towards the side table. Phil walked over without thinking. Eyedrops and a syringe, all neat and tidy. 'Three of them?' he queried. 'Must have been quite a family.'

'Yes, it was,' she returned wryly. 'But they've all grown up, and the last one was married off just yesterday.' She picked up the syringe and came back. 'Lean back in the chair,' she ordered. He took off the glasses and settled back. She picked at the edge of the tape, and managed to free it. Black eyes, almost as black and deep as his hair. She hesitated. The past few minutes of conversation were whistling around in her head.

'Well,' he complained gruffly. 'I don't want major surgery.'

'No,' she returned. *What do they call you—battleaxe?* He must think I'm fifty years old—an old hag who cracks the whip down in the cellar of the building. Well, it serves him right! The drops cascaded out of the syringe. One or two lucky ones hit his eye. The others ran down his neck.

'Hey, I didn't ask for a bath,' he roared.

'It's all right,' she soothed, in the same tone she had used time after time with the girls. It worked. He settled back as she tidied up the mess with a tissue. 'And now the other one. Don't blink like that. I can't get the drops in while you flutter your eyelashes.' Long lashes, she noted. Curling up at the ends. I'd give my right arm for real lashes like that! Three precise drops flooded his other eye. He spluttered, blinked and reached up a hand. She stopped it in mid-flight.

'None of that,' she ordered. The hand stopped. She dabbed at the excess forced out on to his cheek, then carefully replaced the pads and the tape from the fresh supply on the table. 'There now.'

'That's a good boy,' he chuckled as he sat up. 'You forgot that part. You could be my mother, the way you talk.'

'I doubt that very much,' she sighed. 'And you can't see a thing?'

'Shapes. Light and dark. Movements,' he said. 'It's nothing permanent. So you wouldn't want to be my mother?'

'I should hope not.' It was hard to keep the disapproval out of her tone. And I really don't have any reason for disapproving, she reminded herself. He acted like a boor and a bully, and he apologised very nicely for it all. So either he's the world's biggest fake, or he's been raised with the nicest manners, or—lord, I don't know, do I?

'Thank you,' he offered. She jumped. While she had been debating, he had left his chair and was standing directly in front of her. He was not a huge man. Slender, whippet-like, and about a head taller than herself. Which isn't any great height, she told herself. But tall enough for me. If he hugged me, the top of my head would fit just under his chin! It was a fine supposition, but she was more than startled when he proceeded to demonstrate how true it was.

'What are you doing?' she snapped. It wasn't a gut reaction. She had some experience with hugging. From time to time over the past ten years she had found time to date a man—and to fight off a hug or two. Three times, to be exact. Raising three girls took a great deal of effort!

'I can't see you,' he grumbled, 'and I need to know something about you. I have to do it in Braille.'

'That's a good excuse.'

'I'm glad you think so.' He hadn't noticed her sarcasm, evidently. 'But I do wish you'd stand still. I can do this all by myself. You needn't wiggle against me.'

'I wasn't wiggling *against* you,' she stormed. 'I was wiggling—stop that!'

His hands had wandered through her hair, surrounded her pert round face, touched on eyes, nose and mouth, and were now diving over her chin and off into space. They landed on the tops of her well rounded breasts, paused for a second, and then trailed down her sides, over her swelling hips, and—

It had taken her that long to recover from the surprise of it all. From the surprise, and from the shock of wild-running senses which his touch had evoked. Her hand moved automatically, bouncing off his cheek with a satisfying thud, driving him back a step or two.

'Hey,' he protested.

'Hey is right, Mr Wilderman,' she stormed. 'I don't allow people to take liberties with my—with me. I don't see any reason why you should want to get to know me better, because I doubt if I will be seeing you any time in the near future. Mrs Simmons—'

'Mrs Simmons will be out for the day,' he returned. 'For a sweet little old lady you've got some marvellous figure.'

'And a strong arm,' she threatened. 'And I never said anything about being a sweet little old lady.'

'No, you never did,' he chuckled. 'I'll strike out the sweet, if you object. Why don't you run along to your little cell and get that work out?'

'Yes,' she snapped, happy that he couldn't see the rose hue that coloured her face. Blushes she had never learned to suppress. She started for the door.

'You even walk softly,' he called after her. I'm darned if I'll take that at face value, she told herself. The man had a tongue that's hinged in the middle. One side sweet, the other sour. She reached for the knob.

The door was one that swung inward. Just as her hand moved forward the door swung open, catching her in the stomach. She staggered back a step, lost her balance, and sat down on the floor with a thump. 'This makes my day,' she groaned.

'Now what?' he asked. She turned to look at him. He had left the security of the desk and was fumbling his way across the room.

'Don't do that,' she called.

And behind her, at the door, a young voice. 'Don't do that, Dad!'

'Robert? What the devil are you doing here at this hour? And what happened to Peabody?'

Phil turned around. A boy stood in the door. A teenager, from the look of him. Painfully thin, blond hair neatly combed, wearing a suit and tie. A thin face. You could almost count the bones. Dad? He was a carbon copy of the man, in every way.

'Robert?'

'I—I think I knocked your—your lady over. She's sitting on the floor.'

'Well, help her up—or—come over here and lead me to her! Hurry up. She has fragile bones!'

Oh, do I? Phil ran a hand up and down her 'fragile bones'. Everything seemed to be in order, but her bottom gave notice of bruising to be reported later. The boy sidled around her as if she were a poised rattlesnake, and hurried to his father. The pair of them came over to her. 'Give me your hands, Peabody,' the father commanded.

She reached up hesitantly. 'I can get up for myself,' she said quietly.

'I'm sure you can,' Wilderman returned. 'Hands!'

She offered them both, smiling as they were swallowed into his. He might not be a big man, she thought, but his hands are for giants. How would you like them to—

He interrupted her wandering mind by moving around in front of her. The boy was doing his best to fade into the background. 'Put your foot up against mine,' he ordered. It hardly seemed worth a protest. She complied. 'Now, upsy-daisy.' His hands tightened on hers and up she went, as effortlessly as if he had been handling a five-pound parcel. 'There now. OK?'

Those darned hands again, sweeping up and down her body, brushing at her skirt, touching her in places where they had no right to be. She slapped at the hands, and he withdrew them.

'That's better than the last time.' He was so close that his whisper echoed in her ear.

'Don't press your luck,' she retorted. But his hands dropped to her shoulders, and before she could duck out of the way he planted a light kiss on her forehead. 'Don't do that,' she muttered through clenched teeth.

'Robert?' He turned Phil around in the approximate direction of the boy, who moved a step or two closer.

'Robert, I want you to meet Miss Peabody. She's the nice lady who has been helping me out.'

'She looks like—' the boy started to say. His father silenced him with an upraised hand.

'Don't say it,' he was admonished. 'She's a lovely lady. Shake hands.'

Phil worked up a smile, and offered her hand. The boy moved away and clasped both hands behind his back. Like that, huh, Phil thought. Shake hands and come out fighting? Well, have I got a surprise for you, sonny. I don't give a darn!

'I want you two to be friends,' his father said, evidently thinking the handshake had been effected.

'Yes, I can see that,' Phil retorted. 'And now if you *gentlemen* will excuse me, I have work to do.'

His ear caught the sarcasm this time. He looked down at her, puzzlement written over his face. She shrugged herself loose from his hands, picked up her scattered pads and equipment, and rushed out of the door, leaving it open behind her.

'But, Dad, she looks like—' The boy was trying it again as she whizzed down the corridor. All of a sudden, the upper reaches of the Pacific Mine and Metal Corporation had taken on a threatening atmosphere. She dived for the protection of her own little empire on the ground floor.

CHAPTER TWO

BY the time the weekend rolled around, Phil was happy to stay at home. Her trip to the executive suite had not been repeated, but images had hung in her mind. Strange images, that caused her more than one dreaming moment when she should have been working. His face, bad manners and all. His eyes, that pulled at her pity, his hands that stabbed at her raw emotions and left her wriggling on her chair. The boy. Thirteen going on fifty-five. Rigid speech, formal airs, and an unhappy shadow trying to hide behind his eyes. A strange pair.

To keep them out of her hair on Saturday she house-cleaned. Polished, scrubbed, dusted, until the old house sparkled. There was nothing to be done outside. Even in California, February spells winter, and many a night the temperature would be down to thirty degrees, just below the frost line. So she had bedded all her flowers in early December, burying them under a load of seaweed imported up the Sacramento River from the ocean, ninety-five miles away.

A walk through the remains of her orchard helped a little. There were branches on the ground from the ancient olive trees and the equally ancient walnut trees. The orchard was so small as to make harvesting, except for her own use, a complete waste of time. At the end of her land she stopped for a breath. The fog had lifted shortly after noon, and there was a sweet clean smell about the earth. She rested one hand on the gnarled tree-trunk nearest, and glared out to where another high-rise office building was under construction. Sacramento was surely expanding, like a rising loaf of bread gone mad.

Sunday was a lazy day. She slept late, then drove down into Rancho Cordova to St Clemens, the Episcopal Church on Zinfandel Drive. And then it was Monday.

'He wants you.' Betty Pervis, in early for a change, with a wide smirk on her face.

'He?' Phil struggled out of her jacket and swiped ineffectually at her fog-damped hair.

'Him. That Mr Wilderman.'

'What would he want me for? Don't tell me Mrs Simmons is out again?'

'No. I saw her come in twenty minutes ago. He wants you, Phil. I bet the minute he saw you he flipped.'

'Stop it, Betty. That's fairy-tale stuff. Besides, he never did see me. His eyes were bandaged all the time I was there.'

'Well,' the young girl pouted, 'it's happened before, you know.'

'What?' Phil was still trying vainly to control her curls. When wet they coiled up like little springs all over her head, and then jingled and bounced as she walked. 'What's happened before?'

'You know. The millionaire boss marries the typist?'

'Oh, sure he does. Daydreamer. So what did he say? What did he want?'

'I told you. He said he wanted you—and then he hung up like to burst my ear-drum. You'd better hurry up. He hates to be kept waiting.'

MRS SIMMONS was in her appointed place, every iron-grey hair in place, her mannish tailored suit impeccable, her hands poised over the keys of her electronic typewriter. 'He

wants you,' the older woman said, and nodded towards the
door.

'That's getting to be the most hated quotation of the cen-
tury,' Phil returned, smiling. 'He wants me for what?' Mrs
Simmons shrugged her shoulders and smiled back. Phil
shook her head in disgust and headed for the inner office.

His hearing must have improved. He heard the door as it
opened. 'Well, damn it, isn't she here yet? How far is it to
that typing pool?' A papa-bear growl, from an office almost as dim as a cave. He was at his desk. His son Robert
was sitting on the divan in the corner. The boy got up silently, with not a wisp of a smile on his face.

'Yes, she's here.' Phil replied in her most serene tone.
'The typing pool is on the ground floor, a hundred miles
from here.'

'Oh, a wit, no less,' he growled. Phil had already lost her
desire to prick his bubble of conceit, regretted her poor attempt at humour.

'Well, you're half right,' she said wryly. She stood quietly in the middle of the room, eyes swerving from father to
son, waiting. The boy was fidgeting, moving his weight from
one foot to the other.

'Come over here.'

'Yes, Mr Wilderman—'

'Penn. Mr Wilderman is my father.'

Silence. Phil could think of nothing to say.

'You can't manage a simple name like that? Let me hear
you say it. Penn.'

'I—Penn.'

'That's a start,' he laughed. His entire appearance
changed. The worry-lines disappeared from his face, taking years off his age. The dark glasses, sited at a jaunty angle on the bridge of his nose, seemed to be laughing at her.
Not maliciously. Happily. Breathe, Phil commanded her-

self, and relaxed as air poured into her lungs. His fingers beckoned. She moved slowly towards the desk until she was up to the typist's chair that stood beside it.

'No further?' he asked.

'No.' It wasn't exactly a whisper, neither was it a full-blown statement. I'm losing my nerve, Phil snarled at herself.

He was up from his chair before she could assemble her defences. Up and in front of her, inches away, with both hands trapping her head between them. Fingers moved up her cheeks, into her hair, and paused. Her agitation ceased. The hands were stroking, calming. Altogether—wonderful, she thought, and blushed at her own statement.

'Good morning, Peabody,' he said softly. 'The records tell me it's Philomena—is that right?'

Tongue-tied, Phil struggled to reply and gave up. His fingers read her struggle, and moved down to cup her chin. 'Do I frighten you?'

'Yes,' she managed. And then more bravely now that the dam was broken, 'Yes. I wish you would stop pawing me, Mr Wilderman—Penn. I—'

She managed to get to the chair as his hands dropped away. That uneasy feeling crowded almost everything else out of her mind. It bothered her because she could not define it, and definition had circumscribed her life for so long she felt lost.

'What do you want of me?' she asked impatiently.

He went back to his chair and sat down. He moved with more confidence, more agility than he had the previous week, she thought. He stood a little taller, straighter, and there was an aura of power surrounding him. 'How are things in the typing pool?' he asked.

It was not what Phil had expected. She squared around in her chair, set both feet flat on the floor, and stiffened her spine. 'Work is slow,' she said in her office voice. 'On Monday it's always slow. By Tuesday, when the engineers have had a chance to think, work picks up.' And now what? Did he want to fire a couple of the girls? Save a little money in the over-inflated budget?

'That's good,' he said. Which again was not quite what she expected. Executives about to fire somebody don't usually start off with 'That's good.' She stole a quick glance at the boy. He had sat down when she did. Better manners she had never observed before in a teenager. And that was one of the problems. He was just too unnaturally quiet for an American teenager!

'We have a problem.' Penn broke in on her thoughts.

'*We* do?'

'Robert and I. We have a problem.' And I'll bet that's the understatement of the year, Phil told herself. She sat up even straighter, not willing to contribute a comment, and waited.

'You don't seem to care?'

'I'm sure you'll tell about it when you're ready,' she returned primly. To emphasise the point she put her pencils away in her pocket and folded her hands in her lap. He cleared his throat, as if not accustomed to such rebuttal.

'Robert is growing out of all his clothes. You can see that, I suppose.'

'Yes.'

'I'm not boring you, am I, Philomena?'

'No, but nobody calls me that. I—'

'I should call you Miss Peabody? By the way, it *is* Miss, isn't it?'

'Yes. I mean, yes it is, not yes you should—' Another tangled tongue. She swallowed hard to clear the obstruction. 'I mean—you should call me Phil. And yes, it is *Miss* Peabody—Phil.'

'I'm glad we've settled that,' he chuckled. 'How in the world did you last as a *Miss* all this time? You seem to be a nice companionable lady.' Phil almost strangled over the words that wanted to pour out.

'Oh, never mind,' he conceded. 'None of my business, is it? What I want, Phil, is for you to take Robert out on the town this morning and get him a new outfit.'

'I—'

'No, I know it's not in the union contract. I'm asking for a favour.'

'I wasn't going to say that,' she retorted angrily. 'All I meant to say is I don't have any experience buying for men. All my expertise is with girls!'

'Boys, girls—' he grumbled. 'This is the unisex age. I don't see what difference that makes.'

'A lot you know,' Phil told him. 'The unisex age is almost over. The pendulum is swinging madly in the other direction. Girls look for the very feminine. Boys look for the very masculine.'

'And skirts are longer this year,' he chuckled. 'Or so they tell me. Why any woman with good-looking legs would want to wear skirts at mid-calf is more than I can reason out.'

'Perhaps that's to keep them from being ogled by men,' Phil said primly. 'And all that is beside the point. We were talking about Robert's clothes. He's old enough to pick out what he wants for himself. At most, you might have his mother go along with him to supervise.' A silence settled over the room. Penn Wilderman drubbed his fingers on his desktop. Robert Wilderman was staring at his father, his eyes wide open, and an anxious expression on his face.

'Robert,' the father finally broke the silence, 'would you please go out to Mrs Simmons' office for a moment. I need to speak privately to Peabody.'

'About my mother?' The belligerence was unmasked. The boy had no intention of sharing his mother's secrets with another woman, Phil thought, and he was making no bones about it.

'Robert!' A stern command that snapped like a whip, but left all the scars internally. The boy got up slowly from his chair, looked as if he might voice an objection, and thought better of it. He slammed the door behind him on the way out. The whole thing was too mediaeval for Phil to accept.

'I don't want to hear any of his mother's secrets,' she exploded. 'That's a terrible way to treat a child of his age. Terrible!'

'I didn't ask you in here to criticise my life-style—or my family's,' he snapped. 'Just shut up and sit down.'

'I am,' she fumed. 'And don't tell me to shut up. I can always get another job. Sacramento is crying out for experienced secretaries.' Just for emphasis she stuck her tongue out at him, and then had a hard time smothering the giggles brought on by her own silliness.

'I don't doubt you could get a hundred jobs,' he thundered. At least it seemed like thunder. It wasn't very loud, but it shook the furniture—and Phil—in a manner she was not eager to repeat. 'In fact, I might offer you a better job myself. Now just listen. OK?'

'OK,' she whispered, her fit of rebellion suppressed. Despite what she had said, it wasn't all *that* easy to get a new job—and she had worked for Pacific Mining for almost ten years now.'

'My wife and I are divorced. Robert is our adopted child. My wife was awarded custody. Now my former wife has remarried and Robert had become an—obstruction, I guess you would say. So she shipped the boy to me, not even waiting to find out whether I was in the country or not. My

son is a bright young man, but so thoroughly stamped down
that he hardly appears normal. I'm sure you've seen that?'

'Yes,' she admitted. It was a hesitant agreement. His
world of darkness seemed to be closing in on her, disorder-
ing her usually logical mind. Just for a minute she wished
she had the nerve to get up and open a curtain. Outside the
window Sacramento roared and chugged and whined its way
into the future. Inside, she was swathed in a thousand veils
that shrouded and blinded her to all but this man. This man
who was suddenly turning from grouchy bully to loving,
concerned father.

'So now I have a difficult problem,' he continued. 'I can't
stand this man my wife—my former wife—has married, and
I wouldn't want Robert to be within a hundred miles of
them. Yet, to get the court order rescinded, I have to be able
to provide a home life for him myself. And today is a beginning. You are obviously the motherly type. You don't
think yourself too old for Robert?'

'Me?' she gulped. There it was again, that obsession he
seemed to have about age. 'Why—why no, I don't think of
myself as too old for Robert, but I—I would hardly classify
myself as a motherly type.'

'Come off it,' he chuckled. 'You brought up three
girls—'

'Three sisters,' she insisted firmly. 'They were my younger
sisters.'

'So all right, your younger sisters. Children none the less.
You saw them through their scrapes and bruises and teens?'

'I—well, yes, so to speak.' It was technically not true.
Sally was only eighteen—but his statement was close enough
to the truth to be accepted.

'Then there you go,' he nodded. 'The motherly type. No,
I don't see this as being any big thing. Your department is

in the doldrums. You hop in the car, take Robert to some place where clothes can be had, and outfit him. Easy.'

'Not that easy,' she sighed. 'What sort of outfit? How many things? How much money are you willing to invest in all this? Children's clothes come higher priced than adult clothes these days.' Again that prim maiden-aunt tone. And I wish I could wash *that* out, she told herself fiercely.

'I want him to have a complete wardrobe,' Penn rumbled. 'It's up to you what he gets. As for money, there's a company credit card in my wallet here.' He squirmed around to reach his wallet out of his back pocket and laid it out on the desk. 'Take it with you. I don't really care how much things cost. Spend what you need to. Anything up to five hundred dollars, I would say. If you need more, give me a call from the store.'

Phil almost swallowed her tongue. Accustomed to nursing money as if it were a sick relative, she could have outfitted three boys the size of Robert for five hundred dollars. And have change left over. She fumbled for the card.

'I—I guess I could manage,' she returned softly. 'I'll take him over to the K-street Mall in my car, and we'll—'

'Nonsense,' he said. Again that roll of thunder, that threat hanging in the background. 'My car is downstairs. Harry is probably ruining his lunch by chewing on doughnuts in the cafeteria. He'll drive you. Off you go.'

Off she went, indeed. It was like being swept out of the kitchen by a particularly big broom. Robert was standing at Mrs Simmons' desk, having said not a word, apparently. When she tapped him on the shoulder he followed. Not until they entered the lift did he speak.

'You're really going to buy me some clothes?'

That disdainful look, meaning *how can a mere female buy clothing for me?* His father's look all over again. The pair of them would be great candidates for monkhood, Phil

told herself. I'd like to give them both a hot-foot to upset
that darn dignity. How can a thirteen-year-old boy be such
a stick? 'No,' she responded. 'I wouldn't dream of buying
anything for you. I'm going to take you somewhere where
you can buy yourself some clothes—and your father's going to pay for them. Do you have any objection?'

He thought about it until they reached the lobby. 'No,' he
said, as they stepped out of the lift.

A short bandy-legged man was leaning against the reception desk. He looked like an out-of-work jockey with grey
hair and no semblance of uniform. When he saw Robert he
sauntered over to them, spread both feet apart, and issued
a challenge.

'You the broad gonna take Robbie shopping?'

She glared at him, eyeball to eyeball. It wasn't hard. They
were both about the same height. 'Yes,' she snapped. 'I'm
the—er—broad that is taking Robert shopping. Are you
Harry?'

'Who else?' he sighed. Another woman-hater, Phil noted.
That makes three. They must be a close tribe, the Wildermans. I wonder if there are any more at home? 'Well,
c'mon,' the little man drawled, 'I don't have all day.'

'Do you not really?' Phil drawled in return. 'Have to get
your bets in at the track, do you?'

'Well,' he stuttered, embarrassed by her directness. 'I—
hey, the car's out front in a no-parking zone.'

'Where else?' She did her best to present a royal cold
stare, but just the doing broke her up. When she giggled he
smiled back at her. Out of the corner of her eye she could see
the boy smiling too.

The car was one of those stretch-Cadillacs, two blocks
long, with shaded windows for one-way viewing. Hollywood style. Phil classified it all as she scrambled into the
back seat. Robert dithered a moment or two, and then de-

sire overcame manners. He scrambled in up front, next to the driver. Mark it down, Phil, her subconscious demanded. He's really a thirteen-year-old kid. Give him the chance and he'd have the engine out and in pieces on the pavement. All that dignity is faked!

'Where to?' The little man needed a pillow under him to see over the steering-wheel. His voice had the gravel-sound of those who do a great deal of shouting in their lives. 'Where to, Miss—?'

'Peabody,' Robert told him, using his father's inflection.

'To the lower K-street Mall,' she said. 'I don't rightly know how you'll get there. They're tearing up that whole area to put in the Light Rail vehicles, and—'

'I know,' Harry grunted. 'Been drivin' in this town for twenty years or more.' That seemed to be that. Phil buttoned her lip and relaxed into the soft springy seat, planning her strategy. Unfortunately she found it hard to give Robert's needs her full attention. His father's face seemed to haunt her. *And I don't know when I've met a more despicable man,* she insisted to herself.

Harry proved to be some sort of driving genius. He managed to deliver them to the back of the Mall without scraping a fender, or killing anyone in the middle of the mad traffic jam which normally haunted the Capitol Mall when the California legislature were in session. Phil began to breathe again when Harry pulled over to the kerb in a no-waiting zone and opened the door.

'Lose your breath, lady?' he asked as he handed her out.

'I always do when someone else is driving,' she apologised. A real smile was her reward. 'I don't know how long we'll be,' she hazarded. He shrugged his shoulders.

'Makes no mind,' he returned. 'I'll be around here somewheres. You come out, I'll find you.' Robert climbed out

without assistance and stood fidgeting, as if he had never
been in downtown Sacramento before.

'Over this way,' she called, and led him across the grass
and tree-lined open mall. Her goal was the classic simplic-
ity of Macy's, but before they made it to the front doors the
boy stopped and stared.

'What's that?' he asked in awe. Phil looked up. As a per-
ennial shopper she tended to ignore the obvious these days.
The boy was standing almost underneath the Indo Arch, a
mass of steel formed vaguely in the pointed-arch shape of an
Indian Temple door. Soaring forty feet above the surrounding mall, it was the starkly symbolic gate between the
modern State capital and the rebuilt park area known as Old
Sacramento.

'You've never been here before?' she asked.

'I've never been anywhere around here,' he returned bitterly. 'There never was any time. My—she was always busy
at something or other. She never had time.'

How about that? Phil mused. She spent a few minutes
explaining about the arch, and the reconstructed Old Sacramento.

'I'd like to see that some day,' he said. Not enthusiastically, just a general comment. Which made it even more
strange to her when she heard herself say, 'Maybe we could
come. I'd be glad to take you.'

He looked at her as if she were some curious sea-monster.
As if he had heard but could not believe. 'You mean that?'

'I said it,' she said grimly, wishing she could take it all
back. They marched into the store without another word.
From long practice, Phil knew her way around. She led him
unhesitatingly to the Men and Boys clothing area, and then
stopped him with a small hand on his wrist.

'Now you have to decide just what you want to wear,' she
told him. He was the slightest bit taller than she, and it was

unnerving to see how his grey eyes studied her. I wonder what colour his father's eyes are, she pondered as he thought out an answer.

'You really mean that? I can decide for myself?'

'Why not? You have to live in them. What's your favourite?'

'Jeans,' he replied immediately. So what else is new, Phil chuckled to herself. Give a kid enough rope and he'll buy—blue jeans. She waved her hand towards the proper aisles, and followed as he plunged down them like a young colt just unleashed into fresh pastures. Jeans. They come in all sizes and all styles and all colours, and he just couldn't make up his mind.

'If you're sure of the size,' she prompted, 'try on one pair, and then take a couple of each.' That broke the log-jam. He actually smiled. With his whole face *and* his eyes, he smiled. As with his father, it changed his whole appearance. The solemn formal stick figure turned into a glowing teenager. He was gone into a fitting-booth before Phil could add another word.

She sank into a chair, glad to rest her feet. If this expedition were to be anything like a shopping trip with her sisters, she would need arch-supporters before the day was done. It was—pleasant—just to sit there, watching people buzz around her like a hive of angry yellow-jackets. She was surprised when Robert came out of the booth and stood in front of her.

'Do you think this would do?' he asked hesitantly. She smothered her smile. This was not the time for it. The waist band was comfortably loose, although the jeans clung to him like a second skin. The legs were a little too long, but a quick needle would turn up the cuffs with ease.

'Do you like them?' she countered.

He strutted back and forth, did a couple of deep knee bends, all without bursting out of the pants, and then came back. The smile was flickering, as if he expected a denial. 'I like them,' he said fiercely.

'So we'll get—oh—six pairs,' she commented casually. 'Choose the rest of them, but make sure they're this same size.'

He flashed away again, thumbing through the racks as if he were a seasoned shopper. In fifteen minutes he had accumulated an armful, and the smile seemed permanently fixed.

'And now shirts, socks, and underwear,' she announced. He nodded happily. 'And one suit, for dress-up.' She expected rage, and got acquiescence. It took another hour to complete his outfit. The credit card was somewhat more worn than when she first received it. *But,* Phil told herself, *if it were Sally, we would have one dress by now, and I'd be exhausted.*

It was warm outside. The sun had finally broken through and dried off the fog. Aircraft seemed to be stacked to preposterous heights, waiting to be called in to the landing pattern of the Metropolitan Airport, to their north. A few pigeons, paying absolutely no attention to the sanitation rules, were dive-bombing the pedestrians. And Harry was waiting for them beside the Arch.

'Bought a lot, did you?' the little man asked. For some reason the gravelly voice seemed more friendly than before. He came up to Phil and relieved her of all her packages, without offering help to the boy at all. *And he's doing that on purpose,* she told herself. Robbie was tired. She could read that on his face. But there was a stubborn determination there too. The first one to offer him help would get a first-class set-down! But women are entitled to be tired, she chuckled to herself, and put on such a demonstration that they both believed it.

The ride back was different. When Phil climbed in to the back seat, Robbie was close behind her. Harry took the long-cut, around the Capitol building and the park that lay behind it, then wandering eastward past the reconstruction of Sutter's Fort, north around the cool green of McKiney Park, east again to circle the scattered buildings of the Sacramento branch of the University of California, and then back in a twisting path through the back streets, until they were in front of the Pacific Mining and Metals building.

'Leave them packages in the car,' Harry instructed.

'Someone has to do a little sewing on the trouser legs,' Phil told him. 'They need to be taken up about an inch. Can you get it done?' He looked doubtful, but helped her out of the car and then drove off.

'I know your mother would have been a better help for you,' she told the boy. His face hardened. She fumbled to a stop.

The boy was bursting with something he wanted to say. It tumbled out in all the bitterness of a thirteen-year-old mind. 'My mother hates me,' he announced, and strode off towards the front door of the building.

'Now wait just a darn minute,' she called after him. He stopped. She walked over to confront him. 'Don't you ever say anything like that,' she lectured. 'You don't know everything there is to know about your mother and the world. What do you suppose your father would say if he heard that?'

The boy was close to tears, but his pride was bigger than his frame. 'He wouldn't care,' he said. 'He hates me too.'

CHAPTER THREE

PHIL made sure that Robbie got to the right lift, then turned back and hurried to the typing pool. It was after one, and the girls were gradually drifting back to work. 'While the cat's away, huh?' She grinned at them and headed for her own work station. A surprising amount of work had come in, for a Monday morning. She thumbed through it all and made a distribution among them.

'Not El Dorado again,' Harriet groaned as she scanned her assigned workload. 'It's a devil of a note when a company can't take gold out of its own mine!'

'Type,' Phil chuckled. 'Yours not to reason why. El Dorado county had become a suburb since the old days. The new residents are householders, not old miners. You can't blame them for not wanting us to reactivate the old mines.'

'I can,' Harriet returned. 'I don't make enough money to move out there. Why should I feel sorry for them? They work on the idea that *I've got mine, and to hell with anybody else*. They don't want to listen to the fact that the mines on the Mother Lode were there before *they* were.'

'Oh, wow,' Phil laughed. 'That sounds definitely like sour grapes. Or is it Lionel again?'

Harriet waved her comment aside. 'Lionel is long gone,' she said, bending over her word-processor keyboard. 'It's Frank now. And yes, he's a pain in my—stomach. Oooh!'

'Oooh?'

'Look who just came in!'

Phil whirled around. The entire room was quiet. Only one keyboard clicked. Penn Wilderman stood at the door, his hand resting lightly on Harry's shoulder. It was the first time she had seen him in full light. His face, screened by the inevitable dark glasses, was narrower than she had thought. The black hair tumbled in some profusion, to curl slightly at the back of his neck. He went from broad shoulders to narrow hips, reminding Phil of the boy. There was an aura about him, a feeling of poise, of command. His grey three-piece suit was immaculate. His tie, slightly loosened, flamed red against the white of his shirt. Not a huge man, not at all, but big enough.

Harry led him down the narrow aisle that separated the work positions. 'Peabody?' Penn said.

'Yes?' Her stomach quivered. She took a deep breath to calm it. You've been doing a lot of that lately, her conscience nagged.

'Lunch,' he announced. The keys in the background stopped clicking, as all the typists listened unabashedly.

'I—I have a packed lunch,' she stammered. 'The boy—'

'The boy is on his way home to try out his new clothes. And now you and I are lunching. There's something I want to talk over with you.'

'Oh!' Well, what else do you say? To Phil's certain knowledge the boss of Pacific Mining had never ever come down into the typing pool. Neither father nor son. And now, oh so casually, *lunch!*

'Mr Wilderman—'

'Penn.'

'Ah—er—Penn. I don't go out for lunch, and it's—'

'I know. It's not in the union contract. But you'll come anyway because it's a favour.'

'I—yes.' It wasn't a question of making up her mind. That area was totally vacant, spinning around in an upset such as her twenty-seven years had not known before. And tumbling out of the vacuum her voice had given its own answer.

His hand transferred to her shoulder. 'Get the car, Harry,' he ordered, and then urged Phil down the aisle towards the door. Behind them a buzz of conversation rose. 'They'll have enough gossip to last a week,' he told her softly as the door sighed shut behind them.

'Well, I don't relish being the subject of it,' she grumbled. His hand squeezed her shoulder—partly warning, partly command. She stepped off briskly towards the front door.

His magic carpet of a Cadillac whisked them over to L street in a matter of minutes, and into Frank Fat's restaurant, the favourite eatery of the Republican administration. He must have called ahead. A table was waiting for them. They moved through the crush like an elephant train, first the *maître d'*, then Phil, and slightly behind her, hand on her shoulder for a guide, Penn. He seemed to have a good many friends in the late-lunch crowd. People called out to him from both sides as they passed, but he signalled her forward.

'I'm really hungry,' he said as he fumbled at the back of her chair, then trailed a hand around the table to the opposite side. 'The Beaumonts quit this morning. That's the third couple I've lost in six weeks.'

'I'm not surprised,' she muttered.

'What?'

'I said I'm surprised,' she lied cheerfully. The frown on his face indicated disbelief.

'Yes, well—I want the steak, please. The special, with onions and oyster sauce. Philomena?'

'Please,' she cringed. 'Someone might hear you. Phil is my name. And I couldn't possibly—oh, bring me the Chef's Salad, please, and a cup of tea.'

'Now, where was I?'

'The Beaumonts quit this morning?'

'Yes. And Harry is such a terrible cook.'

'Didn't you know that slavery is against the law? It seems to me that Harry is around day and night.'

He smiled at her, tilting his head in a truly attractive move. 'Harry and I go a long way back,' he told her. 'He's one of my father's old war buddies. I think he's shared everything I've ever done—except for Vietnam. Ah, I love the smell of Fat's steak special. Sure you won't have some?'

'Of course not,' she sighed. 'I'd be a balloon in three weeks if I ate like that. After a moment she stopped eating, staring at his dexterity. He attacked his food with vigour—just as he does everything else, she thought. That hank of black hair kept sliding down over his forehead. Phil squeezed her own hands together to get rid of that traitorous impulse. Leaning across a table to brush the hair out of his eyes was just too much to expect of an employee!

He managed about half of his steak, then laid his utensils aside and dabbed at his mouth with his napkin. 'Well?'

She was caught by surprise again, idly tracing the line of his chin with her eyes. 'Well? Well what?'

'So are you going to help us?'

'I—guess I don't understand, Mr—er—Penn.'

'Robert and Harry and I are living in a big house. We need help.'

'Oh. Yes, I suspect you do. You want me to find another couple to take care of the house, is that it? I'm not really in the personnel business, but I suppose I could ask around and see if something can be arranged. There must be *some-body* willing to put up with you!'

And there goes your big mouth, she yelled at herself. What sort of a way is that to talk to your boss? *Somebody might be willing to put up with you. Hah!* 'I—I really didn't mean that, Mr Wilderman,' she stammered. 'I don't know what came over me.'

'I do,' he rumbled. 'You've got a terminal case of honesty. That's one of the several things about you that I like.'

'But—' She gave thanks again that he couldn't see her mad blushes. If there were anything about herself that she hated, it was that blood-surging blush that gave her away in many a tight corner.

He was off on his own hobby-horse. 'I like you because you're quiet,' he enumerated. 'You tell me the truth. You are eminently practical. You know how to handle children. You know how to handle grouches and bullies. You know how to handle other women. You're a fine figure of a woman. And you're old enough not to be bothered with all this first flush of love and emotion. You are altogether a fine person, Philomena.'

Her first confused reaction was, 'Hush, people are listening'. And then her flustered mind marshalled all his statements, everything seemed fine until she ran into *and you're old enough to*—that was the phrase that stuck in her craw. She threw up her hands in disgust, and pushed her plate away.

'Finished eating?' He had returned to the work at hand, and was proving to be a fine trencherman.

'Yes,' she sighed. She put both elbows on the table and rested her chin on them, trying to read his face. She waited until he had completely dismantled the lunch, and then, 'Just what is it you want me to do?' She tried to keep her voice cool and low. The couple at the next table were taking an inordinate interest in *their* discussion.

'Simple,' he said. 'I want you to come live with us.'

'You want me to *what!*'

'Hey, keep your voice down,' he chuckled. 'We don't want everybody in the place to know what we're talking about, do we?'

'I—no!' Phil collapsed back into her chair and dabbed at the residue of the overturned water glass, a victim of her outraged jump to her feet. 'No.' More softly, but hissing with her anger. 'Say that again. You want me to what?'

'I said, we want you to come and live with us. Surely for someone of your age and charm that's not a surprise?'

'Well, a lot you know,' she hissed back at him. 'What has my age and charm got to do with it! I—'

'All right. Don't blow a fuse. It's not all that complicated. I thought you wouldn't mind coming over and looking after our house—and us. You have kept house before, haven't you?'

'Yes,' she snapped, 'for my own family. All girls. And you have the nerve to—I—'

'I didn't think it took a great deal of nerve.' She slashed a look. His face was solemn. There might be laughter behind the words, but his face was solemn. Her hand waved in her natural gesture, and she looked at the upset glass by her plate.

'I—you startled me,' she sighed. 'I spilled—'

'I hope it's water,' he interrupted. 'It's running down the leg of my trousers.'

'Oh, my,' Phil gasped. She snatched at the two other place napkins and rushed around to his side, madly sponging at his trouser-leg.

'I think I'd rather be wet than notorious,' he grumbled. 'I suppose now that everyone in the restaurant is looking at us?' Phil's empty hand flew to her mouth as she straightened up and glanced around. Everyone was. Clutching desperately at the wet napkins she sidled around the table and back to her seat.

'I—I'm sorry.' She had to make do with a whisper. It was all that would come out. 'They're all—staring. I'm sorry!'

'For God's sake,' he returned. 'I'm not asking you to give up the world and enter into seclusion. You have a holiday coming, don't you?'

'I—yes. Four weeks. But I thought I would save it for the summer, and then I could help my sisters with—'

'So give me two weeks of it now. Your job will be protected for you—and at the end of that time we could see how it's going.'

'I—' She closed her mouth with a snap. If I give him a word off the top of my head I'll regret it, she thought. It's too easy to say yes to this—this aggravating man. He seems to have some sort of mind-control over me. Or have I been missing someone to care for these days? All I know is that I want to say *yes*, but I'd better not! So she compromised.

'I think that's too much for a quick decision. Mr Wilderman—er—Penn. I'll have to think it over very carefully.'

'Why?' He was going to pound at her defences, and she grew more wary because of that. 'You know me. I'm the world's biggest grouch, right?' Phil shook her head in agreement, and then thanked heaven that he couldn't see. 'Are you afraid of me?' She shook her head again. 'Can't say anything?'

'I—it's Robert I don't know. He could be a bigger problem than all three of my sisters combined.'

'I don't see why you say that. He's just a normal thir-teen-year-old kid.'

'Hah! A lot you know!' She hadn't meant to say that. It slipped out. But having said it, the rest had to follow. 'Rob-ert is a mixed-up child. He thinks his mother hates him.'

'She does. Almost as much as she hates me. That woman would do anything in the world to do me in. Well, maybe that's an exaggeration. I think she would draw the line at hiring a hit-man to get rid of me. That would be like killing the chicken that lays the golden eggs.'

'Goose,' she advised absent-mindedly. 'Goose that laid the golden eggs.'

'Yeah,' he noted. 'Our divorce settlement gave her a quarter share in Pacific Mining.'

'I—but a mother can hardly hate her own child. That's just biologically not an in-thing.'

'Robbie is an adopted child,' he reminded her. A chill seemed to gather around Phil's heart. The way he talked about his wife was pure venom. But this casual reference to Robbie was like a chunk of ice. *It's true,* she told herself. *He hates the boy too! And they look so much alike. Carbon copies. His illegitimate child?*

'I—I need to think about it,' she maintained stubbornly. His sigh shook them both.

'All right.' He wadded up his napkin and threw it down. 'Then there's no need for us to remain here, is there?' He hardly waited for an answer, but scraped his chair back and stood up. The waiter hurried over.

'Madame did not care for her lunch?'

'What the hell—didn't you eat anything?'

'I wasn't hungry,' Phil said quietly. The waiter held her chair as she stood up. 'Shall we go now?' She moved over to him, and lifted his hand to her shoulder. It lay there for a second, and then closed in a harsh grip that hurt her. He seemed to be in the grip of some strong emotions. She bore it until a whimper was forced out of her, at which point the grip relaxed. No apology came. Phil struggled to control her facial muscles. It would be adding to the gossip if she led him through the crowd with tears in her eyes. He waited patiently.

The Cadillac carried them painlessly back to the office building, where Penn scrambled out. Phil followed, helping him to the door. 'The reception people will take me the rest of the way,' he said gruffly. 'You go home. You've some considerable thinking to do.'

'But it's only two-thirty,' she said. Being late, quitting early, shirking the hard jobs—these were just not the things that the Philomenas of the world did. But he insisted.

'I do believe I have a little influence with your boss. That's Henderson, isn't it—in Administration?'

'Yes. I had to take two days off for my sister's wedding, and Mr Henderson won't like it if—'

'Mr Henderson will think it's just grand,' he chuckled. 'He'll be so pleased he'll do handsprings. Go home. Harry?' The wiry little man came over to them. 'Harry, take Miss Peabody to her car. And while you're at it, check the damn thing over. I hear that most women in this town drive junk.'

'Well, I really—' Phil stamped her foot and prepared to give him a piece of her mind, but it was too late. He went through the doors, and the two receptionists were fawning all over him. Just watching turned Phil's stomach.

So, like Cinderella, Phil rode around the corner in great style, to be deposited beside her rusty old car. The coach had turned into a pumpkin faster than any fairy godmother could swing a wand. Harry got out with her and circled the ancient Subaru, making *tch tch* noises as he went. Phil stood by the driver's door, key in hand, waiting as if she expected a death sentence from him.

'It's an old car,' he commented as he came up to her.

'I know that.' It's hard not to *sound* exasperated when one is. She did her best, but he caught the inflection.

'If it was a horse we would've shot it four years ago.'

'You don't have to be a critic,' she snapped.

'Brakes work OK?'

'Of course they do.' Righteous indignation, followed by an immediate amendment, because the truth must be served. 'Well, perhaps they're a little bit—soft?'

'Turn on the engine.'

She slid into the driver's seat, flustered, and was unable to find the ignition lock. 'Take your time,' he offered sarcastically. Which made her angry enough to do just that.

The key finally achieved its purpose. The engine rumbled, turned over a couple of times, and then caught with a ragged roar. The car body shook. It was all so normal that Phil smiled. Until the little man stuck his head in the car window.

'Four-cylinder engine?'

'Yes!'

'Only runnin' on three. Been that way a long time, I suppose?'

'I—leave me alone,' she muttered as she reached for the gear-lever. He backed away, looking as if it would all blow up when she moved it.

'Lights work?' he yelled as she moved slowly out of her parking slot.

'Yes,' she roared back at him. It was a definite lie, but since she never drove after dark, she felt it could be marked down as a minor misdemeanour. She snatched a quick look at him in the rear-view mirror. He was laughing.

'Darn nuisance,' she muttered as she turned right on Fifteenth Street and headed for Route 50. During the entire trip home to Rancho Cordova she spent ninety per cent of her time painting images of the jockey and his boss in her mind, and throwing mental darts at them. Which left only ten per cent of her brain to navigate the car—about par for the course with California drivers.

The car squealed to a halt in the familiar driveway, throwing up pebbles and dust in all directions. She got out and walked around the steaming vehicle, trying to see what Harry had seen. It wasn't hard. She was driving a piece of junk, she told herself. She kicked at the left tyre to relieve her anger.

SUPPER WAS as simple as one could get. Two fried eggs shoved into a sandwich, and a glass of cold milk to go with it. Then back out to the living-room to ponder. Channel 13 news was on. She watched it with half an eye, deep in thought. Come live with me. Of course, he didn't mean it the way it sounded. Give up your typing job, and come and be my housekeeper was what he meant. Which gave it all an entirely different slant. She loved her job. On the other hand there was something to be said for staying at home and keeping house. I wonder where he lives. What *kind* of a house is it that needs keeping? The questions piled up, while the answers receded.

Along about ten o'clock the telephone ruined her chances to see—again—the old black and white movie, *Raffles*. She snapped off the set with a twinge of regret and went out into the hall to answer the call.

'Phil, this is Debbie.' Phil groaned, Debbie lived about five miles away, on the edge of Fair Oaks, and only called when she wanted something. As in this case.

'Phil—John and I have a chance to take a wonderful trip up to Tahoe on the weekend, but we can't take the girls!' *I'll bet you can't,* Phil thought. *Two more monstrous kids I've never seen. Real hell-raisers.* 'So we thought we'd let their aunt really get to know them,' Debbie continued. 'How about if I bring them over on Friday night, and we'll pick them up Sunday night late?'

And that will shoot my weekend for sure, Phil thought. *A whole lovely weekend baby-sitting for somebody else's children. So their aunt can get to know them? Their aunt knows all she wants to know about them. They expect me to clothe them and feed them and nurse them, and nobody will ever say a word about payment.*

John is a senior architect, and they're looking for a free baby-sitter! Good old dependable Phil! It was hard to tell which one of the sisters was most surprised at the answer. The little family push had been just enough to make up Phil's mind for her. She would accept Penn Wilderman's offer—because she was curious, and to please herself for a change. Just herself, no one else. Because she wanted to find out what would happen. And here was the perfect opportunity to burn her boats before she could change her mind back again.

'I'm really sorry,' she said, 'but I won't be available this weekend.'

'Oh, Phil!' Under the usual procedure. Debbie would cry a little, Phil would simmer, and then relent. *Not this time, sister.* 'But Phil, we counted on you!'

'How about the week after?'

'Not then either, Debbie. Why don't you hire a baby-sitter! There are plenty available.'

Deep silence from the other end, then an off-telephone conference. John came on the line. 'Phil, you just have to do this for us. Debbie needs a vacation, and—'

'So do I, John. I haven't had one in ten years. But I intend to take one now.'

'Hey Phil, what's got into you?'

'It's hard to tell.' She managed to work up a chuckle. 'But whatever it is, I like it. Do have a good time, John. Call me when you get back and tell me all about it—oops. I forgot. I won't be here. Well, I'll be in touch.' She laid the receiver down on to its cradle with a broad smile on her face. Her brother-in-law was still spluttering as she disconnected.

'One nail in my coffin,' she teased herself as she went for coffee. 'Now, if the family grapevine is working—'

It was. No sooner had she made her mug of instant coffee and added the skimmed milk than the telephone rang again. *They'll push me over the top, to where I can't possibly back out!* She smiled as she picked up the instrument.

'Phil, just what are you up to?' Imperious Samantha. Being a doctor's wife was next door to coronation in Sam's mind.

'Up to?' Phil queried. 'Why, I can't honestly say that I'm up to anything much. What makes you ask?'

'Debbie called me. She's all upset, Phil.'

'Is she really? How terrible.'

'Phil, you *are* up to something. I can smell it.'

That's some nose. Phil wanted to say, but didn't Samantha and her husband lived downtown, adjacent to Mercy Hospital, more miles away than the cows cared to fly in a California winter.

'I can't imagine what gave you that idea,' Phil coaxed. 'The truth of the matter is that I'm tired of having all of you lean on me, Sam. I almost feel as if my life stopped when Mother died—and I took her place. Now it's ten years later,

I'm twenty-seven, and people treat me as if I were fifty. I want something more out of life, Sam.'

'Phil! You've lost your head! And besides—what will we all do without you?'

For the first time a serious note crept into Phil's voice. 'Why, I guess you'll all learn to grow up just a little bit more,' she sighed. She was going to have to use stronger ammunition to make them see things her way, Phil decided. And the language they all understand and respect is: 'I've found a man,' she said softly. Her sister made a curious noise at the other end of the telephone and hung up.

'And now,' Phil announced to the house at large, 'they'll both be over here tomorrow to bring me back to the straight and narrow. But neither of them gets up early enough to catch me before I go off to work, so all I really need to do is be gone by the end of the day. The coward's way out, Philomena. Just exactly what I need!' That night, still dithering, she packed a bag. And so to bed.

The day blessed her decision. The sun was up bright and clear. The early morning fog had dissipated before seven o'clock. The highways were cluttered, but not jammed. One or two dare-devil sparrows could be heard above the hum of civilisation. Phil started earlier than usual, just in case either of her sisters made the supreme sacrifice. Which was just as well.

The doors to the building were already unlocked, but nobody was in reception, and the typing pool was still locked. She fumbled with her key and propped the door open while she felt the inside wall for the light switch. The rows of fluorescent lights flared. And the voice at her elbow said, 'Miss Peabody, they don't fit.'

She dropped her bag, startled, and whirled around. Robert was directly behind her, a rebellious look on his face. A dirty face, at that.

'What don't fit?' She was struggling for time. Never an early-morning person, Phil required a little prompting to get moving.

'The trousers. They don't fit.'

'But that's only the cuff,' she said solemnly. 'I told you yesterday. Every pair of jeans has to be turned up. It won't take but a minute or two with a sewing machine, and not more than ten to fifteen minutes by hand.'

'Really?' A faint appeal stalked that thin face. *And that's something I can do for him,* Phil told herself fiercely. *He hasn't an ounce of confidence in himself! Or anyone else, for that matter!*

'Really,' she repeated. 'What did your father—'

'His father said why didn't you stop at the tailor's.' Penn Wilderman came stalking in from out of the dimly lit lobby. 'So why didn't you?'

'Because I don't think Macy's has a tailor on tap,' she said fiercely. 'And even if they did, this isn't the sort of thing you need a tailor for. Anybody can sew a cuff. Anybody!'

When he laughed she knew he was laughing at himself, and her happy grin flashed back at him. 'Evidently not quite everybody,' he returned. 'I tried last night, and Harry did too.' He looked down at her with his head tilted—that crazy boyish look on his face—and only the dark glasses to distort the happy picture. She was mesmerised by that smile. It tugged at her heart, and her head had no chance.

The water's too deep, she whispered to herself. Way over my head. But she dived in anyway. 'When we get home tonight I'll fix it,' she said.

CHAPTER FOUR

PENN allowed Phil all morning to straighten out the affairs of the typing pool, and to leave Harriet a notebook full of advice. That, of course, left her no time to call either of her sisters. Which helped her guilt feelings immensely. They could hardly interfere when they knew nothing about what was happening. Robbie, demonstrating his confidence in absolutely nobody, sat near her in the work-room. 'To make sure I don't escape?' she asked him.

He returned a tiny smile, and continued to play around with one of the spare word-processors. He did generate a little stir when, along about ten-thirty, he managed to break the corporation's access code and went wheeling and dealing among the corporate memories. Phil caught the action out of the corner of her eye and hustled over to him.

She leaned over his shoulder and turned off the set. 'And just what do you think you're up to, young man?'

'Nothing.' He sat there rigidly, hands still on the keyboard.

'Nothing? That access code is designed especially to keep people out of our records.'

He swivelled around in his chair and looked up at her. His narrow face was flushed. 'It's a stupid code,' he announced. 'Any *hacker* could solve it in twenty minutes.'

'But you took a whole hour?'

'Well, I'm only thirteen, for goodness' sake. What do you expect of a kid?'

'Yeah, kid,' she chuckled. 'Don't do it again—today, that is. Promise?'

He studied her for a moment, looking for—something. 'Well, OK. Promise.' And still those eyes staring, judging. Phil walked away, trying to look confident, but actually keeping her fingers crossed. *Too bright,* she told herself. *He may be adopted, but he's a chip off the old block for all that. What am I letting myself in for?*

There was no more time to ponder. Penn arrived at eleven o'clock. Phil was not watching, but the sudden silence was enough to announce his appearance. She finished the sentence, gave Harriet a quick 'God bless', and headed for the door. 'I have my car in the car park,' she said. 'I'll follow you.'

'Suitcases?'

'In the boot.'

'Harry, transfer the suitcases and have someone bring her car along. Robbie's waiting in the limousine, Peabody. Let's get a move on.'

She was still fumbling with 'But I' when they reached the lobby, his hand firmly on her shoulder. Harry had already disappeared. They were out on the pavement before she could muster up a 'This isn't right.' And even then it hardly contained enough indignation to make it worth while. He pulled her to a halt. 'The flowers,' he asked brusquely. 'What kind?'

She sniffed the air. From long usage she had forgotten them, sited in large pots on either side of the entrance inside the lobby.

'Camellias,' she said. 'It's like a little artificial garden. Your father loves them, they say. The gardener keeps changing them whenever the cold gets to them. There's a greenhouse somewhere. Haven't you ever been here before?'

'Not me,' he laughed. 'I was always the kid they sent out into the field. When my father decided I was seasoned enough to run the company I was no longer interested. I wouldn't have come back—except my mother laid it out for me, too. A very domineering woman, my mother. Come on.'

'Wait,' she said softly, and slipped out from under his hand. The blooms were profuse. She picked one of them and was back at his side.

'Now what?'

'Stand still,' she ordered, stretching for his lapel. 'Darn. You modern men have ruined a good custom. No button hole in your lapel. Here, I'll tuck them into your jacket pocket.' His warm hand closed over hers and carried both up to his lips. It was a fleeting kiss. Just a touch of warmth that made her shiver. 'You're a strange one, Peabody,' he chuckled. 'Whoever would have thought? Flowers in February. I'll have all my suits altered. Button holes coming up!'

'Now *you're* being silly,' she laughed. 'Robbie is getting impatient. Come on.' As they went across the wide walkway she kept cadence to herself, 'Button holes, button holes, button holes.' And for some strange reason it warmed her heart.

The ride was smooth, like drifting in a canoe down a slow-moving river. It was comfortable, too. She was in between Robbie and his father, and the width of the seat provided plenty of room. 'As soon as we get home I need you to put those drops in my eyes,' he said as they circled around down the one-way maze that led to Fifteenth Street.

Phil had already lost track of their route. 'Does it hurt much?'

'Hardly,' he grunted.

'And you can't see a thing?'

'Hey, don't work up that pity bit,' he chuckled. 'I can see. Shapes, outlines—but everything is a little fuzzy. It's getting better. The doctor says it's sort of like getting a bad sunburn. Another three weeks and I'm sure everything will be cleared up. These pads are just a precaution.'

'That's a relief.'

'You were worried about my dad?' The boy was trying to puzzle something out.

'Of course I was worried.' Phil tried to keep it all on a casual basis, but for some reason that was becoming a hard thing to do.

'But two weeks ago you didn't even know him.' The boy had the bit in his teeth, and meant to run with it.

'That doesn't stop me from worrying now that I *do* know him.'

'You're funny.'

Penn's hand came over and squeezed hers. *A warning, or a comfort? Maybe both?* At least I can hope, she thought.

They were in a part of Sacramento Phil had never seen. A little enclave of winding roads, scattered houses. A sign said South Land Park Drive. Another, swathed in old trees, said 12th Street. Directly ahead was the Sacramento River, masked by the trees. They were in the old section of the city, where residential land sold by the foot, not by the quarter-acre. They turned left.

'You don't live here?' A hesitant question begging for denial.

'I believe I do,' Penn answered.

'But—this is where all the millionaires live!'

'I do believe you're right.'

'I—' The car turned off the street, through a set of wrought-iron gates that opened on a small circular drive. A stone wall circled the block-long property. Bushes and trees

hid the house from the street. The car came to a stop in front
of a massive building that sparkled with windows.

'You don't live here!' An angry statement, defying an
answer.

'I do believe I do.'

'Well!' A large sigh to accompany. 'How in the world do
you think I can housekeep such a monstrous house all by my
self?'

'My mother did.'

'Well, she must have been some sort of—I don't believe
it. It's just not possible. For a house like this you have to
hire half a dozen servants!'

He was pushing her out. 'Not quite. Only five, I think!'

'But you—you—said that Mr and Mrs Beaumont had
quit and that you wanted me to—' She turned around and
faced up to him. Nose to chest, so to speak. The closer she
got the taller he seemed to be. 'I think you had better tell me
just what you want *me* for, Mr Wilderman!'

'To fix my trousers,' Robbie answered from behind her.

'That's one good reason,' Penn chuckled. 'There are half
a dozen more. What I really want is for you to get these
people of ours organised so there's some order and effi-
ciency and quiet in this crazy house. I don't expect you to
peel the potatoes and make the soup or sweep the floor. Or-
ganisation, Philomena!'

'Oh!' She bit at her lip, wished that her car were there for
a quick get-away, and alternately wished she had worn
sharp-pointed shoes, so she might kick him in the ankle.

'Now, shall we go in?' He tucked his hand under her elbow to emphasise the fact that the invitation was purely
rhetorical. The house was a stranger to the Sacramento area.
Built along the lines of an old Spanish *hacienda*, it would
have fitted better into the softer climate of southern California. But the walls, the trees, the isolation, hid it from all

its neighbours, of whom there were few. Pillared arches provided a porch, and swept around the sides of the house to form an open mall. The house itself was deep-set within this portico, with wide arched windows flanked by huge wooden shutters. Around the entire second floor a narrow balcony ran, railed with filigree iron. Phil could barely see the curved red tiles of the roof, topped with four sets of twin chimneys. Penn seemed to read her mind.

'Conspicuous consumption,' he said. 'My great-grand-father had it built, when gold was still pouring out of the Mother Lode. Impressed?'

'Frightened,' Phil returned. 'I just keep wondering what happens to me at midnight. Pumpkins and mice?'

He chuckled and hurried her into the house. Robbie trailed behind them, while Harry struggled with her bags. A young girl was waiting for them in the bright hall. Seventeen, perhaps, or eighteen. Short curly black hair, held precariously in place by a white ribbon. A round full face, with smooth tan complexion. Mexican, somewhere in her background, and pretty, Phil concluded.

'Philomena, this is Cecily. Where's Mrs Waters?'

'In the kitchen. She's doing lunch.' A touch of liquid accent, the soft caress of Spanish mingled with the drawl of the American South-west. Altogether nice, Phil thought. Her smile was returned four-fold.

'Mrs Waters is our cook, Philomena. You can meet her later. Cecily works the morning shift. Mary comes on from three until seven. Frank is the handyman, and George is the gardener. They'll all be around the house somewhere, after lunch. Why don't you go up to your room and settle in? Cecily?'

The girl nodded and headed for the broad sweep of mahogany stairs that curved gently around to an upstairs landing. There was a painting on the wall, half-way up. A portly pirate, with short black beard, piercing eyes, and a gold watch chain prominently displayed across a half-acre of stomach. It almost seemed there should be an earring in one of his lobes, but of course he wasn't that sort of pirate.

Harry, right behind Phil, with the bags, said, 'The old Boss. He built the place. Been nothin' like him in the family until Penn come along.'

And I can surely believe that, Phil thought. Isn't that the claim—there's a throwback in every family come the third generation? The room to which she was led was almost at the head of the stairs. Cecily threw back the double doors with a touch of grace and stood aside. Harry stopped behind them in the hall. Both waited for Phil's reaction.

'Oh, my,' she murmured as she walked slowly to the centre of the room and looked around. 'Oh, my goodness.' Cecily smiled broadly. The bedroom was four times the size of her own, back home in Rancho Cordova. The walls were pink, the wall-to-wall carpet beige, and the bed covered with a Coat-of-Joseph quilt. Four floor-to-ceiling windows made up one wall, facing west towards the river. The windows stood slightly ajar, inviting her out into the sunshine on the balcony. She resisted. There was too much to be done, too much to be learned.

'I think you've made a mistake,' prim little Philomena said. 'I'm the housekeeper, not the daughter of the house.' But you don't want to change to something else, Phil, her conscience shrieked. Don't be so darn positive!

'No mistake,' Cecily laughed. 'The best room in the house, yes. Mr Wilderman picked it out himself. This one, he said, this one is for Peabody. He calls you that?'

'Yes,' Phil laughed. 'But everybody else should call me Phil. You too, Harry.'

'Sure,' the little man said as he swung her bags up on to the bench in front of the dressing-table. 'He hears me call you that and the balloon goes up for sure. Well, maybe when he's not around.'

'The lunch is in twenty minutes,' Cecily offered. 'You want help to unpack?'

'Me?' Phil could just not hold back the giggles. 'I don't have enough in those bags to—well, I don't. But please do stay. I want to ask a question or two.'

Harry took the hint, and left. Phil opened her cases, and transferred the dresses slowly into the huge armoire that took up one corner of the room. It was true, she hadn't brought many clothes. And those she had brought were of two kinds, simple suits for office work, or take-aways from Good Will Industries. At least they looked that way. Cecily watched, somewhat disappointed.

'Tell me about Robbie,' Phil asked. 'Does he go to school? Does he ever see his mother? Is he happy here?'

'*Ay Dios mio,*' the girl laughed. 'First, yes, he goes to school. But they have vacation. A private school, no? The boy is too sharp. He knows everything. And in his room the computer—you wouldn't believe. He is in trouble once. The police came. Something about tapping into the City's computer system illegally. He—his mother—that is hard to say. His mother has the right to him—you know—the court control. The guardian? But I don't think—especially now that she is remarried—well.' She shrugged a very expressive shoulder. The girl sat down on the corner of the bed. 'It is money, I think. The mother has an income from the Company. The boy also. His mother can't stand to have him around—until she needs money. His money. Then she comes here with much noise and loud argument, you know? And takes him back. Mr Wilderman, he tries now in the court to get permanent control of the child. But the lawyers say you must have family. There must be the home life, and parents. It is a puzzle. There must be action quickly. The court is—ruling? Next week.'

'You mean the case has to be decided as quickly as all that?'

'Yes. I think so. Mr Wilderman, you know, he don't tell us, but we hear. And Mrs Wilderman—well, I don't know. She does not want the boy for love, you understand. She would rather he live with his father. But then she would lose the money. I think—it has been peaceful here for a week. I think something is bound to explode very soon.'

'And Mr Wilderman? He really wants the boy?'

'Of course.'

'For an adopted child he looks very much like Mr Wilderman.'

'But of course. I—oh—the bell. I must serve the lunch. Excuse me—I forgot to say, Welcome.'

'Thank you, Cecily. I'll be down in a minute.'

It took much longer than that. She stopped long enough to scrub herself in the white and gold bathroom, then slipped into one of her better cotton dresses. It was a distinct contrast to her working clothes. A dress warm enough for the mild winter, but sparkling in spring buttercup. Her head was already starting to ache with all she had learned—and had not learned. She pulled out the pins in her hair and unbraided it, setting it straight with a few quick passages of her brush. It made a world of difference to her appearance, but that was something she had failed to notice in the haste of the past ten years.

Fifteen minutes later, she started back down the stairs. Sunlight glittered off the stair-runners and played echo off the little glass squares suspended from the massive chandelier. Behind, on the darker wall, another picture hung. A life-sized oil, it appeared, of a young woman in the spring of her life. She was dressed in a long ball-gown, and was

poised looking to her right, a happy smile on her face.
Something tugged at Phil's mind. There was something
about the picture—but she could not place just what it was.
A young woman, with golden hair, smiling at the world! She
shrugged her shoulders and went down.

Robbie was waiting for her. 'The dining-room is at the
back of the house,' he said. 'When are you going to fix my
trousers?'

'Just as soon as we finish lunch,' Phil said casually. The
boy looked at her sceptically, his solemn thin face a mixture of hope and doubt. He stood there for a moment, then
turned and walked away down the hall.

Phil was distracted as she followed him. There were more
paintings on the walls. Not family pictures, but works of
some merit, hung too high for her to read the names of the
artists, but not so high that she could not appreciate their
excellence. When she turned her attention to where she was
going the boy had disappeared. At the end of the hall were
a pair of double doors, closed. She was looking down the
lateral corridor, wondering where Robbie had gone, when
she reached for the knob and went in. Actually she was half-
turned, not paying attention to her path. And she smashed
into Penn.

His arms came out, almost automatically, and kept her
from falling. More than that. They wrapped themselves
around her and pulled her in solidly against his vibrant
strength. All his actions seemed programmed, not real. He
held her close, muttering something she could not make out.
She relaxed against him, enjoying the feeling.

One of his hands wandered to her hair, tumbling through
it like a leaf in a mill-stream. The other moved to the small
of her back and pulled her closer, ever closer. The warmth
and comfort of it all had taken her completely by surprise.

The hands moved up to cup her head, and his lips brushed across hers gently.

Gently, at first. They came again, insistently, demanding, drawing out of her all the emotions she had stored for twenty-seven years. Stored and never shared. Until now. It was too much of a demand. Her own hands were trapped against his chest. She wriggled them loose and felt them follow the flow of his ribcage, around his back as far as she could reach. And then, as suddenly as the assault had begun, he pushed her back, away from him. 'Who?' he asked bitterly. And all her castle of dreams collapsed.

'Philomena,' she quavered.

'Damn!' He stepped away, widening the gap beyond touch. 'I don't know what came over me,' he sighed. 'I was thinking of something, and there was the smell of your perfume—damn it, Peabody, it reminded me of someone. I'm sorry.'

She had managed to regain her breath by then, and some semblance of her mind. There was a feeling of loss involved—what had tasted so sweet was bitter. But she was determined not to let it show. 'No need to apologise,' she said primly. 'I've been kissed before. To be honest, I rather enjoyed it.'

'That's kind of you,' he chuckled. 'And honest. I like that. But I want you to know I don't run around the house assaulting elderly ladies.' He offered an arm. For himself, she knew, but it felt warmingly good. 'They're about to serve lunch.'

She led him to the table, wrestling all the way with her own thoughts *Elderly lady!* Good lord, he's got me thinking that way now. Philomena Peabody, twenty-seven going on fifty! It was nice, that kiss. She did enjoy it. She had been kissed by men before—but so long ago she could hardly associate name with face in her memory. And I mustn't let him think—what he's thinking.

'I'm not really *that* old,' she told him. If he wants to pursue the subject, now's the time!

'No, of course not,' he rumbled. 'Sit over here next to me.' He held a chair for her. Phil slipped into it, biting her lip in disgust. He *didn't want* to pursue it—or her, for that matter. Why should that seem important to her? A gong sounded out in the hall. Robbie came in, thumping in his seven-league boots. Harry was not far behind.

And there's another question answered, Phil thought. Harry eats with the family. So he's not a servant, he's a— what? And Robbie, sitting all hunched up at the far end of the table, looking as if he expected to be poisoned by the cook. His hands were grimy, and there was a streak of something—chocolate? —on his chin. Phil's household soul rebelled. She beckoned to the boy. He looked sullenly, then got up with much reluctance and came around the table to her side. She pulled his head closer so she could whisper in his ear.

'I do the trousers, you wash the hands,' she said. 'And the face too, for that matter.'

The boy considered. He had his father's habit. His head was tilted to one side as he thought, but not an inkling of a smile crossed his face. 'OK,' he said, and thumped out of the room.

'OK?' Penn, looking at her but not seeing, the pads behind his dark glasses still fixed in place. Silence. 'I know it has to do with Robbie. I never realised how noisy he is when he walks. What's going on?'

'He's doing me a favour,' Phil replied. 'We have this bargain going. And all teenagers sound like a herd of buffalo. Even the girls.'

'At least he didn't yell. You're a good influence on that boy, Peabody. You could have been his mother.'

She had her water glass at her lips when he said that, and almost drowned as the fluid went down the wrong pipe. He bent over the corner of the table and patted her back a couple of times. Patted, in his style, Phil thought. A couple more of those and he'll break my back. *I could be the child's mother?* Robbie is thirteen and I'm twenty-seven. So it's biologically possible, I suppose. But again, that urge to tell him—if he wanted to know. 'Me being Robbie's mother is faintly possible,' she offered with a touch of whimsy in her voice. 'But just barely so. There's this matter of age between us.' And having thrown out the gauntlet for the second time, she relaxed in her chair, waiting to see what he would do.

Cecily came in at that moment with a serving-tray, and set it down in front of him. 'Don't go on about your age, Peabody,' he said firmly. He reached for the carving-knife, and, as Phil held her breath, did an adequate job of carving the roast. And that, she told herself, is the last time I'm going to bring up the subject. When they take the pads off his eyes he'll know better, and I'll be back at my word-processor faster than he can say *who the hell are you!*

She ate more than she had intended. Lunch was usually a sandwich. Mrs Waters was obviously a cook *par excellence.* Phil wandered out to the kitchen for an introduction. The cook was a good advertisement for her wares. Short, well-rounded, flushed cheeks, grey hair. Somebody's mother, looking for a family to love. 'Been here thirty years,' she admitted. 'Mr Waters was the gardener here—before George. But, the war and all, and we never had children, so I stayed. I seen Penn grow up. He was a happy young man, until his sister died. Since then—well, he's changed. Needs some lovin', that man.'

'His sister died?'

'Boating accident. The pair of them used to race up and down the river in those speedboats and all. Neither one never listened to what nobody had to say. Hit a piece of driftwood, she did. Turned the boat over, broke her neck. She was racing him. He never forgot that. Killed her man too. But he wasn't a Wilderman.' The tone of voice gave to indicate that *therefore the husband didn't count in the scheme of things*.

Robbie came through the swinging doors. 'I washed my hands,' he said. 'And ate all my lunch. Now?'

'Now,' Phil laughed. 'Thank you again, Rose. We'll talk later on. Come on, Robbie.' When the door swung shut behind them Rose Waters stopped what she was doing, put her hands on her hips, and contemplated the back of the door. 'Well,' she said 'I *do* declare. Make a nice housekeeper, that one—make a better wife!'

Not even dreaming of such a fate, Phil and Robbie tumbled up the stairs and into her room. Cecily had resurrected an old pedal Singer sewing-machine from somewhere in the attic, and it stood rather forlornly in the middle of the beige rug. But it worked. 'Up on this chair now, Robbie,' she ordered. The boy, still suspicious, climbed up on the low flat chair and moved as she directed. While she measured and pinned she tried a little conversation.

'When does your school open again, Robbie?'

'Pretty soon.'

'Like it, do you?'

'Ummph.'

With a mouthful of pins Phil could hardly question him at length. 'What do you want to be when you grow up?'

'An adult.'

She looked up quickly, and caught him in a smile. He did his best to erase it, but failed. The grin spread gradually across his face as she made a mark in the air with her finger. 'One for you,' Phil told him. 'But watch yourself, wise guy. Two can pun as easy as one.'

'Well, stupid people keep asking me that,' he returned. The sulky expression was back.

'And that puts me in *my* place,' she chuckled. 'Skin out of those trousers now, and I'll get them sewn.'

'I—I didn't mean you, Miss Peabody,' he defended. 'And I don't take my trousers off when there's girls in the room.'

'Thank you on both counts,' she chuckled. 'But I'm not a girl—I'm a woman.'

'I—I don't think I know what the difference is.'

'I don't think I do either,' Phil returned. 'Scoot out of here now. I'll have all of these ready in about an hour.' The boy managed one more tiny smile, and was gone.

Her first major task of the day finished, Phil decided to wander. She saw Cecily leave, driven off by Frank the handyman in a very plebeian Ford. The sun was bright outside. At the end of February, in the sun, the temperature stood at seventy degrees. It would get colder at sunset. Even worse if clouds settled down from the mountains to the east. There was snow in those mountains, deep snow. Lake Tahoe was under a blizzard, the weatherman had said at midday. And that only a couple of hours away by road. But now it was worth a walk. Phil strolled out on the veranda, and wandered around to the back of the house.

It was all too confusing, this house, the Wildermans— husband and wife fighting over the boy. Not exactly what you could call a tug-of-love case. Maybe Robbie was right. Maybe they both hated him. But why? He was an adopted child, but he resembled Penn so closely—could that be the

source of the bitterness? And if Mrs Wilderman was intent
on getting the boy back, what would she do next? I just
hope, Phil told herself, that I'm done and gone from here
before the inevitable explosion.

CHAPTER FIVE

THE remainder of the week was a string of little scenes, as Philomena put her hands to organising the household. There was the early morning uproar that brought her up in her bed. It came from behind the connecting door which she had noted but not checked. She slipped into her robe and padded barefoot in the general direction of the problem. The door was unlocked, and on the other side Penn, dressed only in pyjama bottoms, was vainly trying to avoid Harry's ministrations. The bedroom was dim, almost dark.

'I don't want a bath,' Penn said grimly. 'For God's sake, Harry, can't you get the eye drops closer to the eyes?'

'I could if you would stop wigglin' around like a fish on a hook.'

'Oh, so now it's my fault?'

'Look, boss, it's been your fault for two weeks. I hadda refill the prescription four times already. Everybody in the drug store thinks I'm drinking it.'

'Ah. Afraid of your reputation, are you?'

Phil ghosted across the floor. 'Let me do that,' she told Harry. He surrendered the dropper without an argument. 'Sit still. Stop acting like a little baby,' she warned Penn. Harry almost swallowed his tongue, and faded out of the room.

'Baby, is it?' He was a tiger now, all sleek and deadly. She paid his objection about as much attention as she had her sisters' under similar conditions.

'I call it as I see it,' she said firmly. 'Hold still.' Her thumb forced his eyelid up, and two precise drops fell on to his eyeball. 'Is that any better?'

'Lucky,' he grumbled. 'So you got it all. Lucky.'

'You bet,' she chuckled. 'We'll try for two.' Her thumb went out again. He shrugged away, and almost got the digit in his eye. 'I said sit still,' she commanded.

'Yes ma'am.' A very docile comment, that foreshadowed troubles to follow. A tiny grin flicked at the corner of her mouth as she repeated the eyedropper exercise.

'There now, that wasn't too bad, was it?'

'No, Mommy.'

'Don't be a smart-aleck,' she warned.

'Or you'll turn me over your knee? How about a little retribution?' He lunged at her, managing to find one wrist, and pulled her down across his knees. 'Now, Miss Know-It-All, try this one for size.'

It wasn't her time of day, frankly. She did anything better in the afternoon. But there wasn't a great deal of time to object. He had her trapped, pinioned, and crushed up against his naked chest before she could catch her breath. It was about as close as she had ever been to a naked man, and the lack of experience told on her. What followed replaced at least two of her normal three cups of coffee. His lips came down on hers again, softly, gently. His breath smelled like warm clean breezes. *And I haven't even brushed my teeth,* she thought wildly. It didn't bother him. The gentle assault became mental torture. He sealed her off from every outside contact, forcing her to complaints—rioting complaints. They were ignored. The hand behind her head was no longer needed to lock her in place. She had totally surrendered. And then it was over.

She struggled to sit up. At least it was affecting him also, she noted. He's as out of breath as I am. And something more. That strange expression on his face, as if he had tried something awful and found he liked it!

'Damn it, Peabody,' he muttered. 'You've done it again!'

'Of course,' she returned, as the experience whirled from pleasure to bitterness. 'It's all my fault, right? I took advantage of you.' Her hand reached out against her will, and stroked the curling hair on his massive chest.

'Right,' he grunted. His two hands under her armpits lifted her straight up and set her down on her feet. 'For the sake of my peace of mind, please get the hell out of here!' She fled back into her own bedroom, slammed the connecting door behind her, and frantically fumbled with the key.

It spoiled the whole morning, but the next day, and every day thereafter, he appeared politely at her door, eyedrops in hand. She would lead him over to her bed, sit him down comfortably, and administer his daily dose. And as each day passed, she wished crazily that he might pull her down into his lap again.

With Robbie, things were a little different. The first three days the boy gloomed around the house in his new jeans, disappearing into his room whenever she tried to make conversation. 'Hiding with his computer,' Cecily told her. 'It talks back, but it can't give him any orders.'

On the fourth day she trapped him in a corner and refused to let him go. 'I mean to talk to you, Robbie,' she insisted. 'And if it means that I have to follow you all over the house, even to the bathroom, I'll do it.'

'I'll go in my room and lock the door,' he muttered.

'I've got a key to every room in the house,' she returned jingling her key-ring at him. He thought about it for a minute or two, and then gave up.

'So talk.'

'Don't you have any friends, Robbie?'

'Not around here. In St Louis, yes. I talk to them through the computer network.'

'Lord, that must make a tremendous telephone bill.'

'He doesn't care so long as it keeps me quiet. Didn't you know that?'

'I know that your father is very worried about you,' Phil snapped. 'Between the lawyers and the court case, he's about to go through the roof. Do you *want* to go back to your mother?'

'No. No, I don't.' The defiance had disappeared. He was just a lonely little boy.

'Then you have to help, Robbie. You have to get out in the sunshine—get a little exercise. How about touring the city with me?'

'Well—I'd rather play with my computer.'

'I'll pull out all the fuses in the house if you don't get outside,' she threatened.

'Why are you so serious about all this? I'm nothing to you.'

'Of course you're something to me. Everybody is something to everybody. Don't they teach you *anything* in that school of yours?'

'No, they don't. I don't understand you. Women are like my mother—and you're not. I think you've got a crush on my—on him!' Those dark eyes bored through her like daggers. She caught her breath.

'That would be a likely way to commit suicide,' she returned, even though her heart wasn't in it. 'Get yourself a jacket while I see if I can rustle up a car.'

'You are funny, Peabody—er—Phil? You rustle cattle, not cars.'

'Not where I come from, buddy. The clock is running. Scoot.'

Phil's life had been marvellously improved by the reappearance of her car. It arrived three days after her, and seemed to have been—perhaps resurrected would be the best word for it. The engine had been tuned, the brakes re-lined and adjusted, it sported four—no five—new tyres, and the whole rackety thing had been repainted. The only thing she could object to was the colour. An ancient Japanese car masquerading in Kelly Green was just not her cup of tea. But it ran.

They made their first visitation to Sutter's Fort. Once it had stood on a hill, distant form the confluence of the Sacramento and the American rivers. Now the city had grown up around and past it, its ruins had been reconstructed by the state, and it stood its vigil just a short distance up Capitol Avenue from the State House.

The wall around the fort looked newer than it ever had in Sutter's time. The original wall had been eighteen feet high, made of adobe. The replacement was lower, of painted brick. The central building, the trading post, glowed in a new coat of paint. And the low workshops that stood against the inside of the walls now sold souvenirs. Robbie was impressed but not very. His reaction fell into that gap that Phil defined as 'underwhelmed'.

'Junk,' he commented. 'Tourist stuff. And I read somewhere that John Sutter was a fake.'

'Did you now,' Phil chuckled. 'I thought the jury was still out on that. So maybe he wasn't a Swiss nobleman. You can't dispute that he established the first white settlement in Northern California, and if it hadn't been for the Gold Rush in 1849 he would have been a very wealthy man.'

'That don't make sense, Phil.' She smiled at him. Her name had come out naturally—and that was a start. 'How could he go broke because of the Gold Rush?'

'It wasn't hard,' she returned. 'Thousands did. But John Sutter had his own way. He wanted to make his money from wheat. There were plenty of customers. Bread cost a fortune in the Gold Rush days.'

'So what was the problem?'

'Wheat has to be planted, tended, and harvested. In the end every labourer that Sutter recruited gave up the agricultural work and went off to pan gold for themselves. Sutter went so far into debt that there was no escape. Want to see some more?'

'Like this?'

'Well, it's hard not to be like this, Robbie. Everything from the old days went to wrack and ruin. It's only been in the last few years that things have been reconstructed. But there's a lot to learn. How about if we go down to Old Sacramento?'

'It's your car,' he grumbled, but she could actually see him relax. So she drove west, skirting the traffic problems on the Capitol Mall, the wide expanse of road that ran from the Capitol building itself down to the river, on the order of the great boulevards of Paris. She also had to dodge the traffic around the K Street Mall, a shopping district that was being overhauled to allow the use of LRV's—light rail vehicles.

They left their car parked in the underground facility in the mall and walked across into the Embarcadero area, the flat plain between Route Five and the river. Reconstruction of the old city was not yet complete, and might never be, but as they walked from block to block they saw it all as it might have been when this little corner of the world was the gateway to the goldfields. There were drapers and drugstores, grocers and hardware, mixed together with saloons, gambling halls, and banks. Not to mention the Hastings building, and the statue which marked the Western terminal of the Pony Express.

'You mean to tell me that they actually lifted the whole town up over fifteen feet?' Robbie's scientific mind found it all improbable.

'More than that in some places,' Phil laughed. 'You know the original city was almost swept away several times in the early days. But instead of just moving away, they dredged the river, lifted all the buildings with hydraulic jacks, and filled in underneath them. And if you think all of that is fairy tales, young man, just run across the street there. You can still look down at the original building, below the present street level.'

Phil stayed where she was and watched as he ran the gauntlet of traffic to have a look. She had had enough. Her feet hurt. If the Bee had suddenly predicted a twenty-foot rise in the river level, Phil was prepared to stand and drown rather than move another step. Robbie walked back slowly.

'Convinced?'

'Yeah. I'm convinced. It's hardly believable though, is it? How could they afford all that?'

'You have to remember that in those days, Robbie, practically all the gold mined in the United States flowed through this city. And a little of it stuck on every hand it passed through. So now, what have you learned?'

He pulled himself up out of his normal slouch. 'I've learned that sightseeing is hard work. My feet hurt.'

Which led them back to the house in a companionable mood, about four o'clock in the afternoon. 'I'm gonna go watch television,' the boy commented. He made himself up a bologna sandwich and a glass of milk, and wandered off.

'Television?' Phil asked. 'I didn't see any antennae on the roof. Have they run the cable out here yet?'

'Nope,' Rose laughed. 'Satellite antenna. Out behind the swimming-pool it is. Gives us one hundred channels twenty-four hours a day, and not a worth-while programme on any of them.'

'But Robbie likes it, I suppose?'

'He sure does. A mite more companionable, the boy is,' Rose commented as she prepared the dinner. 'Roast lamb tonight. Can I give you a hint, Phil?'

'You bet, Rose. Shoot.'

'Maybe you ought to,' the cook muttered. 'Shoot, that is. Find out what Mary is doing.'

'Well, according to the schedule she's supposed to be cleaning the downstairs rooms. Cecily does the upstairs in the morning and serves lunch. Mary does the downstairs in the afternoon and serves dinner. No?'

'That's what the schedule says.'

'I see.' Phil bit her lip. The only thing she hated worse than trouble was letting a little trouble go long enough to become big. 'I'd better go change and clean up,' she said. 'And then I'll see.'

'You bet you will.' Rose was not going to say any more, so Phil got up, stretched, slipped off her shoes and went off, not expecting to find that there was a serpent in the Garden.

The house seemed very still as she made her way up the stairs. *It's like one of those Gothic horror stories,* she told herself as she paused in front of the portrait on the wall. 'You wouldn't haunt me, would you?' she asked the picture. The old pirate seemed to grin back at her. With that reassurance she went, barefoot, up the rest of the stairs.

The door to her room was closed. She could not remember shutting it, and Cecily had long since gone home. So perhaps the wind blew it, she thought, as she pushed her way in. Across the room a figure was bent over the bureau, and all Phil's clothes were lying in disarray on the floor.

'What in the world are you doing!' She was across the room like an avenging angel. This surprising invasion of her own privacy was almost as bad as a physical attack. Sick to her stomach, Phil clutched at the woman's shoulder. It was Mary Treadway, the second maid. A middle-aged thin woman with iron-grey hair, Mary was the sort of person who could easily be someone's spinster aunt. Instead she was the mother of a large family, always in need, always complaining.'

'I—I was just cleaning up,' the maid stammered.

'Cleaning up? Here? It looks as if you're *making* a mess, not cleaning one up. And why up here? You know the programme. Your job is to clean downstairs. Cecily takes care of everything up here.'

'I—I must have forgotten.'

'How could you forget? It was only yesterday that I went over the complete list of duties with you!'

'I don't have to listen to any talk like that.' The thin face was diffused with anger. Real or false, Phil asked herself.

'No, you don't,' she returned quietly. 'You can always quit.'

A flash of alarm came over the woman's face. 'I—I can't do that,' she almost cried. 'I need the money.'

'Then I think you'd better get yourself downstairs and do the work you're assigned.' Phil felt grim, and her voice reflected her feelings. She watched as the older woman hurried out of the door.

And what do you suppose that was all about, she thought? She forgot? Not a chance. It's true she used to clean this room, until I changed the schedule, but forget? Never. So then what? Checking my clothes? To what purpose? Or maybe it's just snooping; an incurable urge to know everything about everybody. If so, all she found out is that I like expensive underwear. How about that?

Still puzzling, Phil stripped off her clothes, took a quick shower, and climbed into her working-clothes. She made a quick tour, as she did every day, of all the rooms on the second floor. They were immaculate, as usual. Cecily was a cheerful and thorough worker. Phil left Penn's room for last. *Because it stands next to mine,* she told herself. It was as good an excuse as any.

His room was slightly smaller then her own, with none of the frills. Its colour-scheme was bronze and gold. The windows opened up on to the same balcony. His clothes were hung neatly, all in a row, more suits than she wanted to count, but all in what she classified as 'Corporation' colours—navy blue, grey, pinstripes. As with his son, until Phil had worked over the boy's wardrobe, he tended towards formality. And yet, he was not always formal. She had a few glimpses of the man beneath the disguise. Wonderful glimpses, that left her staggered. She sat down on his bed, and then fell over on to his pillow.

There seemed to be some residual comfort from it all, some warmth. Left over, of course. He had been gone from the house for hours, and the pillow cases had been changed. *What are you diddling about,* she accused herself, and could not find the answer. A wry smile played on her mobile face. *Back to the salt mines, lady!* She laughed at herself as she swung her feet back on to the floor, brushed down the counterpane, and went downstairs.

There was that feeling again, that mood of Gothic doom. She stopped in the bend of the stairs, concentrating this time on the painting of the young woman on the opposite wall. There was some ethereal vagueness about the girl. She looked like someone. *Someone I know!* Again it escaped her, and she went on down.

Robbie was in the game-room at the back of the house, glued to the ten thousandth re-run of a Tarzan movie. A youthful Johnny Weissmuller swung through the vines, chasing after Jane. Phil stayed for a moment. She liked the really old movies, and the dialogue was just right. 'Me Tarzan, you Jane.' What a lovely bunch of writing that was! Chuckling quietly she ruffled Robbie's hair and headed for the door. To her surprise the boy followed her movement, and smiled.

Her tour of inspection swept on, through the dining-room, where there was dust on the sideboard, into the living-room, where the cushions were in some disarray, and out into the hall, hunting Mary. And found her.

The maid was talking to someone on the telephone. Talking softly, swiftly, with her eyes continually sweeping the hall. As soon as she saw Phil appear she downed the telephone and did her best to look industrious. Phil was tired of being the disciplinarian. She swept by Mary without saying a word, and went out into the afternoon sunshine looking for Mr Yu, the gardener. There was something very comforting about sharing the old man's garden—and his dry wit.

Dinner that night was more relaxed than meals had been since she came to this—palace. Penn was in a good mood, allowing her to administer the eyedrops before the meal with not a single quibble. 'Things went well today?' she hazarded.

'They surely did,' he said, 'but I can't carve this darn roast.'

'I'll do it,' she offered. 'You don't have to be totally independent. Not here.'

He tendered her the carving-knife and fork, and a big smile. The last so startled her that she almost dropped the other two. He leaned back in his chair. 'We settled a part of that business out at the Mother Lode,' he said. It was the first time he had ever introduced business into a casual conversation. Two firsts for the day, Phil crowed to herself. Robbie smiled at me, and Penn said a few nice words!

'I never did understand what it was all about,' she tempted.

'You know, of course, that we own a dozen or more small mines in El Dorado county. They were open into the 1930s, but the costs of extracting gold were just booming, so my grandfather closed them. There's plenty of gold left there, mind you, but it just cost more than it was worth to get it out. The United States government had pegged the price of gold at thirty-five dollars an ounce, and there it stayed. Now, things have changed. The government no longer tries to control the price of gold. Of course extraction costs have gone up, too. But today, one ounce would cost us about one hundred and sixty dollars to extract—and gold prices are pretty firm in the neighbourhood of three hundred and thirty dollars an ounce. So, it could be profitable.'

'But?'

'Yes, there's a *but*. But the people who live in El Dorado county are suburbanites. They don't want the massive machinery that we would need for open-pit mining. Well, some of them don't. Today we made agreements with three of the towns which allow us to reopen four of the mines, provided we don't go to open-pit mining. I think we can still make a profit. How did your day go?'

'I think I wore out a pair of shoes,' Robbie interjected. Another surprise. To that moment he had never said a word at the table. 'She took me sightseeing. I must have walked fifty miles!'

'Poor you,' Phil teased. 'I think it was more like five.'

'But I got even,' the boy returned, grinning. 'I think her feet hurt more than mine did.'

'That must have been a sight to see, all by itself,' his father commented. The two of them launched into a heated
discussion about places they had been and admired, leaving Phil sitting in a conversational back-water, happy to hear
them making real family talk. Harry was out of it too. She
caught him once with a big smile on his face, and he winked
at her, as if she might be responsible for breaking the log-
jam. Which of course I'm not, she told herself regretfully.

At the end of the meal she threw them a bombshell,
without meaning to at all. 'Tomorrow is Sunday,' she said
as a reminder. 'All the help has the day off, and—'

'All except George Yu,' Penn told her. 'He comes into the
house and we eat Chinese for the day.'

'Well, that had me worried,' Phil said. 'I have to go home
tomorrow.' A heavy silence fell at the table. All three of the
men laid down their utensils and stared at her. 'Did I say
something terrible?' she asked.

'Yes,' Robbie returned.

'I think so,' his father added. 'We hadn't expected you to
leave us, as if you were hired help.'

'Well, that's what I am,' she returned defensively. 'And
besides, it's only for the day. I have to check up on my *own*
house, and pick up some more clothes. And my sisters! Sally
will be back from her honeymoon, and the other two will
want to beat me up, I'm sure.'

'Well, I won't let them,' said Robbie, his face flushed,
both fists formed and resting on the table-top.

'I'm just joking,' she hastened to add. 'I don't mean
they'll beat me up—I'm older than they are.'

'And they respect your grey hairs,' Penn chuckled.

'She don't have any—'

'That's enough, Robbie. If Philomena needs a day off to
go home, we must consider ourselves lucky to have her the
rest of the week. What time do you want to go?'

'Early, I suppose,' she said, trying to hide her own groan. 'There's nothing I like about the word early, but I've a lot to do.'

'I'll bet there is,' Penn said. 'By the way, I brought your pay-cheque home.' He handed her an envelope. She tucked it under her plate for the moment, and waited for dessert to be served.

Despite her hatred of things early, she was up and dressed by six-thirty. There was a noise at her door by seven. Penn, wanting his eyedrops administered before she disappeared, 'Just a week and a half more,' he said quietly as she went about the job with dispatch. 'Dr Morgan says everything is coming on fine, provided I just don't rush things. I can see much better.'

'Well, he's right,' she sighed as she applied new pads. 'After all this time it would be silly to take chances. Whatever took you to the Antarctic in the first place?'

'Government secrets,' he chuckled. 'They were looking for coal, so they imported a mining expert.'

'But—coal isn't your line!'

'Hey,' he laughed. 'After ten years in our typing pool and you don't know that Pacific owns open-pit coal mines all over the West?'

'Well, I don't read all that stuff,' she huffed. 'I just type it. Most of you people write as if you had swallowed a dictionary. You need more warmth in your correspondence!'

His hand trapped hers, and his other joined, sliding over the softness at her wrist, and up her forearm. 'Warm, like you,' he muttered. He was looking at something beyond her ken, feeling something more than her arm, dreaming something? It would have been simple for her to pull away. Robbie had come out of his own room and was staring at them. But Phil just did not want to. There was too much pleasure to be had from his hands. Pleasure like nothing she had ever experienced before.

'Well, I won't keep you.' He disengaged her gently, lowering her hand rather than dropping it. 'Have a good day.'

'I will,' she promised softly, and stared after him as he made his way back to his own bedroom, using the wall as a guide. It amazed her how proficient he was. How strong. How gentle. How— 'Dear lord, Phil,' she muttered to herself. 'It isn't as if you were going to *eat* him.'

'What did you say?' She turned around, startled. Robbie was still standing there, fully dressed.

'Nothing,' she improvised. 'I was—just clearing my throat.' She managed a dismal hacking cough to illustrate. 'And what brings you out so early, young man?'

'You.' He partnered her as she went down the stairs.

'Your car is out front.' Mr Yu, dressed in slacks and white shirt, held the door for her. 'Frank filled up the tank and checked the oil.'

'Silly,' Phil remarked, but was warmed just the same. After all, she had only driven the car forty miles since the last time Frank had checked it out. She strolled down the stairs. Robbie went right along with her. As she reached for the door handle she looked over at him. I do believe he's growing like a weed, she thought. His eyes are dark grey! Dark, intense eyes.

'And just what are you up to?'

'I'm going with you.'

'Not *may* I go with you?'

'No. Just I'm going. You need somebody to look after you. Dad said last night you are really a *little* thing.'

'I'm not all *that* little.'

'Well, I'm going anyway. You're a girl—a woman. Whatever. Somebody's got to look after you.'

Phil knew when she was beaten, and surrendered gracefully. 'How kind you are.' The boy seemed to swell up just the slightest bit. He ushered her into the driver's seat, closed her door behind her, and went around the car to climb in. As she drove away a peculiar thought hit her. The boy. Is he going just to keep me company, or to make sure I come back? Is it possible that I mean something to him? As he means something to me? She chewed on the idea all the way out to the house in Rancho Cordova.

'That's an old house,' Robbie said as they drove up into the yard. 'Funny kind of a house to see in the middle of all this.' Phil followed his waving hand. It *did* seem that a dozen more high-rise buildings had come into existence in the short time she had been away.

'It's a farmhouse,' she said as she led the way up to the front door and fumbled for her key. 'When I was a little girl this was all a big farm, and my daddy was a farmer.'

'But it's not now?'

'No,' she said softly. 'My father had no sons—only girls. It takes a great deal of muscle to be a farmer. Muscle and brains. And Dad left so many debts we had to sell the land. But that's last year's news. Come in, Robbie.'

He stepped over the pile of mail lying on the floor behind the mail slot. She stopped to pick it all up. Bills, advertisements, magazine subscriptions—she sorted them all out on the way to the kitchen.

'Now the first thing we do,' she told the boy, 'is open a few windows. The house smells as if it hasn't been lived in for years!' And so the day began. There was dusting to do, some washing—somehow the living-room furniture had accumulated jelly fingerprints—and some laundry to be done. Robbie followed her around like a shadow. It wasn't until midday that Phil got around to the mail. Most of it was disposable. But there were four or five hand-delivered envelopes, with no stamps. She tried the first.

'We're home,' the first note said. Sally. 'I'll have to call her,' Phil told Robbie. 'That's my youngest sister. The baby of the family.'

'How about that,' Robbie returned. 'I'm the oldest *and* the youngest in my family. I wish I had a little sister.'

'It could happen,' she told him absent-mindedly. 'Your Dad's still a young man. He could marry again. Look at this!' Four of the envelopes were identical. 'Call me!' the first one said. 'Call me!!!!' the fourth one said. And the ones in between were the same, but with fewer exclamation marks. 'My sister Samantha,' Phil explained to a giggling Robbie. 'She's impatient.'

'Me too. No lunch way out here?'

'Not much,' she returned. 'A can of spaghetti? I never keep lunch stuff around.'

'I'll take it,' he said enthusiastically.

While he was eating she dialled Sally's new number. The response was electric. 'It's wonderful,' the girl gushed, and then invested ten minutes in the details, concluding with, 'Phil, you've just *got* to get married!'

'And who would have a spinster like me?' Phil returned through the forming tears. 'I've got a mint of work to do before I go back, Sally.'

'You're at home?'

'Yes, for a little while.'

It should have been no surprise, but when the doorbell went at three o'clock, and she opened it to all three of her sisters, Phil was almost in a state of shock. One at a time she could handle—three were just too many. She fell back into the living-room, and all three of them started yelling at her at once. There came a terrible clatter down the back stairs, and Robbie was standing close in front of her, fists half-raised, his face flushed.

'Don't you yell at Philomena,' he roared. They all stopped, with mouths half opened. After a pregnant moment Samantha said, 'And who in the world is this?'

Phil put both hands on the young man's shoulders. 'This is Robbie,' she said warningly. 'I told you I had found myself a man, didn't I?'

'And you'd better leave her alone,' the boy threatened, 'or I'll get you all.'

'Phil, I just have time,' Deborah interrupted. 'Our trip to Vegas is on, and I can bring the girls over here in no time. We'll be back on Wednesday.'

'I hope you don't,' Phil said firmly. 'I won't be here. Robbie and I are leaving in about twenty minutes—'

'And she's never coming back,' the boy threatened. Debbie managed an impatient laugh.

'Come on, Phil, the joke's over,' she grated. 'Let's get life back to normal in this family.'

'And Phil,' Samantha interrupted. 'Albert and I have just got to talk to you about the terms of the Trust. He—I—want enough money to open a new office in a better district, and—'

'Sally,' Phil ordered. 'Take Robbie out in the kitchen, will you.' She watched as her baby sister complied. 'Now, you two. Things have changed around here. I don't *want* to go back to the old ways. I have my own life to lead, and it doesn't include baby-sitting, or trying to break the terms of Daddy's will. You two tear at my heart. You know Mother told me to take care of you. I've done a terrible job. I don't know when I've met two more selfish people in my life.'

She stopped to stab at a tear forming in her eye. 'Now you both have families to look after, and jobs to do. Just go and do them. When I get back on an even keel I'll contact you.

But don't hold out any wild hopes. Things have changed permanently.'

The two of them stared at her for a moment, and then picked up their bags and left. Moments later Sally came out of the kitchen. 'Atta girl,' she said softly, kissing Phil on the cheek. 'You should have done that years ago. You know what Charley and I want from you?'

Phil's tears were really rolling now. She looked at the blur that was her youngest sister and waited. 'What *we* want is to love you.' And with that Sally was gone too. Robbie came out of the kitchen.

'You forgot this,' he said, waving another envelope at her. She managed to dry up the storm, and tore open the plain white envelope. Inside was a cheque, made out in her name, for four times her usual salary. The tears started again. She dropped into the armchair and let them flow. Robbie came around in front of her, with both hands in his pockets.

'What's the matter now?' he asked patiently.

'I don't know,' she admitted. 'I just don't know.'

'Girls are funny,' he said conclusively. 'Let's go home now.'

CHAPTER SIX

PHILOMENA devoted the drive back to the city to deep thought. Robbie climbed into the car without a word, his face relapsing into his typical teenage scowl. The inbound traffic was light because it was Sunday afternoon, but they were still serenaded by the city-dwellers' bird-song—the whiz and hum of tyres as cars passed, the rattle of gratings as heavy vehicles hit the overpasses at speed, the blinking of headlights as fools tried to exceed the fifty-five-miles-an-hour speed limit, and the occasional blasting wail of a horn as one bad driver signalled curses at another.

It was all background. Phil had her own problem. She went back over all that was said between sisters, and still believed herself to be right—but at a painful cost. Little sisters don't become spoiled by themselves, she told herself fiercely. It takes two to tango. They are what I made them. And now, having laid down the law to my own, I'm darned if I'm not running off to somebody else's family, all set to take up the burden again! And how big a fool does that make me?

Harry waited for them at the bottom step. He opened her door. Robbie made some sort of grunting noise that might, under the wildest circumstances, be interpreted as a 'Thank you,' and then scrambled out of the car. Phil required a great deal more care. Before she left the house she had changed into one of her best dresses, a light wool that matched each of her curves gently, and clung just above the knees. Which made scrambling out of tiny cars something of an adventure. Harry tried to act as if he hadn't noticed the large amount of thigh on display. She tendered him a wry smile, and went up the stairs ahead of him.

It had been a long hard day, and Penn was not quite able to assemble it all. A day set aside out of the rush of time. The sort of splendid day that could be spent outdoors, in the heated pool—damn those eye pads—or just piddling around and listening as George Yu commented on the world, the planets, and the Raiders. Until they had insulted half the world by moving to Los Angeles, the Oakland Raiders football team had been the old man's pride and joy.

But there had been no relaxation in it all today. Mr Yu seemed grumpy. Something about his camellias, and the up-coming flower festival. Something too about how quiet the house seemed without Miss Peabody in residence. And just hearing it said had startled Penn into breaking away and stomping off into the house. 'Bad enough, for God's sake,' he muttered as he fumbled his way into the lounge, 'to be thinking stupid things like that myself, without hearing everybody else in the house come down with a terminal case of Peabody.' He splashed what he thought was Scotch into a tumbler, discovered it was Bourbon, and sipped at it any-way. The whole picture bothered him. Her reaction to Rob-bie, and to himself, and—his reaction to her. Damn, it bothered him.

Along about four o'clock in the afternoon Harry found him, slumped down in the old Morris Chair in the front sit-ting-room, still nursing the same glass of Bourbon, down more in spirit than in spirits.

'Ain't nobody set in here since the old man died,' Harry commented softly.

'I know.' There was a time of silence, punctuated by the clink of ice in Penn's glass. 'Have something, Harry?'

'Not me. You know what the doctor said.'

'Yeah, I remember. No wine, no women, and not much song?'

'That about covers it. Funny feeling around the house today.'

'No, don't *you* start that. That's all I've heard all day from George Yu.'

'Crazy Chinaman.' A soft comment, not a criticism, but more like the underlining of a long-held pleasantry.

'Like a fox, Harry. He could have been a stockholder in Pacific Mines and Metal, but he didn't want it. Too much responsibility, he said. I remember him arguing with my father about that. Responsibility brings ambition, ambition brings worry, and—I forget the rest of it. Some Chinese philosopher before Confucius' time. Where the hell is she?'

'Who?'

The glass in Penn's hand seemed to crumble, spreading shards all over the carpet. His reflex action knocked over the bottle of Bourbon at his elbow. It fell to the carpet beside the glass, dumping its contents over his coat sleeve and trouser leg. 'Damn!' Harry moved rapidly over to his side and picked up the flaccid hand.

'Just a nick,' he reported. 'Needs a plaster. What's bugging you? The hearing?'

'Among other things. Next Thursday, Harry, and it's going to be one tough struggle. These bandages don't come off until three days later. I'll walk into that courtroom, the Juvenile judge will take one look at me, and everything goes down the drain. All I've got going for me is character witnesses and past history. Nobody in their right mind would give custody of a child to a blind man. What I need is—damn it, Harry, if I had my sight it would be no problem at all. I'm sure of that! But—'

'But what?'

'Her. What do you think, Harry?'

'I wish I knew what the hell you're talking about, Penn.'

'Peabody, damn it. Philomena. What do you think?'

'Nice lady. The kid don't let on, but he likes her. Nice shape. Built classy, not one of these skinny broads. Always used to hate those skinny ones. Every time you try to hug one you get splinters. Not this girl.'

'She's hardly a girl, Harry. And that's the problem. What about the age difference between us?'

'Oh, I don't know, boss. It's hard to tell with a good-looking broad. I'd say there can't be more than eight or ten years between you both. Nothing to worry about. Hardly anybody would notice, these days. Just what are you thinking about?'

'I'm thinking—you'd better find me another glass. And put Scotch in it. I can't seem to find the Scotch bottle.'

'OK, if that's what you want, but that's her car coming up the drive now, and you—'

'And I stink of Bourbon. Good lord. Get this coat off me. Do I have anything right here?'

'That smoking-jacket thing—the one you swore you'd never wear because—'

'Never mind what I swore I'd never—give me the damn thing and get out there and make her welcome!'

All of which brought Harry to the front door all in good time, and left Penn to fumble around madly trying to rid himself of the Bourbon smell, and at the same time stuff himself into the scarlet smoking-jacket his former wife had given him. The jacket clung, and so did the smell. Draconian measures, he told himself, as he poured the carafe of water over his trouser leg. Better water-wet than Bourbon-wet. It had suddenly become important to make a good impression on a certain lady.

Phil looked back towards Harry as she moved up the stairs. 'You're sure it's OK to leave my old car parked in front of the house?' she asked. There wasn't time for an answer. Moving faster than usual, for some reason she still did not fathom, she cannoned off the solid steel of Penn's chest, rattled around a time to two, and was finally rescued by those arms. For a second she was about to relax, to let it all happen. But then he seemed to pull her closer, to bury her nose against the soft suede of his smoking-jacket. And the smell hit her.

'My lord,' she muttered, wriggling furiously until his surprised arms unfolded and turned her loose. 'Drunk by Sunday evening?' It was hard to hide the disgust in her voice. Drunks and smokers were her favourite hates, and she had no plans for staying close to either category.

'No, I am not,' he returned indignantly. 'I've had one drink today, and managed to spill it all over myself. And just supposing I were? Who are you to—dammit!' She could see him try to suppress his words. His angry throat seemed to choke up in sympathy with his swollen angry cheeks. It was a momentous struggle. She watched, spell-bound, having never seen an autocratic man swallow his own words. Her moment of anger had passed. But perhaps the chuckle was a mistake. His hands seemed to find her by radar and fastened on her shoulders, holding her stiffly at arms' length.

'Funny, Peabody?' he asked warningly.

'Er—no, of course not.' After all, he was the boss. She had never held a doubt about that. 'I—I think you must have spilled something,' she offered tentatively, a sort of good-will gesture. It was amazing how quickly he snapped up the olive-branch.

'Yes,' he returned gently. The hold on her shoulders became a gentle squeeze, and then a tentative caress. 'We've missed you, it seems.'

There was nothing she could think of to say. Especially when he leaned forward on a straight line, kissed the fringe of her hair, then corrected his aim and lightly touched her lips. 'Dinner's ready,' he grinned. 'Won ton soup and Mandarin chicken. Mr Yu's been worrying about it all day.'

It was the grin that undid all her resolves. So he smelled like the Jim Beam Distillery—that lopsided little grin took years off his age, charmed her prejudices, soothed her worries—and gave her something to say. 'Great,' she enthused. 'I'm sick of my own cooking! Give me ten minutes to freshen up.'

'Better make that twenty,' he chuckled. 'I need to do some freshening myself.'

'We're going in the same direction,' she chuckled, taking his arm, 'so why don't we share a stair?'

'Poetry?' he groaned but followed her lead into the house and up the stairs. From the kitchen she could hear a great banging of pans, and a few delectable Chinese phrases that required no translation. As usual, her eye was caught by the haunting painting on the opposite wall. The girl-woman's eyes seemed to follow Phil as she came to a gradual stop. The artist had caught an expression—was it happiness— congratulations? Almost it seemed as if the girl in the painting were at least wishing her well.

'What is it?' he asked, tugging at her arm.

'The painting. The girl—' She struggled for words and found none. His massive head swung in the direction she was looking. It almost seemed that she could see tears beneath the eye-pads, but that was ridiculous. Phil started them up the stairs again. 'It's just that the—she—'

'Robin,' he said in a low tired voice. 'Her name was Robin.'

'Was?'

'Yes.' A blunt word, that cut off the conversation. She escorted him to his door, then returned to her own room. A quick brush-up, that was all she wanted. A quick wash, a struggle with comb and brush through her long curly hair, the briefest of touches from her lipstick, and a knock on the connecting door. Startled, she walked over to it. In all her time in the house she had never thought to lock the connecting door into his bedroom.

'More drops in your eyes?' she asked as he came in.

'Well—it wouldn't hurt, I suppose.' It was the first non-positive statement she had ever heard him make. He was a man who made up his mind quickly, and spoke it immediately. And now, 'I suppose,'—as if there were other objectives to be reached.

'Sit here on the edge of my bed.' She guided him around the furniture. He dropped down, and the old four-poster seemed to groan at the weight. Phil smiled at the thoughts that ran through her brain. He couldn't see, so there was no need to hide the hungry look in her eyes. And he couldn't read minds—she hoped.

Phil feasted on him for a moment, then went over to her own dressing-table where she kept eye-droppers and his prescription. On the way she detoured by the windows and drew the curtains, darkening the room. The dosage was as usual, but her hand shook just the slightest amount.

'Lost your nerve, doctor?' he chuckled.

'It does seem so,' she returned ruefully as she re-loaded the dropper. Make conversation, her mind demanded. But it was hard. He was beginning to have an effect on her that puzzled her. 'I had a little squabble with my sisters,' she offered as an explanation. 'Well, with two out of three. Don't blink, for goodness' sake.'

'Well, don't stick your thumb in my eyeball,' he snapped. 'Two out of three? That's not bad at all.'

'Shows you what a really terrible mother I turned out to be,' she quipped, turning his head so that she could get at the other eye. 'I raised two adult delinquents. This darn pad is sticking to your eyebrow. Whoever put it on this morning wasn't too careful. That didn't hurt, did it?'

'Of course it did,' he laughed. 'You tore off half my eyebrow there, lady.'

'Just not my day,' Phil mourned, 'Hold still, for goodness' sake! You're worse than a basket of kittens!'

'Nobody's ever told me *that* before,' he said as she returned the medications to their proper place. 'Come sit by me, Phil. There's something I need to say to you.'

Her skirt rustled as she complied. The bed complained. 'I'm not sure this bed was made for two,' she teased. Her thumb ran over the edge of his eyebrow, smoothing down the hairs. 'I didn't really pull any hairs out at all,' she mused, accusingly. 'You made that up. Can you see any better today?'

'If you've got all the lights on I'm losing ground,' he said.

'They're not,' she laughed. 'I don't have a single light on, and the curtains are drawn.'

'In that case I'm making marvellous progress. Monday week, that's when the doctors promise the great unveiling.'

'A week from Monday?'

'That's what I said—Monday week.'

'Stop wriggling, or this pad will have the rest of your eyebrow,' she threatened. Her fingers gently smoothed the pad in place, and then, for luck, she kissed the tip of his nose. He reached out for her, but she dodged, giggling.

'I'm not your fourth sister,' he said darkly.

'Oh, do I ever know that,' she sighed. He waited for an explanation—which she had no intention of giving. Why confess to this—this arrogant man—how much he had come to mean to her? She longed for the privilege to brush the hank of hair out of his eyes, to kiss each of his damaged eyes, to—and of course, that was the problem. When the day came to remove those pads, the day when he was fully restored to the light of the world he ruled, Philomena Peabody would become just one of the dull shadows in his life. Someone unnoticed until needed, and then in an absentminded way. And then what will I do, she asked herself. Go back to my sisters and apologise?

'What are you thinking about?' Again that gentle fumbling sound, as if he had a point and hadn't the courage to come to it.

'Oh, nothing,' she sighed. 'My sister Sally, Won ton soup, Robbie's next protest march—I don't know.'

'Sit down here again.' He patted the bed beside him. She sank down gracefully, closer than before, and tucked her legs up under her.

'I have a problem with Robert,' he said. 'A legal problem.'

'Yes, I know.' Almost unconsciously she captured his hand and moved it to her lap, between her own warm sympathetic fingers.

'There aren't any secrets in the world?' he asked.

'Not in the kitchen.'

His fingers squeezed hers gently. 'I don't get rid of my blinders until Monday next,' he repeated softly, as if retelling an old story. 'The Juvenile Court hearing is scheduled for this Thursday.'

'Yes?'

'If I go into court on Thursday I've two strikes against me. First, I can't see; secondly, I don't have a real home for Robert. God, who could believe it would all end up this way?'

'You might as well be honest,' Phil added quietly. 'You've three strikes against you already.' He sat up, rigidly, waiting. 'Robbie thinks you hate him.'

'Oh God, not that too,' he muttered. 'You know this?'

'He told me. He thinks both of you hate him. Both of you.'

'He tells you lots of things?'

'Whoa up,' Phil chuckled. 'It's not that way. He's a crazy upset adolescent. He doesn't like me any more than any of the rest of you—he just sort of—hates me less.'

'But you do get along with him. And that's more than I can do.'

'Or his mother either?'

'I told you once before. His mother's dead.'

'Yes, well, that's more confusion than I want to know about—please don't explain anything more to me about it. What did you really want to talk to me about?'

'I—' He coughed to clear his throat—or his mind. It was hard to tell which. 'I'd like to hire you for another job, Philomena.'

'I—' A sudden fear clouded her mind. 'I'm only a typist,' she moaned. 'I—what other job?'

'I want that boy.' His hands snatched at hers to emphasise. Her little whimper brought him back to reality. 'I'm sorry,' he said bitterly. 'That's all I seem to do—hurt the people closest to me.' And then it all came out, in a machine-gun burst of words, without pause for breath.

'My only hope is to walk into that court on Thursday with a capable, happy wife on my arm, and a son willing enough to go along with the gag. My only hope. By Thursday morning I've got to be married. That's a pretty hard thing for a temporary blind man to do when he's been away for a long time, has no available choices, and no time to ponder about it. I need somebody who will act the part, is on the scene.' He paused for a moment, his head cocked to one side as if waiting for some comment. She offered nothing. He took a deep breath and continued. 'Somebody who—er—is willing to accept the temporary nature of the whole affair, and that's why I want you to marry me, Philomena.'

She took a deep breath to match his own. 'You want me to—?'

'Marry me. On Tuesday, if I can arrange it.'

Well, she sighed to herself, at least he didn't call me 'Peabody'. That's one step in my favour!

'Well?'

'I'm thinking,' she blurted out angrily. 'Surely you don't expect a girl to hear something like that and promptly fall at your feet in rapture? I'm thinking.'

'I'll wait.'

'Don't be *that* darn patient,' she snapped. 'I don't expect to get through thinking about it in the next thirty minutes. Why don't you go downstairs and have your meal. I can hear Harry coming up to look for you.'

'We'll both go.' He stood up. The bed creaked in relief. He tugged at her hand, but she refused to budge.

'Go ahead,' she sighed. 'I'm suddenly not hungry any more.'

'But you are thinking about it?'

'I am. But—from where I sit it's all for Robbie, and I have to talk to him first.'

'It's not *all* for Robert,' he returned. 'I'll see you right in all this, Philomena. I—I seem to like you very much. When I get my bandages off, I'll fix things for you. You'll never have to work again, believe me.'

'Ha!' she snorted. 'You think being a mother to Robbie Wilderman is some sort of lead-pipe cinch. And with *you* thrown into the bargain besides?'

'I swear there will be proper compensation for it all,' he said. There it was, that pompous 'I am the head man' tone again.

'Yes,' she snapped. 'I'm sure there will be, and it's only temporary, and now before you really make me angry, go get your supper.'

He mumbled something about 'women' under his breath as he stumbled towards the door. She made not a move to help him, but Harry was just outside, in the hall, and rescued him. Phil sat where he had left her, and tried to think it all out.

Men! He hadn't even attempted to put icing on the cake. He just set it out there in front of her and dared her to accept. Marry me and save Robbie. A most objectionable man, with a most objectionable son. Good lord, am I some sort of masochist? I've put up with a decade of playing mother—and didn't do too good a job at it, either. And now I'm supposed to dive into a worse mess. How long is temporary? What happens when he takes those darn pads off his eyes and really sees me? And having learned to survive through adolescent sisters, is any of that experience transferable to a sulky-boy type? Oh lord.

She sat there for more than an hour, knowing all along that there was something she had not entered into the equation. It had something to do with *him*—and every time she approached the subject her mind shied away from it like a nervous mare! Finally, about seven o'clock, she gave up the argument and went to do the one thing she knew had to be done.

Robbie's room was just a few doors down from her own. A stereo system was blasting at high intensity from within. Although all the walls were thick, almost sound-proofed, this penetrated. Phil shrugged her shoulders. Only four years ago Sally had been swept up into hard rock—heavy

metal as it was known as on the street. She knocked on the
door without response, gave it a moment or two, and then
barged in. Robbie was sitting at his computer table, hard at
work on some word-game. The stereo blasted away from a
desk beside him. His right foot was tapping on the rug
matching the primitive rhythm of the music. His unruly hair
looked as if it had been exposed to perhaps ten seconds'
worth of shower. He was wearing a blue pyjama top and his
favourite jeans. When she leaned over his shoulder and
flipped the stereo off he jumped.

'Hey,' he yelled, and then stopped in mid-sentence when
he recognised her. He dropped back into the chair again,
and went on punching keys on the computer board.

'I need to talk to you, Robbie,' she said softly. That sullen look swept over his face. He refused to turn around. Phil
looked around for the power switch, and shut it down. The
computer rumbled a couple of times, its internal blowers
slowed to a stop, and quiet reigned. He turned around. A
swivel chair, she noted. A poor under-deprived kid.

'Now I've lost the entire computer program,' he growled,
but avoided her eyes.

'You'll think of it again some day,' she said very compla-
cently. 'I have some questions, and I need some straight
answers. Listen up.' The last two words had a snap to them
that brought him up to the mark. It works on boys too, Phil
noted, with some pleasure. Maybe I learned how to be a
mother after all!

'So?' A touch of insolence, but overlaid by curiosity, and
curiosity was winning. Phil looked around. There were four
chairs in the room, all loaded with clothes, books, video-
tapes, and what-have-you. She picked the nearest, dumped
its computer magazines on the floor, and sat down.

'Hey,' he protested again. Her eyes roamed around the
dishevelled room. He had the grace to blush. 'So it's not

neat,' he grumbled. 'I can't have those *women* coming in here every day and getting everything out of order.'

'You sound like your father,' she commented softly, showing just enough steel in her voice so that he knew it was there. 'Starting tomorrow you pick up in here, or Cecily will, or *I* will.' He got the message. If Phil had to come in and clear things, shortly thereafter there would be hell to pay.

'Is that all you came for?' he grumbled. 'Breaking up my program just about that?'

'No,' she said, showing more steel. The boy was becoming agitated. He moved back into his swivel chair as if to re-establish his position. She didn't give him the time he needed.

'Your father,' she said. 'For some reason he likes you.'

'No, he doesn't,' the boy returned bitterly.

'He does,' Phil continued relentlessly. 'He told me so. I don't know why he would. You're a real cactus.'

Robbie's head snapped up. 'What's that mean?' he demanded fiercely.

'Well, look at you,' she continued. 'When you love people you want to hug and kiss them once in a while. Look at you. You're just like a cactus, loaded with spines and prickles. Some hugger you'd make! Let me tell you something, Robbie. The world is full of people who don't want to be loved—so nobody loves them. You have to give a little to get a little.'

The boy turned all this over in his mind. She could see the gears creaking. 'My father likes me?'

'Of course he likes you. Why do you think he's going through this fire-drill with the court?'

'Because he needs the money,' the answer came.

Phil stifled a giggle. You can be hard with adolescents. You can be direct. You can be bitter. But you can't laugh at them. 'Your father's got enough money to buy out the US

Treasury,' she commented. 'And maybe a couple of other countries to go with it. He *wants* you. I don't know why. Do you?'

'Yes,' he returned after a pause. 'I think I do. I haven't been hugged since—since a long time. I suppose that's something you have to put up with when you have women around the house?'

'I suppose so. And you've got a problem, Robbie.'

He watched expectantly.

'Your mother wants to keep you, and she has a new husband. You like him?'

'I can't stand him,' the boy returned. 'He doesn't like to go fishing or swimming or anything. And he don't know a thing about computers. Can you imagine that?'

'Yes,' Phil returned. 'I can imagine that. So you don't like your mother's new husband, and—'

'She's not my mother,' he interrupted bitterly.

'Ah. I had forgotten.' Another moment of silence. 'Did you know that your Dad is planning to get married again?'

The little head snapped around. 'To a woman?'

'Well, that's the usual thing.'

'No, I didn't know.' There was a look of appeal in his eyes. 'I know I won't like her.'

'Well, that *is* too bad.' Phil got up, brushed down her dress, and moved toward the door. 'I thought you and I might become—well, perhaps not friends, but—'

'You mean he wants to marry *you*, Phil?'

'Is that so bad? So I'm not a movie queen. Yes, he wants me to marry me.'

'I—and are you going to?'

'I don't know, Robbie,' she told him bluntly. 'It all depends on you. If it's going to start a revolution, then no, I won't marry him. If you and I could live peacefully together, why I thought I might give it a try. What do you think?'

The boy was up from his chair, moving towards her. Awkwardly, but with a hint of his father's feline grace. Thirteen, and he was already an inch taller than she. Much taller, if she slipped out of her two-inch heels. She did just that.

It was just the right touch. Suddenly towering over her, bigger, she could see his face lighten as he came closer. The dominant male, she giggled to herself. At all ages. Now what?

He took her by the hand. 'I want to show you something,' he said. She followed him out into the hall and down towards the stairs. George Yu stood at the bottom.

'You don't eat?' he called up to them. 'Neither of you to eat, and the boss all grumpy. You two come down to the kitchen. I got left-overs. The soup is still hot.'

Phil stopped at the head of the stairs. Robbie looked down and actually smiled at her. His tugging hand led her half-way down, and stopped at the bend.

'There.' He pointed across to where the painting of the woman was half hidden in the shadows.

'There? I like that painting very much. Who is it?'

'That's—that's my mother.' There was a catch in his voice, as if he had some trouble with his throat. Phil dropped to the stair and pulled him down beside her. They both stared at the painting through the interstices of the banister.

'So that's your mother,' she sighed. 'There's something about her—the—picture—that's bothered me for two weeks. Something familiar—but I know I've never seen her.'

'Me neither,' the boy returned. 'She died when I was one year old.'

'So long ago,' Phil sighed. 'And you've never been hugged since then, I'll bet.'

The boy cleared his throat, and relaxed his stiffened back. 'No,' he whispered, 'I guess not.' It must have been an unconscious movement. He slid over on the stair until he was touching her, and then suddenly he collapsed in a heap, tears streaming down his face, his head close on Phil's shoulder. Her arms went around him, comforting. She murmured consolation in his ear, and he cried it all out there on the stairs.

The storm went on for minutes, then gradually decreased to a hiccup, and blew its way out. He fumbled for a handkerchief to wipe his eyes. Dirty, Phil noticed, as any good housekeeper would. He coughed a couple of times, and cleared his throat.

'You didn't get any prickles,' he said, 'so I can't be a real cactus.'

'I guess you can't be,' Phil said in pseudo-amazement. 'Could I have been wrong? I was wrong once before—let me see now—that would have been eighteen years ago.' He managed a chuckle. She flowed gracefully up to her feet and pulled him with her. He wrapped both arms around her, and pulled her close, her soft cheek against his, for comfort.

'I still don't see why that picture bothers me,' she repeated a moment later.

He released her, laughing. 'It's because you look just like her, Phil, didn't you know?'

'I like this hugging business,' she returned. 'How could she look just like me?'

'Well, maybe not *just*,' he said, 'but kind of—well, you know!'

'I'll have to take your word for it,' she giggled. 'And now I'm really hungry. Why don't we both sneak down to the kitchen and try some of the left-overs?'

'And what are you going to tell my father?'

She was all solemnity again. 'What *should* I tell him?'

'I think—I don't know. I suppose you might make a nice mother for some kid. I don't need one myself, but you'd make a great mother.'

'But not for you,' she probed. That stubborn, sullen look flashed across his face. 'Well, at least have a little sympathy for my elderly bones,' she sighed. 'Take me to your kitchen and feed me—before I have to decide what to tell your father. You won't advise me?'

'Nope.' He went over to the table and sat down, burying his face behind a huge soup spoon. Phil stood in the kitchen doorway, both hands on her hips. Well, I almost got you. And there's always a next time, kiddo. She had already decided what she was going to say to Penn.

CHAPTER SEVEN

WHAT with one thing and another, it was late evening before Phil tracked Penn down. The warmth of the sun still lingered. He was lounging out behind the house on a comfortable swing-sofa, with no one else around. She stopped on the edge of the grass to absorb the picture of him. He was leaning back in the swing, both feet planted firmly on the cement that surrounded the pool. His sports shirt was unbuttoned, his raven hair flopped to one side, and worn jeans clung to his supple hips. There was a little frown tugging at his mouth. Altogether too handsome, she told herself. The fingers of his right hand came up and tugged at the pads that covered his eye.

'No!' The half-scream was involuntary. She dashed across to where he sat. 'Don't do that!' she ordered.

'Don't do what?' He was laughing, and that boyish look was on his half-tilted face.

'Don't touch those pads,' she gruffed, doing her best to swallow her fears. 'It's just a week to go. If you take those pads off out here in the bright sun you'll—you'll—'

'I'll what?'

'Don't tease me,' she muttered. 'You know darn well I don't know what would happen. I'm not a doctor or a nurse. But I'm sure you'll—'

'But you're sure I'll do something wrong?' Definite laughter. The frown was gone. And then he gave her a set-down. 'I don't remember any of my employees who worry about me the way you do, Peabody.'

One of his employees, that's the way he thinks of me. So much for all those lovely dreams last night! She stood silently beside the swing, her hands twisting nervously behind her back.

'So you came to tell me something.'

'I came to tell you—I—I talked with Robbie about—about—what you said.'

'So it all depends on Robbie, does it?'

'Well, doesn't it? That's what you told me in the first place!' He reached out a hand in her general direction. Without even thinking, she put her own in his. He tugged at her gently, until she settled down into the swing, as far from him as she could get.

'I put it all very badly, didn't I?' he said softly.

'Yes, you did,' she returned grimly. His hand still held hers, and it disturbed her in some way which she couldn't comprehend.

'I'm not much for speech-making, Philomena. It wasn't *all* for Robbie. Some of it was for me. I need a wife, need one very badly.'

'And that's what you'll get if you make blind choices,' she snapped. 'You'll get one very badly.'

'Low blow,' he returned gravely. 'Blind choices? Semantics, Peabody, or do you mean it?'

'I—I'm sorry. I wasn't thinking. I—'

'Just blurted it all out?'

'Yes.' She had composed herself by this time. Both his hands were on her one, toying with it. 'I'm sorry. You were saying?'

'I was saying I need a wife, Philomena. A woman like you. I happen to like you very much.'

And that, she told herself, sounds about as exciting as a peanut butter sandwich. But it was better than nothing, wasn't it? Because I—I like him very much too. Her resolve returned. She added her other hand to the pile. 'I came out to tell you that if you still want it, I'll marry you—Penn.'

'Ah.' There was a whole host of satisfaction in his one word. He slid over on the swing, agitating it as he moved, until he was sitting hard up against her. *Which was just the way she wanted it.* His hard thigh crushed up against her, his warm arm around her shoulders, gently squeezing. She used her free hand to snatch at the sofa arm as the swing jerked and bounced. Her feet no longer reached the ground, but for some stupid reason her heart was as high as the clouds that temporarily brushed across the sun.

'So now we're engaged?'

'I—I guess so.'

'Good. Now where the—where did I put that thing?' His struggle to get a hand into his pocket without moving away from her was agitating her—not the swing. His elbow kept brushing against her breasts, sending shivers up her spine. 'Ah!' The hand came out of his pocket with a small box. He snapped it open with one hand, and held it out to her.

She stared at the diamond ring, stunned, not knowing what to say. It was a small but perfect diamond, set in a circlet of sparkling diamond chips, the whole gleaming on a platinum ring.

'This is where the heroine says *For me?*' she managed.

'That's the line,' he chuckled. 'See a lot of movies, do you?'

'No.' She had finally managed to clamp down on her emotions, and her usually cheerful spirit was leaking through. 'No,' she repeated, 'but I read a great many books. What do I—'

'Now you don't do anything,' he said. His strong tactile fingers snatched the ring from its nest and held it out towards her. Wordlessly she extended her left hand. He fumbled for the right finger, found it, and slipped the ring on.

'It just fits,' she reported, astonished.

'Of course,' he chuckled.

There, she told herself. Of course it wouldn't dare not fit. Not if Penn ordered it! But instead of that surge of anger that had teased her for weeks in such situations, this time she felt marvellously better—happier.

'It's lovely,' she managed to breathe.

'Of course,' he commented.

'Did you ever think that if you keep talking like that somebody might just—hit you?'

'Somebody will, I'm sure,' he agreed. 'But not you, Peabody.'

'No,' she sighed, giving up the war after one battle. 'Not me, I guess. Were you *that* sure of me?'

His arm was around her shoulders again, tucking itself under her left arm, with the tips of his fingers just inches from her breast. She leaned over against him, resting her head under his chin. 'Sure of you?' he said. 'I don't believe I've taken such a risk in many a day.' She started to raise her head. 'No,' he ordered, 'don't move.' She dropped back, sighing. It was pleasant to be coddled. His free arm came across her, resting on her stomach, hand clutching at her hip.

'You're a great deal of woman, Philomena,' he whispered into her hair. 'A great deal of delightfully designed woman. We'll make a good pair, you and I.'

Surely we will, she told herself fiercely. Until my option runs out, we'll make a great team. And after that—well, I won't think about that. Not right now. She snuggled closer, pulling her legs up under her. He used one foot to start the swing rocking gently. Somehow or other his right hand had moved from her hip and was cupping her breast, weighing it. The pleasure of it all overcame her reluctance, but only for a moment. When her hand moved his away from her breast back down to her waist he sighed deeply.

'Not accustomed to giving samples?' he asked. There was something wrong with his voice. It sounded as if some—passion—were choking him, fighting him. 'Not even for your fiancé?'

'How could I know?' she answered, her own voice husky with strain. 'I've never been engaged before. Perhaps I just don't know the drill?'

They rocked back and forth for minutes. Her muscles relaxed as the tension faded. She lay against him, savouring the warmth, wondering whether she should have—but the chance had passed.

From out of the mist of her day-dreams his voice finally penetrated. 'And then on Tuesday we can be married,' he was saying. 'Judge Caldwell will do it for us in Chambers, I'm sure. Then comes the hearing, followed by a short honeymoon at home. I'll send Robbie off with Harry, and give the others a vacation.'

And that, she told herself, puts a period to all the dreams. Orange blossoms and a long white gown, and music—'Here comes the bride—' All down the drain. She nestled closer to him, and hid her face against his shirt. After all, he's only a man, she thought fiercely. What can he know about a girl's dreams!

'God,' he muttered. 'I don't understand what you do to me, Peabody. We'd better go into the house and—tears? Why?'

She sniffed back the last drop, and used a knuckle to clear her eyes.

'Why?' he repeated.

'Nothing,' she stuttered. 'Sometimes women feel like crying. It isn't every day that—that one gets a proposal—or—oh lord, I can't hold it in!' The tears came again. She wrestled free from his embrace and raced back to the house as fast as her feet could carry her. Blinded, she fumbled her way down the hall and into the kitchen, where George was still at work.

'Why, what's the matter?' the old man asked, as he opened his arms and Phil came into them.

'I—Penn and I—' she stammered through the tears. 'We're going to be married.'

'Which is certainly a good reason for a girl to cry her heart out,' Mr Yu murmured, laughing over Phil's bent head.

Penn made all the arrangements. Or perhaps his super-efficient secretary did. In any event on Monday Doctor Hanson came to the house, took a blood sample, gave her a smile of approval, and went off mumbling to himself about laboratory schedules and tons of work to be done. But Harry, who drove the doctor to the house, gave Phil a wink as if assuring her that all medical men have such troubles.

And so when Rose came to her at one o'clock in the afternoon with a puzzled frown on her face, Phil saw no real problem. 'So if your niece is that sick,' she assured the cook, 'Frank can drive you down to San Francisco right away. No, it's no real problem. Harry said he and—Penn—would be home early, and Mr Yu is out at the back somewhere.'

Frank managed to combine his errands. He took Cecily home on the way, and promised to stay in the city until Rose was sure he was not needed.

That left Phil rumbling around the house until Robbie came in from school at two o'clock, with Mary, the afternoon maid, right behind him. At which time, Philomena told herself, somebody has to get dinner for the master of the house, and that somebody is obviously me. And off she went to the kitchen.

She heard the noise in the front hall at about three o'clock. The big front door slammed, and feet echoed down the hall. A quick smile flashed across Phil's face. She wiped flour off her hands on to one of Rose's super-sized aprons. Penn was home earlier than she had expected. Her hands fumbled with the ties of the apron. Ordinarily when she was cooking she thought nothing of welcoming guests in an apron. But Penn, on the day before their wedding? Nothing doing! She struggled, but the loop around her neck got caught in her hair, and it was a pretty dishevelled housekeeper who finally made it to the hall. It wasn't Penn.

Mary stood in the alcove leading into the library, a strange couple stood at the foot of the stairs, and Robbie was frozen in position half way down.

The woman was tall and aristocratic, her blonde hair piled up on her head in the latest fashion, wearing a mink coat despite the heat. The man was tall, thin, trying to hide a narrow face behind a full beard and moustache. Not one of that kind, Phil moaned, as she positioned herself between Robbie and the intruders.

'And you are?' she inquired in her best deep voice.

'Oh, none of your business,' the woman stated flatly. 'I don't have to dispute the world with the hired help. Come, Robbie, we're leaving at once.'

'No,' the boy shouted, backing up the stairs. 'They can't make me go, Phil?'

'No, they can't make you go,' she answered.

'I'm the boy's mother,' the woman snapped. 'Come down here, Robert. At once, do you hear.'

'So that's it,' Philomena grated. 'Possession is nine points of the law? Well, Mrs whatever your name is now, *that's* the boy's mother.' She gestured over her shoulder to the picture that gleamed against the wall. 'And there's no way you're going to get Robbie out of this house without his father's approval.'

'We don't have to put up with this nonsense,' the woman returned. 'Donald. Get the boy. Now.'

'Mary, call the police. Report an attempted kidnapping,' Phil called. All eyes turned to the maid. She was standing just by the hall telephone, but made no effort to pick it up.

'Eloise?'

It was obvious that Donald really didn't want to play the game. 'Get the boy,' the woman snapped. 'They're all alone in the house.' She turned her attention back to Phil. 'And don't think we don't know about you. Living in his house. In the next room, for that matter. You just wait until the Judge hears about *this*. We've got pictures!'

Donald had finally made up his mind. He moved past Eloise and headed for the stairs. Phil backed up directly in front of him, slowing him down. 'Robbie,' she called over her shoulder. 'Into your room. Lean out the window and yell for Mr Yu.'

Donald stopped, one foot in the air. 'Mr Yu?' he asked over his shoulder.

'The Chinese gardener,' Eloise supplied. 'He's eighty years old at least.'

Robbie had gone by this time, his boots clattering on the stairs as if heralding the Light Brigade. Donald put his foot down on the next riser. Phil backed up slowly, directly in front of him. 'You're the one who's going to get hurt. Although when I get through with you I might save up a punch or two for your lovely wife. That would sound good in court, wouldn't it?'

He hesitated again. 'Get on with it,' his wife ordered. He began the pursuit. This is silly, Phil told herself. Here I am being stalked by a rabbit! But he is big. What I need is a weapon. They were in the second-floor corridor, inching gradually down toward Robbie's room. She could hear the boy yelling out of the window at the top of his lungs. His bedroom door was open. Phil backed into the room, and found exactly what she needed.

It was something one finds in every American child's bedroom girl or boy, when they get to a certain age. A baseball bat. She hefted it, found the balance, and moved briskly back to the door. 'Don't bother, Robbie,' she called over her shoulder. 'Everything's in good order now.'

'That's what you think.' The man in the door was trying to show a little bravado. He hadn't seen the bat as yet. 'I intend to take that brat with me, little girl, and—oooh.' The bat, wielded like a quarter-staff, had just slammed into his solar plexus. He dropped to the floor, gasping for breath.

More footsteps clattered on the stairs. High heels. Eloise stormed down the corridor, her face rigid with anger. 'Get up, Donald, and get that child,' she screamed. 'Donald? What happened to—?'

'You'd better pick him up and go home,' Phil grinned at her. 'Donald has suddenly decided not to do any kidnapping today.' The worn end of the bat wiggled in her hands. Eloise carefully started to back down the hall.

'You'd better take Donald with you,' Phil insisted. 'They don't collect garbage in our neighbourhood for another two days.'

'I—wait until I tell the judge about this,' Eloise threatened. 'Now I'm sure we'll get custody of the boy.' She had been sliding steadily towards the stairs, ready to abandon her new husband, when she backed into George Yu.

The old man had sufficient strength to force Eloise back up the hall, and sufficient wit to take in all the evidence. 'Kidnappers,' he chuckled. 'You want me to use judo on them? I could break a few bones?'

Eloise paled, her face so white that the patches of rouge on her cheeks gleamed like fire. 'No, no,' she gasped. 'We're going. It was all a terrible mistake. Get up, Donald.'

Donald looked as if he would rather stay where he was, but when Mr Yu bent over towards him he scuttled along the floor a few paces and staggered to his feet. The Chinese gardener pointed toward the door, and the pair of them fled. The three conspirators waited until they heard the front door slam, and then broke into laughter.

'Would you really use judo?' Phil asked through the giggles.

'Me?' the old man returned. 'What do I know about judo? I spent all my life in California. Baseball I know—judo, no. That's Japanese stuff. Besides, what did you need me for? I was busy with the camellia beds. Exhibition next month. I *have* to get the blossoms ready.'

'Well, I'm sorry,' Phil said very primly. 'I couldn't find the baseball bat, you see.'

Mr Yu smiled, bowed, and retreated down the hall. He moved like a shadow, without a noise. What a marvellous man, Phil told herself, and then, unable to contain it, told Robbie, 'He'd make a wonderful grandfather.'

'Mr Yu?'

'Who else?'

'Why did you do that?' the boy asked. 'You didn't have to fight him just for me. He was a lot bigger than you.'

'Yeah,' she giggled, 'but I had the bat.'

'And you did it just for me?'

'Just for you. Hurts, does it?'

'Yeah. Sort of. I'm not accustomed to—' That tiny smile edged at the corners of his mouth. He saw his reflection in the wall-mirror and quickly replaced the smile with his normal frown.

Philomena whistled as she took the stairs two at a time, stopping to pay tribute to the Pirate King, and Robbie's mother. Mary was struggling into her coat by the front door.

'Leaving?'

'I—guess I'd better,' the maid replied. 'I—'

'I know. You've been spying on us for them all the time.' There was no bitterness in Phil's voice. She understood the woman's need. 'They paid you to call them?'

'Yes. I—I needed the money. I hate to lose my job. It's the baby.'

'Yes. I know all about it, Mary. I looked into it all last Friday. It wasn't such a terrible crime, what you did, provided it doesn't happen again. There's no need to give up your job—unless you can't stand us here.'

'No need to—?'

'No need to. And next week, when things settle down, I want you to sit down with Mr Wilderman and see if he can't work something out. I know it's all been a shock. Go on home. Take a few days off, and come back when you're ready. Nobody need know except you and I, and I have the most atrocious memory you ever saw.'

There were genuine tears in the woman's eyes. She thought for a moment, nodded her head, and turned to the door. 'I'll be back Wednesday,' she said softly, and went out.

'And that leaves the whole blinking house to me,' Phil lectured herself. There was a smell invading the hall. 'Oh my heavens,' she wailed as she ran for the kitchen. 'My pies!'

There was no need for her elaborately prepared explanation, concocted over a tray of hot biscuits to go with the salmon loaf. Robbie clattered down the stairs as soon as Penn's car purred to a halt, and poured the whole story into his ear before Phil could even get her apron off.

Dinner went well, but there were so many questions to be answered that Phil hardly managed a bite before everyone else was finished. The whole affair was topped off when Frank stomped into the house in the middle of the meal.

'Wasn't any emergency at all,' he grunted. 'Nothing wrong with anybody in Rose's family. Somebody's playing games with the telephone. Rose nearly blew a fuse when she found out. I brought her back and left her at home.'

Later that night, exhausted, Phil tumbled out of the shower, slipped into her shorty nightgown, and stood by the window to watch the full moon chase the evening star across the sky. Up in the mountains, forty miles away, it was snowing. Down in the protected valley where the Sacramento and the American rivers flowed, spring was showing signs. By craning her head she could see the reflected light of the dome of the State Capitol. And this is how the rich people live, she chuckled to herself. Here I am in the middle of the city and it looks more like country living than actually being out in the country.

Behind her there was a light knock on the interconnecting door. She left the view behind her reluctantly. There was no need for a robe—Penn couldn't see anything. She opened the door and extended her hand.

'What are you doing?' he asked casually.

'Just looking—the window,' she murmured. He came to her as if he had all his faculties, slipping one arm around her waist, and walking her back to the window. There was nothing at all wrong with his sense of touch, she told herself, alarmed. His hand was broadly open, resting in that declivity where her narrow waist swelled outwards into her rounded hip. His finger tips moved.

Not a sweeping caress, just a sensuous application and release of pressure, almost as if he were playing a drum. And if his fingers were the drummer, her skin came taut under the pressure, as if she were the drum.

'So you hit Donald with the baseball bat,' he murmured into her mass of hair.

'Well, it seemed the logical thing to do at the time,' she returned. 'She said—that it would help *their* case in court. I hope it doesn't?'

'I don't think it will,' he reassured her. 'The more I think of it the funnier it all seems.'

The conversation seemed to be going on at two levels. The verbal she could handle—if she put her mind to it. The other, the pleasing assault of his fingertips, was beyond her experience, and her automatic response, moving closer against his side, did nothing to help her resolution. Her nightgown, lightweight, felt almost as if it were not there. His hand rested just inches above its hem. She felt a crazily mixed feeling—remorse and relief—when it lifted and moved higher. And gasped as it kept going upwards, to rest on the lower slope of her breast. And the conversation went on.

'Tomorrow is our wedding-day.' A casual statement of fact from him that caused her mind to somersault. In all the madness of the day she had forgotten!

'Yes—' she managed to stammer, 'Yes, it is. I—I hope the weather's nice.'

'That's my girl,' he laughed. 'Tomorrow is our wedding-day and you want to talk about the weather?'

'It—it seemed to be the safest subject.'

'Ah. I never thought of you as wanting to be safe.'

'Well, I do,' she insisted. 'Every woman does. It isn't the same for a woman as for a man.'

'What isn't?'

'Getting married. It's too wrapped up in responsibilities and—and passions—'

'I understand.' Those pernicious fingers smoothed the firmness of her breast, touched lightly on its proud peak, and faded away. Regretfully.

'I just wanted to say good night. Everything will be all right, Philomena. I shall keep you safe. Guide me back to the door.'

'I know you will,' she sighed as she led him back to his own room. There was no sleep to be had that night. She tossed and turned, feeling the trail of those fingers all night long, wishing mightily that there could have been no need for him to stop.

She came down to breakfast with him on Tuesday, before he went off to work. They were all quiet. Robbie squirmed in his chair, almost smiling. Harry was his usually gloomy self, and Penn seemed to be wrapped up in something deep in his mind. As she had done for weeks now, Phil picked up the morning paper and began to read him the headlines. But none of the stories caught his interest, and when she stopped short of the whole reading, he didn't urge her on.

'I'll send the car for you,' he told her briefly. 'Along about midday, I suppose, and I'll meet you there.'

She stood in the door for ten minutes after the car had gone. What a wedding, she groaned to herself. I'll meet you there. Well, I suppose when you stretch the truth a little, that's what happens at a *normal* wedding, right? The groom waits at the church, and the bride comes to him. *Normal*, hah!

So it was all rather a surprise when the doorbell went at about ten-thirty, and Cecily, a big smile on her face, ushered her sister Sally into the living-room. Sister Sally and half a million packages.

'Well, you certainly fooled us all,' her sister said as she slumped down on the couch to catch her breath. 'Lord, I've been running around like a head with its chicken cut off. That man is crazy, Phil.'

'That man?'

'That man that you're going to marry. Now we'd better try everything on. Mrs Ralston is waiting just in case something needs to be adjusted.'

'Mrs Ralston? Waiting where?'

'She's the head seamstress from Balmain's, silly—'

'And she's up in your bedroom,' Cecily interrupted. 'And she didn't look like a wait-around person.'

'But you—' Phil sighed as she took her youngest sister's hands. 'Stop just right there. What the devil is this all about?'

'Well, you could have knocked me over with a feather when he telephoned me yesterday morning. Of course I had all your measurements. So he sent that sexy car around after me, and he and I went down to Balmain's—boy, is he a choosy guy. It took hours. For me they never would have stirred a stump. For him they jumped every time he opened his mouth. What the devil does he do—own a gold-mine?'

'Several dozen,' practical Phil inserted deftly. 'And I still don't know what you're talking about. Let's go upstairs—at least we shan't keep Mrs Ralston waiting for whatever it is.'

Her bedroom had been taken over. Mrs Ralston had brought two assistants, who were busy emptying boxes, and stuffing their contents into her wardrobe, and her bureaux. Noting her anxious look, the seamstress said, 'Your future husband insisted on a complete trousseau, Miss Peabody. A little of everything, he specified. And this, of course.'

A dressmaker's dummy stood by the open window, and Phil's heart did a sudden jump at the dress it displayed. Orange blossom and white lace, demurely seductive, revealing a little, promising everything. She could almost hear the wedding march being played in the background. A tiny gold coronet—pure gold it would be—the idea broke through her trance, and left her giggling like a fool. A long train, the veil, everything! It was too hard not to cry—and when she started they all joined in—all except Mrs Ralston, who had other things on her mind.

A few alterations were required. Well, Mrs Ralston thought they were, and Phil had given up the struggle long since. It was easier to just drift down with the tide. 'Just a little lower in the cleavage,' the dressmaker insisted.

'A little more and I'll get pneumonia,' Phil protested feebly.

'The lace will protect you,' the practical answer came. Sure, Phil thought. The lace was like a transparent film, hardly real enough to stand a fingerprint. Sure it will protect me. You bet!

And when it was finally completed, they all insisted she take it off again. And come down to lunch!

'I couldn't eat a thing,' she sighed for the tenth time.

'Got the willies?' Sally laughed. 'Me too. But if you think it's bad now, wait until tonight!' They all laughed.

'Very funny,' Phil groaned.

'So eat something,' Rose insisted. 'It takes a lot of strength to be a bride.'

'Yeah, sure.' But she did manage a pink grapefruit, the smallest corner of the steak she was served, and a piece of toast. 'And Penn did all this?' she asked again.

'All this,' her sister assured her. 'With his fingers, no less. He felt everything from top to bottom, then had me describe the whole ensemble. What a lucky girl you are, Sis. You just wait until he gets those pads off his eyes. Now, I've got to change too. Upstairs, lady.'

'You too? For a wedding in a—' Shut up, Phil, she yelled at herself. You don't know what's going on. Just shut up and do what you're told. You just wait until he gets those pads off his eyes—yeah. You're not what he thinks you are, and nobody, but nobody fools around with Penn Wilderman's sensibilities! There'll be a day of reckoning, little Miss Peabody! She shivered, and Mrs Ralston complained of it as they slipped the magic dress down over her head again, set the train, adjusted the veil, flounced out the fulness of it all, and led her gently down the stairs. The limousine was waiting.

'There'll be a reckoning,' she told herself as she stepped carefully into the big interior. 'But not today, lady. Enjoy.'

The car whispered away, like a magic carpet. She closed her eyes. For some reason she didn't want to see where the judge's chambers were. The ride was longer than she had expected, and the bridal party was tense. The bridal party. Herself, Sally, Cecily, and Rose. Mrs Ralston had gathered all her troops and disappeared.

'We're here.' Sally made the announcement, nudging her sister. Phil opened her eyes. 'It isn't the guillotine,' Sally chuckled. 'Or if it is, you're riding in one fancy tumbril, sis. Get moving. We're five minutes late. And I don't think the man you're marrying is much of a waiter-around either.'

And so she opened her eyes. The car was parked directly in front of her own parish church, Saint Clement's Episcopal. The doors were wide open, waiting. Sally handed her the tiny bouquet of orange blossom, they all fussed with her dress and veil, the organ sounded, and she walked down the aisle towards the altar, where he and Harry and Robbie waited, all kitted out in formal wear. Her arm shook in the crook of Mr Yu's elbow. Her entire frame shivered until that moment when she came close enough to feel the aura, and Mr Yu transferred her hand into that of Penn. Then suddenly it all became a dream, a warm comforting dream, and the shivers left her.

The ceremony passed completely over her head. She must have made the proper answers, because the organ was playing again, and Penn was folding back her veil to kiss her. She walked back down the aisle with him, proud and puzzled. At the door of the church he stopped and kissed her again.

'What's the trouble, Philomena?' he asked softly.

'I—I was surprised,' she sighed. 'The dress, the church. I thought we—you—I was just surprised.'

'I'm not altogether insensitive,' he whispered in her ear. Her hands crept up around his neck, and she pulled his head down to hers.

'Thank you for everything.' And the tears came in little driblets.

'Crying on your wedding-day?' he teased. 'I thought only the bride's mother did that. What's the matter now?'

'I—nothing,' she mumbled, and ducked her head into his shirt front. She had finally puzzled it all out. What a stupid place this was to discover that you've fallen in love with your husband!

CHAPTER EIGHT

THE party was a small one. The group of Penn's friends who had been at the church came home with them. Sally's husband Jim had joined, apologising for missing the ceremony. The old house welcomed her. It seemed to smile, gaptoothed, through its arches at her. Confused, wildly happy and at home, she needed a clean up and a respite from the tight coronet that held her veil. When she went up the lady in the picture smiled at her.

'Wish me luck,' Phil begged as Sally hustled her up the stairs.

'Who, me? I already did that.'

'Not you, sis. The girl in the picture. I have a sort of feeling that if—'

'Don't let it worry you, love. Look at that leer on the Pirate's face, over here. Now if he got you alone in some dark corner you'd have something to worry about!'

Phil dappled her face with cold water while her sister looked over the room in awe. With coronet and veil off, she took down her hair, brushing it out into a gleaming sheath of wild curls. 'Be careful of the dress,' Cecily admonished, giggling. 'You'll need it for your daughter.'

'Yes. Of course.' Why not dream? Phil challenged herself. What law is it that says I can't delude myself if I want to? And so she stood carefully still while her two attendants rearranged the beautiful wedding-gown. One question bothered her, and she could not help but ask. 'How did you know about the wedding, Sally?'

'The wedding? Your—Penn, is it?—Penn telephoned.' And then, in a more serious tone, 'Deborah had already gone. They found a baby-sitter for the week, and took off for Lake Tahoe.'

'Who in the world would willingly watch those two for a week?'

'John's mother and father. I don't say they were happy to do it, but they're doing it.'

'And Samantha?'

'I—I'm sorry, Phil. Samantha and her husband have decided that you are purposely keeping them from *her* inheritance. Sam said—well, she wouldn't come. And after all you did for them! Dammit, Phil, sometimes relatives can be worse than enemies!'

'Don't let it bother you,' Phil said softly. 'I'll survive, and one day they'll get over it. You'll see. Hadn't we better go down?'

The group downstairs was making enough noise for twice its number. Phil hesitated on the bottom stair, took a couple of deep breaths to steady her nerves, and strode into the living-room looking as complacent as if she had done this sort of thing every day. Or at least once a week, she amended as they all turned in her direction and her composure slipped away from her.

Penn was standing in the middle of the room, a glass in his hand, his ears perked. 'Philomena?' She went directly to him, a rush of affection assaulting her. He smiled when she stretched high enough to kiss the tip of his nose, then surrounded her with one arm. Somebody in the crowd filled her hand with a chilled champagne glass.

'A toast,' Penn announced. 'To the loveliest bride ever to come into the Wilderman family.' There were cheers as the wine went down. Not used to wine at all, Phil emptied her glass, and then hiccupped as the sparkling liquid hit her stomach. Penn pulled her close. 'What did you say?' he whispered in her ear.

She hiccupped once more. 'What I said,' she whispered back, 'is that you haven't the slightest idea what you're talking about, Mr Wilderman.' Someone filled her glass. She clinked it against his. 'And here's a toast to the true descendant of the Pirate King,' she whispered back at him. The second glass went down as quickly as her first, but nobody was counting—or noticing—until he handed his glass into the nearest passing hands and swooped down on her with both arms. Her own glass fell to the floor, and there was considerable cheering as his lips touched hers gently, moved away, and then almost as if compelled by outside forces, came back passionately, demandingly, sweeping her out of herself with sweet abandon. It left her weak, trembling, leaning against him for support. He gathered her up again, coddling her head against his chest gently.

'And that's what happens to uppity wives,' he whispered into her hair. 'Want to try for two?'

'I wouldn't dare,' she quavered. 'Not here, with all these people watching!'

'Now that's the right attitude,' he chuckled, releasing her. She didn't want to go. 'We have to mingle,' he chided.

'I—I'd rather do it right where I am,' she confessed, but he gently pushed her away, and she mingled.

An hour later they had all gone. Rose provided a buffet supper for the family. The lobster was delightful, the heart-of-palm salad equal to it, but everything else Phil noted was some hazy world whose borders were too ill-defined for her to recognise them. Never-never Land, she asked herself?

What have I done to me? She was seated between Penn and
Robbie, and they both looked so—so huge, so handsome,
so—

'So now *you're* my mother.' Robbie, bending close to her
ear.

'It looks as if,' she returned, having trouble with all the
syllables. 'Eat your heart out, kid.' The lobster salad splat-
tered all over her beautiful dress.

'I dunno,' the boy chuckled. 'I like neat people.'

'What are you two arguing about?'

'We're not arguing, Penn. We never argue. We occasionally—did I say that right?—we might fight, but we don't
argue.'

'How much champagne have you had tonight, Philomena?'

'Counting this one?'

'Yes, counting that one.'

She gulped it down thirstily and giggled as the bubbles
tickled her nose. 'That makes—three,' she managed. They
were both laughing, and she could see nothing funny about
it at all, as her earnest face showed. 'Compared to all the
champagne you've drunk in your lifetime, that's hardly a
drop, love.' She shivered at the word. Love. Delicious. If
only it were true. Why is my mind so hazy?

She wanted to be sure he understood her. 'Yes, three,' she
said sleepily.

'Yes,' Penn chuckled. 'I understand. You're sleepy, and
you've had three glasses of champagne tonight.'

'No, no.' She waved her hand in front of his face to get his
attention. 'I've had three all of my life. Only two tonight.'

She had spent the whole evening sitting up straight, being the lady. And now suddenly the table was at an angle,
falling slowly up at her. Things were all just very confusing. The salad bowl kept falling up at her, faster and faster,

until Robbie yelled, and Penn caught her by the shoulders, then climbed out of his chair and swung her up in his arms. 'Whoever would have thought of it. She doesn't drink alcohol. Wow!' He shifted her weight in his arms, so that her head rested on his shoulder. One of her arms was around his neck, and a contented smile marked her face.

'She's smiling,' Robbie said softly.

'Is she really? Well, we've got to get her to bed, Robbie. It'll have to be a two-man job. I'll carry and you guide. Right?'

'Right.' They started slowly for the stairs, doing each tread slowly. Half-way up one of those huge eyes of hers opened.

'Penn,' she managed, waving towards the painting. 'Who was that lady?'

He stopped, shifting her weight again, looking over his shoulder. 'I thought I told you before,' he said gently. 'That's my sister Robin.'

That's my sister. That *was* my sister. *That's my mother,* Robbie had said. The words haunted her confused mind. She squeezed the eye shut again and tried to move closer to him.

'Stop wriggling,' he complained softly. 'You'll have us both back down the stairs. I'm not one of these macho Hollywood stunt men.' She became rigid in his arms, which made it worse, and then went limp as he carried her into her room and stretched her out gently on the bed. They *shushed* each other as the door closed behind them.

She squeezed one eye open. 'Shower,' she muttered. 'Wedding night.' The floor rocked abominably, but she made it to the bathroom, shedding items of clothing as she went.

With more luck than skill she managed to cram her curls under her shower cap, and stepped into the cubicle. The hot water sprayed ice-cold, shocking her out of her comfortable daze. Her blank mind began to spin, and even the gradual warming of the water could not help.

'Wedding-night,' she muttered. 'Happily ever after!' The thought twisted like a knife to her heart. He had already set the boundaries to their marriage. Just until he could see again. It would have worked, she thought bitterly, if I hadn't gone and fallen in love with him. Now *that's* a real laugher, Philomena. Poor slow-witted Philomena.

One day soon he'll be able to see again. What will he expect? An old battle-axe? Five-foot-two of stern matriarch? You little fool. He doesn't even know how tall you are. Five foot two, provided you wear two-inch heels. Grey hair. How can he possibly know that it's straw-blonde, that the curls are real, not ironed in? He's braille-read my face, but all he knows is that it's round. He can't tell that I've got green eyes, and a dimple in each cheek. And a too-wide mouth that couldn't be stern if it wanted to. What a mess!

She shut off the water and stepped out into the steamy bathroom. The full-length mirror on the wall confronted her with more than she wanted to see. No, he can't know all that, her mind screamed at her. That's something he'll never see. The freckles on my shoulders, and across the bridge of my nose. The pale white skin that burns when I'm not careful. The full, firm breasts. If I were older he would expect *something* to sag a little?

The narrow waist? No, I stopped him when he got that far in his *research*. The comfortable hips, the tapered legs? Nothing. He'll look for a woman of comfortable age, inches taller than I am, and he'll pass over the little thing I really am, with all my fears and prejudices and *ordinariness* written on my face, and he—and he won't even know me. Or want to know me. And that's what will break your heart, won't it, Philomena Wilderman? Her mind was too muzzy, too filled with fears and tears to continue. She dabbed at herself with the towel, discarded the shower cap, and stumbled back to bed.

THE PALE LIGHT of pre-dawn was outlining the window when she woke up. She was lying flat on her back in her own bed. See, she told herself, you went and got yourself fool-drunk, and nothing bad happened. Here you are, totally naked in your own bed—totally naked? The thought startled her, and she tried to sit up. It proved impossible. A heavy brown arm was thrown completely across her body, locking her into position. The attached hand had taken complete possession of her left breast. When she tried to gently remove it there was an instant groan of protest in her ear. She inched her head sideways, and found herself nose to nose with a man.

It was something she had not expected. Something she had not even thought about. Which proves what an idiot you are, Philomena Peabody, she lectured herself. She wriggled slightly to try to break away. The movement brought another protest, and the hand slowly and gently kneaded her breast, until its roseate peak sprang to full proud life. It brought something else too, a wild incessant hammering at the door behind which she had locked all her passions. And just another minute of this, she knew, would show how weak that lock was. She froze in position again. The hand gradually came to a stop. She stared at the pads that covered his eyes, wishing mightily she might see them without them seeing her.

What have I done? Nothing unusual, her practical mind insisted. That's not just a man—that's your husband. You remember, Phil? Orange blossoms and lace, and *I, Philomena take thee, Penn.* Remember? Harry couldn't find the ring because Robbie had it, and Cecily caught the bouquet, and you stepped out into the sunlight, right in the church doors, and discovered you loved him? Remember? Well, there he is. The man in possession. He's the *possessor,* and you're the *possessee,* lady, and there's no way to back out of it—because you don't want to! He needs a shave. He's got such a heavy beard. Funny I hadn't noticed that before. I wonder how it feels to kiss a man with a beard? Well, it's not really a beard, just a little—lord, isn't it rough! That was her two fingers, exploring, reporting, drawing back quickly when the dragon almost opened an eye. And we're in my bed together, and it's almost morning and he—good lord, he's as naked as I am!

So what I'll do, she decided, is to lie here quietly, making believe I'm fast asleep, until he—but he didn't. Not for another three hours, and by that time Phil was indeed sound asleep again, dreaming wild dreams, sighing sweetly in the toils of the dragon.

On Wednesday morning it was another noise, another male, who brought her up out of the darkness. Sleepily she forced one eye open. Robbie was sitting on the foot of the bed, bouncing. The mattress shook.

'Hey,' the boy called. 'Dad's downtown. He called and told me to get you up. They've moved the hearing up a day. We have to be in court by eleven o'clock!' She gave him a glare and then a smile, and pushed him in the general direction of her door.

She dressed slowly. What does one wear to a court hearing in the morning? Something judgmental? Dark, sober? Her hand reached automatically for one of her two old light blue trouser-suits. Her office uniform, no less. But a sudden intuition stopped her. Instead she chose a demure white blouse with a Peter Pan collar, and imitation gold studs at the wrists. A sturdy corduroy beige skirt, and a pair of dark brown half-boots completed the outfit. She brushed her mass of hair diligently, and let it hang free. A touch of pink lip-gloss, a bit of powder on her nose, and she was ready. 'Into the valley of death—' she quoted haphazardly as she squared her shoulders and went down.

The hearing was to be held in rooms in the Hall of Justice, 'because of alterations in the regular Juvenile court,' Frank explained. They drove down I street, past the City Hall and the Post Office. There was construction everywhere. The city was growing almost before her eyes. Which she could open now, she found. The aspirin had already begun its work. There wasn't a parking place to be had. So what else is new, she asked herself.

Frank drove the limousine right up to the front of the building, parked in the No Parking zone, and held the door for them. Harry was waiting for them on the steps. 'The boss has gone up already,' he said. 'He and the lawyer. Better hurry up. This judge, she don't stand for nonsense.' He took the crook of Phil's arm and hustled her up and into the building.

'She?'

'Yeah. Judge Irene Mulrooney. Not too well liked by the lawyers. She doesn't care for long-running cases.'

'Like this one.'

'Yeah. Like this one. You don't look old enough to be married, Mrs Wilderman.'

'Well!' It was all she could think to say. Twice in one hour. Well! She squared her shoulders and reached back for Robbie's hand. It came into hers. Reluctantly, but it came.

The hearing room was larger than she had expected, but plain. A bare desk in the middle of the room for the judge, with a high-backed swivel chair, and two sets of modern armchairs, facing each other on opposite sides. The empty space in the middle looked like the bullring, waiting. Blood spilled? she asked herself. Will it be one of *those* battles?

Penn knew she was there. Perhaps the sound of her heels, she considered. But she was wearing boots, and the heels were soft leather. But he knew, and he stood up, a smile on his face, and arms extended.

For the audience, she supposed. The opposite side of the room was crowded. Eloise and Donald, and what must have been a whole platoon of lawyers, all glaring at her. Play the game, she told herself fiercely. Play the game.

Her feet did not require orders. They sped up, leaving Harry behind, and in a moment she was safe again, squeezed inside his arms, almost as if it were all true. It is all true, she insisted to herself. It is! We're married—and even if only one of us is in love, there's enough here for two. More than enough. Her sigh gave her away.

'Something bothering?' His lips were at her ear.

'I—I don't know,' she sighed. 'I think I—I'm just not a morning person—and changing the date surprised me. I don't like surprises. I like—neat, orderly—well, sometimes I do.'

'Sounds a little confusing there,' he chuckled. 'I'll see what I can do about providing a safe orderly life for you.'

'Can you do that?' she sighed.

'You sound suspicious.'

'I don't know a great deal about *happily ever after,*' she confessed, pressing her nose into his chest. There might have been more lovely words, but at that moment Robbie caught up to them, exchanged a very adult handshake with his father, and sat down. Harry pre-empted the lawyer's seat in the first row, and relegated that worthy to the second row. Penn offered a brief introduction. 'Mr Whirlmount,' he nodded backward. Phil barely caught a look at the middle-aged blue-eyed man behind them, before Penn seized on her attention, drawing her down beside him.

She scanned his face for some sign that he knew yesterday had been different, and last night had—what? Those gauze pads stared back at her.

'Are you peeking?'

'With these things on? Don't be silly.'

'Did you get your eyedrops this morning?'

'Is this what it means to be married?'

'Yes, it does,' she snapped indignantly. 'I'm entitled to worry about you!'

'Yes. I admit that,' he laughed. 'One of the pads fell off last night. Harry fixed everything this morning.'

'One of them fell off?' Panic. Last night? She squirmed in her chair. 'What—what did you see?'

'A dark night,' he whispered. 'Was there something I should have seen?'

'Oh no!' The judge and bailiff came in at that moment. She jumped to her feet, spilling her purse and its contents all over the floor. The judge looked over at her as she bent to recapture her worldly goods. Judge Mulrooney. About sixty, white-haired, gold-rimmed glasses, tall for a woman. She nodded at both sides of the case with equal chill, and sat down. Phil, still scrambling for her lipstick and key-chain, half under the chairs, decided to leave things where they were. She stood up, brushed down her skirts, blushed an apology at the judge, and sank into the chair next to Penn, hoping she might sink completely out of sight. The judge rapped on the desk top with the rounded end of a ballpoint pen. Her recorder rushed in and handed her a large envelope. She opened it with some disdain. 'The Case of Wilderman Versus Wilderman,' the judge announced. Her court recorder bent over her shoulder and whispered in her ear.

'I stand corrected. The case is amended to read Wilderman versus Worth. Do I understand, madam, that you are

the former Mrs Wilderman and are now Mrs Donald
Worth?' Eloise's platoon of lawyers signalled agreement.

'I'm sure she can speak for herself,' the judge commented wryly.

'Yes,' Eloise returned. Her voice was high and shrill, on
the point of breaking.

'And your former husband, Mr Wilderman, is suing for
custody of an adopted child, Robert Penn Wilderman.'

'Yes,' Penn nodded.

'You, Mr Wilderman, charge your former wife with ne-
glect, child-abuse, and failure to comply with prior court
orders. Now, let me hear the lawyers.' And she did. For an
hour and thirty minutes, like a battle royal, as Phil slipped
lower and lower in her chair, trying to dodge the verbal bullets. The judge handled them skilfully. Probed, when questions seemed half answered. Tapped her pen occasionally
when things seemed to be getting out of order. And then—

'And now, Mrs Worth, I see you have added to your
charges, alleging that your former husband is now, along
with his other problems, guilty of lewd and lascivious con-
duct, by reason of living openly and immorally with another woman. Who?'

'That one. Right there,' Eloise screamed. 'They've been
at it for weeks, with the boy in the house too!'

'Well,' the judge sighed. 'What is the quotation—there
are none so blind as those who will not see? You, young
lady. Are you cohabiting with the plaintiff?'

'Me?' Phil squeaked. 'Am I what?'

'Are you living in the same house as Mr Wilderman
there?'

'I—yes.'

'All right, sit down, I won't bite you.'

The devil you won't, Phil sighed. Penn's hand closed on
hers again, gently. It did a little bit to soothe her spirit, but

not much. The judge was tapping her pen on the desk monotonously.

'I think I understand everything so far,' Judge Mulrooney said softly. 'So now we'll hear from the third party involved. Robert Wilderman?'

The lawyer reached over the row of chairs and tapped Robbie on the shoulder. The boy stood up. In spite of the suit, the tie, he looked like an accident on its way to happen. That sullen teenage scowl was back in full force. He spared one quick look over his shoulder at Phil, and she could see the unspoken appeal in his eyes. She shifted over to be as close to him as possible. He heard the chair shift, and one of his hands reached behind his back. Phil leaned forward and tucked her own in his. It continued to surprise her. Thirteen years old, and his hand was bigger than hers. Bigger and stronger. It closed around her like a vice. The boy backed up, as close to his chair as he could get, and hung on.

'Robert Penn Wilderman?'

'Yes sir—ma'am.'

'Don't be embarrassed. What do your friends call you?'

'Robbie'

'Well then, Robbie. You've lived with your mother, the present Mrs Worth.'

'She's not my mother. My mother is—' The bitterness rolled out of him. The judge tapped the desk.

'Yes, I understand that. But Mrs Worth is your mother by adoption, as your uncle has now become your father by adoption.'

'That's it!' Phil clamped her hand over her mouth as everyone in the court glared at her. But that was it. She remembered. He was carrying her up the stairs, when they looked at the painting. *That's my mother, Robbie had said. And that's my sister, Penn had said.* No wonder they look alike. He's not—how could I have thought that Robbie was his illegitimate child! How could I have thought that! She wanted so badly to apologise to the silent man sitting straight and true beside her, but the judge was watching.

'To continue,' Judge Mulrooney said, 'If I may, young lady?'

'Yes. I—I'm sorry,' Phil stammered.

'And then, Robbie, you lived with your father for some time?'

A very defensive, 'Yes.'

'Now, Robbie, there are three sides to this case. It's your life we are dealing with. You *do* understand that?'

'Yes, ma'am.'

'Good. Now, given your own choice, Robbie, would you prefer to live with your mother?'

'Her? No. I don't want to live with her. She hates me. Her and that—that wimp she married.' More taps with the pen.

'All she's interested in is that I need to be living in her house at the end of each quarter, because that's when the company pays my dividends, and she takes all the money. That's all she's interested in, my money. I'd let her have it all if I didn't have to live with her.'

'All right son. Mrs Worth, is it true that you receive all the child's stock dividends? One eighth of the company stock?' The judge peered at some papers. 'Eighty thousand dollars a year?'

'Well, I—yes,' Eloise began. 'But you know how expensive it is to feed a child these days.'

'Yes, I'm sure I do,' the judge snapped. 'I have three myself. Eighty thousand dollars. How much of that is banked for the boy's future?'

'Banked?' Eloise's troops were in confusion, muttering among themselves.

'Well?'

'None, your honour,' her lawyer interjected.

'But next year we expect to start an investment programme for him,' Eloise shrilled. 'My—Mr Worth is an Investment Counsellor.'

'Next year?' The judge grinned. There was nothing happy about it. It looked like the grin a wolf might offer when meeting Little Red Riding Hood.

'All right, Robbie,' she continued. 'So you would prefer to live with your father?'

The boy agonised for a moment, then shook his head negatively. 'No,' he managed. 'I—he's a nice man, but—my mother was his sister, you see, and he thinks I'm a *responsibility*. I don't want to live where I'm just a responsibility. He's—he's busy, and works hard, and goes places where I can't go, and he never stops to play with me, or anything— but he does send me to a private school.'

'I see. He takes his responsibility seriously, though?'

'Yes, ma'am.'

The judge thought for a moment. 'You leave us with a difficult situation, Robbie,' she finally sighed. 'You don't want to live with your father, and you don't want to live with your mother—by adoption,' the judge hastily qualified as the boy stirred into objection. 'Do you have any ideas?'

'Sure,' the boy proclaimed. 'I've got a perfect solution. I wanna—excuse me—I want to live with Phil.'

A deadly silence fell over the entire room. 'And who the devil is Phil?' The judge leaned forward over her desk to stare at the boy. Philomena shrugged her shoulders. After all, they had outlawed the death penalty. So what else could happen to her? She stood up, still clutching at Robbie's hand.

'I'm Phil,' she announced in her soft ready-for-battle voice.

'And I wanna stay with Phil because she wants me,' the boy interjected swiftly. 'She doesn't have any responsibility—about me, that is, and she doesn't want my money—she just wants me. And that's what I want. I want somebody who wants me.' And with that he slumped back in his chair, pulling Phil down with him, clutching at her hand as if defying the world to separate them.

'Now let me see if I've got this right,' the judge sighed. 'This woman is cohabiting with Mr Wilderman, and you want her to be your legal guardian?' From behind, the lawyer nudged Phil sharply. She turned around. He gestured towards her left hand.

'Your honour,' she offered tentatively. 'If you mean I'm living with Penn and that's a bad thing, it's not, you know. It's really very nice.' Chuckles surrounded her. 'I forgot to tell you my full name. I'm Philomena Peabody Wilderman. Penn and I are married, and I think Robbie should live with us—because—because Penn is the nicest man I've ever known, and it takes two parents to bring up a teenager, and I know because I've had lots of experience in that field, and so—I think Robbie should go home with us.' And she collapsed into her chair again, and tried to shrink into a smaller package than she was. Another hand trapped her, on her left side. She was thoroughly surrounded. Penn on one side, holding her gently; Robbie on the other, clutching desperately, so that her hand ached.

The judge looked at all of them, one at a time, counting, assessing. And finally she tapped on her desk a couple of times with the top of her pen. 'I think maybe you're right,' she finally said. 'So ordered.' That pen again, an extra rap, and the judge billowed out of the courtroom, followed by her marching legion.

Luckily the room had two separate exits, or there might have been blood on the sand after all, Phil thought.

'I'll appeal!' Eloise yelled after them, as half her lawyer-platoon held her from making a frontal assault. 'I'll appeal!' They could still hear it echoing down the hall as they headed for the stairs.

Robbie was still clutching her hand, and it ached so much that she finally could not suppress a whimper. Penn turned around in a flash. He had been walking ahead of them, his arm on his lawyer's.

'It's only my hand,' she said quickly. 'Robbie doesn't know his own strength.'

'Gee, you should have said something,' the boy returned, releasing the pressure. 'Oh, what a mess I made!'

'It's not a mess,' she assured him. 'It just needs a massage and a—'

She stopped in mid-sentence. Penn had turned away and was going down the stairs. She could read anger in the set of his shoulders. It was still there when she followed him into the back seat of the limousine. Robbie—a smiling Robbie—jumped into the front seat, and was quickly lost in conversation with Harry—about machinery, of course. Phil settled back into the seat, and made an attempt to lift up the arm-rest. Penn's heavy hand kept her from doing so.

'So don't bottle it all up,' she said quietly. 'Whatever it is, it belongs out in the open. You won the case. Robbie is yours.'

'No,' he said bitterly. 'I didn't win the case, and Robbie isn't mine.'

'Penn! What are you trying to say?'

'I'm trying to tell you the truth,' he muttered. 'I didn't win the case. You did. The judge didn't appoint *me* to be the boy's guardian, she appointed *you*. And in any case, you were right a week or so ago. You said he hated me, and obviously he does.'

'He doesn't hate you, Penn. He defended you in the court. He laughed with you, and—'

'And he also told the absolute truth,' her husband grated. 'All I ever did was put a roof over his head and feed him. Nothing more. I was always too busy—too wrapped up in the Big World. I kept him away from the river because I remembered how his mother died. I couldn't go with him, so no Little League. No Boy Scouts. With the finest mountains in the world within forty miles of us, I've never once taken him camping. It's all damn true, but it took you to bring it all out, Peabody. Sometimes I'm not sure whether meeting you was good or bad for me.'

The bitterness was more than she had expected. She tried to defend herself. '*I* didn't win the case,' she sighed. 'The judge misunderstood. I was speaking for you!'

'I know that,' he grunted. 'Maybe I could have better spoken for myself!'

It was a cold, flat statement. For the past few minutes she had been hugging herself, congratulating herself, and now suddenly it all exploded in her face. He settled back in his seat, a frown on his handsome face. She studied him. He had the look of a man troubled beyond his capacity. And then, just as suddenly, his muscles relaxed, the frown disappeared. One of his warm hands fumbled for hers, squeezed it gently, and held on to it as the car moved out into traffic on the way home.

'It's not your fault, Philomena,' he sighed. 'It just seemed for a moment that—well, it's one problem out of our way.'

'But your—but Eloise—she said they would appeal.'

'So let them,' he said wryly. 'I can afford to hire more lawyers than that damn St Louis wimp. We'll lead them a merry chase before they get *that* decision overturned. You did a good job, old girl!' Congratulations, but the taste was bittersweet.

How can I be so high up in the air on one side, and so low down on the other, she asked herself. Congratulations—old girl. Darn. I *should* have told him the first time the subject came up. And now I don't know *what* to do! She was still deep in thought when the car drew up at the front door.

CHAPTER NINE

THE atmosphere of tension was still there when she came down to dinner. Robbie appeared with clean face and hands, and something that might be called a smile on his face. Harry was his usually glum self, and Penn had withdrawn somewhere inside that darkness of his, and no amount of conversation would bring him out. After the meal Harry guided him into the library, and before the door closed behind them she could hear the hum of conversation.

'So that leaves you and me, Robbie,' Phil offered tentatively. 'Or have you got something on too?'

The boy shrugged his shoulders. 'I was going to watch *Dr Who* on television, but if you and—Dad—I thought both of you would like to be alone for a while, so—'

'No, don't disturb your plans,' she returned hastily. 'I've got a million things to do. You just go ahead.'

He proffered a real smile this time, and when he walked by her chair he stopped long enough to kiss her cheek. 'It takes some getting used to,' he said, 'but maybe I could like having a real mother around the place.'

'Well, don't get over-enthusiastic,' she returned. 'Who knows? Given enough time I might be able to put up with you.' She reached up, ruffled his hair, and giggled.

'You don't plan to disappear now, do you?'

'It all depends on how you mean that,' she said. 'I *do* intend to disappear. Out into the garden, before it gets dark. Run along, kid.'

It was still light outside, in those minutes after the sun had gone but before the dark had taken over. She wandered slowly down into the garden, towards the hot house. Mr Yu was still working inside, and she was in no mood for casual chatter. She turned back and sat down on the sofa-swing. The tip of her toe barely reached the ground. The whole construction was adapted to long-legged men, she accused. Two blue jays refused to accept her comment, and fled, flying low over the shrubbery in the direction of the park. In the background she could hear Mr Yu singing. She braced herself and gave the swing a shove, then coiled her legs up beneath her and tried to relax.

Being a wife, if only a temporary one, was proving more nerve-racking than she had thought. His offer had puzzled her as much as her own acceptance—until that moment on the steps of the church. But the fact that she loved him was no guarantee that he felt the same. Something temporary, he had said. Until the problem with Robbie was disposed of, and he gets his sight back. Well, Robbie was—settled, not disposed of. And on Monday morning the doctor would remove his pads for the final time. And then what?

Her mind balked at the jump, and left her wandering around in her head as the gold on the western horizon began to fade into the blue and purple that heralded the end of day. Although she was in the centre of the city the trees and purposefully curved streets cut out the traffic noises, and left only a certain empty tranquillity on her ears. The swing squeaked a little as she lowered a foot and gave another push. Mr Yu's song had a haunting familiarity about it, but the name escaped her. She nestled back in the corner of the swing, and wrestled with her devils again.

'Mrs Wilderman?' Harry, standing on the little ridge that overlooked the pool area. Just a shadow now.

'Here,' she answered softly. The little man sidled down the hillside in a rush of gravel.

Mrs Wilderman? What a nice sound. She had heard it so seldom these last two days. 'What is it, Harry?'

'I have to go now.'

'I—what?' Harry was a part of the family. A fixture in the house. Every minute of every day, where Penn was, there was Harry. It was almost impossible to think of Harry as having to 'go now'! She dropped her foot to the ground and braked the swing to a stop. 'You have to *go?*'

'A ten o'clock flight,' he returned.

'But you—how the devil can Penn get around if you—?'

'He has you now.'

An overwhelming statement. He has me now. If only it were true! 'I—I don't understand, Harry.'

'It's simple enough. I have to make a trip. I'll be gone two or three days—well, to be exact I expect to get things wound up by Sunday. But my plane leaves in a couple of hours, and he needs you now.'

'I—yes. Yes, of course, Harry. Where is he?'

'In the living-room.'

'I'll go in at once. And Harry?'

'What?'

'Have a safe trip.'

The little man had disappeared before she could gather her wits about her. Mr Yu was making closing-for-the-night noises down in the greenhouse. And Penn was waiting for her? She jumped up, setting the swing into a wild creaking and groaning. The gravel of the path crunched under her sandals as she made her way back up to the house.

The house was quiet, as if it had gone to sleep. Penn was sitting on the big couch in the middle of the room, facing the door. Somehow he sensed her. She stopped to scan his face, uplifted in her direction. There was something dear about it, something heartwarming. She floated over the distance between them. He was holding out a hand. She took it, and followed his direction as he tugged her down to sit beside him.

'Well, Mrs Wilderman.' The second time in one night! She pinched herself, just to make sure, and then settled back. His arm automatically came around her shoulders.

'Well, Mr Wilderman?' she sighed.

'What we need now is a nice fire in the fireplace.'

'Yes.' She snuggled closer to him. 'What fireplace?'

'The one right in front of us.'

'That's a door,' she offered.

'You need more imagination,' he returned. 'A big stone fireplace. And the flames? They're blue on the top, a flickering blue.'

'Silly. It's still a door. A double door, I grant you, but there aren't any blue flames.'

'Pragmatic Philomena?'

A deep-throated chuckle. 'The girls called me Practical Pill.'

'Pill?'

'Well, it was hard to say Philomena when they were young, and then when they got older, they thought Pill was more appropriate.'

'Tell me about them.'

So she did, emphasising the good, making herself the butt of the bad, not knowing how clearly she silhouetted her own loneliness, demonstrating how quickly her youth had fled. 'And now it's your turn,' she concluded.

'Not much to tell,' he assured her. 'Compared to you I'm practically a stay-at-home. Although they did call me the "Wild Man" when I was younger. A dare-devil fool, that's what my father called me. Up until—'

'Until your sister's accident?'

'Ah. You know about that too?'

'Kitchen gossip,' she said, feeling a compassion for him that went beyond all bonds.

'She never would have gone out on the river if I hadn't teased and dared her. Never could let things alone. She always had to do everything big brother did. And the race was the most stupid thing imaginable. There was debris in the channel. She must have been going ninety miles an hour when her boat hit the floating tree trunk. It threw them both almost a hundred feet. They were both dead before—well— it was all my fault, and the cloud has hung over me ever since. If only I could have that little time to live over again.'

'And that's what drives Penn Wilderman?'

He crushed her against him with one strong arm. She could feel his fingers sink into her shoulder. 'And that's what drives Penn Wilderman,' he said bitterly. 'I'd better get to bed.'

His hand relaxed. Phil rubbed her shoulder where the fingers had dug craters, and then stood up. As soon as he heard her move, he came up too. Holding his hand, she guided him up the stairs and into his own bedroom. Still holding her, he took himself to the big armchair next to the bed, and sat down.

'Eyedrops,' she offered, trying to get a little normality into her voice.

'Yes, please. Not many more times to go,' he answered. 'Lord, doesn't that sound good?'

She dimmed the overhead lights, found the drops on his dresser, and administered them. 'Hey, what's the hurry?' he grumbled. 'No sooner do you get the pads off than you flood me. I wanted to get a look at you.'

And that's just what I *don't* want, she told herself. We've gone this far in the dark, and I want to keep it that way until the last possible minute! 'Don't touch those pads,' she warned. 'It's just a few days before the grand unveiling, and all will be revealed!'

'You make it sound like a Hallowe'en project,' he complained.

'Well, this is no time to ruin weeks of work,' she told him. 'Be optimistic, Penn.'

'Oh, I am,' he returned. There was just a touch of sarcasm, just a touch of despair. 'But have you ever thought—suppose I go down to the doctor on Monday, in all my darkness, and he takes the pads off—and the world is still dark?'

'It won't happen,' she assured him. 'I just *know* everything will be OK. Here are your pyjamas, at the foot of the bed. I have to check up on Robbie.'

'Damn that kid,' he said. 'You married me, not Robbie.'

'I know, but he needs somebody to—'

'So do I,' he snarled at her. 'Go ahead!'

The depth of his anger reached her. She reacted by running. None of her experience had taught her how to deal with an angry husband. But kids—

So Robbie, still following a horror movie on Channel Six, was quickly disabused of the notion that his sweet lovable mother would let him sit up until midnight. She hustled the boy into the shower, picked up the clothes he had strewn across the floor, and went back to her own room.

An hour later, bathed, perfumed, but not yet calm, she stood by her window. Her translucent pink nightgown, the one that reached her ankles, but hung loosely at her shoulders on two shoe-string bands, flared around her. Half dreaming, she watched the star patterns. There was a noise from next door, a strangled cough.

Surely Penn must be asleep by now, she told herself, but could not stop the movement that carried her through the connecting door into his bedroom. Penn was in bed, apparently asleep, but the lights were still on. And *his* clothes were strewn around the room. He has an excuse, she told herself fiercely as she bent to the task, and then laid out the clean things he would need in the morning.

He stirred in the bed as she finished. She froze in position, sure that her vague movements, her mutterings, might have awakened him. When he became quiet again she edged cautiously over to the door and flicked off the light switch. The change from light to dark blinded her. She blinked her eyes, holding fast until some of the darkness became less dark, some of the shadows became more distinct. Gently, she whispered across the rug towards her own room, then stopped and came back to kneel beside him. Her gentle hands brushed the lock of hair back from his forehead, and offered a loving kiss. And before she could move both his hands snatched at her.

'Gotcha,' he whispered, pulling her closer.

'Darn you, I thought you were asleep! I—'

'I wanted to see you.'

'I'm not going to have you take those pads off your eyes,' she stormed at him. 'You're worse than Robbie is, for goodness' sake!'

'I don't need to see you with my eyes,' he contradicted. 'Be still.' It was a command she could not refuse. She didn't want to refuse. His hands had given up their imperious grip on her upper arms, and were now shaping her face, running through the softness of her long hair. She knelt there beside the bed, ignoring the complaints from her leg muscles. Hardly receiving them, for a fact. All the lines of communication to her brain were tied up in the sensual assault those hands were making as they dropped gently down on to her shoulders, pushed the straps of her nightgown away, and coursed down on to the proud pulsing mounds of her aroused breasts. Somewhere in the distance she could

hear the hiss of his breath as he caressed and measured the
fullness of her, the proud upward tilting of her woman-
hood.

One of his hands slipped downwards brushing the gown
off her hips, as it explored the softness of her rib cage, the
sharp inward curve of her waist, the burgeoning outward
bulge of her full hip. And then back upwards again, to torture her breast.

Madness raced through her mind as she fought herself.
One half of her screamed for more. The other half kept at a
litany. *It's only a temporary marriage. It's only temporary!*
There was little doubt which half might win—until he
laughed. 'No doubt about it, old girl,' he commented, 'You
are a whole lot of woman.'

'No doubt,' she whispered bitterly as she scrambled away
from the bed and restored her nightgown. Dear old girl.
There's nothing special about *this* man, she told herself.
He's just like all the others. All cats look grey on a dark
night! Damn him! It was hard to lock in the whimper of
anger and frustration.

He sat up in the bed. She could see the shadows moving,
and took another step backwards. 'I didn't mean to make
you cry,' he said somberly. 'Come back here.'

'Well, you managed to, no matter what you meant!' She
retreated into her own room and slammed the door behind
her. It wasn't *all* his fault, her conscience proclaimed.
Maybe not, she thought angrily, but if I don't blame *him*, I
have to blame myself—and I don't want to do that! Weari-
ly she stumbled across the room in the dark and flung herself down on the bed.

It was a wasted effort. She tossed and turned all night, but
sleep would not come. When the fingers of dawn light
touched on the trees outside she gave it all up, went for a
quick shower, and hastily crammed herself into fresh un-

derwear, a pair of old dungarees and a T-shirt. Rose and the
maids were off on vacation. Harry had gone. Frank lived
out in an apartment over the garage, and Mr Yu would be
coming in. The old man would make the dinner, but breakfast and lunch were in her hands. Make-up was not worth
the effort, but she did take time to brush out her hair before she went down to the kitchen.

The only solution, she decided, was to keep her fingers
busy and her mind empty. She scavenged up utensils, broke
half a dozen eggs, and scrambled them. Sausages went into
the microwave. Bread went into the toaster. The coffee pot
began to bubble. She scattered a few plates on the huge
kitchen table, added coffee mugs, and plodded deter-
minedly back up the stairs to serve as Penn's guide. He
hardly seemed to need one. She went into the room and
closed the door behind her. He was just coming back into
the room, followed by a spiral of steam from his shower. He
was using his towel to scrub at his unruly hair.

It was a sight she had never seen before. The dominant
male, in all his naked glory. A week ago she would have
screamed and run. Today she stood with her back against
the door, trying to breathe so softly that he could not hear.
And admired. He was every bit as male as she was female.
Sleek, muscular, broad shouldered, narrow hips. Strong
heavy thighs—and everything else, beautifully proportioned. He fumbled for a moment at his clothing, and she
almost broke away from the door to help. Almost. His
groping hands found everything where she had placed it the
night before. Very slowly, it seemed, he balanced on one leg
at a time and struggled into his shorts. Slacks followed, and
then a sports shirt.

She was congratulating herself on not being discovered as
he bent to lace up his shoes. 'Enjoy the show, did you?' he
asked casually. He stood up and brushed at his slacks as he

turned directly toward her. Startled, she looked at his eyes. The pads were still in place.

'Damn you,' she muttered.

'The door squeaks,' he told her as he started to move towards the sound of her voice. 'See everything you wanted?'

He was within reach at that moment. Her hand seemed to move involuntarily. It jumped to his forehead, and her fingers combed through his hair, smoothing and shaping it. 'That's nice,' he said. 'We must do this more often.'

There was just enough sarcasm in his voice to bring her back to reality. She snapped her hand back. Her finger tips were burning. 'I suppose you've come to take me to breakfast?'

'Damn you,' she sighed. His hand dropped on her shoulder. She turned, opened the door, and led him out into the hall and down the stairs. Robbie clattered up behind them, half shouting a greeting, passed them on the stairs, and hesitated just long enough to give his 'new' mother a light kiss. He was gone into the kitchen before the pair of them reached the bottom step.

'Damn kid,' Penn commented. She almost jumped, startled by his first words outside the bedroom.

'Don't talk like that,' she retorted fiercely. 'He's a sensitive boy—and both words are operative.'

'Me too,' he chuckled. 'I'm a sensitive boy too. And he's stealing my act.'

'I don't know what you mean,' she snapped. He demonstrated. But his kiss wasn't aimed at her cheek, and in no way could it be called fleeting. When they both came through the kitchen door Robbie, who was half-way through the scrambled eggs, laughed like a fool.

She guided Penn over to his chair, and then glared at the boy. 'What are you laughing at, you—' She stamped her foot on the hard floor, too late to remember she had no shoes on.

'You and Dad,' the boy chuckled through another mouthful of food. 'You don't *hafta* hide in the hall to get kissed. I know all about that stuff. Why is your face so red, Phil?'

'Because you don't know all you think you know,' she snarled. 'And there's nothing I hate worse than cheerful people in the morning! Leave your father some sausages!'

Robbie and Penn spent most of the morning together in his library. Conspiring about something, Phil thought as she rushed through a brief dusting and rearranging, and then went upstairs. I'm angry. Why? At whom? And had no answer.

Robbie had heard the 'cleanliness' message. His room was as neat as a new pin, bed made up, magazines put away, clothes on hangers. And we'll see how long that lasts, Phil snorted, as she made her way down the hall to Penn's room. Everything was as it had been earlier—except that that magnificent body was missing. She picked up the wet towel. It was a crazy thing to do, but she rubbed it gently against her cheek before dropping it into the clothes hamper. His pyjamas were still huddled up at the foot of the bed, unused. She re-folded them and put them back in the drawer. And then the bed.

It was a very difficult bed to make. Not that it was overlarge, oddly formed. Every time her hand reached for a pillow or a sheet or a blanket it just seemed to linger, as if some sustenance could be drawn from its emptiness. 'Come on, girl,' she told herself. 'You're going down with something. Get to work.' It might have taken something more than words—horse whips, perhaps—but a thump of feet on the stairs served instead. She finished making up the bed in twenty seconds flat, and ran for her own room. She spent the rest of the day trying to avoid everyone else who lived in the house. And since they all suddenly appeared to be very busy, it wasn't too hard a job.

Saturday night Robbie served as his father's guide. Phil could hear them from her hiding-place next door. There was considerable laughter. It served to warm up a very tiny portion of her chilled heart. For all the muddling, all the interference, all the upset she had caused, at least one good thing had resulted. Robbie and his father had come to appreciate each other.

Exhausted from a sleepless night and a fugitive day, Phil went to bed early, slept the sleep of the just, and awakened to a household already in motion. She could hear multiple thumps up and down the stairs, banging noises from the area of the kitchen, and motor noises from a car at the front door. She checked her bedside clock. Seven o'clock. Sunday morning? It seemed impossible. She threw back the covers, snatched at her heavy blue robe, and cautiously peered into Penn's room. Empty.

Through his room, just in case, and out into the hall. Empty. Down the stairs and into the kitchen. Robbie was stuffing his face with buttered toast. His father, fully dressed, across the table from him, was deep in thought. Harry was back, standing by the sink, a big smile on his face.

'Tarpon?' the boy asked through a mouthful of bread.

'Bonito,' Harry returned. 'Everything.'

Robbie looked up just in time to catch Phil standing in the door. 'Isn't it great, Mom?' he cried.

The two adults turned in her direction. 'Yes,' she managed. 'It's great. What?'

'Fishing,' Robbie said. 'Dad's arranged for me to go down to Catalina for a week of deep-sea fishing! Harry's coming with me, and we'll camp out on the boat and—wow!'

'Wow indeed. You'll need more breakfast than that.'

'I can't wait. The plane leaves at eight o'clock. We've only an hour to get to the airport, but I'm all packed, and—Mom? Didn't anybody tell you?'

'No, I guess not.' Phil tried to sound cheerful. It was bad enough to have to smile at seven o'clock on a Sunday morning, but—no, nobody had told her, had hinted, had even suggested. Tomorrow his father comes out from under the bandages. Today we ship Harry and Robbie off for a week of deep-sea fishing. Mr Yu is too old to travel but lives in his own little house out at the back. Frank is required to take Penn to the doctor's. And that leaves only me, she thought. What about me?

But none of her agitation showed in her voice. 'No, that's OK,' she told the boy. 'I get seasick just thinking about water. A whole week. I'll bet you'll have fun.' She slipped into the chair between her two 'men' and snatched at the last piece of toast on the plate. Harry thumped a mug of black coffee down in front of her.

'Yeah, well, women have that kind of trouble,' Robbie pontificated from the depths of his thirteen years of experience with life. 'Only—I wish Dad were coming. But of course, with his eyes and all—next time, Dad?'

'Next time, Robbie.' It was the first time Penn had spoken, and it didn't sound all that enthusiastic—or is it something else, Phil asked herself. She was straining, these days, to register nuances—to read behind the words. And there was definitely something there to be read.

'We gotta go,' Harry contributed. 'All the stuff's in the car. Come on, kid.'

The car was moving before Phil could get to the front door. She waved a belated goodbye to the back of the vehicle, and was rewarded when Robbie stuck his head out the window and blew her a kiss.

Penn was still at table, nursing his coffee-mug, a dour look on his face. Phil plumped herself down in the nearest chair and pulled her mug over in front of her. The coffee had cooled just about to the edge of drinkability. 'It'll be all right,' she said softly. 'He'll enjoy every minute of it. And he will be safe, won't he?'

'He'll be safe,' he returned gruffly. 'Happy, I don't know. Safe, I'm sure of.'

'So what brought all this on so suddenly?' She leaned both elbows on the table, the coffee-mug treasured between her hands. Penn was wearing that office mask, a look of non-committal interest that gave nothing away. His fingers were drumming on the table-top. She remembered where they last had drummed, and blushed. 'Is there something wrong, Penn?'

'Wrong? How the hell could there be anything wrong?' he roared at her. His chair fell over as he moved violently away from the table. 'I'm going back upstairs. You needn't come. When Frank comes back from the airport send him up to see me.' He stomped out.

She heard him stumble on the stairs, and repressed the urge to run after him. Somehow or another, she knew, he was not prepared to accept any help from her this day. This is strange, she told herself as she started to clean up the kitchen. Sometimes I feel very married, and sometimes I feel—like a stranger in their midst.

It was another sunny day—the first day of March, for a fact. Spring was hustling about in the valley where the American and the Sacramento rivers met. She snapped on the kitchen radio as she worked. Ski-ing conditions were still perfect up in the mountains, forty miles away, with deep-packed snow. She stretched up on tiptoe to look out of the small kitchen window. Mr Yu was transplanting flowers out of his greenhouse into the beds in the back garden. In the middle of the garden a pair of robins were strutting. She felt the need to share, dropped the rest of the dishes hastily into the dishwasher, and dashed upstairs to dress.

SHE WANDERED around the gardens all the remainder of the morning, and then went back in, having promised Mr Yu that she would see to the evening meal. The house was like a tomb.

As she headed for the kitchen Frank came out of the living-room and started for the front door. 'He's in the library,' he said in passing. 'He tells me to get out and take the rest of the day off. You be OK?'

'Me? Oh, yes.' Just to be sure, after Frank had left Phil went along to the library and cracked the door slightly open, just enough to see her husband sitting at his desk, a glass paperweight in his hands, and an almost-lost look on his face. As gently as she knew how, she closed the door and went back into the kitchen.

They shared dinner in the kitchen. 'It's not worth carrying everything to the dining-room just for the two of us,' he said when she went to get him. He looked tired, as if all the little tensions had become one big one. There was no discussion at the table. He ate the Western omelette she put in front of him, drank the coffee, enjoyed a slice of the apple pie, and said nothing.

An hour later, having stood the silence as long as she could, she got up and started on the dishes. It was growing dark outside. She took a quick look. Thunderclouds obscured the setting sun. She could hear the boom and rumble in the distance, as the storm did its work.

'It looks like a bad storm,' she commented. 'I think I'll have to put the light on.'

'Yeah, you do that,' he said bitterly. 'At least one of us might as well be in the light.'

'Oh Penn,' she sighed. 'Please. It will all be over tomorrow. You'll see.'

'You're damn well right,' he returned. 'Everything will be over tomorrow. I'm going upstairs.' Fighting the chill in her heart, Phil came around the table and offered her hand. He brushed it aside. 'I don't need any guide dogs,' he grumbled as he pushed back his chair and felt his way along the wall to the door. 'Just keep out of my way.'

She collapsed in a chair. It was worse than she had ever expected. *Just keep out of my way! Tomorrow it will all be over!* Her head ached, as if the storm had shifted to the inside of her head. 'Oh, Penn,' she moaned as she dropped her head into her arms on the table. The tears that followed upset her more than anything else. Practical Philomena just didn't cry. The world was too full of things to be done. There was no room for cry-babies. She knuckled the last drop of water from her eyes, and marched out into the living-room.

By nine-thirty she had read the same page of her novel over for the twentieth time, her headache had abated slightly, and she hadn't heard a sound in the house since seven o'clock. 'Well, there's no use struggling,' she lectured herself. 'Staying up late won't put off tomorrow. It's going to be, come hell or high water.'

Phil got up, stretched mightily, and then performed the nightly ritual, going around the house, locking windows and doors, and setting the burglar alarm. It was something that Harry usually did—and just the doing of it reminded her that Harry and Robbie were far away. Another little stab in her heart, that. If Robbie were at home perhaps they might have talked together—played games—built up some camaraderie? She turned off all but the night lights, and went upstairs slowly, feeling like some old hag whose days were numbered. There was no sound from Penn's room. The thunder was still working its way around the basin of the valley, and rain was thundering for admission. Not one to be plagued by storms, she felt something different in this one. Some evil, trying to reach out and pluck her from the safety of her home.

She closed her door behind her, then trailed clothes across the floor—doing just what she hated most when Robbie did it. By the time she reached the bathroom she had completely stripped.

The hot water revived her. Shower cap tucked tightly around her mass of hair, she revelled in the beat of the water on her skin. The sounds of the shower shut out the storm—and everything else. The soap felt sensuous as she lathered her hands and rubbed them up and down her body—and dreamed. If it could be Penn's hands? Penn's arms? Too much to hope for. She reached for the cold water and smashed the dream to bits under an icy deluge.

The bath towels were immense. She used one to dry herself, then wrapped the other around her, sarong-fashion. Her hair was dripping at its ends, where the shower cap had failed its mission. A little brushing, she assured herself, and walked out into the dark bedroom. There was someone there. Penn. Standing by the windows, listening to the rush of water against the panes.

'Penn? You wanted something?'

'My eyedrops.'

'Oh! I thought you said yesterday that you wouldn't want another—'

'Well, I do.' How could everything that seemed so warm and loving turn into such coldness, she asked herself. Have I done anything to deserve all that?

'All right,' she returned, using her softest voice. 'Sit on the bed here, and—'

Whatever it was he wanted, it wasn't eyedrops. He seized her proffered hand and yanked her up against him. She backed away and he followed. Backed until the inside of her knees banged into the side of the bed. 'What—I don't understand,' she managed. 'What do you want, Penn? Have you been drinking?'

'Not a drop. You don't really understand, Philomena? I'm you husband, and it's dark inside here. I want a little comfort.'

'Inside? You want me to put on a light?'

'I want you to *be* a light, Philomena!' He pushed. Trapped against the bed, she fell over backwards and suddenly he was on top of her.

'What—Penn!' The towel was gone. Ripped away and discarded over his shoulder. His robe followed. 'Penn!' Not a scream, but a soft reproach. 'I didn't expect this. It wasn't part of our—'

'Bargain? This is a marriage, not a bargain. Did you expect I could lie there next door to you and never have an inclination?'

'Is that what it is, Penn? Just an inclination? You need someone to pick on, and I'm nearest? Is that why you sent Robbie and Harry away?' It was getting harder to talk, to reason, than she had ever supposed. His hands were roving over her face, along the line of her neck, down to her breasts. His weight was no longer a burden, but some sort of promise. That's all you need do, she told herself fiercely. Talk to him, be calm, keep cool. But her traitorous body wanted nothing of the kind.

She could hardly suppress the moan as his hands shifted lower to her hips and below, and his lips took their place at her breast. The breath blew out of her as wild spasms shot through her nervous system, and reported in to her brain. So many feelings, so many reports, that her control centre was at the point of overload.

'Don't. Please, Penn—don't.' A weak effort—her strained voice trying to give one answer while her rolling hips gave another. His hands stopped.

'You don't want this?'

'I—no!' That last word took all her remaining control.

'Then fight me off,' he snarled.

She was fully stretched out, her nerves jangling, perspiration pouring from her, her legs spread. 'I won't fight you,' she sighed. 'I can't. But it isn't part of our bargain *or* our marriage, Penn.' The hands started moving again, his lips followed. Not a mad physical assault, but a teasing that drew her out from herself, sent her tossing and turning out of control.

'You don't want me to do this?' A hiss out of the darkness. Her eyes were shut tight. She could not muster an answer, but her tossing, squirming body told him all he wanted to know. Those lips teased at her, nibbling her ear-lobes, running channels of fire down to her breasts, across her stomach, until she could stand no more. Her hands snatched at his hair. He hesitated for a moment in his wild pursuit. But instead of pushing him away she pulled him closer, hard against the softness of her. Her mouth was half open. It was hard to breathe. When he came into her it was like a benison.

There was a sharp momentary pain, hidden quickly in the glory that followed, as their wild passion drove them up to and over the edge. She screamed at the joy of it, wrapping arms and legs around him, refusing to let him go. After that one last surge he was strangely quiet, his hands holding his weight up off her. The fever in her mind gradually subsided, until she recognised the real world. *So that's what it's all about, she told herself. How wonderful!* She felt a tiny chill as air moved across her wet skin. *What wonders marriage can bring. I love him more than ever.* The glory of it filled her. And then he spoiled everything.

He rolled away from her and sat up on the edge of the bed, holding his head. 'Penn?' she queried. 'It was—'

'I didn't mean that to happen, Philomena,' he groaned. 'I didn't expect that you would still be a virgin—not at your age. I—I'm sorry. I'll try to make it up to you.'

She sat up carefully behind him, feeling the ache in her bones and muscles, feeling the despair sweeping over her. *It was all a mistake, that's what he's telling me now? He may have wanted it but he doesn't want me. Oh, God!*

'Make what up to me?' Her voice was like glass, ready to shatter at any moment.

'All of that,' he returned. 'I don't even know what to call it.'

The glory had gone out of life. She felt as deep in blackness as he must, behind those terrible pads. *He wanted a woman,* she told herself fiercely, *and I'm the only one available!* 'The word they commonly use is rape,' she said, and the bitterness rolled off her tongue, poisoning every word. 'Rape,' she threw after him as he stumbled off in the darkness to his own room. 'Rape,' she whispered against the door that he slammed behind him. It wasn't rape, and she knew it without question. Seduction, yes, but not rape. She was trying to hurt him with words as much as he had hurt her. He had turned all that beauty, all that wonderful experience, into something that animals do, without feeling. Something precious had died in that dark room. She wept for it.

CHAPTER TEN

DESPITE the agonies, the tears, the recriminations, Phil finally fell asleep, and when she awakened the California sun was bright in the sky. She sat up quickly. The room and bed showed the ravages of the previous night. Her bedside clock reported ten in the morning. All she could think of was Penn. This was the morning he was to have his eye pads removed. She had to be gone before he came back. The idea rolled over and over in her troubled mind. She had married him to help keep Robbie in Sacramento, and that task had been accomplished. He had always said it would be a short marriage—a temporary device. But she had not counted on falling in love with him!

And last night, wasn't that the confirmation? He had taken her to emotional peaks of which she had never dreamed, and then cruelly dumped her off the mountain. She dressed hurriedly. Slacks and sweater, her long curls tied back carelessly into a pony-tail, and low-heeled shoes. A few personal items crammed into a case. Leave the rest, but hurry! Down the stairs for the last time, pausing to salute the Pirate and squeezing out one last tear for the Lady. Steal by the kitchen door. Rose is at work, singing at the top of her lungs. Hurry.

No time for goodbyes. Robbie would just have to understand. Out of the door into the sunshine, around the house to the garage. Her little car, shining like new, started immediately. As soon as the engine settled into a regular beat she drove around the house to the front door.

Up the stairs, into the hall, where her suitcase waited. Back to the door—too late. She could hear the imperious purr of the Cadillac as it swept around the drive and halted just behind her own car. Too late. Her hand moved towards the doorknob, but before she could grip it, the door flew open. Penn.

He stood in the doorway, staring at her. The pads were gone. A pair of dark sunglasses covered eyes that could definitely see. Eyes that followed her as she shrank against the left wall, out of his reach, out of his way. He had that facial expression that one sees on the statues of Caesars—autocratic, commanding, solemn.

'You can see again,' she managed to whisper.

'Who the hell are you?' he snapped. He took off the glasses. Dark brown, almost black eyes searched her up and down. 'What's going on?' he snarled. 'I know you, but—' Some thought snatched his attention away, he strode down the hall and started up the stairs. She heard him stop, halfway up.

It was worse than she had expected. 'Who the hell are you?' I guess that's a great way to sum up a marriage, she gibbered to herself as she grabbed the suitcase and ran. She was in the car, engine running, when he came back to the door. 'Hey, you!' he yelled. The old car jumped as she jammed it into gear. Gravel spurted as the wheels spun. She accelerated down the drive, one eye on her rear-view mirror. He came down the stairs, hastily restored the dark glasses to the bridge of his nose, and watched, hands on hips as she turned left and disappeared from sight.

Traffic was heavy, as it was every Monday morning in the centre of the city. Phil found it hard to concentrate. 'Running away from your husband.' The phrase kept repeating itself, pounding in her ears like a dirge. 'Yes,' she yelled to the world at large, 'and if he catches me—' And then she came to her senses. What do you mean, *if he catches me?* Whatever gives you the idea that he is even going to try? You know where you rate, Philomena. But just in case!

Just in case, she swung the wheel hard left on P Street, heading westward towards the river. The parking lot at Pacific Mines and Metals seemed full. She pulled up in front of the building and parked in the No Parking zone. A guard came out of the building, waving his hand, and came to a full stop when he saw who she was.

'Good morning, Mrs Wilderman. Will you be here long?' Listen to the anxiety, she told herself grimly as she powered past him into the building. He's helping me break the law, and doesn't dare do otherwise because of Penn. If it were not for Penn, he would have thrown me in the river and had my car towed away. The idea made her angry, and anger overcame fright. She stalked into the typing pool as if she were a queen. All the noises stopped. She gave them all a vacant smile, a quick wave, and slid into one of the empty booths. Her fingers were slippery with perspiration. Phil wiped them off on her slacks, punched up the computer terminal, entered the Personnel Access Code, and sat back as the computer unrolled all the names of employees starting with the letter P. P for Peabody. She slapped at the stop key.

And there I am, she snarled at herself. One entry in a thousand. Peabody, Philomena Mary. File Number 621. Address and telephone number. Date of first employment. Pay increases. Promotions. Commendations. Health record, next of kin. Ten years of work, all summarised in green on the display panel. She glared at it, doing her best to hold back the tears. You can't drive in California while crying, she told herself. It's against the law.

'Phil?' She looked up over her shoulder. Harriet, the new supervisor, stood there, and the last thing I need, Phil told herself, is a long conversation—or someone looking over my shoulder to see what I'm doing. The screen glittered at her as the electronic circuits waited for further instructions. Her hand moved to the keyboard and typed Peabody, Philomena Mary, File Number 621. ERASE. She slapped down hard on the command. The computer ruminated for a second, then flashed a message: 'Are you sure?' She dragged her hand back for just a second and typed 'Yes'. *Peabody Philomena Mary,* glared at her a second, then disappeared from sight and from memory. Just to be sure, when the computer displayed the query sign she ordered it to search for Peabody, Philomena Mary, File Number 621. The machine grumbled for a second, then reported 'No such file exists'. Now—he'll never find me, she told herself as she turned off the terminal and struggled to her feet. *If he ever wants to!*

'Have to hurry,' she mumbled to Harriet as she brushed by her and headed for the street. 'Double-parked.'

It was a long slow drive out along Route Fifty, heading for Rancho Cordova. Twice she had to pull off the highway to wipe her eyes. 'I won't cry,' she told herself. Nobody seemed to notice, not even the Highway Patrolman bustling by her on his motor-cycle. Crying on the highway was *not* a crime, it appeared. A stop at the local shopping mall brought enough food for her to hibernate for a few days. At one o'clock, when she let herself into the old farm house, she was dead tired. Too tired to carry in the groceries. She snatched out the milk and the frozen orange juice, put them in the freezer, and stumbled off up the stairs to bed. And that took care of Monday.

Gloomy Tuesday. The skies were packed with thunderheads, close enough to rattle the windows in the old house.

Philomena managed to climb out of bed and paddle her way down to the kitchen. Coffee was the only answer. Her head felt as if an elephant had stepped on it. Her nose was stuffed up, cheeks red, and eyes rimmed with black. 'Change the bed,' she reminded herself as her hands fumbled for the makings. 'You've cried the pillow-case to death.' As the pot perked she huddled herself up into a little ball on the window seat, and stared out to where the garden once had been. All gone. The garden, the farm, the clump of willows that stood by the creek. And even the creek itself, diverted to make room for another high-rise.

Her conscience nagged her. 'Rape,' she had shouted after him, and it hadn't been. Seduction—well, yes—but there's no law against seducing your wife. And she had so enjoyed it all. All except the last five minutes, when his words had spoiled all his deeds. But it wasn't rape, and her accusation had no foundation. 'I owe him an apology,' she told herself as she reached for the telephone. Her hand stopped before she picked up the instrument. Talk to him? I'd sooner wrestle an alligator! I don't *dare* to talk to him. Or face him, for that matter. I'll—I'll write him a nice letter?

Thirty minutes and two cups of coffee later she was still reaching for the telephone. I've *got* to call somebody, she told herself as she dialled her sister Sally's number. There was no answer. She tried it again three times during the day, with the same result. Disgusted with the world, she suddenly remembered the groceries, still stacked in the car. Wrapped in her faded old green robe, she ventured out. It was raining as if someone had broken a dam somewhere in the sky overhead; coming down in sheets.

'Sunny California,' she muttered as she dodged back into the house, dressed, squeezed herself into her heavy rainwear, and went back for the groceries. And felt as stupid as she must have looked. While she was forcing herself into her sou'wester coat the thunderstorms had rolled on towards the mountains, and the sun was sparkling at her.

By Wednesday she felt well enough to eat a decent meal. Put it all behind you, she ordered. It's time for Practical Pill to get her feet on the ground and go about living. She had a place to live, no job, and not a devil of a lot of money in her bank account. The house—well, it belonged to all the girls, not just to herself. To sell it would require action by the Trust, a couple of bank officials whose names she had already forgotten. So the first order of things must be to get a new job. She settled down with copies of both Sacramento papers and began to scan the sits. vac.

A very hard job that, scanning the ads. The print was small, and behind it lurked Penn's face. Smiling, laughing, accusing, pursuing, loving Penn. His face swam in miniature behind the advertising, then grew and grew until it filled the page, and held her, bound her, until the tears came to blot it all out. When she dried her eyes, the cycle started again. She threw the paper down and dialled Sally. Still no answer.

There were still two sisters left. But Deborah had gone to Tahoe for a ski-ing vacation, and if Samantha were actually at home she was not the person with whom Phil could share a confidence. So she put the telephone and the papers away and threw herself into a fury of house-cleaning. Her mind steadied under the diversion. At four o'clock that afternoon the doorbell rang, and she found herself running down the stairs in eagerness, almost singing. He had finally come!

She threw back the lock and opened the door expectantly. And there, standing on the bottom step, so that his eyes were just at the level of hers, was Penn. She brushed away the tears and stared. Black eyes, focusing on her, sending out pulses of anger, massive anger.

'Mrs Wilderman, I believe,' he said, in a voice that sounded like a steel rasp at work. She backed slowly away from him as he came up the steps and into the hall. It was as if Penn's anger were a terrible wind, forcing her backwards step by step down the hall, until she ran into the back wall. *I need to make a decision,* she screamed at herself. *No you don't,* that inner voice assured her. *The decision was made for you, a long time ago.*

All of Phil's resolution and fierce independence disappeared in one crashing collapse. She abandoned dignity and pride. With tears streaming down her face she ran straight ahead and threw her arms around her husband's waist. 'Oh, God, Penn,' she groaned into his sweater. 'I need you.'

He stood rigidly still for a moment as she huddled herself against him. *He's going to refuse me, she thought in panic.* But she was mistaken. His arms came around her, pressing her even tighter into the safe nest. His lips brushed lightly against her hair. So lightly that she could barely feel it. 'It's all right, love,' he said. 'I'm here. Everything will be all right.'

And she knew it would be so.

It took more time for the tears to slow and all the time he held her close, crooning into her hair.

'You didn't forget,' she finally stammered. 'I thought you had forgotten me!'

'I've never forgotten anything about you, since the day we met,' he said, suddenly very solemn, very believable. 'Everything except what you looked like, Philomena. You've been a rascal, *young* lady.'

'Yes,' she admitted freely. 'I—I didn't know how to tell you, and—'

'No matter,' he laughed. 'If I fell in love with you blindly—how much easier it is to love what I can see. There's an old Roman poem that goes something like *How much stronger Love must be, sweeter the touch, the kiss, the mind, if Love be blind.* You're a beautiful woman, Mrs Wilderman. Come on. Blow.' He offered her a handkerchief that seemed half an acre in size, then tucked her under his arm. She squeezed up against him, unwilling to be an inch from her anchor.

'I'm sorry,' she offered tentatively.

'I'm sorry? Is that all I get from my run-away wife? I'm sorry?'

'I—I don't know what else to say.'

'If it's conceivable, after all the things I've done to you, Phil, for you to say *I love you,* that would be a good place to start. Can you forgive me?'

'I—I don't need to forgive you.' Happy for the first time in days, she almost giggled at his serious face looming over her. 'I love you. I'm pretty stupid. I didn't find it out until the day we were married, Penn, but—I love you.'

'That's enough for now,' he returned as he leaned over and kissed her gently. 'Let's go home, wife.'

'Whatever you say,' she said, and did not recognise the proportion of her surrender until they were at the front door. The telephone rang behind them in the living-room. She stopped, and used the momentary break to quell her panic.

'Leave it alone,' he grumbled, reaching out for her.

'I—I can't,' she stammered, stalling for time to regain control of her very scattered senses. 'I—I have this thing about telephones. If I don't answer it, I'll have bad luck all the rest of the day!'

'That's about as crazy an excuse as I've heard,' he chuckled. 'The telephone is your servant, not your master.

You don't *have* to jump every time it rings at you.' He did a quick scan of her worried little face. 'Or maybe you do. Well, I'll give you two minutes to get back out here.'

'Or else?'

'Or else I'll come and get you, wife.' He added a small push in the middle of her back to get her moving. She ran the rest of the way.

'Phil? It's Sally here. I think you're in a lot of trouble. Phil? Are you there?'

'I'm here, dear. What trouble could I be in?'

'Well, we just got back from our trip to Los Angeles about three hours ago, and the telephone was ringing when we drove up to the house. Your husband, it was. Mad as a hatter. Wanted to know where the family home was. I gave him the address—Phil, if you're in trouble, you'd better get out of there quick. He means to get you.'

'You're too late,' Phil giggled nervously, not quite sure of the status of things. 'He's already got me.'

'What in the world is going on, Phil?'

'I—you wouldn't believe it if I told you, Sally. I—I think I've managed to get him just where he wants me. I can't talk now. He hates to be kept waiting. Call me here tomorrow. If I answer you'll know I'm in a lot of trouble. G'bye.'

She barely managed to get the instrument back in its cradle. Her feet were busy running before her hand was finished 'putting down'.

'Relax,' he said, catching her on the fly, like an expert outfielder. 'You've still got thirty seconds.'

'Oh,' she sighed, out of breath and courage at the same time.

'But there's no need to waste all that allotted time,' he continued smoothly, and proceeded to kiss her very thoroughly. Even more shaken than before, she leaned against his arm as he helped her out to the Cadillac. Frank held the door for them. It was not until they were enclosed in the moving cocoon, out on the highway, that she regained a little aplomb.

'You used more than thirty seconds,' she accused him, doing her best to glare. 'What if we were really in a hurry?'

'First, lady, you need to remember that the boss doesn't have to account for his time. Got it?'

'I—yes. I—I've got it.'

'Good. Secondly, Robbie and Harry will be back tomorrow morning on the nine o'clock flight.'

'But that's—that's hours away.' The spirit was willing to dare, but her shaky voice demonstrated her weakness.

'Yes, isn't it?' A broad grin spread across his face, and a devilish look gleamed in those dark, dark eyes of his. She shivered. Whatever it was he was planning was bound to be—bound to be! She shifted uneasily in her seat, clenched her hands together in her lap, and did her best to admire the scenery.

They were back at the mansion before she could account for the time. Penn helped her out of the car, and before she could muster the scream that ought to have followed, he swept her up in his arms and carried her up the stairs to the door. 'Put the car away, Frank, and take the rest of the day off,' he called over his shoulder.

Murder, she thought wildly? He's getting rid of all the witnesses? He's going to kiss me to death? Phil's head kept spinning as he kicked the front door closed behind them and bustled her into the living-room. The couch bounced as he dropped her there.

'Now then, Philomena.' He pulled one of the straight-backed chairs over directly in front of her, reversed it, and sat down with arms resting on its back, almost nose to nose with her.

'Yes?' Calm, cool Philomena—well, almost. With those pads on his eyes, and then his glasses, she had never noticed how neat and precise his nose was. How—Roman? It was irresistible. She leaned forward and planted a kiss on its end.

'Now cut that out,' he growled. 'First, we have a great deal of talking to do, you and I.'

'Dictatorial,' she muttered. 'Pompous. What you mean is you're going to talk and I'm going to listen, right?'

'No, it's not right,' he sighed. 'So I'm a little pompous. You're a whole lot impulsive. And neither one of us is really going to change.'

'I—suppose so,' she returned apologetically. 'Mama always said you can't marry a man, meaning to change him to what you want. What did you want to talk about?'

'You and me,' he said. 'Your mother was some smart cookie. How old were you when you became housemother?'

'I—seventeen. I was old for my age, though.'

'Of course you were.' His hand ruffled through her loose hair. 'And you kept on being older than your age, didn't you? That was a mean trick you played on me.'

'I—I didn't,' she returned indignantly. 'It was all in your mind. I never said I—you decided right away that I was some old biddy—what Harry called, an old broad!'

'But you knew what I was thinking, and you never set me straight. Why?'

'I—at first I thought it didn't matter. We wouldn't have met again, ever. Until you suddenly had to have a new wardrobe for your son. It's your fault! How did I know Robbie needed clothes, for goodness' sake?'

'He didn't.' There—in the background. He's laughing at me, she thought. I can hear it. Her temper was climbing, rescuing her from being a shrinking violet. A blush flooded her cheeks.

'What do you mean?' she said very slowly, very firmly.

'I mean Robbie had a cupboard full of clothes that we had to get rid of. It took me two or three days to think up that excuse.'

'Excuse? You sent me off with that little—with that boy as an excuse!'

'I had to think of something to get us back together again,' he chuckled. 'You have no idea what you put me through, Philomena Wilderman. There I was with this crazy feeling, for some—old broad—that I couldn't even see. I *had* to find some excuse to keep you close by until I could get all those crazy feelings under control. Instead, I kept getting deeper and deeper in the mud. But that wasn't the height of my scheming. The wedding—that was my centre-piece. A real out-and-out scam, that almost backfired.'

'You—you—rascal!' she gasped. 'You—the wedding—it wasn't because you needed a wife for the court hearing?'

He got up and spun his chair out of the way, and sat down on the couch beside her. One arm went around her stiff shoulders, the other covered both her hands, twisting and straining in her lap. 'Oh, I needed a wife,' he whispered in her ear, 'but not just for the hearing.'

'But—but you said it was only temporary—that after the hearing and all—you said—you'd make it all worth my while. That's what you said!'

'Well, in for a dime, in for a dollar,' he chuckled. His hand had come off her shoulder, and was toying with her ear lobe. 'I somehow had the feeling that you wouldn't buy the package without an escape clause.' And then, much more seriously, 'Do you want to escape, Phil?'

'Me?' She was struggling between laughter and tears, and the laughter won out. She relaxed, and snuggled up against him. 'Not me. I never had it so good!'

About five minutes later, while she struggled to regain her breath, he tickled her chin. 'I love kissing,' he chuckled.

'Well, don't be too free with your favours,' she snapped. 'I don't share.'

'Hey now, love, I don't either. We were lucky, you and I.'

'Lucky?'

'Of course. Robbie was always a problem. There was no way our marriage could work if you hadn't won him around.'

'It wasn't all my doing,' she sighed. 'The poor mixed-up kid thought I looked like his real mother. That picture of your sister—it seemed to connect us all. It gave me a first advantage with Robbie. And it gave me my first bad opinion of you. I thought that Robbie might have been—your illegitimate child, or something. And it wasn't until we went to the court hearing that I found out you were really his uncle. You could have told me outright, you know.'

'Sure I could have,' he chuckled. 'And would have lost your interest completely. I knew the boy had your attention, and as long as you thought I was his father you were hanging in there. I had few enough strings on you to afford to let one go. But you're right in one aspect. The painting did tie us together. When I came home Monday without the pads on my eyes I just couldn't wait to find you, to see what you looked like. And what did I see? My sister Robin standing in the door. I thought I had lost my wits, or something, so I rushed up the stairs to look at her portrait, and by the time I came down again you were gone. I thought— well, I was high—on excitement, not alcohol—on Sunday night. And when you yelled rape at me and then ran away, I figured I had really blown the works.'

'It wasn't rape,' she sighed, and moved as close as she could. 'I knew it at the time, and I know it now. It was just that—well, afterwards—you seemed to be so disgusted with it all that I thought—I just wanted to hurt you back, and that's why—I'm sorry, Penn. It wasn't rape. I'm your wife, you were very gentle, and I did enjoy it so much. I—I never thought I could—I just didn't know about that sort of wonderful excitement.'

He heaved a sigh of relief after the explanation. 'I thought I really had done us in,' he told her. 'I thought I deserved to be miserable—that I ought to let you go.'

'I'm glad you didn't.'

'Well, that was only for a couple of minutes that I had that crazy idea,' he laughed. 'And then I called the office, and lo and behold, someone had erased all of Philomena Peabody's records. Who could have done that?'

'Who indeed?' she murmured in a very quiet voice. There were some interesting patterns in the wallpaper. She studied them carefully. Anything rather than look into those eyes.

'And then your sister—I had her telephone number, but nobody answered. Do you realise that I had two secretaries at the office doing nothing for three days but dial your sister's telephone every fifteen minutes, day and night?'

'It must have cost you a fortune in overtime.'

'Don't be sarcastic,' he laughed. 'I'll get it all back. I'm a persistent guy.'

The wallpaper lost its interest. She turned around to face him, treasuring his face between her two soft hands. 'I'm very glad for that,' she confessed. 'I'm a very stubborn woman. I might have held off from calling you for—oh—at least another week. Maybe two.'

Confession is good for the soul, she told herself a few minutes later. My, doesn't he taste good! But there's something going on around here that I can't quite figure out. He's up to something! She shivered deliciously, in anticipation.

He raised his hand to check his wristwatch. 'Three o'clock,' he announced. 'And Robbie will be back tomorrow. I should have arranged for the kid to spend *two* weeks fishing.'

'Why—that's unkind, Penn. That's my son you're talking about.'

'So it is. Well, I think you'd better run up to your room and have a nap, Phil.'

'Nap? I'm not tired. I'm so excited I couldn't sleep. I—why?'

'I'm glad you're not tired,' he chuckled. 'Scoot upstairs.'

She went, but reluctantly, dragging her feet, stopping to smile at his sister's picture, winking an eye at the Pirate King. By the time she wandered into her room he was right behind her, with two glasses in his hand.

'Champagne,' he said. 'Let's drink a toast to the time when the pompous overcame the impulsive.'

'Or vice versa,' she giggled, gulping the contents at one swallow. 'Oops, I forgot.' She hiccuped. 'What are you doing?'

'How does this damn thing come off?'

'There's a zipper in the back,' she whispered in a very tiny voice. The glass slipped out of her hand and fell, but did not break. Her blouse slipped off her shoulders. His warm breath on her skin started her quivering. He needed no other invitation.

An hour later, satiated, she lay stretched out flat on her back, all her limbs askew, like some wanton Eve. He lay on his side, facing her. Perspiration stood on his forehead. She used a finger to trace letters in it, then dried it off with her loose hair.

'What are you writing on me?' he asked.

'A message,' she responded. '"Penn Wilderman Belongs To Me." I intend to have one made for each of your cars, and two to go in your office.'

'Are you really? Pretty possessive, aren't you, Mrs Wilderman.'

'I—yes,' she stated very firmly. Practical Pill was back in action. Everything seemed under control. Except—it had been a wild hour, but how could she know if it had been as wild for him as it had been for her?

'Penn?'

'Yes. I'm still here.' His hand was tracing circles in her hair.

'Penn, that wasn't too shabby for—for an old broad, was it?'

'For a beginner I'd rate that as a ten plus,' he laughed. 'Were you worried? I never would have thought that you would catch on so quickly. And that's enough with the *old broad* business.'

'I—well. I wanted to talk seriously—stop that!' His index finger was probing at the spot just under her ribcage—the only spot on her entire body that was ticklish. She squealed as she wriggled away from him and seized the punishing digit. 'Don't do that,' she giggled. 'I hate being tickled.' Her hand pulled his finger up to her mouth. She snapped her sharp little teeth at it without touching, and then kissed it gently.

'Hey, for a minute there—' He rolled over on his stomach, half on top of her.

'That's just to remind you that I don't put up with any foolishness,' she giggled.

'Even from your husband?'

'Especially from my husband. I wanted to talk seriously about something.'

'Now? Here? Boy, you can always tell who the amateurs are, can't you.'

'Amateurs? I thought I had just become a professional. Stop that!' Two tickling fingers this time, one on either side. She snatched them both up and held them. Talk fast, you fool, she told herself. Talk fast.

'It's about Robbie.'

'Oh.' His fingers stopped wriggling. 'Even in our bridal bed? *What* about Robbie?'

'It's just that—I think it's a bad mistake, having an only child in the family, and I'm not really getting any younger, so if we intend to do something about it we'll have to be fairly quick, and—what are you doing?' A *frisson* of alarm in her voice, as he rolled over again, on top of her, and began that tickling assault.

She did her best to squirm away, but his weight pinned her in place like a butterfly in a showcase. 'What are you doing?' Barely forced out, this time, because of the wild giggling she could not suppress. He stopped.

'What am I doing?' That Voice of Doom tone of his, suddenly broken off in the deep bass of his own laughter. 'You presented me a problem. Robbie needs a little sister. These things don't come easily. I may have to work on it for some time to come.' Those hands again, not poking, not tickling, moving slowly up to the under-curve of her breasts.

'You silly man,' she said in a soft, love-filled voice. The fingers moved on and his lips came down on her. Everything else was lost as her world dissolved in flames.

She dared not take a chance on love.
If she ever *saw* the man who'd stolen her heart,
she'd have to give him up.

WHEN I SEE YOUR FACE

Connie Bennett

PROLOGUE

THE GUNSHOT WAS entirely unexpected, and in Ryanne Kirkland's opinion, totally uncalled for. It reverberated through the shadowed warehouse, echoing in the near darkness long after the man in the rumpled suit had clutched his chest in surprise and pitched to the concrete floor, dead. The other man—the one with the gun—calmly replaced the weapon in the pocket of his tailored worsted jacket, bent over, and then pried the briefcase from his victim's lifeless fingers. Except for the unusual, stark surroundings, the two men could have been stockbrokers conferring on a deal; a deal that obviously had gone very sour.

Hidden in the shadows watching every gruesome move the murderer made, Ryanne suppressed an insane desire to scream. She wasn't a screamer by nature. In fact, the last time she could clearly recall doing so she had been six years old and her mother had just informed her she was too young to travel across the country to see the Beatles in concert. The resulting tantrum had shaken the rafters, and it wasn't until her father had quietly emerged from his study and told Ryanne how disappointed he was in her that she had calmed down. Disappointing her father was one thing Ryanne could not bear, and that had been her last temper tantrum.

Now, however, Ryanne felt justified in screaming. It wasn't every day that she witnessed a cold-blooded murder, nor did she often find herself alone in a deserted warehouse with a stranger who had no aversion to using his very deadly gun. She was relatively certain that even her calm, practical father would have forgiven her for screaming in this instance... probably.

The scream welled in her throat, burning and begging to be released, but she somehow managed to hold it back. With or without her father's approval, she had to. No one knew she was hiding in the shadows of the warehouse of a chemical processing plant in one of the less reputable areas of Chicago. Her decision to follow Vinnie Perigrino, the man in the rumpled suit, had been an impulsive one. The man who had killed him didn't know she was here, thank goodness; his ignorance was the only thing keeping her alive. One ear-piercing scream was the quickest ticket to kingdom come Ryanne could have purchased, so she swallowed the painful yell and tried to think rationally about what to do next.

And, of course, the answer was astonishingly clear: she would stay here, hidden in the darkness, until the murderer left.

It was a simple plan that did not require her to do anything, which was good, because Ryanne wasn't sure that her legs would have held her up had she come up with a plan of action that required action. She'd been crouched behind the fifty-gallon chemical drums that read Flammable in big red letters for what seemed like ages, and her legs felt watery and trembled. Staying put was definitely the best plan all around.

The man with the gun would leave through the same downstairs door he'd come in by. After waiting a decent interval to make sure the coast was clear, Ryanne would follow. She would run to her car, parked out of sight just around the corner, and drive like a bat out of hell to the nearest pay phone. There, she would call her editor on the city desk at the *Examiner* and report what she'd just seen, then she'd call the police.

Or maybe she'd call the police and then phone her editor. Yes, police first, she finally decided. Old habits were hard to break, and for a reporter the first instinct was always the story, but Ryanne swore that if she got out of this mess, common sense would prevail and she'd give the police the first crack at the case. And while she was waiting for the police to arrive, she'd call her editor.

Patting herself on the back for having made such a rational decision at a time when there didn't seem to be a rational bone in her body, Ryanne tried to keep her breathing under control; it was showing a marked tendency to be harsh and erratic. She mentally repeated the litany *Stay calm, stay calm* and waited for the gun-toting man in the worsted suit to leave so that she could follow the scenario she'd just plotted.

Only Worsted didn't follow the script. He was supposed to leave, but he wasn't showing any signs of hotfooting it out. Instead he placed the briefcase on the floor and started dragging the body away from the clearing in the center of the room toward the wall opposite Ryanne's hideout. More drums lined that area, stacked three high and who-knew-how-many deep.

Now why on earth would he do that? Ryanne wondered. Certainly when the work crew came in tomorrow morning and found a dead body in the middle of the floor it would put a pall over the day's activities, but Ryanne doubted that Worsted was concerned about the delicate sensibilities of the workmen. If murder didn't faze him, why would he care where the body was found as long as he was well away from the scene of the crime before that happened?

Unless, of course, finding the body wasn't inevitable.

Ryanne felt a shudder of apprehension ripple down her spine and that barely suppressed scream welled again. Those bright red letters, *F-L-A-M-M-A-B-L-E*, jumped out at her and everything suddenly became clear. Worsted didn't want his victim found, and the best way to ensure that was to place the body next to several thousand gallons of highly flammable chemicals and set off an explosion. When those drums blew, there wouldn't be enough of Perigrino left to know he'd ever existed. And when Vinnie disappeared, so would Ryanne Kirkland.

Douglas Sutherland, Ryanne's city desk editor, was bound to take a dim view of one of his reporters getting herself blown up, even if there was a good story in it. It was Douglas's very pragmatic theory that reporters did a better job when they were functioning well enough to write down the facts, and in this instance, Ryanne agreed wholeheartedly with her boss. She'd grown rather fond of living these past twenty-eight years. She had good friends and a great job, her Aunt Rose seemed to have forgiven her for being an old maid, there were two gold fish depending on her as their only visible means of support and her best suit was ready to be picked up at the cleaners.

Disappearing without a trace would definitely put a crimp in her life-style.

Vinnie's dead weight was forcing Worsted to labor over his job of disposing of the body. He was getting closer to the opposite wall, and Ryanne quickly began evaluating her options. There weren't many of them, and the time to exercise them was definitely *now*. The second floor of the warehouse was a three-sided affair, like a gigantic horseshoe, and the fourth side—to Ryanne's right—was nothing more than one long drop to the lower floor.

There were two enormous, open freight elevators that were obviously used to carry the chemical drums up or down as the situation warranted, and on either side of the elevators, a safety railing led to vertical steel ladders at both ends. It was one of those ladders that had allowed Ryanne to follow Vinnie upstairs, unseen. He'd unlocked the side door and left it conveniently ajar, leading Ryanne to believe he was going to be meeting someone else in the warehouse. At the time, Ryanne had hoped that Vinnie would lead her to someone a little higher up on the syndicate ladder. Now she just wanted to get out with her hide and her story intact.

Perigrino was a small-time hood who'd fallen in with bigger-time hoods who ran an illegal gambling operation. Ryanne's best sources on the mayor's organized crime unit had informed her that the police were planning to put the squeeze on Vinnie in the hopes that he'd lead them to the uptown banker who was laundering the syndicate's ill-gotten booty. Knowing a banner headline story when one was tossed into her lap, Ryanne had used a few more contacts to find Vinnie, and had followed him to the darkened warehouse because it was Friday night and she had nothing better to do.

Taking the unlocked door as the next best thing to an engraved invitation, Ryanne had silently followed Vinnie into the warehouse, keeping to the shadows, never once pausing to wonder if she was doing the sane, logical, reasonable, *safe* thing. Like her Pulitzer prize winning father before her, Ryanne thought first, last and always of the story.

An hour ago she'd thought this one was getting more intriguing by the minute. Visions of a substantial raise in pay had danced in her head as she'd watched Vinnie step onto one of the freight elevators and ride to the second floor. When he'd disappeared, Ryanne had quietly sprinted through the shadows to one of the ladders and scrambled up like a monkey. She'd found a convenient hiding place from which to watch whatever proceedings were about to unfold, and she'd waited.

Worsted had arrived moments later. He'd ridden the elevator up, stepped off and moved directly to the center of the room where Vinnie had stood so casually he might have been waiting for the crosstown bus.

Too far away to hear more than muted murmuring, Ryanne had watched. Vinnie gave Worsted a briefcase, and they chatted some more, like old college chums at their twenty-year class reunion…until Worsted calmly, and in the most civilized manner imaginable, pulled out a gun and decreased Chicago's population by one—a body count that was very shortly going to double if Ryanne didn't act fast.

Though Worsted was facing her as he tugged the uncooperative body, Ryanne knew she'd have to take her chances. The shadows were deep and Worsted was some distance away. Also, he was understandably distracted. No matter how composed he appeared to be, lugging around a man he'd just murdered had to be a little unnerving.

Ryanne stood slowly and tested her shaky legs by flexing her knees. Normally she was in excellent physical condition, but terror had a way of making even the strongest legs a wee bit unsteady. Thankfully they felt more substantial than warm Jell-O.

The Nike running shoes she'd been known to wear with even the classiest pieces of her limited wardrobe enabled her to move quietly, and she retreated a little farther into the shadows, then began inching her way toward the ladder. A rabbit warren of corridors among the stacked drums provided suitable cover, and she merely retraced the route she'd taken when she arrived. But the makeshift tunnels soon ran out, and she stopped, peering across the room toward Worsted, who had almost succeeded in draping Perigrino across the top of a chemical drum. Obviously he was leaving nothing to chance.

As though Vinnie had looked down from somewhere in the great beyond and seen what was about to happen to his former self, the dead man grew even more uncooperative and slid off the drum with a deadening thud. Ryanne heard what she assumed was a muttered curse from Worsted, and she glanced furtively at the ladder. It was twenty feet away, and the room offered only a few paltry shadows to protect her. Why that twenty feet hadn't seemed so open and desolate when she'd been headed in the opposite direction she couldn't say; she just knew that now it did.

But there were no alternatives open to her and she glanced at Worsted one last time. Miraculously, his back was to her and she knew she'd never get a better opportunity.

Keeping as close to the wall as possible, she moved out of her rabbit warren. One step at a time, flattened against the wall, her heart pounding out the cymbal crashes from the *1812* Overture, she forced herself to keep going. Another step, fifteen feet to go, then twelve . . . nine . . . seven . . .

She might have made it if Worsted hadn't turned.

CHAPTER ONE

Douglas Sutherland
Chicago Daily Examiner
Michigan Ave.
Chicago, IL

Hugh MacKenna and Assoc.
Private Investigators
La Cienega Blvd.
Los Angeles, CA

Dear Hugh:

Enclosed are the newspaper clippings and copies of the old police reports you said you'd like to see, and I've enclosed a couple of photos as well. The gorgeous redhead in the eight-by-ten glossy is Ryanne Kirkland, and the one who looks as if she gargles with lemon juice is Judith Tremain, Ryanne's secretary. They'll be arriving in Los Angeles on Monday, and Ryanne has promised that she'll call you just as soon as they get settled into the house at Malibu. If you can take a look at the security system in the house she's sublet and make sure it's in good shape I'll be forever in your debt. Ryanne is very special to me and I'll rest a lot easier knowing you're going to be looking out for her while she's in L.A. working on her screenplay.

In regard to the clippings and the other stuff I've enclosed, I think you'll find it all interesting, probably even fascinating, but overall, the incident is a dead issue. As long as Ryanne is blind the man who left her for dead in that warehouse five years ago has no reason to try to kill her again, but I really appreciate the thorough approach you've taken to this simple favor. I like the idea that someone out there knows her history and understands what she's been through.

One word of caution, though: for both our sakes; don't let on to Ryanne that I've told you everything. She has this cockamamy notion that if people know the whole story they will pity her more than she thinks they already do. If she knew I'd told you, she'd serve my head on a platter to that guide dog of hers, so mum's the word, okay? If Ryanne wants to tell you the story, fine, but you didn't hear it from me!

Well, that's about it for now. If you have any questions please give me a call. I'll be right here, chained to the city desk as always. Take care of yourself—and Ryanne.

Love,
Uncle Doug

Uncle Doug? Hugh looked at the endearment again and smiled ruefully. Douglas apparently thought he was asking his "nephew" a pretty big favor; it had been twenty-five years, at least, since Hugh had called his father's best friend "uncle." Hugh's parents had still been married then, living the Ward-and-June-Cleaver myth in a quiet Chicago suburb. Everything had been simple and innocent. Unfortunately his parents' ugly divorce had proven to Hugh that few things were simple, and no one stayed innocent for long.

Tossing aside the letter and the unbidden memories it had provoked, Hugh reached into the manila envelope and extracted the rest of the material Douglas had sent. Ryanne

Kirkland's picture was on top and Hugh looked at it objectively. Douglas hadn't exaggerated. It was a beautiful face. But then, what else would one expect given the amount of reconstructive surgery she'd had after falling off that warehouse ledge and landing flat on her face? Given that kind of challenge, how many plastic surgeons in the world would create an ugly face?

But beauty, artificially achieved or not, was still beauty, and Hugh knew how to appreciate it with the best of them. Her face was rounded in a gentle oval and her features were soft, her lips prettily bowed. The fiery mane of red hair that framed her face was attractive, too. Ultimately, though, Hugh found it was her eyes that he could not avoid. They were enormous, bright blue eyes that stared beyond the camera straight into his own.

Eyes like those could reduce a man to cinders in a matter of seconds, Hugh decided. Then he remembered that those lovely eyes couldn't see.

"New case, Hugh?" Mo Johnson stepped through his boss's open door and took a chair without benefit of an invitation.

"No, just a little background work on a favor I'm doing for Douglas Sutherland, an old buddy of Dad's from Chicago. He's got a friend moving into a house a mile or so up the beach from my place and he wants me to check out her security system and keep an eye on her while she's in L.A."

Mo quirked one eyebrow. "Normal caution against Sin City crime, or is he expecting trouble?"

Hugh leaned back, tapping the photo thoughtfully against the edge of his desk. "Maybe a little of both. Doug's the overprotective, fatherly type, but he may have reason to worry. You ever heard of Ryan Kirk?"

"The mystery writer? Sure. I never miss a book. I hear they're turning his latest into a movie."

"Not 'his,'" Hugh corrected. *"Hers."* He tossed Ryanne's picture across the desk.

"You're kidding." Johnson looked at the photograph in disbelief. "You mean to tell me this gorgeous lady is Ryan Kirk, writer of the grittiest, seamiest detective novels since Mickey Spillane?"

"That's right. Her name is Ryanne, with an *a-n-n-e*, Kirkland. Until five years ago she was a reporter, and according to Douglas, a damned good one. She didn't start writing the Cameron Lawe mysteries until after she lost her sight."

"You mean she's blind?"

"Yep." He shoved the second picture across the desk. "This is her secretary, Judith Tremain."

Mo studied the middle-aged face that might have been attractive if Ms. Tremain had learned how to smile. "Definitely not the type I'd like to meet in a dark alley."

Hugh smiled. "Doug says she's a real dragon lady."

Mo looked at the photo of Ryanne again and shook his head. "Ryan Kirk is a woman. How about that?" He returned the pictures to the desk. "How'd she go blind?"

"She was working on a story about a nickel-and-dime gambling syndicate and saw a small-time hood get waxed by one of his associates."

"So the guy blinded her to keep her from testifying?" Mo shuddered. "That's positively medieval."

"No, no. She was trying to get away from him and fell off a ledge in a warehouse. The fall smashed her head up pretty badly," he said, remembering his conversation with Douglas the previous week.

Mo made a noise that signified his disgust. "Did they get the guy who did it?"

"Nope. Ryanne had never seen him before. Doug says the police are pretty sure they know who he is, but a blind eyewitness tends to make a poor impression on juries. As far as I know, the guy was never even charged."

"Any chance she'll get her sight back?"

Hugh shook his head. "The doctors say no way. Something about irreparable damage to the optic nerve because of the fall. But I think Doug is a little nervous about Ryanne right now because she's been having headaches and has decided to go to a big specialist out here. The top neurological man in the country or something like that. Doug thinks the killer has been keeping track of her all these years and might get the wrong idea about why she's seeing the doctor. He may think there's a chance she'll get her sight back."

"And try to kill her," Mo added, though it was unnecessary because they both knew the implications of what Hugh had just said.

"It's a possibility, though I'd say a very remote one. I can't imagine this creep taking the risk of icing Ryanne unless he's got proof she's going to see again, and Doug says there's no chance of that."

"So where do you come into all this?" Mo asked.

"I'll just go over her security system and play good neighbor Sam. Make sure she gets settled in comfortably, drop in for a friendly visit from time to time."

"Sort of a one man Welcome Wagon."

"Something like that."

Mo glanced at the picture of Ryanne again and sighed. "Why is it you always get first crack at the gorgeous damsels in distress?"

Hugh pretended to be appalled. "Are you suggesting that I might try to seduce a poor little blind girl? I can feel my Boy Scout merit badges tarnishing as we speak."

"I didn't think they let subversive types like you in the Boy Scouts," Mo said teasingly.

Hugh chuckled at the jibe, but instead of taking up the gauntlet he glanced at the other photographs Douglas had sent. There was an attractive shot of Ryanne Kirkland dressed in shorts and a halter top, romping on someone's lawn with a cute golden retriever nipping at her heels, and another shot of her and the dog nose to nose that was too schmaltzy for words. The next picture brought Hugh up short, though, and he forgot to be cynical about the sentimental shots. It was Ryanne in a dramatic evening dress that bared one shoulder and clung to every curve of her fragile, slender body. Her hair was upswept, her face was glowing, and by her side, in harness, was the same carefree retriever from the previous photographs. He wasn't her pet, he was her guide dog—her eyes.

Once again, Hugh was captivated by the clear, unshadowed beauty of Ryanne's blue eyes, but something unusual caught his attention and he flipped back through the pictures. In all but the one he'd handed Mo, Ryanne was wearing glasses.

"That's weird," he muttered under his breath.

"What?" Mo asked.

Hugh handed over the pictures. "Why would a blind person wear glasses?"

"Camouflage?"

"You're a big help."

Mo ducked his head modestly. "I like my job, so I do my best to please the boss. So tell me, boss . . . are we going to sit around here all day looking at pictures, or what?"

Hugh grinned. "Are you trying to tell me you're bored, Mo?"

"Hey, I'm a detective. I get paid to detect."

Hugh tossed the pictures aside and pulled a slim file from his desk. "In that case, why don't you sink your teeth into this."

"Ah-ha!" Mo's eyes lit up. "What is it? Blackmail? Arson? Industrial espionage?"

"None of the above," Hugh told him. "It's a little old blue-haired Beverly Hills matron who thinks her husband OD'd on Geritol. She wants to know how he's spending his time away from her."

Mo groaned in misery. "I had to ask." He stood and moved toward the door. "She wants pictures and everything?"

"And everything."

"Oh, brother." Mumbling something about investigating employment opportunities in life insurance sales, Mo left and Hugh went back to the photos Doug had sent.

He saw a pretty lady who'd had a hard life—pretty pedestrian in his line of work—yet Hugh suddenly felt a deep foreboding that Ryanne Kirkland was about to change his life. He sluffed the idea off as maudlin claptrap, but this was one premonition he should have listened to. Closely.

CHAPTER TWO

"JUDITH!" Exasperated, Ryanne jerked her head and torso from the empty cabinet, misjudged the distance, and banged her head on the shelf above her. "Damn!" Rubbing the latest of her growing collection of bumps and bruises, she settled back on her haunches to wait. Pots, pans and a varied assortment of baking dishes fanned out around her in a cluttered but well-organized circle.

"Aren't you finished yet?"

The thickly padded hall carpet had muted Judith's footsteps so that Ryanne hadn't heard her coming, but she was much too familiar with her secretary's perpetually irritable voice to jump at the sound. Until Ryanne's "accident" as she euphemistically referred to it, Judith had been secretary to the circulation manager at the *Examiner*. Ryanne had known the older woman for years. When her new career as a novelist had taken off and it became apparent that she needed a combination secretary, assistant, and companion to help keep her life in order, Judith had been Ryanne's first choice. Despite their constant bickering, Ryanne had never regretted hiring her.

She turned toward her indispensable friend. "Never, as long as I live, will I sublet another furnished house."

"You called me out here to tell me that?"

"Yes."

"I'll make a note of it."

"In braille, please."

"Naturally."

The floor squeaked ever so slightly as Judith turned to leave, but Ryanne protested. "Wait a minute! I need your help."

Judith gave the array of cookware a dismissive glance. "It's your mess—you clean it up."

"Just tell me where that enormous stew pot is, okay? I put it right there—" she pointed unerringly to a conspicuously empty spot on the floor "—and now it's gone."

"Well, I don't see it, either. Are you sure you didn't put it back in the cabinet?"

Ryanne rubbed the bump on her head. "I'm sure," she replied tightly.

"Then it's vanished," Judith pronounced helpfully.

"Great. As if a furnished house isn't bad enough, it has to be a *haunted* furnished house as well."

"You know, if you'd just left things as they were you wouldn't be having this problem," Judith commented, bending down to the cabinet to see for herself whether or not the elusive pot was there.

"If I'd left things as they were, I'd be spending the next six months not knowing where anything is. Do you see it?"

"Nope." She moved on to the next bank of cabinets. "You probably put it in one of these thinking it was a teapot."

Ryanne sighed heavily. "Judith, I may be blind and temporarily disorganized, but I do know the difference between a three-gallon enamel stew pot and a whistling teakettle." She reached into the box sitting next to her, poked around for a moment and came up with a huge blue enamel lid. "See, here's the lid. I just need the pot it attaches to."

Judith let the cabinet door shut with a bang and Ryanne made a studied attempt not to jump at the sound. Even after five years loud noises still bothered her, and though Judith was well aware of the minor phobia, she rarely went out of her way to protect Ryanne from the small upsets. In fact, Ryanne was certain her companion leaned in the opposite direction, making loud noises deliberately. It was as though she was subtly trying to reassure Ryanne that not every bang meant imminent danger or death.

"Not in there, either? Don't tell me I'm going to have to hold a seance to find it," she quipped, ignoring the shudder down her spine that accompanied the banging of cabinet doors as Judith continued to search.

"No, but it has to be here some—" As she turned around, the dining area fell into Judith's view, and underneath the chrome-and-glass table sat the stew pot—just inches from the twitching nose of Ryanne's dozing golden retriever. "Aha! That stupid dog pilfered it. You don't need an exorcist, you need an obedience school."

"I should have known," Ryanne muttered. "Aggie came sniffing around here a few minutes ago and I shooed her away. She must have nudged it over there while I had my head in the cupboard."

"All the evidence points in that direction." Judith went to pick up the pot and moved to the sink to wash it.

"Is she asleep?"

"Under the table," Judith confirmed.

"Well, don't wake her until I get this job finished."

"Are you kidding? If I had my way I'd put her to sleep permanently."

Ryanne clucked her tongue reproachfully. "Now Judith, you love Aggie as much as I do. Admit it."

Ryanne could almost visualize Judith drawing herself up indignantly. "I'll admit no such thing. I loathe the beast."

Across the room the familiar clatter of Aggie's choke collar warned both women that the guide dog had heard herself being discussed. The canine padded across the floor and poked her nose into the back of Judith's knee. "Get away," she growled, but Aggie only wagged her tail happily and nudged her again. "Stupid dog can't even tell when she's not wanted."

"Aggie knows who loves her and who doesn't, don't you baby?" Ryanne cooed, and the dog responded instantly and predictably to her mistress's voice. Before either woman could stop her, the affectionate retriever was plowing through the cookware and planting her cold, wet nose and scratchy tongue on Ryanne's face.

"Aggie, no!" Ryanne squeaked, but the dominoes had already started to fall. Her wailed protest only made Aggie think it was playtime, and when Ryanne jerked away, trying to restrain the dog, her backward movement overturned a set of saucepans. Startled by the crash, Aggie skittered to one side, landing squarely in a well-stacked pile of cookie sheets. Her feet skidded out from under her as she tried to find solid ground again and the box of lids tumbled and clattered all over the floor.

Panting, her golden eyes wide, Aggie finally stepped back and looked at the mess she'd created. Ryanne, who'd landed squarely on her bottom, threw up her hands in abject frustration, and Judith, who had stood patiently waiting for the chaos to subside, merely smirked. "Shall I call Guiding Eyes for the Blind and tell them you want to return one slightly clumsy, extremely idiotic dog?"

"Stuff it, Judith. Clumsy or not, Aggie stays. You, on the other hand..."

"Yes?" she prompted expectantly. It was unusual for her to make it through a day without being fired, so she figured it would be just as well to get it out of the way this morning.

"Can help me clean up this mess," Ryanne finally finished. "You wash and I'll dry and put away. And we'd better hurry. Hugh MacKenna is going to be here in less than an hour and I've got to change clothes."

Resigning herself to the task ahead, Judith bent and began reassembling the pieces of cookware, placing them on the counter next to the sink. "I thought he was supposed to be here at eleven."

"That's right," Ryanne said, groping at her feet for errant pots and pans.

"Well, if you're going to change you'd better do it soon because it's ten forty-five right now."

Ryanne's head shot up. "You're kidding?"

Judith sighed patiently. "I've known you for most of your adult life and you still haven't learned that I never kid."

"Omigod, Judith, what am I going to do? I can't meet a man who has a voice that sounds like smooth Kentucky bourbon looking like this! When we talked on the phone yesterday I thought I'd died and gone to heaven."

"Don't worry about it, Ryanne," Judith advised. "If he's one of Douglas Sutherland's friends, Hugh MacKenna has got to be at least sixty years old. He's probably as bald as a billiard ball with a gut that hangs over his belt and peeks out from under his sweaty, tattered T-shirt."

"Don't be ridiculous. This is Hollywood, land of the beautiful. They don't even let you on the Ventura Freeway without checking for an even tan. And besides, what do I care what he looks like? It's his voice I'm in love with."

"Uh-huh. The last time you fell in love with a voice, it had a wife and two children."

"Ah, but what a voice it was. I spent many a sleepless night over that one, let me tell you." She grinned in the general direction of her companion, who was busily washing by this time. "Unrequited love has taken a rap through the centuries, but I can tell you from personal experience, it ain't all that bad. I've yet to meet a man who can match my fantasies of him."

"I don't want to hear about your fantasies," Judith informed her.

"Judith, old duck, what you need is a man of your own. Then we'll talk about fantasies."

"No thanks. I've had my turn. Romance is only for the very young or the very foolish. I am neither."

"Nonsense. Romance is universal."

"Is that why you live like a nun?" Judith asked shrewdly. "Or are you planning on letting old bourbon-breath change all that?"

"That's bourbon *voice*," Ryanne corrected. "And I doubt he'll change anything about my life because I plan on worshiping him from afar."

"Well, unless you go change your clothes, I'd make that very far, because you look like something the cat dragged in."

"I'm changing, I'm changing," Ryanne promised, heading out of the kitchen. "Just leave those things in the drainer and I'll put them away when old bourbon-voice leaves."

"All right, but next time you get down on the floor, put Agnes the Menace on her bed chain!"

"Yes, sir!"

With Aggie at her heels, Ryanne breezed confidently down the long hall, pleased that there was at least one place in this unfamiliar environment where she could move at her normal, breakneck pace. The rest of the house was one gigantic obstacle course, with tables, chairs, ottomen and other evil accoutrements that jumped out at her with annoying regularity. She'd been in the house four days, and had spent the biggest portion of her time trying to memorize the layout of the place and the whereabouts of the insidious, shin-eating furniture. If she concentrated completely, she could move fairly well through her bedroom, its adjoining bathroom and the kitchen, but the huge living room that was separated from the kitchen by an open bar, and the office Judith was still trying to whip into shape were maddeningly elusive. But before the week was out, she would conquer them. She had to—it was a matter of honor. No mere house was going to get the best of Ryanne Denise Kirkland!

Counting the doorways in the hall as she passed them, she rushed into the master bedroom, then paused to take stock. Judith had described every room to her in minute detail, and she knew the enormous suite stretched out on either side of her, with a luxurious king-size bed to her right, and beyond that, floor-to-ceiling windows and French doors that led to a cedar deck. The deck ran the entire length of the back of the house, which overlooked the ocean.

In front of her was a small, comfortable sitting room, and to her left, a walk-in closet and the door to the most extravagant bathroom Ryanne had ever encountered. Just thinking about the gigantic whirlpool bathtub made her mouth water, but there was no time for indulgence now.

Moving slowly she resisted the temptation to run her hand along the mirrored closet doors as a guide, and instead she listened for the subtle change in air pressure that signaled the opening to the bathroom. Guided by the hollow sound, she hurried in as quickly as she dared, and stripped out of her T-shirt and cutoffs, tossing them into the hamper. She laid her glasses on the counter as she filled the marble basin with water and began washing the morning's residue of grime from her face and arms.

Ryanne knew that she was facing a mirror that ran the length of the seven-foot vanity, and as she toweled off, she wondered absently exactly what it was the mirror saw. Friends told her that her face, which had once been pretty but unremarkable, was now beautiful. Even crusty Judith had declared that it was "passable," which had to mean this new face was something special indeed. But to Ryanne, it was a mystery—even though she had memorized every line and contour with her hands. She knew her nose was a little shorter than it had been, her chin and jaw not quite as obstinate and her cheekbones a little more distinctive, but how all those elements fit together she didn't have a clue. And she never would. It was strange having to rely only on imagination to picture how other people looked, and Ryanne thought it was downright eerie to know that if she miraculously got her sight back she wouldn't even recognize her own face.

From the kitchen, Ryanne's human alarm clock shouted that it was ten fifty-four, and Ryanne retrieved her glasses and hurried back toward the bedroom. In her haste, she misjudged the location of the door and bounced off the frame like a pinball off a bumper pad. With a muttered curse, she adjusted her position, this time giving way to the temptation to feel her way along the wall, around the corner to the closet. She had worked hard to make her movements as close as possible to those of a sighted person, and that meant using sound cues instead of touch whenever possible to determine the location of a door, a room, or an object. Since she was short on time, though, Ryanne abandoned her vanity in favor of making it to the closet in one piece.

There, her entire summer wardrobe stretched out before her, and since clothes had never been a priority in her life, it was a pretty short stretch. With her hands she quickly skimmed over the sections of blouses, pants and jeans, until she came to the small selection of dresses. Old bourbon-voice deserved something special, Ryanne figured, and she was going to give it to him. Somewhere in here was a pastel blue outfit consisting of a cap-sleeved bolero that would adequately cover the scars on her shoulder, and a calf-length sundress that would hide the black-and-blue on her shins, her constant reminders that she moved too fast and with too little caution.

Searching for the gauzy, gathered cotton set, she dismissed the first few dresses until she came to the short-sleeved bolero.

Working quickly, she removed it from the hanger, laid it carefully aside, then did the same with the thin-strapped sundress. The gathered, lace-edged half slip she wore under the dress was attached to the hanger with clothespins, and she hurriedly slipped it on. The dress went over her head next, and for once, the zipper did what it was supposed to and zipped without a snag. As the bolero went on, she bent to the shoe rack and rummaged around until a pair of delicately strapped sandals appeared under her agile hands. She slipped them on hurriedly, reminding herself that in them she'd have to walk slowly and carefully or she'd have a broken toe to match her bruised shins.

"It's eleven-o-four," Judith hollered from the kitchen. "He's late!"

"So am I!" Ryanne yelled back as she emerged from the closet. She felt her way back into the bathroom, groped for her hairbrush and gave the wild mane a quick once-over. Though she couldn't see it, her hair was one thing she had no trouble visualizing, since it had been giving her problems all her life. Knowing that without a curling iron it was useless to try to subdue it, she merely pulled it back from her face and secured the sides with tortoise-shell combs. With no time for makeup she decided she'd just have to trust that her plastic surgeon had been diligent about natural beauty.

Back in the bedroom she snatched Aggie's lead from the closet hook where the guide dog's harness was stored, and took off for the kitchen.

"All finished. How do I look?" she asked as she entered and whirled in a pretty pirouette. When Judith answered from the living room, Ryanne realized she'd been wasting her smile on the refrigerator.

She turned toward the voice that informed her, "You've looked worse."

Coming from Judith, that was high praise, but Ryanne couldn't resist a dry, "Gee, thanks."

"What do you want, a medal? You look fine, and even if you didn't, there's no time to do anything about it. Jack Daniels just pulled up in the driveway."

"Wonderful!" Ryanne moved toward the window where her sentry was spying. "Is he driving a snazzy little sports car?"

"No, he's in a nondescript black van with a gaudy logo that reads MacKenna and Associates."

Ryanne smiled at Judith's irritable tone. "So tell me, what does he look like?"

Judith peered through the blinds as she assessed their visitor. Hugh MacKenna was tall, broad shouldered and lean hipped, with just enough masculine arrogance in his long-gaited walk to make a woman—any woman—take a second look. His light brown hair was so perfectly groomed that the ocean breeze wouldn't have dared disturb it, and the expression on his handsome, classically sculpted face said he knew it. All in all, he was one of the most attractive men Judith had ever seen.

Of course, not even bamboo shoots under her fingernails would have forced her to admit it.

"Judith, come on," Ryanne prodded. "Describe him to me."

Judith let the blinds fall and turned toward her friend. "Form a mental picture of Quasimodo wearing huaraches."

A picture of Charles Laughton as the Hunchback of Notre Dame wearing an Izod sweater, cotton baggies and trendy Mexican sandals popped into Ryanne's head and she burst out laughing. Knowing Judith's perverse sense of humor, Ryanne was certain her secretary's assessment meant Hugh MacKenna was inordinately good-looking, but the mental image wouldn't go away and she struggled to bring her laughter under control. She almost succeeded, but then the doorbell chimed, sounding like a muted version of Quasimodo's cathedral bells and she started laughing all over again.

"You get it, Judith, and I'll hold on to Aggie," she instructed, fighting back laughter as she attached the dog's lead to her choke chain. *"Quasimodo wearing huaraches?"* The image assaulted her again. "Come on, admit he's not that bad."

"Are you kidding," Judith scoffed, refusing to confess. "Tanned or not, they wouldn't let this guy anywhere near the Ventura Freeway."

CHAPTER THREE

Laughter? Hugh glanced around as he neared the front door. Somebody inside Ryanne Kirkland's house was definitely amused about something. The burst of laughter on the other side of the door cackled and rolled, and while Hugh couldn't have said it was a pretty, musical sound, it certainly was infectious. He just couldn't keep from smiling.

"I guess I don't have to wonder if anyone's home," he muttered under his breath. "Just whether or not anybody in there is sane."

He pressed the doorbell and thought he heard another, quieter laugh, and he waited. His hand was poised in midair, ready to ring again when the door finally cracked open. A pair of grimly suspicious eyes glared defiantly at him as though trying to make him feel guilty for having had the audacity to ring in the first place.

The lines around the woman's mouth were drawn into a perpetual frown and he'd have bet his life there was no way the burst of laughter had passed between those forbidding lips. She had to be Judith. The picture Douglas sent hadn't done her justice.

"Yes?"

Hugh put his most confidence-inspiring smile in gear. "Mrs. Tremain?"

"Yes."

"I'm here to see Ryanne Kirkland. I'm Hugh Mac-Kenna."

She looked him over dispassionately. "Can you prove that?" she challenged.

"Certainly." Somewhere behind the door, out of Hugh's narrow range of vision, a chuckle was winding down, as though someone was trying to regain control of their funny bone. Hugh's questioning smile acknowledged the sound, but Mrs. Tremain remained oblivious. He reached for the slender wallet in the inside breast pocket of his jacket, noticing when he glanced down that Judith's right foot was wedged tightly against the back of the door. Anyone who wanted to get past this lady uninvited would have to break her foot to do it. A formidable woman, indeed; Ryanne Kirkland would never have to worry about door-to-door salesmen.

Judith accepted the open wallet and carefully inspected the driver's and investigator's licenses that rested one above the other.

"Do I pass muster?" he asked amiably.

Judith took a step back and opened the door wider. "You're late."

Hugh's smile didn't falter. "Yes, I apologize for that. I was out in the valley and got caught in a traffic pileup on the Ventura Freeway."

That was too much for Ryanne. Laughter bubbled over again as Hugh moved into the living room. He watched as she clutched her dog's leash in one hand and put the other over her mouth in an attempt to control her giggles.

"Was it something I said?" Hugh asked dryly.

Ryanne could feel the heat of embarrassment rising in her cheeks. "I'm sorry," she managed to gasp, knowing she was making a spectacle of herself. "Really..." She finally managed to regain control. "It was just something Judith said earlier that struck me as funny. Please forgive me. I'm Ryanne Kirkland." She stepped forward and held out her free hand toward the voice that sounded even sexier in person than it had on the phone.

"It's a pleasure to meet you." Hugh accepted her firm handshake and resisted the temptation to hold on a little longer than was necessary. The pictures Douglas had sent of Ryanne hadn't done her justice, either. The attractive features were the same, and her eyes just as crystalline blue, but no photograph could have captured the effervescence of her smile or the infectious nature of her laugh. Ryanne Kirkland was like an uncorked bottle of champagne, bubbly and beautiful. Just looking at her, Hugh felt as if the champagne cork had popped him right between the eyes.

With great reluctance he released her hand, only to find it filled again with the enthusiastic wet nose of her golden retriever. Always ready to overwhelm a new audience, Aggie lunged toward Hugh, and Ryanne gave the lead a firm snap.

"No!" she commanded, her voice low but gruff. "Aggie, sit."

"It's all right," Hugh reassured her. "I like dogs."

"Shh! Don't let her hear you say that or you'll never get rid of her," Ryanne warned him. "Unlike Judith, Aggie doesn't know the meaning of the word stranger."

"She's a beautiful dog."

"Thank you. Despite her excess enthusiasm, Aggie is a sweetheart. I don't know what I'd do without her."

Behind Hugh, still stationed near the door, Judith expressed her opinion of that statement with a loud harrumph, which Ryanne deliberately ignored.

"Why don't you have a seat, Hugh. I'll tie this monster down to keep her out of your way. Believe me, you'll thank me for it later."

"I trust your judgment." Hugh grinned and moved to the sofa.

Ryanne listened carefully as he moved and when she had accurately placed his location, she chose a seat for herself at the opposite end of the couch. She fastened the lead around the sturdy leg and Aggie pondered this new limitation for a moment before settling down on top of Ryanne's feet.

That chore completed, Ryanne turned her attention back to her guest. "Would you like coffee? I'm sure Judith would be happy to brew a pot."

Hugh took a quick look at the secretary and decided Ryanne couldn't have been more wrong. "No, thanks."

Ryanne smiled at him. "I appreciate your coming by like this. I have the feeling Douglas Sutherland coerced you into giving me the VIP treatment."

"I wouldn't say that, exactly, but he did make it clear that if I didn't do my best to see that you got settled in comfortably he'd tell my father I was being a bad boy."

Ryanne laughed lightly. "That sounds like Douglas. He and your father are old friends, aren't they?"

"They survived World War II together and haven't let anyone forget it since. Dad runs a deep-sea fishing charter on the gulf in Mississippi and they get together every year to invade the beaches at Normandy."

Ryanne nodded, smiling. "I remember Douglas's yearly vacations while I was working at the *Examiner*. He always returned with a sunburn and a fish story even Herman Melville would have envied."

"If you think Doug is bad, you should hear Dad. Nobody can weave a fish story like Webb MacKenna."

"I'll take your word for it." If only because she enjoyed the sound of his voice so much, Ryanne would have liked to question Hugh further about his family, but since she felt guilty about taking up his valuable time, it didn't seem appropriate to sit and chat. "Douglas told me you're a private investigator, Hugh. And he also said you're an expert in security installation and maintenance.''

"Let's just say I do a lot of that sort of work."

"Well, I appreciate your willingness to check out the system I inherited here. I tried to tell Douglas that it wasn't necessary to bother you, but he insisted I give you a call."

"I'm glad he did," he reassured her. "It's no problem, believe me. I imagine Douglas also told you I live right up the road."

"Yes. That seemed awfully convenient to me," Ryanne said teasingly. "Considering the fact that a real estate broker friend of his in Chicago used her connections to help me get this place. I'd say one or both of us was set up."

"You think Doug is playing matchmaker?" Hugh asked wryly. The only thing that surprised him about the thought was that he hadn't considered the possibility himself. It was clear from the sudden frown that appeared on Ryanne's face, however, that that particular idea had never crossed her mind. Apparently the thought didn't please her, but she recovered quickly and managed a smile. "No, actually, I just thought maybe he was playing mother hen again. He's so overprotective sometimes that I want to strangle him. It would be just like him to appoint a watchdog to keep track of me out here."

Hugh laughed as though the thought was farfetched, yet he mentally saluted Ryanne. She was obviously a keen judge of character. To keep her from carrying her watchdog theory any further, Hugh changed the subject smoothly. "Yesterday on the phone you mentioned that the owner of this house subscribes to the Malibu Security Watch System, isn't that right?"

"Yes. Before Mr. Reston left for Europe he sent me copious instructions on the system," she answered, noting that Hugh's conversational transition had been a little too brisk.

Obviously she'd been right about Douglas—he *had* appointed Hugh MacKenna as her guardian. She'd have to do something about that, and soon. For the time being, though, she'd play the game and see where it led. She smiled sheepishly. "I've been practicing activating and deactivating the system, and I have to tell you, I'm really impressed with the security officers who respond to the alarms. They're remarkably forgiving when you accidentally set it off. Being blind does have certain advantages at a time like that. They may think I'm an idiot, but they wouldn't dare say it to my face."

Hugh chuckled appropriately at the bit of self-deprecating humor, but Ryanne could tell it was nervous laughter. It was always that way in the beginning, she had discovered. Until people got to know her they were never really sure whether or not there was an edge of bitterness to her references.

"Have you committed the Security Watch phone number to memory in case of an emergency?" Hugh asked.

"Yes," Ryanne confirmed. "And I'm a whiz at 911 for police or an ambulance."

"Good." He looked at her, wondering if she could tell he was returning her bright, impish smile. Her face was turned precisely toward him, their eyes nearly meeting. She was so good at looking directly at him that until she'd reminded him he'd nearly forgotten she was blind. "Frankly, Ryanne, the Security Watch System is about the best protection you can have in this neighborhood."

"That's nice to know."

"The only real problem with the system is that the sensors tend to go bad pretty quickly because of the sea air around here. As I'm sure you've already discovered, most of the houses on Malibu Beach are only a stone's throw from the ocean at high tide and the sand and salt spray can really get to them. I'll check out all the alarm sensors inside and out and if there's a problem Security Watch will send out a maintenance man to fix it."

"I appreciate your help."

"As I said before, it's no problem."

Ryanne heard Hugh stand and she followed suit. Aggie, never one to be left out, jumped up as well. "Is there anything I can do to help you?" Ryanne asked, realizing as the words came out of her mouth that it was a stupid question. Even if she could see, she still wouldn't have the vaguest notion of how to assist him.

But Hugh didn't seem to think it was a dumb question—or at least he didn't let on that he thought it was. "No, thanks. It's a pretty simple job, really. I'll just get my equipment kit out of the van and call Security Watch to let them know what I'm up to." He stepped around the glass-and-chrome coffee table.

"I'll leave Aggie tethered to the sofa so she won't pester you to death, and if you need to know where anything is, just ask Judith," Ryanne suggested.

"Fine." Hugh started toward the door, then stopped. "By the way, one of my associates, Mo Johnson, is a big fan of yours. When he found out I was coming here today he asked me to tell you that in his humble opinion your Cameron Lawe mysteries are some of the best detective novels being written today. He says you write gritty, realistic violence like nobody he knows."

For just a second Ryanne's pleasant smile slipped. "Tell him that's because I've seen a lot of violence. Close up and firsthand."

A small, dismal silence fell over the room, but before Ryanne had the chance to kick herself for what she'd said, Judith took charge. "It's almost noon," she announced. "Are you going to get this over with or am I going to have to fix lunch for you, too?"

Hugh looked at the secretary. Her face was set in a belligerent frown, but her eyes were firmly focused on Ryanne. They were filled with a concern Hugh was certain she'd rather not have anyone else see, and he decided that despite Mrs. Tremain's rude, obnoxious behavior, he liked her a lot. "This is going to take a while, ma'am," he informed her placatingly. "Please just go on with whatever you have planned and don't pay any attention to me."

"Easier said than done," she muttered, moving toward the door to open it for him. "Just ring when you're ready to do the inside—and try not to track in any sand, would you?"

CHAPTER FOUR

WHILE HUGH WORKED, Ryanne tackled the mess she'd left in the kitchen and Judith retreated to the office, muttering unkind epithets about men under her breath.

True to his word, Hugh's inspection did take quite a long time, and it wasn't until Ryanne finished the cupboards that he finished his rounds upstairs. What with all the clanging of pots and pans, however, Ryanne had lost track of his movements through the house, so when he suddenly spoke to her from the hall entrance to the kitchen she jumped.

"Hi. Have you finished reorganizing?" he asked.

Ryanne put her hand over her pounding heart. "Are you part Indian or something? You didn't make a sound coming down those steps."

"I'm sorry if I startled you."

"Don't apologize. But if you keep it up I'm going to have to hang a bell around your neck."

Hugh grinned. "That would give a whole new meaning to the phrase, 'I'll be there with bells on,' wouldn't it?"

"I suppose so." Ryanne chuckled. "Could I tempt you with a cup of coffee now?"

"That sounds good."

While Ryanne searched for a mug she heard Hugh move to the end of the Manhattan-style bar and pull out one of the stools. "So, tell me about this security system I inherited," she suggested, then turned her attention to the coffee.

"You'll be happy to know it's in fairly good shape."

Ryanne turned toward him and narrowed her eyes comically. "Why do I not like the sound of *fairly* good?"

Hugh laughed again. "Don't worry, it's no big deal. The system checks out fine except for the west window in the master bedroom and the doors to the upper deck. The pressure sensors there aren't nearly as responsive as they should be and they need to be replaced, that's all. I'll call Security Watch and have them send someone out. I'd do the work myself but they get a little testy when unauthorized personnel start replacing their equipment."

"That's okay, really, Hugh. You've done more than enough already. I'll call them later and request the repairs."

Hugh started to protest that it was no trouble. He knew it could be days before Security Watch got someone out on call unless a little pressure was applied, but Ryanne had a stubborn look that he knew better than to challenge. She was an independent lady who had to depend on others too often because she was blind, so she made up for it by doing as much as she could for herself. He felt his already considerable respect for her go up another notch. "All right," he acquiesced. "But if you have any trouble or get any flack, please let me know. The owner is a friend of mine and he owes me a favor or two."

As they had talked Hugh had watched Ryanne, mesmerized by the ease with which she had managed to fill the two coffee cups with exactly the same amount of coffee—and not spill a single drop. The only clue he had that she couldn't see was the way she moved slowly toward him with the back of her free hand held slightly in front of her body so that it came into contact with the bar. She swept her hand gently over the tabletop next to him, making sure the space was empty before setting the cup down.

"Thanks."

"You're welcome." Ryanne moved back to the opposite counter for her own mug. "It's not as good as Judith's coffee, but it's drinkable."

"Your secretary is very. . ."

"Rude?"

Hugh chuckled. "Formidable was the word that came to mind."

"You should try for a career in the diplomatic corps," Ryanne suggested. "Don't take her attitude personally. It's just her way of keeping the world at arm's length. You get used to her after a while."

"You'd have to. I got the impression from Doug that they don't get along too well."

Ryanne waved an airy hand. "That feud is all for show. They're both so overprotective of me that they constantly disagree about what is or is not in my best interests." Since Hugh seemed in no hurry to leave, Ryanne changed the subject, wanting to find out a little more about him. "Tell me more about your work, Hugh. Somehow you don't fit the normal image of a crusty old private eye working out of a seedy upstairs office. What kind of cases do you handle?"

"Oh, the usual. We get a few divorce cases, but mostly it's security installation and corporate espionage. I have a computer expert on staff who specializes in computer fraud cases and I handle personnel security clearance for several large firms around the country."

"You travel a lot, then?"

"Some," he admitted. "Enough to make it cost efficient to keep my own jet hangared out in Burbank."

"You make it sound very routine."

"Most of the time it is."

Perched on a stool around the corner from Hugh's, Ryanne plied him with more questions about his work and finally got him to admit that he did occasionally handle unusual, even dangerous cases. Hugh wasn't the first private investigator Ryanne had ever met, but she quickly discovered he was one of the most interesting.

Part of her mind was focused fully on everything he said, but the purely feminine side of her was listening intently to the way he said it. His voice was rich, almost hypnotic, and there was a warmth to it that exuded trustworthiness. Without her sight to guide her, Ryanne had learned to depend on voices to tell her what she needed to know about a person. After she'd known someone for a while, their actions spoke louder than words, of course, but in the beginning, she trusted her instincts about voices, both what they said and what they didn't say. And Hugh MacKenna's voice was speaking directly to Ryanne's libido right now.

Given what Judith had said about his Quasimodo looks, Ryanne was certain Hugh was a very attractive man; she certainly hoped so at any rate. Fate played funny tricks sometimes, as Ryanne was acutely aware, but it just wouldn't be fair if a voice like Hugh's didn't have a face and form to match it.

"Well, have I bored you to tears yet?" Hugh asked when Ryanne temporarily ran out of questions.

"Hardly. You try to downplay it, but you really do lead a fascinating life." Ryanne slipped off the stool and picked up her cup. "Would you like some more coffee?"

"Just half, please." He placed the mug in her outstretched hand and watched her as she moved. Again she poured their coffee with amazing effortlessness, and before he even realized the words were out, he asked, "How do you do that? No, wait, I'm sorry. That was rude," he apologized, unable to believe he'd spoken without thinking. He wasn't accustomed to saying anything that wasn't carefully thought out in advance, but Ryanne Kirkland was having an unusual effect on him. Already more than once he'd had to force his thoughts back into line when they'd wanted to wander off and concentrate on the wisps of red hair that teased her forehead and framed her lively eyes behind those mysterious glasses.

Ryanne could tell he was embarrassed by his own question and that he wasn't a man accustomed to being embarrassed. If there was one thing she'd learned how to do well, though, it was ease the discomfort people felt at asking such natural questions. "Don't be silly, Hugh. You can ask anything you like. I can't pretend not to be blind, and you can't pretend not to notice."

"All right, then, how do you do it?"

Ryanne could hear the easy smile in his voice. "The same way you learned to come down creaky stairs without making a sound, I suspect. Lots of practice and knowing the right technique. First of all, I know exactly how much coffee is coming out of the spout and how much the cup will hold. And also, I can feel the heat on my fingers as the coffee level rises. My favorite technique, though, is just listening. Any vessel has a hollow sound when it's empty, and as you fill it with liquid, that sound rises in pitch. Try it sometime with a glass of water, but unless you want to embarrass yourself the first few hundred attempts I'd advise you to practice when you're alone."

"I'll give it a try," he promised.

Ryanne returned with their coffee. "Any more questions?"

"Even personal ones?" he asked, his voice softer, his smile no longer evident.

Ryanne had heard that tone too many times not to know what was coming, and she sobered as well. "How did I become blind?" she asked for him.

"Yes."

"What did Douglas tell you?"

She heard him shift on the stool before he answered. "Only that you were a reporter until you were blinded in an accident five years ago," he replied, hating himself for not being able to tell her the truth. Yet instinctively he knew that Doug was right about Ryanne. She would not appreciate knowing that Hugh was aware of her whole, tragic history. In fact, he suspected that if she did know she might withdraw from him completely, and he most definitely did not want that. Something about Ryanne was drawing him like a magnet and Hugh, who had always found himself attracted to smart, independent, savvy women, wanted to get to know this one better.

Ryanne leaned back on the stool and crossed her legs, carefully adjusting the full skirt over her bruised shins to give her time to think about what to tell him. She had pat answers on this topic—one for every occasion. All she had to decide was whether to tell him the simple cleaned-up-cocktail-party version of her story or the *Reader's Digest* condensed version that was grim but not gory. There was, of course, the unvarnished truth, which included how it felt to know she was going to die, a description of the searing pain of Worsted's bullet as it entered her shoulder, and a recounting of her long, torturous road to recovery. But no one had ever heard the unvarnished truth, and probably no one ever would. It was a living nightmare that replayed endlessly in Ryanne's head, one that she couldn't share.

In this case, though, the cleaned-up version didn't strike her as appropriate, so she opted for something in between versions one and two. "Actually it happened while I was sticking my nose in where it didn't belong," she began. "I was following the subject of a police investigation and one of his cohorts took exception to the fact that I saw him commit murder. In my attempt to make a fast getaway I fell off a steep ledge in a warehouse loft. I'm convinced the only thing that saved my life was the fact that I fell on my head—it's far too hard to allow any life-threatening damage."

"And the fall caused your blindness?"

"Uh-huh." She pointed vaguely toward her head. "Neurological damage to the optic nerve."

She said it casually, without bitterness or recriminations, as if she were just stating a simple fact. Hugh had known women who spoke more passionately about a broken fingernail than Ryanne did about her blindness. Was it a front? he wondered. How could she not be bitter? "Did they catch the guy?" He already knew the answer, of course, but Ryanne didn't know that and if he didn't ask questions she was likely to get suspicious. And, too, Hugh wanted to hear the story from her so that he could see if she was coping with the tragedy as well as it appeared.

"No. The police are pretty sure they know his identity, but I'd never seen him before so they couldn't make a case. All I could give them was a description that matched Worsted's—and about a million other men in the Chicago area."

"Worsted? That was his name?" Hugh asked, pouncing on the piece of information that hadn't been included in the sketchy reports Doug had sent him.

Ryanne chuckled. "No, that's not his name. I labeled him that at the time because he was wearing a worsted business suit, and the name just stuck." She turned her head away from Hugh's slightly and he realized that she wasn't as casual about the topic as she pretended. "I know it sounds silly, but it's easier for me if I call him Worsted rather than his real name."

"Why?"

She shrugged. "Somewhere in Chicago there's a man who would sleep a whole lot sounder if I was dead. I'm never going to get my sight back, but I can't imagine that he's one hundred percent positive of that. In a small way, I'm still a threat to him."

"So you think of him in the past tense and refer to him by a name you made up because it makes him seem a little less...real."

"Exactly." Ryanne turned her face to him again, amazed that he'd caught on so quickly to what she meant and how she felt. "So...any more questions, or have I depressed you enough for one day?"

"Just one more...for now." The way he said it let Ryanne know that since there was a *now* there would definitely be a *later*. Strangely, the idea was a lot more appealing than she would have liked.

"Ask away," she invited.

"Why do you wear glasses?"

The puzzlement in his voice was so acute that Ryanne couldn't help but laugh. "Philodendrons," she replied, then waited for the inevitable.

"Philodendrons? Why on earth—"

"Think about it," she insisted. "Where do you usually find philodendron and other annoying potted plants?"

Though he was certain there was a connection between her eyeglasses and potted plants, Hugh still hadn't made it, and he didn't like being in the dark. "I don't know.... In houses, restaurants, lots of places."

"And *where* in houses and restaurants are they usually to be found?" she prodded.

"On tables, in hanging baskets...Oh." The light finally dawned and he laughed.

"Exactly." Ryanne laughed with him. "When I first got out of the hospital and was stumbling around like an idiot I moved back home because I figured if my family couldn't be counted on to feel sorry for me and allow me to wallow in self-pity, who could? Unfortunately my aunt who raised me after my parents died had other plans. And she had *plants*, too. Dozens of them hanging everywhere. Walking through her house was like navigating a macrame obstacle course. I never knew when some branch was going to whip out and poke me in the eye."

"You mean she didn't take them down?" he asked, astonished that anyone could be so cruel to a woman who'd just suffered a major trauma. He also wondered what had happened to her parents, but now didn't seem like the right time to ask.

"On the contrary. She left them right where they were and told me to get used to it. And when I finally snapped and began yelling at her to take them down or I'd rip them down with my bare hands, she calmly said—" Ryanne raised her voice a pitch in imitation of her Aunt Rose "—'Is that how you're going to live your life, Ryanne? Making the rest of the world alter itself to suit you, or are you going to make alterations and learn how to fit the world?'"

Her voice returned to normal. "The next day I started wearing sunglasses, but when I realized they fit the stereotype of a blind person with a white cane I switched to regular glasses with shatterproof plastic lenses. I thought I'd try wearing the shades here in L.A., though."

They both laughed, and Ryanne leaned forward as though about to confide a secret. "In case you hadn't noticed, Hugh, the world has been booby trapped. When you least expect it, up pops a hanging plant, an untrimmed hedge, a low hanging branch, an open cabinet door..."

Or a man who tries to kill you, he added silently, trying to squelch the pity he knew Ryanne wouldn't want. Aloud, he commented only, "So you practice self-defense against the booby traps."

"Exactly."

Her hands were lightly clasped together, resting on the bar as she leaned forward. Her face was glowing with life and humor, and Hugh couldn't resist the impulse to reach out to her and cover her hands with his own. "You're a remarkable woman, Ryanne Kirkland," he told her softly, his voice intimate and filled with respect.

Ryanne felt the strength and warmth in his firm hands; heard those same qualities in his voice, and for a moment she was stunned. Mostly to irritate Judith's puritan ethic and to amuse herself, Ryanne joked about men and fantasies often, but it had been over five years since she'd let a man get close enough to touch her. Oh, Douglas and one or two of the reporters she still kept in contact with occasionally gave her a hug or patted her on the shoulder, and because she knew she could trust them she looked forward to that type of casual contact.

But this was different. Hugh MacKenna was a virtual stranger, and no matter how pleasant Ryanne seemed on the surface, always lurking underneath was the knowledge that the next stranger she met could be Worsted. He could walk up to her, engage her in conversation, laugh at one of her jokes—and put a gun to her head without her even realizing that the man who haunted her dreams was blowing her brains out.

That kind of fear and an instinct for self-preservation had been Ryanne's constant companion for five years now, and to prevent disaster she made it a habit to avoid being alone with strangers. As time passed the danger lessened, but an ingrained habit had been formed. The only reason she'd let her guard down with Hugh was that Douglas trusted him implicitly and had instilled some of that trust in Ryanne. She'd been prepared to like Hugh because of Douglas, and she had no objection to swooning a little over his gorgeous bourbon voice. Letting him touch her like this, though, making her heart beat faster because she liked his touch... that was out of the question. Hugh was just feeling sorry for her and pity was one thing Ryanne couldn't tolerate.

Stiffening, she pulled her hands abruptly out of his and seized on his compliment as a way of discouraging him. "Just what is it, Mr. MacKenna, that makes me so remarkable?" she asked with flat practicality, slipping off the stool. "Is it because I can do parlor tricks and pour coffee without making a fool of myself? Is it because I'm blind, and any blind person who doesn't sit cowering and weeping in a corner is to be commended? Just what makes me so remarkable?"

Hugh knew he'd made a mistake the moment he'd reached out to her. He'd felt the tensing of her body—an instinctive, repulsed response to the touch of a stranger. He regretted the action, but not his compliment. Whether she knew it or not, blind or not, Ryanne Kirkland *was* remarkable.

He kept his voice even and calm when he told her, "What makes you special, Ryanne, is the way you light up a room when you smile. And the fact that you've been through so much and have survived with that light still shining—that's remarkable. But I'm sorry if I offended you."

He was so sincere, his voice such a compelling caress, that Ryanne couldn't hold on to the defensive anger she was using as a shield. "No, I'm sorry, Hugh," she said after a moment. "I usually leave the barking to Aggie and the biting to Judith. I didn't mean to take a piece of your hide."

"Don't worry about it," he reassured her with a little laugh. "My hide is as tough as your head."

"Wanna bet?" Ryanne challenged. She held out her hand. "Give me your mug and you can have one more cup of coffee for the road."

CHAPTER FIVE

"ARGH!" Frustrated, Ryanne plopped her forehead on the top of her typewriter and resisted the urge to smash all the keys down at one time.

"What's *your* problem?" Across the room Judith swiveled around from her word processor and scrutinized her employer. "You're supposed to be writing, not resting. There's a difference, you know."

"Yes, I know," Ryanne said, lifting her head. "Unfortunately this stupid screenplay isn't cooperating."

Ryanne heard Judith's heavy sigh. "What is it this time?"

"I'm trying to transform the shoot-out in chapter six into a viable movie scene and it just isn't working! What made the scene so gripping in the book is that the reader knows everything Cameron is thinking—that he really doesn't care if he comes out of this confrontation alive. But in the screenplay all I've got is action—just a lot of bullets and blood."

"Then you've got to find a way to illustrate how reckless Lawe has become."

"That's right," Ryanne snapped, "but how do I show that? Ooh, I hate writing movies! Why on earth didn't I just tell them to let someone else adapt the book?"

"Because you wanted to maintain the integrity of your creation, you wanted the challenge of writing a movie script and you wanted a free trip to Hollywood. Not necessarily in that order," Judith replied testily. She'd lived through too many of Ryanne's creative temper tantrums to take this one seriously. "Why don't you get out of here for a while so I can get some work done? It's no picnic for me to transfer what you write into this complicated screenplay format, you know. Go take a walk on the beach or something. I'm sure your pitiful excuse for a guide dog could use some exercise, and I could certainly use some peace and quiet."

Ryanne nodded. "That's a good idea. Maybe I'll get inspired."

"There's a first time for everything," Judith said dryly. Her chair whined as she swiveled back to her computer, not so subtly telling Ryanne she'd been dismissed.

"Come on, Aggie. Let's go for a walk." The guide dog, resting at Ryanne's feet under the table, jumped up eagerly as Ryanne stood, and together they took off down the hall.

Ten minutes later, Ryanne had changed shoes, harnessed her dog and the two of them were tramping briskly down the beach. The ocean sounded gentle today, she noted, just a whispered sigh as the waves whooshed in, and she relaxed almost immediately. She'd been in Malibu for a week now and because she and Aggie had walked the smooth stretch of beach every day she was confident her guide dog would not lead her astray. Out of long practice, part of her mind kept track of how far they'd wandered from the house, but another part was free to focus on the problems she was having with the adaptation of her book.

She'd met with the producer and director of the movie several days ago, so she knew what they wanted and she knew what she wanted. It was just a matter of getting it on paper without losing that indefinable something that made the Cameron Lawe mysteries so special. Judith was two-thirds correct about Ryanne's reasons for wanting to do the script herself. The trip to Hollywood had been far from free, but it was important to Ryanne that the integrity of her cre-

ation be maintained, and she relished the challenge of doing something new and different.

Of course, with that challenge also came the fear of failure, but Ryanne had long ago learned that fear was something to be faced and conquered. As a child, she had been
so afraid of the dark that she'd had to keep a night-light
burning in her room to chase away the monsters that came
out of the closet to watch her sleep. Now darkness was all
she knew, and the monsters were no longer imaginary. The
fear she lived with was real, but she met it head-on every day
and managed to survive because there was no alternative.

Ryanne estimated that she and Aggie had been walking
for nearly a half an hour when the guide dog stopped
abruptly as though waiting for instruction or warning her
mistress that something was impeding their progress. The
sound of the waves coming into the shore had changed, informing Ryanne that they had reached the breakwater—a
little peninsula of stones that jutted out into the ocean. With
Judith's help, Ryanne had studied the beach and taught
Aggie that this particular spot marked the end of their hik-
ing trail. Aggie was telling her it was time to turn around and
head back down the beach.

"Good work, Aggie!" Her voice full of praise, Ryanne
reached down and patted Aggie lovingly on the head to re-
inforce the dog's training. "That's very good! Okay, we'll
go home now." She turned the dog around. "Beach house,
Aggie. Hup-up."

"Ryanne! Wait up!"

Startled, Ryanne stopped and turned back up the beach.
Even from a distance the deep, whiskey-smooth timbre of
Hugh MacKenna's voice was unmistakable. A smile that was
half surprise, half pleasure spread across her face and she
waved. "Hugh?"

"Hello, Ryanne." Only slightly winded, Hugh jogged up to her.

"Where did you come from?" Ryanne asked, wondering if her delighted smile looked as idiotic as it felt. She hadn't heard from Hugh since he'd stopped by to inspect her security system four days earlier, and she had mixed emotions about his absence. Her logical self had told her she didn't have time to waste on whiskey-voiced private investigators, but her purely feminine side had been disappointed that he hadn't found an excuse to call or come by for a visit. This wasn't a chance meeting, she was certain, and her feminine side was delighted.

"I called your house and just missed you," he explained. "Judith reluctantly told me you'd gone for a walk up the beach, so I decided to jog down and join you. Unless you'd prefer to be alone."

"Don't be silly," Ryanne said a little too quickly. "Of course we'd like your company. Aggie and I were just about to head back, though."

"No problem." Together they turned back down the beach.

"How near here do you live?" Ryanne asked.

"About a mile and a half on up the coast. I'm just outside the Malibu city limits."

"Then you must know this beach fairly well."

"Like the back of my hand. There's a stretch of rocky shoreline just north of my house that has some interesting tidal pools. I'd be happy to show them to you if you ever get tired of this endless expanse of sand."

Ryanne laughed. "Is that the L.A. equivalent of 'come up to my apartment and I'll show you my etchings'?"

"Precisely." Hugh chuckled. "Until I moved to the beach I never realized what an aphrodisiac the ocean could be. One look at my tidal pools and all the women fall breathless at my feet."

Or into your bed, Ryanne thought. After Hugh had left her house the other day Ryanne had cajoled Judith into giving her an accurate description of Hugh, and now she knew that his voice wasn't Mr. MacKenna's only astonishingly attractive feature. She'd learned that his hair was a soft, satiny brown and his eyes were an odd shade of amber and gold. She'd already determined for herself that he was quite tall, but according to Judith he had an athletic physique that was very impressive. Judith had said his features were as firm and classically sculpted as the rest of him, and the picture that had ultimately formed in Ryanne's mind was that of Michelangelo's David, not Victor Hugo's Quasimodo. Listening to his voice now, feeling his magnetic presence beside her, and remembering Judith's description, Ryanne suddenly wished that Michelangelo had been a little more modest and provided David with a pair of trousers.

"So tell me, Ryanne, has Security Watch fixed your faulty sensors yet?" Hugh asked.

Considering her keen physical awareness of him, Ryanne was tempted to tell Hugh that there was absolutely nothing wrong with her sensors, but then she'd have to explain the pun and she didn't think it was particularly wise to let him know the detour her thoughts had taken. Instead she answered, "As a matter of fact, they haven't. I called them right after you left and they never showed up. Yesterday I sicced Judith on them and even that didn't get results."

"They're probably too intimidated to show up now," he joked. "Would you be offended if I offered to give them a call for you?"

Ryanne smiled at him sheepishly. "No, actually, I'd be grateful. If I hadn't been so stubborn the other day you could have played Sir Galahad then and saved me a lot of bother. Do you mind calling?"

"Of course not. I wouldn't have volunteered otherwise. I'll call as soon as we get back to your place. As I told you, the owner owes me a favor or two."

"If you get results, I'll repay you with the libation of your choice," Ryanne promised. "My larder is now fully stocked—I have coffee *and* tea."

Hugh's voice lowered fractionally. "Actually I had something a little more substantial in mind as payment."

His seductive tone had warning bells ringing in Ryanne's head. She stopped abruptly, tilting her head coolly toward Hugh. "Oh?"

"I was hoping you'd allow me to escort you on a tour of Los Angeles."

"Oh." She relaxed and laughed lightly.

"What did you think I was going to suggest?"

"Something wicked and thoroughly indecent."

"Who me?" he cried, feigning injury. "What kind of a cad do you think I am, anyway?"

"A very nice one," Ryanne answered, resuming her walk down the beach.

"Then you'll accept my invitation?"

She sighed. "Oh, Hugh . . . I don't think so."

"Why not? You can't spend a few months in Hollywood and not see the sights—" His voice died abruptly. "Sorry. That was a stupid thing to say."

Ryanne stopped again and Aggie gave a patient, heaving sigh as though she wished her mistress would make up her mind. This time she sat on Ryanne's command and waited.

"Hugh, the word 'see' doesn't bother me. It's so much a part of everyone's vocabulary that I'm really not even conscious of it anymore. I still 'see' things, you know. I just don't see them the way everyone else does."

Hugh looked at her closely, admiring her courage and the simple sincerity she used to put people who said stupid things at ease. He also admired the long, shapely curve of her newly tanned legs and the way her slender, feminine figure filled out the shorts and camp shirt she was wearing. So much so, in fact, that he was beginning to feel like the lascivious cad she'd almost accused him of being. He forced his attention back to their conversation. "You have a very philosophical way of looking at it, Ryanne," he told her softly. "I'm not sure if I could be quite so... accepting if I were in your position."

Ryanne considered that for a moment. "No, you wouldn't be. Not at first, at least. I certainly wasn't. But eventually you learn to adjust, to adapt. Being blind doesn't mean that you stop enjoying life or caring about people. It doesn't diminish ambition or curiosity or any of the things that motivate people to move forward with their lives."

"Really?"

"Yes, really," Ryanne said, a little surprised that Hugh would question what she thought was a statement of obvious fact.

"Being blind doesn't curtail curiosity?"

"No."

"Then in that case, how can you possibly turn down my invitation to tour Hollywood? Aren't you the least bit curious to see the Walk of Fame and Grauman's Chinese Theatre?" He leaned close enough that Ryanne could smell the faintest trace of his musky cologne and lowered his voice to a deliberately tantalizing, seductive whisper. "If you'll go with me I promise to let you stand in John Wayne's footprints."

Ryanne squelched her laughter and matched his tone. "You're using the wrong bait, MacKenna. If you'd offered to let me stand in Harrison Ford's footprints I might have been tempted.''

Hugh snapped his fingers. "Shucks. I don't think they've gotten around to cementing him yet. Would you settle for R2D2 and C3PO?''

Ryanne laughed. "It's not quite the same. I do have to thank you, though. You could have simply told me they were Harrison's footprints and I'd never have known the difference.''

Ryanne felt Hugh's swift change in mood even before he spoke, his voice low and sincere. "I'd never lie to you, Ryanne. Or mislead you. It's not a good way to earn someone's friendship and respect.''

"No, it's not,'' she agreed quietly, inordinately pleased that Hugh wanted those things from her because she realized that she wanted them, too. But being friends implied placing a certain amount of trust in another person and that was something she found very difficult. Particularly when that other person was a charming, attractive male. She decided the best course was to change the subject. "Tell me, Hugh, what brings you out to the beach in the middle of the business day? Are you playing hooky or has MacKenna and Associates fallen on hard times?''

Hugh recognized an evasive tactic when he saw one and he decided not to press the point—yet. "I'm playing hooky—it's the boss's prerogative. I finished a missing husband case this afternoon and decided to take the rest of the day off so I could check in on my favorite new neighbor. How's the screenplay coming?''

Ryanne moaned and threw her head back in misery. "You had to remind me.''

"That good, huh?''

"Oh, don't pay any attention to me. I'm not happy unless I've got something to complain about.''

"What seems to be the problem? Maybe talking about it to an impartial observer will help."

Pleased to have a willing listener, Ryanne recounted the problems she was having adapting her novel into a viable screenplay. Though he hadn't read the book, Hugh seemed to understand, and he was surprisingly good at helping Ryanne get to the heart of the trouble. He had an instinctive grasp of what was important and what wasn't, and Ryanne was impressed with his insight into the business of screenwriting. With his help, she soon had a clear picture of what she needed to do to make the difficult scene work.

"Are you sure you're not a writer masquerading as a private investigator?" Ryanne asked suspiciously. "You're very good at this."

"I've had a little practice," he admitted. "A couple of my cases were used as the basis for a TV pilot a few years back."

"Really? What series?"

Hugh named one of the most popular detective shows on television and Ryanne whistled appreciatively. "I'm impressed."

Hugh laughed ruefully. "Don't be. I still act as a consultant to the writers from time to time, but believe me, the life of the series hero bears very little resemblance to my everyday life."

"You mean 'Any similarity between persons living or dead is purely coincidental'?" Ryanne quoted.

"Precisely."

The brisk pace Aggie set had carried them quickly back to Ryanne's place. As they drew up to the beach house Hugh started to tell Ryanne she had arrived home, but Aggie beat him to the punch. Knowing exactly where she was going, the golden retriever executed a sharp turn that sent Ryanne barreling into Hugh's chest. She stumbled and Hugh grabbed her, steadying her with one arm around her waist.

She felt so delightful pressed against him that Hugh was grateful for the dog's error. Ryanne, however, was far from pleased.

"No!" she said sternly as she dropped Aggie's harness and gave the lead a sharp tug.

"It's all right, Ryanne. No harm done," Hugh insisted.

"No, it's not all right. Aggie's job is to keep me from colliding with persons, places and things, not *cause* collisions, and she knows it. Would you mind helping me reenact that to teach her a lesson?"

Not exactly sure what she had in mind, Hugh nonetheless agreed. "What should I do?"

"Just stand there and I'll bump into you again lightly."

"Hmm...that has possibilities," he mused aloud, and Ryanne tried to ignore the wicked smile she heard in his voice, concentrating instead on her dog. She backed up a step, leaned her shoulder against the hard wall of Hugh's muscular chest, and gave Aggie a firm, sharp, "No!"

Aggie's tail, normally so happily active that it was almost a lethal weapon, dropped dejectedly at the sound of her mistress's displeasure. The movement was so pathetic it was an effort for Hugh to keep from laughing. Obviously as far as this dog was concerned the sun rose and set on Ryanne Kirkland. Somehow, Hugh didn't find that the least bit hard to understand.

Backing several steps away from Hugh, Ryanne ordered Aggie to come to her. The dog obeyed instantly, and when Ryanne picked up the harness and commanded, "Aggie, beach house," Aggie stepped forward smartly, making an exaggerated, wide arc around Hugh, and stopped, as she should have in the first place. Ryanne tapped her foot forward, automatically checking for an obstacle, and finding none, she commanded, "Aggie, right, right."

The retriever responded, navigating Ryanne around Hugh. Ryanne praised her accomplishment so lavishly that Aggie's feathery tail began its happy wagging once again. Now, Hugh did laugh, and he followed Ryanne up the stairs to the enormous deck.

Ryanne lavished more glowing praise on the dog as she removed Aggie's harness and tethered her to the rail. Hugh leaned against the wall opposite her, watching Ryanne's deft movements. Her lustrous red hair curtained her face as she leaned down, and he longed to gather it into his hands and savor the texture. For three days now he had found thoughts of Ryanne Kirkland catching him unawares at the oddest moments. The memory of her effervescent smile and sparkling blue eyes had left him feeling pleasantly anxious and a little out of breath.

It had been so long since Hugh had been this intrigued by any woman that he'd found himself wanting to see her again just to make certain she was as real as the attraction he felt for her. If his missing husband case hadn't taken him on a three-day jaunt through Las Vegas and Lake Tahoe he'd have called on Ryanne much sooner. Now that he was back, Hugh intended to make up for lost time.

"I'll have to give Aggie a good brushing before I let her back into the house," Ryanne informed him as she moved slowly around the deck searching for the patio table. Before she'd left for her walk, she had placed Aggie's grooming comb on the table so she wouldn't have to track sand inside to retrieve it, but now the table was proving elusive.

Hugh watched her grope around, wondering what he should do. It was obvious Ryanne had lost her bearings; she was moving away from the table rather than toward it. For the first time since he'd met her, Ryanne seemed vulnerable, and the reality of her blindness was driven home. It made Hugh's heart ache. For a second he considered sim-

ply retrieving the grooming equipment himself and handing it to her, but he quickly reconsidered. He couldn't treat
her as though she were helpless. Yet he couldn't just stand
and do nothing, either.

"The table's behind you, Ryanne," he said finally.
"About five feet or so."

Ryanne smiled as she moved in the direction he indicated. "Obviously I need to grow eyes in the back of my
head," she quipped. With a sweep of her hand across the
table she located the comb, then turned to Hugh and looked
at him seriously. "Thank you. Nine out of ten people would
have just handed it to me."

"I didn't think you'd want that," he told her, matching
her quiet, sincere tone. A kind of understanding passed between them that made Hugh feel as breathless as he felt
when he saw her lovely smile.

She gave him a softer version of that smile now, but it was
no less effective. "You're right. There are so many things I
simply can't do that it's important to me to do for myself the
things I can."

"I figured that out the other day when you wouldn't let
me call Security Watch."

Ryanne laughed. "And look where that got me."

"Would you like me to make the call now while you're
brushing Aggie?"

"That would be great. The phone is on the bar in the
kitchen."

Hugh knocked the sand off his sneakers but before he
could reach the door Judith appeared and sent him a quell-
ing glance. "I see you found her."

"Yes, thanks to you," he responded politely.

Judith didn't seem to appreciate being reminded that
she'd done something nice. She looked away from him and
spoke directly to Ryanne. "Right after you left, *he*—" she

jabbed an accusing finger at Hugh "—called, and right after that the Security Watch people finally showed up.
Needless to say, I haven't gotten any work done."

"But the security system is fixed?" Ryanne asked hopefully.

"So they said."

"Wonderful!" Ryanne smiled happily at Hugh. "I guess
you don't get to play Sir Galahad after all."

He snapped his fingers. "Drat the luck! Now I don't have
any leverage to coerce you into spending Saturday with me."

Ryanne started to comment, then changed her mind. Instead she turned to her secretary. "Judith, since your work-
day has already been shot, would you mind fixing Hugh and
me something cold to drink? He's going to keep me company out here while I brush Aggie and I know you'd rather
I didn't track sand into the house."

Judith sighed. "All right. What do you want? There's a
pitcher of iced tea already made."

"That would be fine, thank you," Hugh answered as he
moved to the table and sat in one of the cushioned deck
chairs.

"Me, too, Judith. And bring a glass for yourself."

The door slid shut and Ryanne knelt beside her dog to
begin combing the sand out of Aggie's silky golden hair.
Hugh could tell that something was bothering Ryanne, but
her inconsequential small talk gave him no clue as to what
it was. Judith returned shortly with a tray bearing a pitcher
of iced tea and two glasses. She placed them on the table in
front of Hugh, giving him a strange, hard look as she did so.
Her frown was even more disapproving than usual, and
Hugh wondered why she seemed so displeased until he remembered his comment about coercing Ryanne into a date.
Apparently Judith didn't approve.

"Aren't you joining us, Judith?" Ryanne asked as she unfastened Aggie's lead from the deck railing and rose.

"No, thanks. Some of us have work to do in the middle of the afternoon."

"In that case," Ryanne said patiently, "would you mind taking Aggie in for me? I'm sure she could use a drink, too."

Judith sighed and took the lead and grooming comb Ryanne held out to her. "Why not? Come on, beastie." Before she went inside, she stepped back toward the table and tapped the back of the chair beside Hugh's. "The chair's here," she informed Ryanne, tapping it again.

Grateful for the sound cue that kept her from groping around like an idiot again in front of Hugh, Ryanne moved toward the tapping. "Thank you."

Judith grunted and took Aggie into the house. As the door slid shut, Ryanne swept her hand over the table until she encountered the tray. She filled both glasses, placed one in front of Hugh, and settled back. "Now, where were we?"

"We were making small talk until we could be alone and you could say whatever it is you wanted to say to me."

Ryanne chuckled. "You're very perceptive."

"It's an occupational hazard that sometimes spills over into my personal life," he told her seriously. "Do you want to explain why it bothers you so much that I invited you out on a date?"

"Oh, Hugh..." Ryanne took a deep breath and released it as a wistful sigh. "Even under normal circumstances I don't date much."

"What do you mean by normal circumstances?"

"Back in Chicago, on my own turf, working within my regular routine," she explained.

"Why not?"

Ryanne shrugged. "It's just more of a hassle than it's worth. I go out with friends occasionally, but the 'You Tarzan, me Jane' dating ritual is something I don't particularly enjoy. I never have.''

"I see," Hugh said thoughtfully. "What if I promise I won't do my Tarzan yell even once and swear that our date would be strictly platonic?''

Ryanne's gaze was so direct that Hugh was almost convinced she was seeing straight through him. "If you promised that," she said softly, "you'd be lying and I'd be very disappointed." Embarrassed by her own bluntness, Ryanne averted her head. "Sorry. I probably shouldn't have said that. I may be reading this situation all wrong. For all I know, you're just trying to be congenial to me because Douglas asked you to.''

"No, Ryanne," Hugh said gently. "You're not misreading the situation and I'm not just doing Doug Sutherland a favor. You're an intelligent, beautiful, witty woman and I am very attracted to you.''

"And I'm attracted to you as well, Hugh," she admitted. "But the fact remains that for me dating isn't a very good idea.''

"But why not?" Hugh pressed, then pulled back. "Sorry. Look, Ryanne, I'm not trying to railroad you. I admit that taking no for an answer is not something at which I excel, but if you want me to take a hike, I will. If that's the case, though, I'd like to understand why." He hesitated a moment before asking. "Is it because you're blind?''

Ryanne's esteem for Hugh rose several notches. Except for Judith, nearly everyone Ryanne knew was uncomfortable with her blindness and tried to pretend it didn't exist. Hugh on the other hand seemed to accept it as a matter of fact, something to be acknowledged and then dealt with as gracefully as possible. She liked that attitude a lot, because it told her he wasn't feeling pity for her as she'd first suspected. And she liked Hugh a lot, too. Which was one of the reasons she didn't want to go out with him.

"Quit while you're ahead" was Ryanne's motto where men were concerned. Right now, Hugh liked her. He was attracted to her. But if she spent the day with him as he'd suggested, all that would change. Once he got a good dose of what it was like to date someone who was blind, the attraction she sensed emanating from him and the regard she heard in his voice would vanish, and Ryanne would be left feeling inadequate and disappointed.

She couldn't say that to Hugh, of course, but neither could she lie to him. "My blindness has a lot to do with it, yes," she admitted, leaning forward intently, hoping to make him understand. "Hugh...have you ever had a blind date? I mean a real *blind* date? It isn't a carefree picnic in the park. In fact, it can be damned inconvenient at times. I don't know my way around Los Angeles, and neither does my guide dog. Aggie and I both would be almost totally dependent on you. *My* restricted mobility would be a restriction on you. You've only seen me in settings where I'm comfortable—where I know my way around. Once you see me out in the real world I'm afraid you'd be very disillusioned."

Hugh considered her words carefully, but she hadn't said anything that discouraged him. "I'm willing to take that chance if you are."

But I'm not *willing to take that chance,* she wanted to shout. She'd been down this road before, had given in and accepted invitations from people she'd dated before her accident, people she should have been comfortable with. The result was always the same. The moment the novelty of her blindness wore off, disappointment set in. Things became awkward and strained, and the date ended in disaster. And if that was the way it happened with old friends it was bound to be much worse with Hugh, this handsome, charming man who was little more than a comfortable stranger.

Every instinct for the self-preservation of her heart and her ego cried out to Ryanne to say no. Inside her head, though, another tiny voice of hope was saying *Maybe this time it will be different.* And Hugh had issued her a challenge of sorts. Perhaps the only way to prove to him that it was a mistake for them to spend Saturday together was to take the risk and let him see for himself.

Praying she wouldn't regret her decision too much, Ryanne sighed. ''What time should I be ready?''

''How does 10:00 a.m. sound?'' he asked, smiling.

Ryanne heard his smug tone and wondered if his smile was as delightful as it sounded. ''Ten will be fine.'' She paused, then said, ''Do you always get your own way, Hugh MacKenna?''

''Most of the time.''

Ryanne sighed again. ''Let's hope this is one time you don't live to regret it.''

CHAPTER SIX

"Now, you've got plenty of change for a pay phone, and you've memorized the number here, right?" Judith pressed, watching Ryanne like a hawk as the younger woman finished dressing.

"Yes, Judith, I do," Ryanne said tightly, trying not to lose her temper. Ever since Judith learned Ryanne had accepted Hugh's invitation she had made her displeasure obvious, and Ryanne's nerves were strung as tightly as a violin string. She was simultaneously excited and terrified about her date with Hugh, and her companion was only making things worse. "And I'm wearing my most comfortable walking shoes, Aggie has had her breakfast and she's been outside. Except for a few minor details, I'm as ready as I'll ever be, so please stop worrying."

Judith sighed audibly. "Don't get flip with me, Ryanne. This is not Chicago."

"What's that supposed to mean?" Ryanne snapped, turning to face Judith, arms akimbo.

"It means you don't have a home-field advantage. You're going to walk out of here with a man you hardly know—"

"He's a friend of Douglas's—and a private detective, to boot. What could be safer?"

"Staying home."

"Well, I'm not, so would you please get off my back!" Instantly remorseful, Ryanne apologized. "Oh, Judith, I'm sorry. I didn't mean to yell at you. I know you're just worried that I'll be hurt if this date goes badly, but—"

"Your wounded psyche is the least of my worries," Judith returned sharply. "You're not *home*, Ryanne. You don't know where anything is. L.A. is different from Chicago, but it's still a big city and there are a lot of dangers out there. All it would take is Hugh MacKenna carelessly turning his back on you for one minute and you could get so lost we'd never find you. There's not a cop standing on every street corner, you know."

Judith had a valid point, one Ryanne had considered several times herself. Aggie was the perfect example of Newton's law of inertia; once the dog started moving she would continue in a straight line until someone told her to stop, or an obstacle blocked her path. It wouldn't take much for Ryanne to get separated from Hugh and become lost. But Ryanne had calculated the risk involved and decided it was worth it. Now confronted with the issue, she calmed herself and sat on the edge of her bed. "Judith, L.A. isn't a foreign country. English is still the primary language here. If I do get separated from Hugh I'm reasonably sure someone will be able to tell me where I am and direct me to a pay phone. Frankly, though, I don't believe that will happen. I trust Hugh. I think he's capable of being responsible for my welfare."

"It's not a matter of trust or responsibility, Ryanne," Judith argued. "It's a matter of not being familiar with your particular needs."

Ryanne managed a smile. "Then he'll either learn, or get so frustrated and disgusted that he'll call it a day, bring me home and I'll never see him again."

"Which will be very painful for you."

"Aha!" Ryanne jumped up, laughing. "You *are* worried about my wounded psyche!"

There was a long pause and Ryanne suspected that Judith was trying not to laugh with her. When the other woman refused to acknowledge the accusation, Ryanne told her, "Don't worry about me, please. I've got a firm grip on what's happening with Hugh. I think he's just attracted to me now because I'm something a little different from what he's accustomed to. He'll squire me around today until he realizes that I'm more trouble than I'm worth, and that will be the end of it." Her voice was light, but a little stab of hurt accompanied her words.

"And you can handle that kind of rejection?" Judith asked quietly.

Ryanne shrugged. "I have before."

"All right." She turned to leave. "I'll be near the phone all day if you need me."

"Thank you, Judith."

The secretary left Ryanne's bedroom without further comment and Ryanne checked the time, lifting the crystal on her watch and feeling for the position of the hands. Nine forty-five. She had to hurry. She was dressed and had already finished applying her makeup, but she still needed to do something with her hair. On the other hand, Hugh seemed to like her hair loose. Ryanne moved to the bathroom vanity and expertly brushed and fluffed her long, thick tresses. Then, she lightly touched her blue trousers and floral print shirt, staring sightlessly into the mirror and wondering if Hugh would approve. This date with him had become important... far more important than Ryanne wanted it to be. She wanted to be casual about the whole thing, wanted to feel as though it didn't matter to her if Hugh ultimately became disillusioned with her. Other people went out on first dates all the time, discovered they weren't compatible and never saw each other again. But most other people didn't have two strikes against them from the outset, either.

Maybe I made a mistake, not dating more, Ryanne thought. It might have been easier if she'd given herself more chances to adjust to and overcome the feelings of rejection and inadequacy she'd experienced on her few previous dates.

Maybe it won't happen that way this time, she dared to hope. Maybe Hugh would be different. It had been such a long time since she'd been involved with someone that the idea of feeling that wonderful man-woman attraction again was very seductive. She knew instinctively that Hugh MacKenna was a man who could make her feel like a woman, make her feel wanted and desirable. And even though their relationship could last only for the brief period she'd be in Los Angeles, Ryanne was honest enough to admit that she'd take that over nothing.

The doorbell rang and Ryanne put her expectations and her fears aside. She was going to go out with Hugh, enjoy herself while it lasted and take whatever happened—good or bad—as it came.

"THE FAMOUS Grauman's Chinese Theatre has changed ownership since its heyday in the forties," Hugh informed Ryanne in his best professional tour-guide voice. They were walking down Hollywood Boulevard's Walk of Fame, and his running narration included descriptions of the famous buildings they passed, the movie star plaques imbedded in the sidewalk, as well as the colorful people they encountered. "There are more crazies per square inch on Hollywood Boulevard than anywhere else in the world," Hugh had already informed her, and having heard the guitars of street musicians clashing with the chanting of traveling, robed religious groups, Ryanne was inclined to believe him.

Now, though, they had crossed Highland Boulevard and seemed to have arrived at a section of the famous street where the sounds around were more normal—city traffic and gaping tourists.

"It's Mann's Chinese now," Hugh continued. "But fortunately, the architecture hasn't changed one bit. It's still as gaudy and delightful as it was the day Betty Grable sat down and immortalized in cement America's most famous pair of legs." He touched Ryanne's arm lightly and slowed down. "We'll make a right turn here," he informed her.

"Aggie, right, right," she instructed. The dog obeyed and Ryanne could tell immediately that they had entered an enclosure, yet she still had the sensation of the sun shining down on her. The concrete suddenly became rough and uneven, and Ryanne stopped. "Is this it?" she asked, grinning from ear to ear. "Whose famous footprints am I standing in?"

Hugh looked down and laughed. "Actually you're standing in George Raft's famous *hand*print."

Ryanne moved her feet quickly. "Sorry, George," she quipped. "Where are Humphrey Bogart's prints?"

"Over here, I think." Moving slowly, Hugh directed Ryanne around the courtyard, all the while reading the signatures inscribed in the jigsaw configuration of cement blocks. He also described the classic black, red and gold pagoda architecture that towered above them, and Ryanne was enthralled. Hugh's descriptions were so detailed and vivid that she felt she could almost see the building herself. His knowledge of movie star lore was also impressive, and Ryanne spent the entire morning laughing. She was enjoying herself more than she had in longer than she could remember.

They found Rin Tin Tin's paw prints, which did not seem to impress Aggie in the least, and when the crowd for the noon matinee began lining up they decided it was time to move on.

"Aggie, follow Hugh," Ryanne instructed. He led them through the crowd and back out to the sidewalk. "Where to now?" she asked when they stopped just beyond the line of moviegoers.

"Are you hungry?"

"Starved."

"All right. We'll go back to the car now and head down to Farmer's Market. There's a sandwich stall there that serves the best gyro west of Chicago. We can picnic at the La Brea Tar Pits."

"The Tar Pits?" Ryanne looked skeptical. "That sounds . . . interesting."

Hugh laughed. "Oh, it will be, I promise."

Allowing Aggie to set her usual brisk pace, they quickly reached Hugh's convertible, which was parked in a lot just off Hollywood and Vine. As they moved into the flow of traffic, Hugh kept up a running commentary of their location and Ryanne began to form a mental picture of a well laid out city. It was a far cry from the picturesque, winding mountainous road they had taken from Malibu to reach Hollywood.

Los Angeles was certainly a city of contrasts, Ryanne decided. Wooded hillsides overlooked palm tree lined suburban streets, and square city blocks were evidently close to a prehistoric landmark where saber-toothed tigers and mammoth elephants once disappeared in an oozing mire of tar.

They reached the Farmer's Market on Fairfax much more quickly than Ryanne had expected and Hugh led them through the winding labyrinth of covered stalls. The smell of food interested Aggie far more than Rin Tin Tin's footprints had, and Hugh began to wonder if it had been a mistake to bring Ryanne in here. The walkways in the market were narrow and crowded, and it was a struggle to keep Ryanne close while her guide dog weaved right and left, scavenging for bits of food that had been lost or discarded by the lunch crowd.

When Ryanne realized what was happening she disciplined the dog sternly, but Hugh was relieved when they finally reached the Greek sandwich stall. He read Ryanne the menu and when they had their meals in hand, he led her out of the market via a different route. With no food to distract Aggie the dog's performance improved drastically. On the way to the car they browsed the souvenir stands, and Ryanne, with Hugh's help, chose a selection of postcards to send friends back home. Then they inspected the wares at a shop specializing in imported Mexican sculptures and jewelry. Despite Ryanne's protests, Hugh bought her a beautiful pair of carved abalone shell earrings, and asked Ryanne to help him pick out a gift for Judith, as well. He claimed it was a peace offering for the irascible secretary, but Ryanne accused him of trying to buy Judith's affection. They settled on a bracelet of silver and turquoise. Hugh hoped that if the trinket didn't persuade Judith to like him, it would at least provide her with a reason not to slam the door in his face next time he came by.

He lost count of the number of times that strangers—adults and children, alike—approached Ryanne curiously and stopped to pet her lovely dog. Each time, Ryanne patiently repeated the same speech, informing the stranger that a guide dog in harness should never be petted, spoken to, or distracted in any way. She explained that petting the dog, whose natural inclination was to seek approval and affection, diminished Aggie's ability to do her job properly. It astonished Hugh that after the fifth or sixth time someone stopped to admire the dog that Ryanne could still recite her admonition so gently. Hugh was certain that if he'd been in

Ryanne's position, he'd have been barking, "Leave the dog alone, dammit!"

Despite the distractions, though, they made their way back to the car. They piled in again, with Aggie at Ryanne's feet and Hugh behind the wheel, and this time their journey was even shorter. They had gone barely three or four blocks by Ryanne's estimate when Hugh rejoiced at discovering a convenient parking space on Sixth Street.

"Well, here we are," he proclaimed, shutting off the engine.

"The La Brea Tar Pits?" Ryanne asked, her voice once again doubtful. To her right, she heard what sounded like a breeze rustling through the leaves of nearby trees. "A prehistoric tar pit surrounded by trees—in the middle of the city?"

"That's right," he replied cheerfully, climbing out of the car. "Wilshire Boulevard is just one block south of us."

"The tar pits are on Wilshire?" Ryanne asked, incredulous. "I had always imagined that they were somewhere out in the desert."

Hugh chuckled as he opened and held the door for Ryanne. "Not only are they *on* Wilshire, sometimes they are even *in* Wilshire. Every now and then the tar bubbles up and breaks through the pavement. It plays havoc with the traffic."

"I can imagine." Ryanne and Aggie joined Hugh beside the car and waited patiently while he unlocked the trunk. Obviously he had come prepared. He explained what he was doing as he extracted a cooler with soft drinks, and a serviceable blanket.

"Where did you put the bag I brought along?" Ryanne asked as he closed the trunk. "I should give Aggie a drink of water while we're having lunch."

"I've got it right here, too," he informed her, juggling the cooler, the blanket and Ryanne's canvas bag, which contained a gallon of fresh water and a stainless-steel bowl. Ryanne insisted he allow her to carry something, and eventually Hugh relented and handed her the bag containing their sandwiches.

With Hugh in the lead and Aggie commanded to follow, they moved off down the wide sidewalk. Soon they moved onto a paved path amid a grove of trees, and as they wandered in a seemingly aimless zigzag pattern, Hugh described the replicas of gigantic prehistoric sloths. The most remarkable part of the park, though, was the actual tar pit itself, a large black pit that smelled to Ryanne like fresh asphalt heated by the sun. Hugh described the life-size replica of a saber-toothed tiger crouching on a rock that jutted out over the pit, and at the other end of the enclosure, two mammoth elephants seemed to be trumpeting frantically because their baby was mired in the tar. Promising to take Ryanne to the underground museum later, Hugh led the way back to the edge of the grove and found a quiet, shady spot at which to spread out their blanket.

While Ryanne attended to Aggie's needs, Hugh put their sandwiches on paper plates and distributed napkins and a soft drink for each of them.

"You're very domestic," Ryanne complimented him facetiously as she settled across the blanket from him.

"Being a bachelor does that to you."

"You've never been married?" she asked, then took a bite of her sandwich.

"Never."

"Never found the right woman, or are you just allergic to the institution in general?"

"Severe allergy. Deadly, in fact," he told her with mock gravity. "What about you?"

"I've never taken the plunge, either."

"Why not?"

Ryanne shrugged and devoted an undue amount of attention to her gyro. "I was always so single-mindedly devoted to being a reporter that I didn't have a lot of time for developing long-term relationships. And then after I lost my sight...well, it just didn't seem too practical."

"Blind people do get married, Ryanne," he reminded her gently.

"Of course they do," she allowed. "Many have families and lead full, productive lives. But that particular life-style is just not one I envision for myself."

She could have gone on to explain that finding a man willing to encumber himself with a blind wife wasn't exactly easy. And she could have told him about her own reluctance to risk the disappointment she would inevitably suffer if she allowed herself to want to find that man. The dreams of a home and family were ones that Ryanne had forced herself to abandon. Instead she had built a new life and a new career on the premise that her independence was the most important thing in the world to her.

Uncomfortable with their discussion, Ryanne changed the subject, drawing Hugh out first with questions about his father, then carefully probing his life before he settled in Los Angeles. He told her about his restless, vagabond mother who had divorced his father when he was nine. From there, he described the succession of cities, stepfathers and "uncles" he'd been subjected to until he was finally old enough to put his foot down and insist on being allowed to live with his father.

The stories he related about his mother's exploits were all told humorously, but the picture of his childhood that emerged was less than ideal. Apparently Hugh's mother was in love with the idea of being in love, and her constant search for something that always seemed to elude her grasp had made her son's life miserable.

"You must have been a very lonely child," Ryanne commented a little sadly, remembering her own lonely years.

"It forced me to grow up a little faster than I might have liked," he admitted. "But I was born with a streak of independence a mile wide, anyway."

"Where is your mother now?"

Hugh laughed. "I got a postcard from her last Christmas that was mailed from somewhere in the Caribbean. She and husband number six—or maybe seven—were honeymooning there."

"Did your father ever remarry?"

"No. After Mother and I moved away from Chicago, Dad sold his Army surplus stores, bought a couple of fishing boats on the Gulf and became a crusty old seafaring bachelor." Hugh realized how skillfully Ryanne had elicited information from him and he laughed ruefully. "You must have been one helluva reporter, Ryanne. I haven't talked this much about myself in a long time."

Ryanne ducked her head. "Sorry. I have an insatiable curiosity about people and what makes them tick."

"And yet you hate to answer questions about yourself," he noted slyly.

It was Ryanne's turn to laugh. "Oops. I'd forgotten how perceptive you are." The remnants of their lunch had already been cleared away and Ryanne lay down on the blanket, facing Hugh with her left hand propping up her head.

"Perception is about seventy-five percent of my job," he said, reclining to mirror her position.

"What's the other twenty-five percent?"

"Dogged persistence and knowing when someone is trying to divert my attention. Like now, for instance."

She grinned sheepishly. "Sorry. I like asking questions more than I like answering them."

"Then I won't ask if you'd rather I didn't," Hugh told her seriously.

Ryanne shook her head. "No, it's okay. But you see, Hugh, you have a stock of humorous stories that paint a vivid picture of what your childhood was like. You can laugh now at how one of your stepfathers deliberately lost you at a carnival when you were twelve, and if I choose to I can take your humor at face value. Or I can look beyond the laughter to the pain you must have suffered, and get a clearer understanding of some of the forces that made you the man you are today."

"Not many people do that, Ryanne," he told her quietly. "Most are content to laugh at the stories without realizing there's anything behind them."

"And you prefer it that way, don't you?" she asked shrewdly.

Hugh cleared his throat uncomfortably. "As a general rule, yes. With you, on the other hand... well, somehow I have the feeling you'd get down to the truth no matter what I said."

"Don't give me too much credit," Ryanne warned him. "I don't have any mystical powers."

"Or funny stories about your childhood?" he asked gently, steering the conversation back on course.

Ryanne shifted her position, rolling onto her stomach so that her weight rested on her elbows. Clasping her hands she said, "No, I don't."

Hugh moved, too, stretching out on the blanket so that their shoulders were almost touching. "You mentioned once that after you lost your sight you went home to live with your aunt." He paused a moment, then asked gently, "What happened to your parents, Ryanne?"

"When I was twelve my father was killed in a hit-and-run accident. A year later my mother died of cancer."

"I'm sorry."

Ryanne sighed heavily. "So am I. Aunt Rose and Uncle Charley were wonderful to me, but I don't think I ever fully got over that sense of betrayal I felt because my parents deserted me."

"All children feel that way when they find themselves alone, Ryanne. Surely you must know by now that they didn't have a choice."

She frowned and her voice took on a faraway quality. "No, Hugh, they both had choices. Daddy's decision I can understand, but not Mother's. After Daddy died she just gave up on life. When her cancer was diagnosed she refused treatment, not because she was frightened of the surgery, but because she just didn't want to live any longer. Having a daughter who needed her wasn't a good enough reason to fight."

If that were true, Hugh could understand how Ryanne might still feel betrayed by her mother's death, and he told her so. He wanted desperately to reach out to her, but he held that desire in check, fearing she might pull away. Somehow he sensed that if he moved too quickly, presumed too much about this relationship that was still so very fragile, he would lose her.

Reminding himself to go slowly, he concentrated on something she had said that puzzled him. "What did you mean when you said your father had a choice, too?"

Ryanne gave him a crooked smile. "Did I say that?"

"Yes, you did," he affirmed seriously, refusing to be diverted. Something wasn't right and he wanted to know what it was. "How can you blame your father for being in a hit-and-run accident?"

"He didn't have to walk out into the street, did he?" she quipped with morbid humor.

"Ryanne!"

"Sorry," she apologized unremorsefully. She had no intention of talking about how her father had died. It struck her far too close to home. "Look, Hugh, could we drop this, please? Let's just say that both of us survived our somewhat unpleasant childhoods and go on from there."

She sat up and Hugh followed suit. "All right. What's next then?" he asked.

"Well, let's see...." Ryanne thought for a moment, an impish grin replacing the look of sorrow that had marred her face moments earlier. "We could sit here a while longer and keep poking around at each other's deep, dark secrets, or we could complete your guided tour."

"Oh, the tour, definitely. Our secrets can wait until another time."

CHAPTER SEVEN

"Is THERE ANYTHING I can do to help?" Ryanne asked when Hugh came out of the kitchen and joined her on the deck. She was exhausted from their day on the town, but she felt a little guilty about sitting with her feet up while Hugh did all the work.

"Not a thing. Here." He handed her a fluted wineglass and sat in the cushioned deck chair beside her. "The grill's almost ready, the table is set and everything else is just waiting. How do you like your steak cooked, by the way?"

"Medium rare." She sipped her wine and smiled. "You're going to spoil me rotten with this Julia Child impersonation. Judith and I usually share the cooking chores."

"Are you a good cook?" Hugh asked with interest. It was rapidly becoming a consuming passion to know everything there was to know about the fascinating woman beside him.

"I'm terrible. Aunt Rose used to cringe when I put water on to boil. She badgered me all the time I was in high school and college to take home economics along with my journalism courses, but I was still living at home then, and I didn't realize that reporters had to feed themselves."

Hugh chuckled, watching Ryanne's animated face. Just above the horizon the sun hung like a gilded medallion. It bathed Ryanne in amber light and turned her hair to molten gold. She was unbelievably beautiful and he wanted her. Badly. It was a struggle to keep his mind off that growing need and keep track of their conversation. "Earlier today you mentioned something about being single-minded regarding your career," he reminded her, thinking of the quiet, unrevealing hour they'd spent sharing a blanket in the park. "What made you want to be a reporter so badly?"

For an instant Ryanne's expression took on that sad, haunted look he'd witnessed in the afternoon, but she answered him promptly. "My father was a journalist. I can't remember ever wanting to be anything else."

"Because you liked the job, or because you wanted him to be proud of you?" Hugh asked gently.

Ryanne turned her face toward his, capturing his eyes so unerringly that for a moment Hugh forgot she couldn't see. "No," she corrected him, her voice soft. "I wanted to be like him. His life stood for something—he had ideals. He believed in things like honesty, truth and decency at a time when those things were even less fashionable than they are today. He believed in fighting for what he thought was right." *And it killed him,* she added silently, turning her face toward the sunset. "Sounds hokey, doesn't it?"

"I don't think so," Hugh said, touched by the depth of emotion he heard in her voice. "I can only imagine how proud it would make him to know his daughter remembers him with such respect. He left quite a legacy behind. It must have been hard for you to have to give up being a reporter."

Ryanne nodded, pushing away the knife-sharp grief that pierced her whenever she thought of everything she'd lost five years ago. "It was. I loved it all—the interviews, the vague leads that led to big stories, chasing down elusive city officials...seeing my byline under a front-page headline and knowing I was doing something important. I thrived on it." She paused for a moment, her expression becoming wistful. "After the accident Douglas offered me a job on the desk, transcribing stories that came in over the phone from our field reporters, but I'd have gone crazy in less than a week."

For just a moment Hugh glimpsed the enormity of the vacuum blindness had created in Ryanne's life. He felt sorry for what she'd lost, but more importantly, he felt a deep respect for the way she'd put her life back together after what must have been nearly total destruction. "So you decided to write mysteries instead," he concluded.

She smiled. "Yep."

"Do you ever dream about being able to go back to reporting?"

Her smile faded. "No. That's an indulgence I can't afford." She slipped off her glasses, closed her eyes and turned her face toward the horizon again. "The sun's down now, isn't it?"

Hugh looked out over the ocean, letting himself be swept along by the quiet, languid mood that fell over them. "Mm-hmm. It just slipped out of sight. This is my favorite part of the sunset," he told her, rising to walk to the deck rail. "The bright glare is gone and all that's left is a splash of color and fading light. Smog may not be healthy, but it does spectacular things to L.A.'s sunsets."

"Describe it to me," Ryanne requested. He complied, describing the vivid line of scarlet that painted the horizon, then blended upward into hues of magenta and purple. Golden clouds hovered in the foreground and the ocean below grew dark and mysterious. As he described each detail, Ryanne added to the picture in her mind until she had an image that was breathtakingly beautiful. She visualized Hugh as well, imagining his tall, broad-shouldered silhouette in the foreground of the magnificent sunset. She'd ascertained from the sound of his voice that he'd turned toward her. He'd fallen silent, too, and the knowledge that he was watching her caused Ryanne's pulse to quicken.

They were motionless for a moment, caught in the tableau of the silent sunset. It was Ryanne who spoke first, trying to break the tension that suddenly hung thickly in the air, but her voice failed her. It came out as little more than a hushed, seductive whisper. "Are you tired of having to describe everything to me?"

"Not at all," Hugh replied, his voice as soft and smooth as satin. "You make me look at things in a way I never have before—as though I were seeing them for the first time."

Mesmerized by his voice, Ryanne remained silent. She heard him move away from the rail, but she stiffened in surprise when he sat on the edge of her lounge chair, facing her. "There are some things I just can't describe to you, though, Ryanne," he said finally.

There was a hint of a teasing smile in his voice that Ryanne couldn't help responding to. She relaxed and played along. "Such as?"

"Such as the expression on my incredibly handsome face," he said with mock seriousness.

Ryanne struggled to hide a smile. "And what expression is that?"

Hugh leaned closer, resting one hand on the opposite side of her chair. "This is my come hither, smoldering-with-sensuality look."

Ryanne pressed one hand over her heart. "Oh, my! Should I be swooning?"

"Most women do," he replied matter-of-factly.

"Okay." Ryanne threw her head back melodramatically and went limp. "How's this?"

"Your swoon needs practice."

She straightened. "Sorry. I'm not accustomed to receiving smolderingly, sensual looks from incredibly handsome faces."

"I find that hard to believe, Ryanne. Most men probably just aren't smart enough to describe their looks to you."

"Or humble enough."

"That, too."

Ryanne laughed, thoroughly enjoying their playful flirtation. Hugh was teasing her, and yet he wasn't. By making fun of their mutual attraction he was easing the fears she would normally have experienced having someone so close to her. He was making her feel wonderful, and she didn't want that feeling to end. "You know, Hugh, I think the problem is that I really don't have a clear mental picture of a smoldering, sensual look." Boldly she raised one hand and touched his face. "Let's try the visualization by touch method. Give me that look again."

"I never stopped," he informed her, keeping his voice light despite the sudden sharpening of his senses as her gentle, agile fingers lightly caressed his face.

There was a light stubble of beard on the long line of his jaw, Ryanne noted, and he had a small, Kirk Douglas cleft in his chin. Her fingertips brushed his full lower lip and darted away quickly, moving upward before she could allow herself to imagine those lips pressed to hers. His eyes were deep set and his lashes seemed incredibly long. On his forehead she discovered deep vertical lines and one eyebrow was noticeably higher than the other. It took her a moment to realize he was leering at her comically, his face shamelessly contorted. She withdrew her hand and schooled her own face into a reproachful mask.

"If this is what smoldering sensuality looks like I'm almost glad I can't see it."

Hugh straightened as though he was thoroughly insulted. "Obviously you failed to notice my striking resemblance to Robert Redford."

"That's true," Ryanne agreed. "What I got was more like Donald Duck."

"Donald Duck!" He gasped with indignation. "Just for that I ought to kiss you thoroughly and erase that fowl image."

Ryanne's heart began racing but she never gave a thought to escaping. "But sir, I've never been kissed by Donald Duck, therefore, I wouldn't know whether you kiss like him or not."

"Have you ever been kissed by Robert Redford?"

"No."

Without warning, Hugh slipped his arms around Ryanne, pulling her so close that his breath was warm against her face. "Then I can't possibly lose, can I?"

Ryanne's laugh was smothered when Hugh's lips touched hers. A delightful, erotic shock wave coursed through both of them and all playfulness left Hugh's kiss. He drew her even closer, teasing her lips with his tongue, exploring and tasting, just as he'd wanted to from the moment he met her. Stunned by her own eager response, Ryanne placed one hand at the back of Hugh's head while the other tested the breadth and strength of his chest and shoulder. The kiss deepened and ignited fires in both of them, but a cold, wet nose abruptly extinguished them. Aggie, who had been resting peacefully beside Ryanne, took exception to being excluded from this interesting new game and she pushed between them excitedly.

Hugh drew back and looked at the dog trying to crawl onto Ryanne's lap. "I thought they were trained to *guide* their owners, not *guard* them."

Ryanne grinned and ordered Aggie to sit. "They're not. That playful curiosity is just a fringe benefit."

"This could pose a serious obstacle to the development of our relationship, Ryanne," he told her jokingly, but Ryanne took his comment seriously.

"Do we have a 'relationship,' Hugh?"

Lightly, Hugh brushed a lock of hair away from Ryanne's forehead. "We could have. If you want it as much as I do."

"You mean I haven't managed to scare you off yet?"

Her voice was light, but something in her tone betrayed her. "Have you been trying?" he asked in response.

She shrugged and shifted so that there was a little more distance between them. "Frankly I figured I'd accomplish that just by being myself."

Frowning, Hugh stood, retrieved both their glasses and refilled them from the bottle of wine on the serving cart next to the French doors. "Then you were either underestimating yourself or me, Ryanne. I'm not quite sure which."

He touched the wineglass to the back of her hand and Ryanne took it from him, subdued. All their former playfulness had evaporated. "You're angry, aren't you?"

"Angry? No," he said, sitting on the edge of her chair again. "Just confused. You know, the other day you said something about being afraid I'd be disillusioned after I'd spent some time with you."

"That's right."

"Well, we've spent time together now, and I haven't been disillusioned in the least."

"Are you sure?" she asked, wanting to believe him because his friendship had become so important to her.

"I'm sure, Ryanne. If I had gotten tired of you or fed up, or whatever else it is you expected, why would I have invited you here for supper? Why didn't I just drop you off on your doorstep, say *adiós, muchacha*, and beat a hasty retreat?"

Ryanne lowered her head and fidgeted with her wineglass. "Maybe you brought me here for the payoff," she suggested, hating herself even as the words came out. She didn't believe Hugh was like that, but she had to be sure.

"The *payoff*," Hugh repeated disgustedly. He stood and moved away from her toward the deck rail. "Ryanne, in case you haven't been keeping up on current events, let me clue you in. The era of the quick seduction and the one-night stand is over. Women aren't the only ones looking for so-called meaningful relationships anymore."

He took a sip of wine, then continued. "Now I will admit that this poses a few problems for confirmed bachelors like myself, but just because I have no desire to get married and settle into suburbia doesn't mean that I don't crave feminine companionship—not just sex, but real intimacy and friendship, too. I happen to have a particular weakness for attractive, intelligent, fun career women and you fit all those categories very well. Maybe too well."

Ryanne smiled. "What do you do if one of those attractive career women gets a little too serious and wants to replant you in suburbia?"

Hugh pushed himself away from the rail and returned to sit beside her. "That happens a lot less often than many people would think. Usually most of my relationships dissolve by mutual agreement. You'd be surprised by the number of women out there who are just looking for a simple, uncomplicated friendship with a male while they focus on their careers."

Ryanne nodded, understanding what he was trying to tell her. He was laying out the ground rules, and inadvertently explaining one of the reasons he found her attractive. Long-term, lifetime commitments were something he would always avoid, but Ryanne was only in town for a few months. Once her screenplay was finished she would head back to her life in Chicago and Hugh knew it. He was offering her a comfortable, friendly relationship while she was in Los Angeles, and when she left he would no doubt expect them to say "So long" and part with a friendly kiss.

Ryanne was amazed that she found the idea so attractive, but then, she couldn't recall anyone who'd ever attracted her the way Hugh MacKenna did. She had dated regularly in college and during her first years as a reporter, but she'd been too career oriented to involve herself in a serious romance. With the blind optimism of youth, she had always assumed that a husband and children would eventually come along, but she'd been in no rush. And because of the moral values her parents, and later her aunt and uncle, had instilled in her, she didn't believe in sleeping around. Her only affair had been with a good friend in college, someone Ryanne had liked and respected, but whom she had known instinctively would never demand more from her than she was ready to give.

And then she'd had the "accident" that had forced her to abandon her nebulous dreams of a warm, loving man to share her life. She hadn't counted on charming, funny Hugh MacKenna coming along and offering her a short-term, no-strings romance, but Ryanne knew already that she wasn't going to reject the proposition. She would have to guard her heart, of course, and not do something stupid like falling in love. But so far, Ryanne had managed to avoid that pitfall for all of her thirty-three years; surely she could continue that record for another few months. The opportunity to be wined and dined, courted, romanced and made to feel like a woman by an attractive, desirable man was something she couldn't pass up. More importantly, she didn't *want* to pass it up.

There was still one last issue, though, that had to be gotten out of the way once and for all. "Hugh, it really doesn't

bother you that this—'' she pointed to herself ''—purport-
edly attractive, intelligent, funny career woman just happens to be blind?''

Hugh reached for Ryanne's left hand and turned it palm
up. Gently his thumb caressed the small, callused ridge that
her guide dog's harness had put there. ''It bothers me,
Ryanne, because it's made you doubt yourself. It's made it
hard for you to believe that a man could find you special
enough that knowing you, being close to you, would be
worth whatever problems or inconveniences your blindness
might cause.''

Ryanne could tell that it was dark now—the sun was no
longer warming her face—and she didn't think Hugh had
put on any lights yet. She hoped that the evening shadows
were hiding the tears that pooled in her eyes. Leaning forward, she reached out gingerly and cupped Hugh's face in
her hands. Her thumbs lightly brushed his mouth, then her
lips followed suit. She let them linger there for a moment,
and Hugh accepted the kiss for what it was.

''Thank you,'' she whispered, smiling shyly as she pulled
away.

''Thank *you*.'' More than anything, Hugh wanted to pull
her into his arms for a fuller taste of the sweetness he'd
glimpsed so briefly, but he knew it was not the time. This
wasn't a relationship he wanted to rush—it was too special
for that. ''Are you hungry?''

''Does the sea rush to the shore?''

''I guess that means I should put the steaks on now.''
Hugh stood, taking hold of Ryanne's hand and pulling her
to her feet.

''If you don't I may start eating the chair cushions,'' she
warned him.

''Well...that may not be such a bad idea,'' he said, his
voice tinged with remorse.

"Why?"

Hugh tucked her hand into the crook of his arm. "Because I neglected to tell you that *I* can't cook, either."

THE NEXT DAY, in Chicago, a man named Del Michelon looked down at the busy street twenty-seven stories below his office window and contemplated the foolhardy error he had made bringing Arlen Beck into the organization. Behind him, he could hear Beck squirming in the plush chair like a worm on a hook—which was only appropriate. Beck was a stupid, clumsy fool, and Michelon didn't like "employees" with those particular characteristics. Now, more than ever, he wished he had simply disposed of the banker two years ago instead of absorbing Beck's illegal gambling syndicate into his own.

Michelon's silent treatment and that broad back planted firmly opposite him was unnerving, and Arlen finally cleared his throat tentatively. "Mr. Michelon—"

"Shut up, Arlen," Del snapped, not bothering to turn around. "I've got to decide what to do about cleaning up your stupid mess."

"Do you want her killed?" Beck asked.

Michelon finally turned. "No, I don't want her killed, you idiot. This is not the 1920s and I'm not Al Capone. Murder is a messy business and I try to avoid it unless it's an absolute necessity." Michelon eyed Beck critically. "If you'd realized that five years ago we wouldn't be in this position now."

Arlen lowered his head. "I know, sir. But Perigrino had to be disposed of—there was no other choice at the time. He had already made a deal with the district attorney—"

"I know, I know," Michelon snapped. "But you should have contracted the job out—and made sure there were no witnesses. If that girl gets her sight back—"

"But maybe she won't," Beck said, cutting him off hurriedly.

Michelon shot him a withering glance. "Why else would she be going to one of the best specialists in the country?"

"I don't know," he mumbled. "How are we going to handle it?"

Michelon hated hearing Beck say "we." He wanted to tell the glorified punk that it was his own problem, not the organization's, but Del couldn't do that because if Arlen Beck was arrested for arson, murder and attempted murder it would put Michelon's entire empire in jeopardy. In exchange for leniency, Beck would probably give them the head of Chicago's biggest gambling syndicate on a silver platter, and Del Michelon hadn't gotten where he was by losing his head—literally or figuratively.

Grimly he turned his back on Beck again. "*We* are going to wait and see what happens," he said finally. "Is your man in L.A. reliable?"

"Yes, sir. He's one of ours."

Michelon frowned and turned. "Not someone who can be traced to me, I hope?"

"Of course not."

"Good. When is the girl's appointment with that specialist?"

"June twenty-ninth at 11:00 a.m. Six weeks from Monday."

Michelon nodded. "By 9:00 a.m. on the thirtieth I want to know exactly what the doctor said."

"The doctor's reports will be confidential—"

"Then have your man bribe someone in the doctor's office, or have him break in and steal the file! I don't care which. If she's going to see again, I want to know it!"

Beck shrank from his boss's anger. His voice was small when he asked, "And if they can operate on her or something?"

"Then we won't have a choice, will we? We'll have to kill her *before* she gets her sight back and can identify you. Can your man out there take care of it?"

"Yes, sir."

Michelon stared at Beck coldly. "Good. And Beck . . . if it comes down to murder, see that it's done right this time. I wouldn't want to be in your shoes if you botch it again."

"That's not going to happen," Beck promised fervently, rising. "If there's even the slightest chance she'll see again, Ryanne Kirkland will be dead. You can count on it."

CHAPTER EIGHT

"OH. IT'S YOU." Judith stood at the front door, staring at Hugh through narrowed, suspicious eyes.

"It's nice to see you, too, Judith," he said good-naturedly. It had taken a while, but Hugh had finally gotten accustomed to the secretary's peculiarities. On the outside she was as crusty as the barnacles on one of his father's boats, but inside she was as soft as a marshmallow—particularly where Ryanne was concerned. He even suspected that Judith was developing a soft spot for him, but he couldn't be sure. In the month that he'd been dating Ryanne, he and Judith had developed a friendly animosity that kept them both on their toes. "May I come in?"

"I'm expecting the caterers," she informed him firmly.

Hugh nodded as though that explained everything and rephrased his request. "May I come in if I promise not to scare them away when they get here?"

She sighed heavily and stepped back. "I suppose so."

Hugh moved past her into the living room. "Judith, may I ask you a personal question?"

"Only if you absolutely have to."

"Is there anyone in the world you like?" he said teasingly.

Judith closed the door and looked at him dispassionately. "I like caterers."

"Oh. Next time I come by I'll bring food, then."

"In your case it wouldn't help." She moved off toward the kitchen and Hugh followed her, chuckling.

"You're a tough nut to crack, Judith." Aggie came bounding at him down the hall and Hugh bent to scuff her ears. "At least Aggie is pleased to see me," he told Judith with a grin.

Judith's answering look told him how little that endorsement meant to her. "I thought you were meeting your father at the airport today."

"Not until noon. I had an hour or so to spare so I thought I'd drop by and see if you or Ryanne needed any last minute help with the party. Where is she, by the way?"

Judith's disgruntled look turned to one of concern and Hugh swatted Aggie lightly on the rump to send her off. He straightened and moved to Ryanne's friend. "What's wrong?"

"She's in her room—asleep, hopefully. She got another one of those damned headaches this morning."

Hugh frowned. Doug Sutherland had mentioned something about Ryanne's recurring headaches when they'd first talked on the phone more than a month ago, but until a couple of weeks ago that bit of information hadn't really sunk in. He had taken Ryanne to a charming little Italian restaurant out in the valley, and halfway through the fettuccini Ryanne had turned white as a ghost and nearly fainted. It had been obvious that she was in severe pain and Hugh had spirited her home and into bed. Deeply concerned, he'd wanted to stay with her, but Judith and Ryanne had both protested.

"It's just a little headache," Ryanne had told him, trying to make her voice strong and reassuring but failing miserably.

"Ryanne, *little* headaches don't make people pass out."

"I didn't pass out. I just got a bit dizzy, that's all."

"Tell that to the waiter at Viva Italia. He nearly called the paramedics, and I probably should have let him! Ryanne—" he sat on the edge of the bed and took her hand "—obviously this has happened before. Have you seen a doctor?"

Ryanne shook her head and winced from the effort. It had been clear to Hugh that it was costing her a lot just to keep track of what he was saying, but he was too worried to let the matter drop. "Not yet."

"Her headaches just started a few months back, not long before we came out here," Judith told him as she placed a cold cloth on Ryanne's forehead. Then she gave her charge a couple of aspirins and ushered Hugh out of the bedroom and down to the kitchen before completing the explanation. "They were mild at first, but when they started getting worse we decided she should see someone about them."

"Are they related to the fall that caused her blindness?"

Judith shook her head helplessly and poured them both a cup of coffee. "We don't know that yet. The doctor who treated Ryanne after the attempt on her life has retired since then, but she called him anyway. When he found out she was coming to L.A., he referred her to a doctor out here who specializes in neurological disorders. Supposedly he's one of the best in the country."

"Why hasn't she seen him yet?"

"Because he's booked for months in advance, that's why. She's got an appointment on the twenty-ninth. That was the earliest they could work her in," Judith explained waspishly. Obviously she wasn't any happier about the delay than Hugh was.

Hugh's frown deepened as he sipped his coffee. "Why didn't she tell me about this?" he asked, more of himself than of Judith.

"Why should she?" Judith snapped. "Ryanne is convinced they're just plain tension headaches or something. She refused to believe that it's anything more serious. And she's probably right."

At the time Hugh had agreed with Judith's assessment, mainly because he couldn't bear the possibility that something might be seriously wrong with Ryanne. In the weeks that had passed since then, she had had two more bouts with the pain that was so intense it sent her off to bed for hours at a time.

The unfairness of it made Hugh want to strike out at something, but there was nothing to strike, which frustrated him all the more. Ryanne had dealt with so much in her life—her parents' deaths, an attempt on her life that had caused her to lose not only her sight but also the job she loved—and now there was this excruciating pain and the ever-present worry that she might be seriously ill. Ryanne had never admitted that fear, of course, and neither had Judith, but Hugh knew they felt it because he felt it, too.

Ryanne had become so important to Hugh in such a short time that it scared him, yet he couldn't bring himself to back away. She brought him a kind of happiness—a peace and contentment—he'd never known before, and he was determined to allow that feeling to run its natural course.

She was so easy to be with. During the week she worked on her screenplay and had long meetings with the film's director and producers, but many of her evenings were spent with Hugh. They took long walks on the beach or just sat quietly on the deck and shared the sunset. They entertained each other with accounts of the day's frustrations. Ryanne's recounting of the problems she was having with the movie people kept Hugh in stitches. With considerable aplomb, she dealt with their pompous, overblown egos, their daily demands for changes and even an amorous advance or two from the film's associate producer. Hugh had taken the time to read all four of her Cameron Lawe books, and Ryanne had invited him to read her screenplay. He believed her when she told him repeatedly that his insight helped her greatly, not only with her script problems, but with the business of private investigation as well.

The evenings they spent together were simple and pleasant, made up of uneventful moments Hugh had come to cherish. They livened things up on the weekends, though, and Hugh had never enjoyed Los Angeles as much as he did when seeing it through Ryanne's perspective. One weekend he took her to a glamorous star-studded restaurant, and the next they ate hot dogs while standing in line for hours waiting to see the opening of a new science fiction film. Ryanne had followed the story fairly well and had been caught up in the audience's excitement, but Hugh was convinced her greatest enjoyment of it came later when he'd been able to explain the dazzling special effects and describe to her the bizarre aliens that had inhabited the movie.

After that day, Hugh had taken Ryanne to other theaters, to see other major films so that she could experience the pleasure of being part of the crowd. In Hollywood, moviegoing was an event, and audiences applauded and cheered as though they were witnessing a stage production. Nowhere else in the world was watching a film quite the same, and Hugh wanted Ryanne to enjoy the furor. More often than not, though, they watched rented movies on the video cassette recorder at Ryanne's house, where Hugh could stop the action with the remote control and explain any important details she had missed.

Business had called Hugh out of town for an entire week, and the time had moved so slowly for him that he'd thought he would go stir-crazy. His body had been in Boston, but his mind had been firmly attached to the beautiful redhead he'd left behind in Los Angeles. When he'd returned, they had picked up as before, but their time together had taken on a new intensity, as though they both realized what a wasteland their week apart had been. They attended a play at the Mark Taper Forum, and the next night, a concert in Griffith Park. Last week he'd convinced her to take a day off in the middle of the week and they'd left Aggie behind and headed for Disneyland. The guide dog would have been welcome in the park, of course, but she couldn't have accompanied them on the rides, so Hugh became Ryanne's eyes. With her on his arm, Hugh had seen the wonderland with the unadulterated pleasure of a child.

In all the time they had spent together during the past month, though, Hugh hadn't taken Ryanne back to his beach house. Considering his growing hunger for her, he knew that if he took her there again she wouldn't be going home until morning. Ryanne was so precious to him, that he was determined not to rush her into something she might later regret.

"Hugh? Judith, did I hear Hugh's voice?" Ryanne came down the hall moving a lot slower than usual out of deference to the pain in her head.

"I'm right here, Ryanne." He went to her and touched her arm so that she would know he was close. She placed one arm around his waist and Hugh gently drew her to him, kissing her lightly on the forehead. "Judith told me you had another headache."

"The worst of it has passed," she told him, giving in to the desire to lean her head against his shoulder and absorb his warmth and strength. "I thought you'd be on your way to the airport."

"I just stopped by to see if I could run any last minute errands for the party—speaking of which, are you sure you're going to be up to playing hostess tonight? Maybe you should cancel."

Ryanne shook her head gingerly and moved away from Hugh to the bar. "No, I'll be fine in another hour or so." She sat on one of the tall stools and Judith automatically handed her a glass of iced tea. "The food's been ordered, the guests are invited, the bartender has been hired and I'm going to celebrate the completion of the first draft of my screenplay, even if it kills me."

Hugh moved behind Ryanne and began massaging her neck and shoulders. "Well, I must say, Dad is really looking forward to it. He's never been to an honest-to-God Hollywood party before."

Ryanne hooted with laughter and immediately regretted it. She leaned back against Hugh, letting her head loll forward to allow him better access. His hands were strong, yet incredibly gentle, and it felt wonderful to have him touch her. "I hope you told Webb that this is not really a 'Hollywood' party. There's no theme, no tent and no ice sculptures—it's just going to be a few people over for a friendly get-together. Frankly I'm surprised Ted and the other movie people accepted my invitation. Tonight may be a little tame by their standards."

"There you go underestimating yourself again, Ry," Hugh accused lightly. "Who could possibly resist the opportunity to spend an evening with you?"

"You want a list?" she joked.

"No, thanks. I'll just consider myself fortunate that I don't have to fight off a bevy of ardent suitors in order to have you all to myself."

They ignored Judith's disgruntled snort and settled into a discussion of the party. Hugh had willingly agreed to act as host, and Ryanne had already warned him that she wouldn't be able to do much circulating because she tended to trip over people in a crowded room. The guest list was an odd mix, but she really didn't care. Despite their eccentricities, Ryanne enjoyed Ted Braxton, the producer of *Cameron Lawe*, and Malcolm Rissling, the director. When Malcolm had insisted she meet a few of the other preproduction people, Ryanne had decided to throw a small get-acquainted party. Then Hugh had told her that his father, Webb, would be flying in for a week's visit and Ryanne had gladly included Hugh's father. She had even invited a couple of Hugh's associates from the agency. She'd heard so much about their adventures that she could hardly wait to meet them.

All in all, Ryanne estimated that her small get-together had grown to a full-fledged party of some thirty people or so, but she wasn't worried. Hugh and Judith would be there to help her, and she really wanted to share some of the happiness she was feeling these days.

It didn't take any soul-searching to recognize the source of that happiness. It was Hugh MacKenna, pure and simple. She was enjoying the work on the screenplay, but even the fulfillment she got from meeting that challenge was nothing compared to the way Hugh made her feel. He was considerate and charming, intelligent and intuitive. He was as comfortable to be with as an old shoe, but at the same time he made her feel dizzy and breathless—as if she was on a roller-coaster ride. Most of all, he made her feel like a woman, and Ryanne was learning to relish that treatment for the first time in her life.

She joked a lot about being anxious to get her screenplay finished, but in reality she was grateful that she was a long way from having a finalized script because when she did have one there would be nothing to keep her from returning to Chicago. The thought of that always brought a pang of deep sorrow that almost felt like grief, yet Ryanne refused to dwell on the errant emotion. She couldn't afford to. Hugh had made it clear that their relationship was only temporary, and Ryanne had managed to convince herself that was the way she wanted it, too. She simply couldn't let herself fall in love; to do so would mean betraying the pact she and Hugh had agreed to that first night at his beach house. If Hugh ever suspected that she cared more for him than she should, he would end their relationship immediately, so Ryanne kept her growing emotions under control.

It wasn't easy, of course. Ryanne had never met anyone like Hugh. His strength was tempered with kindness and his playful sense of humor was a constant delight. He was caring, compassionate and endlessly patient with the inconveniences Ryanne's handicap caused him, yet never once had he made her feel inadequate or clumsy. In short, he made Ryanne want all the things out of life she'd thought she'd never be able to have.

But allowing her thoughts to move in that direction was dangerous, and Ryanne spent little time dwelling on the future. Regardless of how Hugh made her feel, she had no future with him, and Ryanne had to constantly remind herself of that fact. She told herself that returning to the security of her life in Chicago was vitally important, that her friends were in Chicago and she missed them, that her mobility was hampered by her unfamiliar surroundings, and that the sprawling city of Los Angeles would never feel like home. If she tried hard, Ryanne could come up with a dozen reasons why a long-term relationship with Hugh Mac-Kenna would never work.

Most of those reasons went right out the window when she was with him, though. It took a great deal of effort to live strictly in the present. To reassure Hugh she was keeping their relationship in perspective, Ryanne constantly alluded to her eventual return to Chicago. She fervently hoped he never realized that the repeated gesture was also a desperate attempt to remind herself of the inevitable.

The caterers finally arrived and Hugh left for the airport, promising to return with Webb that evening before the other guests showed up. By the time he kept that promise the house was ready for a party and so was Ryanne, but Judith was still upstairs changing.

"I've got it, Judith!" Ryanne called to her when the doorbell rang. She hurried to the foyer and paused at the door. "Hugh?" she called out. Even her excitement about the party couldn't negate five years worth of caution. Not until Hugh answered did she unlatch the door and step back to admit him. "Good evening, sir."

Hugh stood in the doorway, momentarily speechless. Ryanne was stunning. Dressed in a khaki-colored jumpsuit that was adorned with epaulets and gold buttons, and was tapered at the ankles, she would have looked ready for a safari if not for the way the soft, clingy fabric shimmered and adhered to her every curve. A small cluster of diamonds glittered at her throat, and her fiery red hair framed a face flushed with excitement. What got to Hugh most, though, was the smile that invariably made his heart turn over in his chest.

"You are gorgeous," he said, stepping forward. He took her hands and bent to kiss her, letting his lips linger over the greeting.

Behind Hugh, Webb MacKenna smiled broadly and cleared his throat. "Don't mind me, you two. I'll just stay here in the door and stand guard."

Her face flaming with embarrassment, Ryanne hurriedly broke away from Hugh and extended her hand. "I'm so sorry, Mr. MacKenna. Please come in."

"Dad, in case you hadn't already guessed, this is Ryanne Kirkland. Ryanne, my father, Webb MacKenna."

"It's a great pleasure to meet you, Ryanne. You're everything my son told me you were, and more. I particularly agree with the part about how gorgeous you are." He tucked Ryanne's hand into the crook of his arm and together they strolled into the living room while Hugh closed the door and followed.

"Thank you." Ryanne smiled up at him. Webb wasn't quite as tall as his son, but his voice was just as warm, and his manner equally as open and friendly. Ryanne made a mental note to corner Judith later tonight and ask her if the two men favored each other. "Hugh has told me a great deal about you, as well. Please, have a seat," she invited him.

"No, no. I came to work. Hugh took the liberty of appointing me assistant host for the evening's festivities."

"Wonderful! What exactly does an assistant host do?"

Hugh eased Ryanne away from his father and took her into his arms. "He bails out the host occasionally so that I can spend more time with the host*ess*."

"Oh, how nice!" Ryanne turned her million-dollar smile on Hugh's father. "I hope you're very good at your new job, Webb."

Since there was nothing to do until the guests came, Ryanne insisted they sit for a few minutes so that she and Webb could get acquainted. The bartender Judith had hired arrived and Hugh directed him to the bar while Ryanne and Webb fell in love with each other.

Standing across the room, watching them, Hugh felt an enormous swell of pride. For all his sixty-three years, Webb MacKenna was still a youthful, vigorous man, brimming with life and good humor. He had the uncanny ability to make friends everywhere he went, which probably accounted for the popularity of his charter business. And Ryanne was—well, Ryanne was Ryanne. There was simply no one else like her.

"Did Ryanne finally get smart and dump you for some-one older and wiser—not to mention better looking?" Judith asked quietly as she came up behind him to inspect the young bartender's setup.

Hugh turned to her, ready with the snappy retort he knew she'd expect, but when he looked at her his voice failed him for the second time. Dressed in a casual pastel blue suit with a tapered skirt and unconstructed jacket, she looked like a different person. Her hair, normally a nondescript mass of severe, permed curls, was styled so that it was loose and full, and as a result, all the angles of her face were softened. She had even made a concession to the occasion by wearing a light application of makeup. It took Hugh a moment to take in the dramatic changes and finally find his voice.

"Judith, I hardly recognized you. If you'd learn how to smile I could guarantee that you'd be the second most beautiful woman here tonight."

"Forget it," she said flatly. "If I smiled, the shock would probably give you a heart attack."

"Quite likely," Hugh agreed.

She paused to consider that for a moment. "On second thought, it might be worth the effort, after all."

"Judith, you are one in a million." Hugh laughed and before the secretary could protest he planted a swift kiss on her cheek.

Startled, Judith pulled away quickly and tried not to look pleased. "You do that again, buster, and I'll break both your lips."

"Do I hear my son being threatened?" Webb asked good-naturedly, rising as he noticed Judith. Hugh took Judith's elbow and ushered her across the room. "What has he done this time?"

"He's getting as fresh as a June apple—and just about as sweet," Judith told him sarcastically. "Didn't you ever consider teaching him any manners?"

"*You've* got to be Mrs. Tremain," Webb guessed, chuckling. Ryanne made the formal introductions and the elder MacKenna asked, "Should I take the boy outside and give him a sound thrashing?"

"You should have thought of that thirty years ago." Judith sat and the men followed suit.

Twenty minutes later the guests started arriving, and for the first hour or so Hugh kept Ryanne at his side, her hand resting lightly on his arm as he guided her through the room. Finally, though, Malcolm Rissling captured her for a lengthy conversation about the problems the art director was having finding a suitable location for the movie's primary action sequences. When Malcolm spirited Ryanne away to the settee in the corner, Hugh drifted over to Mo Johnson and his attractive date.

Candy, a tall, leggy blonde who'd started the evening with Rissling, attached herself to Hugh, and though she was exceedingly beautiful, Hugh found the ingenue's conversation a little on the vapid side. He had never been particularly attracted to women who affected Candy's brand of helpless charm, and after a while, her attentions became cloying. He would much rather have been with Ryanne, enjoying her insights into the people around them, her sharp wit, and her own particular brand of seductive allure that was unintentional and unaffected.

When Ben Rosenthal, another of Hugh's partners at the agency, joined them, Hugh quickly turned Candy over to Ben and went off in search of his father. He found him in the kitchen with Judith, arguing over the arrangement of a plate of canapés, and they were having such a good time trading insults that Hugh couldn't bring himself to interrupt. He watched them for a moment and concluded that Webb MacKenna might finally have met his match in Judith Tremain—or vice versa. He wasn't sure which.

Hugh meandered back out to the bar, ordered a scotch and soda, and started mingling again. Ryanne was surrounded by a group of the movie people she'd hoped to get acquainted with, and Hugh wandered in and out of her conversational circle for the rest of the night until the party began breaking up shortly after midnight.

When Ryanne closed the door on the last guest, Hugh and Webb declared the evening a rousing success, and Ryanne collapsed against the door, exhausted but happy. "If it *was* a success, it's all thanks to the host, the assistant host, and the assistant hostess, Judith. Thank you all."

"It was our pleasure," Webb replied.

"What did you think of your first Hollywood party?" Ryanne asked him, forgetting for a moment that it was her first as well.

"A little tamer than I expected, but overall it was quite nice."

"What about you, Judith?" Hugh asked as she started toward the kitchen with a tray of glasses.

"I'm glad it's over. Now things can get back to normal— whatever that is."

Ryanne pushed away from the door. "Speaking of normal, is the house an absolute disaster area?"

"It's not too much the worse for wear," Hugh told her. "We can have it cleaned up in no time."

"No, no," Webb protested, picking up an empty hors d'oeuvre tray with one hand and a full ashtray with the other. "Judith and I will take care of this mess. You two just go out on the patio and get out of our way."

"Webb's right," Judith chimed in. "We can get this done a lot quicker without you two underfoot."

The glasses clanked as she left with the loaded tray, and Ryanne shrugged expressively. "I guess she told us."

"And *I* don't have to be told twice," Hugh replied, taking Ryanne's hand. "Come on. Let's get out of here before they change their minds."

Willingly, Ryanne let Hugh lead her out into the balmy night. Somewhere down the beach another party was still in full swing and a live band was entertaining the entire Malibu Beach colony with Glenn Miller classics. The smooth strains of "Moonlight Serenade" greeted Ryanne and Hugh as they stepped to the rail.

"Finally I've got you to myself," Hugh said fervently. "I thought for a while there I was going to have to get a crowbar to pry little Chuckie Braxton away from you."

Ryanne grimaced, thinking about the amorous associate producer she'd been fending off for weeks. "I told you the producer's nephew had the hots for me."

"And you weren't kidding. He's not the least bit subtle, is he?"

"I don't think Chuck knows the meaning of the word. He's harmless, but he's really becoming a pest. He seems to have the idea that I'm some poor, helpless invalid who needs his protection."

Hugh laughed at that. "Obviously he's not much of a judge of character. You're the least helpless woman I've ever known."

Ryanne smiled, slipped her arm around Hugh's waist, and leaned her head against his shoulder. "That's idle flattery, but I don't mind hearing you say it."

He pulled her closer. "You *aren't* helpless, Ryanne. You manage to be strong and competent, but at the same time, feminine and exciting. I certainly can't fault Chuckie's taste."

Ryanne whispered a thank-you, and turned her face up to Hugh's. He took advantage of the gesture and claimed her lips in a kiss that was as gentle and undemanding as the ocean breeze and the soft music floating around them.

"Dance with me, Ryanne," he murmured, turning her into his arms so that their bodies molded together perfectly.

"I'm not much of a dancer," she warned him, fitting her hand into his.

"Just move with the music," he advised, his voice caressingly low. "This is only an excuse to hold you close."

"You don't need an excuse for that, Hugh." Dreamily content, Ryanne snuggled her head onto his shoulder and they swayed slowly, sensuously, letting the night enfold them. When the jazz band down the beach switched to a lively version of "Little Brown Jug" Ryanne and Hugh ignored the upbeat tempo, but not the physical stirrings that brought them even closer. Hugh sought Ryanne's lips and their slow dance stopped completely. She opened to him without coaxing, and they were both lost.

He gently caressed her back with one hand while the other held her firmly against him, and their kiss quickened, deepened. Ryanne moaned softly as her hand drifted up the broad, lean expanse of his chest and came to rest at the back of his head.

Every kiss is different. The thought registered somewhere in the back of her mind, sharing space with the fever Hugh's embrace always created. His every touch, every word, every movement this past month had told Ryanne how much he wanted her, and every time he held her like this he only made her want him more. Molded against him she could feel the stirrings of his body; they matched her own. She revelled in the delightful tightening of her breasts, the delicious ache between her thighs and the sinking, swirling feeling in the pit of her stomach where she felt the evidence of Hugh's desire pressing against her.... A hunger more fierce than any Ryanne had ever imagined came over her every time Hugh held her, yet she was beginning to fear that she would never know the fulfillment of that desire.

For weeks now, he had come close, then backed off as though some invisible barrier had suddenly sprung up between them. The frustration was driving Ryanne mad; and she knew that tonight would be no different from the other times he'd held her, touched her, kissed her, then left her aching.

"The music's stopped," Hugh murmured, forcing himself to release her. He had to quit now or become completely lost in the passion Ryanne evoked. He took her hand and moved back to the deck railing, too preoccupied with controlling his own fires to notice that Ryanne was fighting an internal battle of her own.

"So it has," she commented tightly, pulling her hand away from Hugh's and crossing her arms in front of her.

"Are you cold?"

Hardly! she wanted to shout, but restrained herself and lied. "Just a little."

"Maybe we should go in, then."

"Fine." Ryanne turned toward the house, but before she could step away from him Hugh touched her arm lightly, forcing her to stop.

"Ryanne, are you all right?"

Am I all right? Of course, I'm not all right, she wanted to shout. *My heart is racing, my palms are sweating, and I want to make love with you so desperately that it hurts. How could I feel like that and be all right?* The heated words were on the tip of her tongue, but she just couldn't allow them to escape. Hugh wanted her. She was convinced of that, but apparently he had a lot more self-control then she did.

Somehow she just couldn't envision embarrassing herself with a breathless, "Take me, I'm yours!" And besides, now was hardly the time or the place, here on deck with Judith and Hugh's father just inside.

Thinking back, Ryanne realized that in all the weeks they'd spent together there hadn't been an appropriate opportunity for lovemaking—since the evening they'd spent at his house, anyway. She couldn't help but wonder why. Was Hugh giving their relationship time to develop, or was he handling her with kid gloves because he thought of her as blind and vulnerable? He'd told her she was the least helpless person he knew, but did he really believe it? If Hugh was going slowly because their relationship was important to him, that was one thing; if he was afraid of taking advantage of her because she was blind—well, that was quite another.

"Ryanne?"

She turned to him and managed a smile. "I'm fine, Hugh."

"No, you're not. Something's bothering you." He took her into his arms. "Please tell me what's wrong."

All of Ryanne's senses were focused completely on Hugh, on his deep, soft voice and the way their bodies fit together. Being in his arms felt so right, how could it be wrong to tell him she wanted to make love with him? It wasn't wrong. In her heart, she knew it, but she just couldn't make herself say the words, not when there were still questions to be answered.

"I'm sorry, Hugh. I—"

"Well, Judith has kicked me out of the kitchen," Webb announced as he joined them on the deck. "Ryanne, as soon as you finish with your screenplay I want you to bring that woman down to the Gulf. We'll spend a couple of days out on the *Mary Ann* where I can boss *her* around."

With a halfhearted laugh, Ryanne stepped away from Hugh and moved to his father, grateful for his interruption. "I don't know, Webb. From what I heard tonight you seem to be holding your own with Judith. You may not need a captain's authority to get the better of her."

"She is an opinionated soul, isn't she?" Webb looked at his son. "Judith told me in no uncertain terms that it was time for us to go home so that Ryanne could get some rest."

Hugh looked indecisively at Ryanne, torn between wanting to clear the air between them and allowing her to get some rest. The look of exhaustion on her lovely face finally pushed him in the right direction. "All right, Dad. You head on out to the car and I'll join you in a minute."

Webb thanked Ryanne for the party and bade her good evening with a chaste kiss, then disappeared back into the house.

"Ryanne—" Hugh took her hands in his "—we'll finish our talk later, all right?"

"Of course." She smiled and touched his face, gently brushing his lips with her fingertips and then her lips. "Thank you for being here tonight."

"I wouldn't have wanted to be anywhere else. I'll call you sometime this week and we'll go out to dinner."

Ryanne nodded in agreement. "If Webb doesn't object, I'll see if I can get Judith to join us. We can have an old-fashioned double date."

"Oh, I don't think Dad will object at all." Arm in arm they sauntered through the house to the front door and Hugh finally, reluctantly, kissed Ryanne good-night.

Once he was gone, Ryanne tried to help with the last of the cleanup, but Judith insisted there was nothing that couldn't wait until tomorrow. Ryanne went off to her room where Aggie was sound asleep, tethered on her bed chain. She woke up as soon as her mistress entered the room and

Ryanne took the dog outside one last time for the evening, then quickly changed clothes and fell into bed.

She was exhausted, almost drained, in fact, but sleep just wouldn't come. She kept thinking of Hugh and the kiss they'd shared, and she wondered how many more restless, frustrating nights she would spend alone.

CHAPTER NINE

THE HOUSE WAS dark and silent as Hugh stepped through the French doors onto the deck. Behind him his bed was a twisted, tangled mess from all his tossing and turning. He wished he could follow the example of his father, who was sound asleep in the guest room. Hugh couldn't seem to find that same peace, probably because the release he craved was down the beach, fast asleep in her own bed—alone. Even a cold, stinging shower hadn't eased Hugh's craving for Ryanne tonight, and he knew that nothing would change until he finally ended this torture and brought her to his bed.

Unbidden, the thought of Ryanne and the way she always came to life in his arms played over and over in his mind, and his body ached with frustrated desire. For a long time Hugh had treated sex casually—as a basic biological urge to be recognized and satisfied. He'd learned, though, that a quick toss in the hay with a faceless stranger was far less pleasurable than the familiarity of a partner with whom he shared something other than the passion of the moment.

That first coming together with a woman who had been courted, who recognized as he did that holding that desire at bay made the moment of completion sweeter, was always exciting. There was a sense of exploration and discovery that heightened the passion, but Hugh enjoyed equally what came later—the camaraderie, the pleasure that came from knowing what made his lover gasp with delight or writhe with ecstasy beneath him. Sexually Hugh gave the woman in his life one hundred percent of himself, using all the skill and control at his command to bring her the same degree of pleasure he derived. Emotionally, though, he'd never learned how to offer the secret parts of his mind or his heart to that woman. He cared, but never loved; not completely, without restraint.

Sensing that, his lover usually withheld that same part of herself from him. The minute either slipped over that fine line where liking turned to loving, Hugh took steps to end the relationship gently. He knew he could never reciprocate, and that to continue would be unfair and eventually painful. And since the women he dated were, for the most part, intelligent and self-respecting, they usually realized further pursuit was hopeless. Hugh could then tell himself the break-ups were "mutual." He'd lived that way for years and had never questioned the validity of his life-style.

Until now.

The warm ocean breeze caressed Hugh's face, reminding him of the way Ryanne touched it—gently, softly, like a sigh. He thought of her beauty, her courage, and her smile, and Hugh felt a desire to possess that was stronger than anything he'd ever felt before. But it wasn't just her body he wanted to lose himself in; it was her soul and her spirit, the essence of everything that made her so remarkable. He sensed that Ryanne would be a passionate lover, and the only thing that had held Hugh back, that had forced him to control his intense need to have her, was the fact that this time he wanted it all, not just Ryanne's passion and companionship, but every part of her—all the things he'd never wanted from a woman before.

He'd moved slowly with her these past few weeks, building their friendship, earning her trust, hoping that somewhere along the way she'd begin to want the same kind of relationship he wanted.

That hadn't happened. Every time Ryanne casually mentioned returning to Chicago Hugh knew that she was still taking to heart the unspoken but mutually understood rules he'd established that night he'd brought her home. Enjoy each other, but don't look for forever after. Keep it light and simple—don't start to fall in love.

He found it bitterly ironic that this time he was the one who'd broken the rules.

HUGH CALLED the following week, and Ryanne was amazed at how little persuasion it took to convince Judith to join her with the MacKenna men for an evening on the town. Hugh insisted they dress casually and they dined on delicious, gooey spare ribs at a little eatery out in the Valley. Afterward they discussed which movie to see, but with scores of choices in Hollywood, the discussion waxed into a heated argument and finally Ryanne settle the issue.

"Miniature golf?" Hugh asked skeptically.

"What's the matter, Hugh? Are you afraid you'd lose to a mere woman?" Ryanne said teasingly, barely managing to keep a straight face.

"Your being a woman has nothing to do with it," he protested. "But if the guys at the office ever heard that I got whipped by a *blind* woman I'd never hear the last of it."

Hugh's casual reference to Ryanne's blindness threw Webb, until he realized that Ryanne treated her disability as a fact and appreciated it when everyone else did the same. Since that was the case, Webb knew he had to do his best to comply.

Though Hugh hadn't said so directly, Webb could tell that his son was falling in love—probably for the first time in his life. Webb blamed himself and his ex-wife, Sherry, for their son's perpetual state of bachelorhood. Though Hugh had always had a steady girlfriend, even in his teens, Webb knew of no one who'd ever gotten under his skin. The way Sherry skipped blithely from one "true love" to the next hadn't set much of an example for Hugh, and Webb realized that his own example had been little better.

Sherry Catlow MacKenna had been a consuming obsession with Webb, and even their devastating divorce hadn't lessened his need for her. It had taken years for the pain of losing her to go away, and he hadn't had the guts to risk another heartbreak like the one Sherry had dealt him. Nowhere in Hugh's life had there ever been a model of what a marriage could be for two people who had that indefinable magic that made a lifelong commitment work. Despite his own dismal failure, Webb was enough of a romantic to believe things like that did happen, and he wanted desperately for his son to be one of the lucky few. With Ryanne Kirkland, Webb thought Hugh might just have that one in a million chance, because she was a one-in-a-million lady.

"I've got a suggestion," he chimed in. "Since Hugh is so worried about his macho image, why don't we team up. Judith and I against Ryanne and Hugh." He clapped his son on the shoulder. "That way, when you lose—and you will, my boy—you can always claim that you were just trying to spare your old man's feelings."

The taunt was as good as a gauntlet in Hugh's face, and the issue was immediately settled. They piled into the car with Judith shaking her head at the insanity of men, and fifteen minutes later they arrived at a large fantasy land of castles, moats, fountains, waterfalls and four separate eighteen-hole golf courses. The interior of the castle was taken up with a teenager's paradise of arcade machines and video games, but once they had passed through that hazardous maze they emerged into the night, and into a cool, green garden where the four courses teed off. At Webb's insistence he paid for their game, and while they waited for a free course, Hugh pulled Ryanne to one side.

"Okay, how are we going to tackle this?" he asked, handing her a putter.

She hefted the club, testing its weight. "You'll have to describe each green to me, point me in the right direction, and then give me a sound cue—tap your putter in the hole or something. Believe it or not, I used to be very good at this."

"That's great," he told her enthusiastically, "because I am the world's worst."

"Just stick wid me, kid, an' I'll make ya a star." Laughing, they joined Webb and Judith just as their turn came up on course number two.

What followed was an exercise in pure hilarity. Not only did Hugh give Ryanne the sound cues she needed in order to putt her way through the eighteen holes, but he also used every underhanded trick in the book to distract Judith and Webb when their turns came around. He stomped and coughed and clapped his hands together to keep them warm. Judith kept pointing out that the temperature was in the eighties, but that didn't deter Hugh. He gave unsolicited advice every time Webb lined up a shot, and in general drove everyone crazy.

They laughed and argued playfully, and were generally so boisterous that Ryanne was glad she'd left Aggie at home. Disciplining her dog in the midst of all the chaos would have been nearly impossible. Also, a guide dog was only invaluable when its owner knew where she was going and what commands to issue. In this zigzagging maze Ryanne was completely lost, and Hugh was far more help to her than Aggie could have been. He was constantly at her side, giving her a feeling of unparalleled security, happiness and contentment.

With Hugh's help, she got a hole in one on the treacherous windmill hazard, but overall her scores were atrocious. Despite Hugh's attempts to even things up with his outright but good-natured cheating, he and Ryanne still lost the match by an embarrassing margin. What they lacked in skill, though, they made up for in fun, and by the time they returned home, even Judith had to admit that it had been an enjoyable evening.

The couples spent two more nights together that week, and by Sunday, when it was time for Webb to return home, Ryanne suspected that Judith was going to be very sorry to see him leave. Despite their constant bickering, a real bond seemed to have formed between them. Ryanne thought it was a shame there hadn't been more time for a little romance to develop as well. Judith had been alone for so long she deserved the attentions of someone as special as Webb MacKenna.

The day of Webb's departure Ryanne invited them over for a farewell luncheon. It took quite an effort on everyone's part not to get maudlin over the occasion.

"I'm really going to miss you, Webb," Ryanne told him as they left the dining-room table Judith and Hugh had just cleared. Webb put his arm around Ryanne and she gave him a hug. Aggie wanted in on the action and jumped up excitedly until Ryanne finally subdued her.

"I'm going to miss you too, Ryanne," Webb told her. "This has been the best vacation I've had in years. I almost hate to go, but I do have a business to run. I want you to know I was serious about that invitation I made last week. Hugh's promised to get you and Judith on that little jet of his and bring you down for a visit."

"I can't speak for Judith, but I'd love to."

Across the room Judith gave a little snort of disgust. "He'll probably get us lost in the Bermuda Triangle and we'll spend the rest of our lives floating around in limbo."

Webb moved to her. "That may be, Judith, my dear, but at least you'll be in good company."

Judith looked past Webb to his son. "I see you come by your enormous ego honestly. Your father obviously had plenty to spare."

Webb grinned. "Judith, you've got all the personality of a barbed wire fence, but I'm going to miss you just the same. Come on. I'd like to spend my last hour in Malibu on the beach. Let's go for a walk."

Judith protested that she had dishes to do, but Webb wouldn't take no for an answer, and finally they left with Aggie yapping playfully at their heels.

"Do you think they'll drown each other?" Hugh asked, taking Ryanne's hand and pulling her with him onto the sofa.

"I doubt it. Despite all their fussin' an' feudin' I think they really like each other. I certainly haven't seen Judith this happy before." Ryanne snuggled into Hugh's arms, resting her head on his shoulder.

"If that's how she acts when she's happy, I'd hate to see her when she's upset." Ryanne chuckled at that and Hugh asked, "Is Judith divorced? I've never heard a mention of her husband."

"No, she's a widow. Toby died about ten years ago. Until she came to work for me she was secretary to the circulation manager at the *Examiner*."

Hugh lifted the long strands of silky hair that cascaded to Ryanne's shoulders and pressed his lips to her throat, causing her pulse to race. "Ryanne?" he mumbled.

"What?"

"Why are we talking about Judith? We haven't had a minute alone since the party and I can think of something I'd much rather be doing."

With one hand at her waist, Hugh urged her to turn toward him, and though Ryanne complied, she couldn't bring herself to melt against him for the kiss he'd hinted at. His mention of the party brought back all the questions and frustrations she'd tried to forget, and Hugh sensed her hesitation.

"That look is back, Ryanne," he told her. "It's the same one you had last week."

Ryanne lowered her forehead to his shoulder. "I'm sorry, Hugh."

"Don't be sorry. Just tell me what's bothering you. Is it something I've said? Something I've done?"

Ryanne raised her head and gave him a rueful smile. "Actually it's more to do with something you haven't done."

With gentle fingertips, Hugh stroked her cheek lovingly. "I can't fix it if I don't know what's broken."

"I know." Sighing, Ryanne slipped out of his arms. "It's just very difficult to talk about."

"Please try." He frowned, steeling himself for whatever was to come. He tried not to think the worst—that she was going to tell him she didn't want to be with him any longer—but a painful twisting in his gut betrayed that effort.

Concerned with her own confusing emotions, Ryanne didn't hear the strain in Hugh's voice. "In a way, it's very silly—not to mention embarrassing." She stood and moved across the room hoping that a little distance would make it easier. "Hugh, last week you told me I was one of the least helpless people you'd ever known. You even said something about my being strong and competent—"

"I said those things because I believe they're true."

"Do you, Hugh? Really?"

"Yes," he answered without hesitation, growing more confused by the minute.

Ryanne sighed again. "All right, then, answer this. I'm sure you don't keep a record or have a standard routine, but...think back to the women you've dated in the past few years—back to the beginning of your relationships with them."

Hugh remembered the direction his thoughts had taken the previous week, when he'd been alone on his deck. Had Ryanne sensed that he was starting to care for her too much? Was she upset because she thought he was becoming too serious? He knew she considered their relationship just a temporary thing, but he couldn't allow himself to believe she was ready to end it now. "Why would you want me to think about other women, Ryanne?"

"Because I want to know how long you waited...that is, when you... If you waited.... I mean—"

Hugh felt the tension drain out of his body. She wasn't trying to say goodbye. "Does that very attractive blush on your cheeks mean you're trying to find a polite way to ask me how long it usually takes me to get a woman into my bed?"

"I wouldn't have put it quite that way, but yes. That's what I want to know. Hugh, we've known each other for almost two months now, and we've been dating for well over half that time. I'm not trying to push you, believe me, I'm not. I don't want you to think that...well..." She floundered again and Hugh refused to bail her out this time.

"Yes?"

Ryanne pursed her lips to hold back an embarrassed smile. "You're really enjoying this, aren't you? God, I feel like an idiot!"

Laughing, more out of relief than amusement, Hugh rose and crossed to her, but Ryanne backed away, holding up one hand to keep him from coming closer. "No. It's not funny, Hugh. I don't care about the other women you've been with, or how long it took you to get them into your bed. What I do care about is us and your attitude toward me."

Hugh could see that she was serious and upset. His smile vanished. "Ryanne, you have to know that I want you."

"Of course I know it, Hugh. I haven't had a wealth of experience in this department, but I'm not some naive Victorian virgin. Without actually saying so you tell me in a hundred little ways every time we're together that you find me desirable. And you can't possibly know how happy that makes me. But you're holding back, and I don't know why. You have to know that I want you, too. You take me in your arms, but you allow me to get only so close and then you pull away, as though I'm some fragile, vulnerable little thing who might faint at the first sign of real passion.

"You're handling me with kid gloves, Hugh," she continued frankly. "And I'm afraid you're pulling away from me because you think you'll be taking advantage of a poor, helpless blind girl who can't take care of herself. If I'm wrong, then I'm sorry. Heaven knows I don't want to pressure you into an intimate relationship if you're not ready to take that step, but I can't bear the thought of being treated like an invalid."

"Oh, Ryanne..." Deep in thought, he stepped away from her, examining the reasons he'd treated her with such extraordinary care. It wasn't her blindness, he was certain of that. He didn't think of her in terms like helpless or frail, or even handicapped, because she wasn't. Again he recalled everything he'd thought about that night on his deck. She *was* special—not because of her blindness, though. She was special because she'd touched Hugh in a way he'd never been touched before. He'd taken their relationship slowly partly out of a need to guard his own heart. Hugh had never been on the short end of a one-sided love affair before, and he had been hoping beyond hope that Ryanne's feelings would eventually match his.

As much as he wanted to, he couldn't allow himself to believe that her willingness to make love with him was the sign he'd been looking for. All he knew for sure was that it was time to stop pulling away.

Ryanne stood waiting for him to respond, growing more agitated with each second that passed. Had she said too much? Had she been too forward? Had speaking out so boldly cost her Hugh's respect? He was quiet for so long that Ryanne lost track of where he had moved to and she suddenly felt almost as vulnerable as the poor little blind girl she was trying to convince him she wasn't.

"Hugh? Are you still there?" she asked finally, unable to bear the silence a moment longer.

"I'm right here, Ryanne. I...was just trying to figure out whether or not you were right."

"Was I?"

"No. If I've been treating you differently or specially, it's because you are special to me. I look at you, think about you, hear your voice, or see your smile, and I want you so badly sometimes that it hurts. But you're right, I have been pulling back from that...desire. I suppose it's because I wanted us to be friends before we became lovers."

"I wanted that as well, Hugh," she told him softly. "And we are friends, I think. I can't believe how important you've become to me in these past weeks. But I'll be completely finished with my screenplay in a month or two and it will be time for me to leave. I don't want to rush into anything, but I don't want to go back to Chicago knowing that I wasted a lot of precious time, either. I want us to be friends *and* lovers, Hugh," she finished, her voice barely stronger than a whisper.

She heard Hugh's footfall on the plush carpet, but when he neared she needed no sound cue to judge his location. She could feel his presence, his warmth, that incredible electricity he created, and she raised her arms to him.

Wordlessly Hugh embraced her and buried his face in her luxuriant mane. Though he hated himself for it, for just a moment he was grateful she was blind so that she couldn't see the haunted expression in his eyes. He'd been only seconds away from telling her he was falling in love, but he couldn't do that now. Ryanne obviously wasn't ready to hear that yet or she wouldn't be talking about returning to Chicago.

Until Ryanne, all of Hugh's relationships had been finite. In her mind, this one was, too. Hugh wondered what it would take to convince her otherwise, and he decided that the first step toward proving to her that she was his would be taken tonight.

"I'll pick you up about eight," he promised.

CHAPTER TEN

AFTER HUGH and Webb left for the airport, the full impact of what she'd said to Hugh hit Ryanne like a ton of bricks. She'd forced the issue and cleared the air, but she'd also committed herself to making love with Hugh—tonight. She didn't regret her decision, exactly, but she didn't feel particularly comfortable with it, either. In fact, she was a nervous wreck.

She wanted Hugh, wanted to make love with him desperately, but as the afternoon crept by and she tried to keep busy and remain calm, everything began to seem planned, calculated. Tonight she would be in Hugh's arms—in Hugh's bed—for the first time, and afterward she wouldn't be able to tell herself that it had been an impulsive act or that she'd been swept away by the passion of the moment.

Feeling like a coward, Ryanne wondered if Hugh would forgive her if she backed out. He probably would, she decided. He was too kind and understanding to sling recriminations at her, but would she be able to forgive herself? The bottom line was that she'd meant everything she'd said to Hugh about desiring him and not wanting to go back to Chicago knowing that she'd wasted precious time.

The thought of leaving Los Angeles created a by-now-familiar pit in Ryanne's stomach, but she refused to think about the eventuality or the feeling it gave her. Neither she nor Hugh believed in long-term relationships, and it was entirely possible that their romance wouldn't even last through the months it took her to finish her screenplay. The mutual attraction could burn out at any time and that would be the end of it. Unfortunately that reasoning offered little more comfort. So instead of dwelling on the future or the past, she focused on the moment—on tonight—and tried to remain calm.

There were some practical arrangements that had to be worked out, and Ryanne dreaded the confrontation that would arise when Judith discovered she was planning to spend the night at Hugh's. Ryanne knew that she had to tell the older woman. It would be unfair to stay out all night without warning her; she would worry. And there was also the problem of what to do with Aggie. She couldn't let the dog wander around loose in Hugh's house all night, and it just wasn't practical to have the inquisitive, excitable animal tethered beside Hugh's bed while they were...occupying it. Aggie would have to stay home, and Judith would have to take care of the dog's needs tonight and tomorrow morning.

There was also another consideration, a very important reason Judith had to know what was going on, and Ryanne dreaded the embarrassment that it would cause both of them. It couldn't be avoided, though, and Ryanne plucked up her courage and went into the living room where Judith was watching an old James Cagney film.

"Judith, may I talk to you for a minute?" Ryanne asked.

"Sure." She turned off the set with the remote control. "All that rat-a-tat-tat stuff was giving me a headache, anyway. What's up?"

Ryanne moved to one of the chairs flanking the sofa and perched on its arm. She had to clear the nervous lump from her throat before she could begin. "Hugh is picking me up later this evening, and I don't think I'll be taking Aggie with us."

Something in Ryanne's tone alerted Judith to her friend's discomfort and she refrained from making her customary wisecrack about the dog. "Fine. If you'll feed her before you leave, I'll take her out and put her on the bed chain before I turn in."

"Thank you, Judith, but...you may also need to take her out in the morning."

"All right," she replied without missing a beat. "Should I feed her, too?"

Ryanne frowned in confusion. "What do you mean, 'All right'? Don't I get a lecture? A warning? A sigh of disapproval? Something? Just 'All right'? Judith, I'm spending the night with Hugh."

"And that's supposed to surprise me?" Judith chuckled. "Honey, the only thing that surprises me is that you've waited this long."

"You approve?" Ryanne asked, incredulous.

"It's not my job as your secretary or my place as your friend to approve or disapprove, Ryanne."

"But that never stopped you from expressing an opinion on any topic before."

"You're a big girl now, and Hugh MacKenna is a very nice man. He cares about you—any fool can see that. In the beginning I was afraid he was on some sort of macho ego trip—that being with you made him feel like the manly protector, but he's not like that. And if you're ready to make the commitment of bringing sex into your relationship, then I know you've thought it through, weighed all the pros and cons, and have decided that being with him is what's right for you." Judith reached out from the corner of the sofa and placed her hand on one of Ryanne's. "You're a pretty sharp cookie, Ryanne. I know you're not going to get in over your head."

Ryanne wondered just how true that was, but she didn't comment on it. Instead she smiled in relief. "Thank you, Judith. I thought you'd be disapproving, or at the very least, a little surprised at me."

"Surprised? How could I possibly be surprised after you typed 'contraceptive sponges' on your shopping list last week? You stuck it in there very casually between 'cotton balls' and 'spray deodorant,' but I noticed it, believe me."

Ryanne laughed, covering her face with both hands. "I suppose that would have been a clue. I didn't realize you'd already filled that list."

"I guess that means you didn't find them, then. I put a braille label on the box and set it in your toiletry basket on the vanity."

"That was very thoughtful of you. Thanks. But no, I didn't run across it. Actually... that was the other thing I needed to discuss with you. You see, years ago I was on the pill for a while, but my gynecologist had me stop, and well... I haven't had any reason... I mean, I've never used these new sponge things before, and... well..."

"You need me to read the instructions to you."

Ryanne shook her head in amazement. "Judith, why is it that you're handling this so well and I'm tripping over my tongue like an embarrassed idiot? For crying out loud, you're twenty-five years older than I am! We're from two completely different generations. You're the one who should be embarrassed about discussing contraceptives, not me."

Judith considered that for a moment. "Well, I'm not the one who's going to be needing them tonight."

Ryanne felt her blush deepen. "You have a point. Come on, let's get this over with." She stood and started down the hall with Judith right behind her.

Together they took care of the practical issue of birth control, and Ryanne was once again left at loose ends with nothing to do but worry about what was going to happen that evening. Would she please Hugh, or would he think she was clumsy and inexperienced? Sex had never played much of a role in her life. She'd certainly never met anyone who affected her the way Hugh did, who made her want to get as close as two people could possibly get.

That intense physical longing scared Ryanne. She kept trying to convince herself it didn't mean she was falling in love; but she knew that she was—that she had. Just a little, at least. Hugh was so wonderful it would have been impossible to do otherwise, and because he was only going to be hers for a short time, Ryanne wanted to savor every aspect of their relationship. Forty years from now, when she was a spunky, gray-haired old maid, she'd be able to reflect back on the wonderful, heady summer when she'd lost her heart to a handsome private eye. Of course, she wouldn't have grandchildren to tell the story to, but she'd have a heart full of wonderful memories, just the same.

The image of the future Ryanne had projected made her smile, but it didn't do a lot to alleviate her mounting fears about the coming evening. And she found herself wondering how on earth she was going to keep Hugh from sensing that she was, in fact, falling in love with him. As the day crept by, she tried to imagine what would happen and how, but that didn't help much. When Hugh picked her up, she asked herself, would they both try to act nonchalant and pretend that this date was as casual as their others had been? Would he make a joke, treat it lightly, and try to put her at ease? When they reached his home would he take her into his arms and whisk her off to bed, or would they sit and try to make small talk? She had no idea.

She tried to imagine Hugh's lovemaking, but that was certainly nothing new. For weeks she'd thought about little else. It was different now, though, because it was about to become a reality. After tonight she wouldn't have to fanta-size about what his flesh would feel like next to hers or how his mouth would feel against her breasts. After tonight she would have memories of Hugh, not dreams, and it was this that finally calmed her somewhat.

She wasn't going to the arms of a stranger tonight; she was going to Hugh. Whether her lovemaking was awkward or naive, Hugh would never judge her and find her lack-ing. He would be patient and kind, gentle and loving. If she told him she was frightened, he would kiss away her fears and replace her timidity with the passion that only he had been able to evoke in her. Above all, he would never hurt her. She knew that as surely as she knew that the sun would rise tomorrow morning, and that she wouldn't be able to see the dawning.

Calmer, filled with a sense of anticipation rather than fear, Ryanne finished getting ready for the evening. She put on a blouse of dark burgundy silk with short, puffed sleeves and tucked the tail into a pair of lightweight black pleated trousers. Her bare feet went into a pair of burgundy san-dals and she spent a considerable amount of time taming her hair, brushing it and smoothing out the unruly curls with a curling iron until it fell in soft layers around her face and onto her shoulders.

"Ryanne?"

Ryanne stepped away from the vanity and moved into the bedroom. "Yes, Judith?"

"Hugh's here."

Ryanne's mouth went dry and the moisture rematerial-ized on her palms. "Oh. Good. I didn't hear the doorbell."

"That's because he came in the back way."

"Up the beach?" she asked, incredulous.

"Yep. And I think he expects to return the same way."

Ryanne laughed and leaned against the door frame. "In that case, I won't be needing these, will I?" She slipped off her shoes and threw them into the huge canvas purse she'd planned to carry. She gave Judith a few last minute, unnecessary instructions about Aggie, said a quick goodbye to the dog, then headed down the hall to meet Hugh.

He greeted her affectionately, taking her into his arms. "You look wonderful."

Ryanne slipped her arms around Hugh's waist and all her earlier fears vanished. This was where she wanted to be. "Thank you. You *feel* wonderful." She hugged him a little tighter and placed her cheek against his throat. "You smell pretty good, too."

Hugh chuckled. "That's my new after-shave cologne. The clerk who sold it to me promised it would make me irresistible."

"He was right," Ryanne told him, tilting her face up toward his.

"Why would you assume it was a 'he'?"

She smiled mischievously. "It had to be. A woman would have known immediately that you don't need any enhancement to make you irresistible."

"Tonight, my darling, flattery will get you anywhere," he murmured, lowering his lips to Ryanne's for a light, teasing kiss. The slight contact was too much of a temptation, and the kiss quickly turned into something more. Judith came down the hall, coughing melodramatically to announce her imminent arrival, and they reluctantly separated. As she passed them she mumbled something about wanting a little privacy, and Hugh took the hint.

"I understand we're on foot tonight," Ryanne said, taking hold of Hugh's hand.

"Uh-huh. I thought you might enjoy a quiet walk up the beach."

"It sounds lovely." She shrugged. "I'm ready when you are."

"What about Aggie?"

"I thought I'd let my conscience be my guide tonight," she told him softly and Hugh groaned at the bad pun.

"In that case, may I offer you my arm, m'dear?"

"Oh, thank you." They bade Judith good-night, received a halfhearted grunt in response, then slipped out onto the deck and down to the beach.

"Judith seemed awfully quiet tonight," Hugh commented as they began their leisurely hike.

"Uh, well . . . I guess that's because I put her in a rather awkward position when I told her I was planning to spend the night with you."

Hugh moaned. "I imagine that went over like a lead balloon."

Ryanne had one hand tucked in the crook of his arm and she placed the other one there as well. "Actually she was wonderful about the whole thing."

Hugh's pace slowed as he looked down at her, his voice filled with disbelief. "You're kidding? I'm amazed she didn't lock you in a closet and throw away the key."

Ryanne chuckled. "That's sort of what I was expecting, too, but she wasn't surprised at all."

"She did know you were talking about me, right?"

"Of course! She even said some very nice things about you."

Hugh stopped dead still. "Ryanne, I think we'd better go back," he told her seriously. "Something is obviously wrong. A mad scientist has kidnapped the real Judith and replaced her with a reprogrammed clone. My God, I've heard stories about this kind of thing, but I never thought it could actually happen to someone I know personally."

Ryanne bit her lower lip, trying to keep a straight face. "Do you think we should try to get the real Judith back?"

"Oh, definitely. This is Hollywood—it's required. Judith must be saved!" he cried, adopting what Ryanne could only imagine was an absurdly heroic pose.

"But Hugh . . . *this* Judith likes you," she reminded him.

"Oh. I see your point," he answered thoughtfully, then started up the beach again. "Obviously the mad scientist is not an evil genius, but rather a great humanitarian bent on doing good deeds to benefit mankind."

"You mean if he thinks you're all right, he can't be all bad."

"Exactly. He may be insane, but he's got good taste."

Ryanne finally gave in to her laughter and wondered why she'd foolishly wasted time worrying. Being with Hugh was as easy as breathing.

They walked slowly, talking or sharing companionable silences that neither felt compelled to fill. The sun was low on the horizon and the serious sunbathers had retired for the day, so they encountered very few people. Occasionally an evening jogger thumped past them, and where the houses sat close to the water, Ryanne could hear music or the intermittent sounds of television. For the most part, though, it was idyllically peaceful, as though she and Hugh were the only two people in the universe.

They left Malibu Colony behind and crossed a short stretch of public beach. Finally the shoreline began to curve outward, and the terrain turned rocky. Hugh stopped, looking down at Ryanne's bare feet.

Realizing the problem, Ryanne starting digging into her purse. "Let me slip my sandals on."

"I've got a better idea." Without ceremony he lifted her into his arms and started up the rock incline that led to his house.

"Hugh! You can't do that!"

"I hate to argue with you, Ryanne, but I think I just did."

"But you'll hurt yourself."

"Humor me, please. I don't get to do my Rhett Butler impersonation very often. Speaking of which, did I ever tell you that I bear a striking resemblance to Clark Gable?"

"Oh, really?" Ryanne asked skeptically, lacing her arms around Hugh's neck. "I thought you looked like Robert Redford."

"Him, too."

"My, my, that's quite a potent combination," she observed, relaxing so that she could enjoy the ride. "Robert Redford *and* Clark Gable."

"And don't forget Donald Duck," he reminded her.

Laughing, Ryanne let her head fall to his shoulder. "I don't know, Hugh, you may be more than I can handle. Why is it that I haven't had to beat a hundred other women off you with a stick to keep you to myself?" she asked just as they reached the deck.

Hugh lowered her onto solid ground but refused to release her. Instead he pulled her close, molding the length of their bodies together. When he spoke, all traces of playfulness left his voice. "That's because I haven't even looked in another woman's direction since the day I met you."

Ryanne felt a flush of heat everywhere their bodies touched, and she could hardly draw a breath to tell him, "Then I'm a very lucky lady."

"Luck has nothing to do with it, Ryanne," Hugh whispered, lowering his head to hers. Eagerly he plied her lips, tracing the bowed upper curve with his tongue until Ryanne shivered involuntarily. She opened to him but drew back her head when he would have deepened the kiss. Instead she met his tongue with her own and mimicked his movement, painting his mouth with delicate strokes until that same shiver of sensation she'd felt rippled through Hugh as well. Only then did she let her head fall back, inviting him to plunder at his leisure.

Ryanne's gesture of surrender inflamed him almost as much as her obvious desire to reciprocate every pleasure he gave her. He pulled her against him tighter, one hand molded to her hips, the other at her back, sealing their bodies together. He plunged deep into her mouth, tasting and teasing, coaxing her tentative tongue to match the fervor of his own. A piercing shaft of heat flooded his loins, and without thinking, he clasped her hips and shifted her upward until she cradled the hardening ridge of his manhood.

Ryanne moaned but the sound was lost in Hugh's kiss. She gripped his shoulders and ran her hands fervently down his back. Then she shifted, arching into him as her own fires ignited and began scorching her with the intensity of her longing. The knowledge that tonight Hugh would finally quench the fire, that she would not go to sleep alone and aching made Ryanne bolder than she'd ever dared dream she could be. Her hands mimicked Hugh's, falling to his hips, letting him know that her heat matched his own.

It was Hugh who moaned this time. The rumble started deep in his chest and rose until it meshed and blended with Ryanne's. Weeks of holding back, of denying himself this pleasure brought Hugh to the brink of his control, and finally, with a wrenching gasp, he tore his mouth away from hers. His chest heaving, brushing against the hardened peaks of Ryanne's breasts, he tried to think rationally, but the effort was nearly in vain.

"This wasn't what I'd planned, Ryanne," he told her brokenly, his lips catching hers between words.

In answer, she arched, seeking the fullness of his mouth, and they were both lost. With a growl of impatience, Hugh

lifted her into his arms again and carried her swiftly into the
house. In the huge, sunken living room a low, square coffee table had been laid out with two place settings, waiting
only for the candles to be lit and the food to be brought in
from the warming oven in the kitchen. The intimate dinner, the soft music and the wine were all forgotten. Instead
Hugh moved swiftly up the steps to the hall and into his
bedroom.

Trying to conquer her uneven breathing, Ryanne buried
her face in Hugh's throat, her lips testing the corded sinew.
She felt his own ragged breathing—which she knew had
nothing to do with carrying her—and when he finally let her
feet slide to the floor she brought her hands to his chest and
felt for the buttons of his shirt that were keeping her from
touching him the way she needed desperately to touch him—
to see him.

The first few buttons fell away quickly and Ryanne felt a
dusting of hair against the back of her hand. Eagerly she
spread the shirt apart and let her hands trace the ridge of
muscle and bone across his chest. The contrast in tex-
tures—the hardness of muscle, the heat of his skin, the
softness of that fine mat of hair—made Ryanne tremble.
With a kind of reverence, she explored the beautiful symmetry of his body, and Hugh ground his teeth together,
praying for the control he would need to bring Ryanne the
same pleasure she was giving him. He tugged at her silk
blouse, pulling it out of her trousers so that he could feel her
flesh against his hands. Her skin was warm and as soft as the
silk of her shirt, but that contact wasn't nearly enough. Impatiently his hands moved to the buttons down the front,
but Ryanne suddenly pulled away, grabbing his wrists gently as she raised her face to his.

"Hugh…has the sun set?" she asked, her voice raspy and
breathless.

"The sun?" He glanced out the French doors at the glow on the horizon that painted the room a faint amber. "Almost."

"Can you close the light out with a curtain?"

Hugh pulled back and studied her face. Was she afraid someone might be watching them? he wondered. There was nothing beyond the doors to the deck but miles of ocean, but if it would ease Ryanne's mind he didn't mind closing the drapes. Reluctantly releasing her, he crossed the room and shut out the fading sunset, then returned to her. He reached for the switch of his bedside lamp, but Ryanne sensed his intent and reached for him, urging him toward her so that she could gently cup his face in her hands. Her thumbs traced his full lips and her voice trembled with barely contained emotion when she whispered, "No light, Hugh, please. Just for tonight, just this once . . . let us be equal. Share the dark with me."

"Oh, love," Hugh moaned, dragging her into his arms, fighting back the tears that suddenly burned behind his eyes. He held her close, fiercely, as though he'd never let go, and then finally, he released her.

He moved away and Ryanne choked back a sob, hating herself for having brought them back to reality. She followed his movements and when she heard the muted click of a door being closed her despair turned to a swell of love so strong it brought tears to her eyes. Another door closed, another curtain slid shut. Hugh was blocking out every trace of light from the room, voluntarily entering her world—not a world of shadows, but a world of blackness.

When he came to her again, Ryanne went into his arms knowing that her heart had already passed the point of no return.

CHAPTER ELEVEN

NORMALLY RYANNE'S PERCEPTION of time was excellent, but wrapped in Hugh's arms, her back pressed snugly against his chest, she had no idea how late it had grown. All sense of time and place had been suspended while they had made love, and now Ryanne was content to float. Hugh's deep, even breathing was as comforting as his arm, which was encircling her and keeping her close to him. His hand lightly cupped her breast as though to claim possession, and Ryanne smiled at the vague, restless movement that had his thumb gently caressing the still-hardened crest. Even in his sleep, he had the power to arouse her.

Ryanne blushed at the memory of how their gentle embrace had blossomed into a passionate fire that had threatened to consume them both. Sharing the darkness, they had undressed each other slowly, exploring and savoring. Ryanne had never experienced such tenderness, and their first joining had been a long, slow, achingly beautiful journey into a maelstrom of sensation that had left her feeling as though she'd flown too close to the sun.

Hugh's arm tightened and he moaned softly. The sound rumbled deep in his throat and Ryanne knew he had awakened even before he buried his lips in her hair. He turned her in his arms and brushed her hair away from her throat, clearing a trail for a leisurely foray across her bare shoulder, up her neck and onto her cheek until he finally found her lips. Ryanne opened to him, welcoming the lazy kiss.

"Are you all right?" he asked, nibbling his way back down her throat.

Ryanne stretched languidly. "Define 'All right.'"

Hugh chuckled as he shifted lower, making an unhurried descent toward her breasts. "Let's see . . . Actually it means several things. Like, are you comfortable?"

His words were muffled as he applied teasing pressure on her already overheated flesh, and Ryanne had to concentrate in order to answer. "How can I be comfortable when you're doing . . . that . . ." She sighed with pleasure when his lips finally closed over the swollen crest of one breast and created a delicious combination of friction and suction. "Any other . . . silly questions?" she managed to gasp.

"Well, are you at least . . . content?" he asked, his own breathing growing uneven. He shifted her like a rag doll so that he could give equal torment to her other breast.

"Not for long." She moaned, reveling in the heat that once again began coursing through her, settling into a magnificent ache between her thighs.

"How about happy?" he suggested.

"Deliriously."

"Sated?"

A chuckle found its way to the surface. "I was until you woke up."

Hugh stopped what he was doing and raised himself, wanting to see Ryanne's face and feeling guilty for desiring something he knew she could never experience. When he spoke again, his voice was soft and serious. "Are you disappointed?"

"Oh, Hugh," Ryanne said, sighing. She reached out, found his shoulder and let her hand trail lightly up to his face. "No one else has ever made me feel the way you do."

And no one else ever will, he told himself fiercely, fighting to keep from saying the words aloud. He had made the rules and he had to play by them—for the time being, at least. He would go slowly with Ryanne, winning her love a little at a time, if necessary, but he knew he was never going to let her go. "I'm glad," he said simply, turning his head so that he could kiss the palm of her hand.

Ryanne turned away and pressed her back against him so that they were lying the way they had been earlier, and Hugh held her close, losing himself in the sweet smelling silk of her hair. Wordlessly he began arousing her again, running his hands down her side, along her flanks, lightly brushing the soft curls of hair at the juncture of her thighs. His fingers ventured further, stroking her intimately and Ryanne arched as a shaft of pleasure pierced her. She groaned and tried to turn to him, desperate to touch Hugh and share the gift he was giving her, but he held her fast until she could think of nothing but the wave after wave of intense heat that rocked her.

Her movements against Hugh and the hoarse sounds of pleasure that whispered in her throat ignited his own fires. He thrust his hips against her thigh and pressed fevered kisses on her back and shoulders, nipping at the sensitized flesh, then soothing it with his tongue. She cried out, begging him to come to her, to take her completely, but he stopped suddenly, leaving her aching and bereft.

Ryanne froze as Hugh's hands moved to the shoulder he'd been exploring so thoroughly with his mouth, and her passion died a withering death. Hugh uttered a muffled curse and leaned away from her, switching on the bedside lamp. She bit down on her lower lip, already swollen from Hugh's kisses, and waited.

Blinking against the brightness of the light, Hugh turned back to Ryanne. Unconsciously she had tightened as though shielding herself and he gently reached out to brush away the hair that had fallen down her back, obscuring the place he'd been kissing. The movement revealed the puckered remains of a wide, angry scar on her otherwise perfect body. He saw the line of a surgical incision, but at its center was the un-mistakable proof that the cause of this injury had been no accident.

Hugh had seen scars like this before, but never on a woman—never on a woman he wanted to love, cherish and protect. A murderous fury, more potent than anything he'd ever experienced swept through him. Trembling with rage, he cursed viciously and forced Ryanne to turn to him. Again he brushed away her hair and found the entry point of the bullet that had ripped into her body, shattered her shoulder, and exploded out of her back.

Ryanne fought back tears as she listened to Hugh's harsh, ragged breathing. He touched her shoulder lightly, then hurled himself off the bed and began pacing furiously.

He cursed and Ryanne held her breath until he stopped at the foot of the bed and spoke to her in a cold, flat voice she never would have recognized as his. "What's his name, Ryanne?"

"What?" Confused, Ryanne sat up, crossing one arm over her body, searching with the other hand for something to cover herself with. She found the sheet and clutched it to her, unconsciously pressing her fist against the scar that had obviously repulsed him.

"I said I want to know his name," Hugh repeated coldly. "I want to know the name of the bastard who shot you!" His voice was as crisp and low as the deadly report of a rifle. He had known all along about the murder Ryanne had witnessed five years ago—in fact, he knew far more than Ryanne suspected he did. But he hadn't known about this. Hugh had assumed that in trying to escape from the murderer she had simply fallen off the warehouse ledge; but this ... this *defilement* was something he hadn't even imagined.

"Why do you want to know his name?" Ryanne asked softly.

"Because I want him dead! I want the bastard who did this to you to pay, damn it!" Hugh whirled away, stopping his angry tirade. Useless threats of violence weren't going to help Ryanne or take away the horror she'd suffered. But right now, the threats didn't feel useless to Hugh. The full extent of the nightmare Ryanne had lived through had just now hit him in a way that hearing or reading about it never had. Until this moment her blindness and the act of brutality that had caused it had been nothing but an abstraction to him. Now it was real.

Reason slowly seeped back into Hugh's mind and he became aware of Ryanne cowered on the bed, shielding herself from his anger. "I'm sorry, love. I'm sorry."

He moved to her, gathering her into his arms, but Ryanne couldn't melt into his embrace. It touched something deep inside her to know that what she had suffered could affect him so deeply, and yet the very intensity of his emotions had frightened her. For a moment she had shared this room with a stranger, someone cold and hard, someone so unlike the Hugh she knew that it was incomprehensible to her that they could be the same man. The steely passion in his voice told her his threats had not been idle and she realized that the kind, gentle man who had filled her life so completely was capable of killing without a second thought.

Hugh sensed her withdrawal and released her. "We need to talk about it, Ryanne," he told her quietly. "I hadn't known you'd been shot."

"Does it make such a difference?"

"Yes!"

"Why? The bullet didn't kill me. It didn't cause my blindness."

"Yes, it did," he insisted. "The impact of that bullet is what knocked you over the ledge of that warehouse, isn't it? *Isn't it?*"

"So what?" she demanded.

"Oh, Ryanne..." Unable to bear the distance between them, both emotionally and physically, Hugh pulled her into his arms again. He settled back against the headboard with Ryanne's head resting on his chest. "I'm sorry. I don't know how to explain what seeing that scar, what realizing you'd been shot, did to me."

"Try. Please," she insisted softly. She wanted the old Hugh back, not the hardened stranger he'd become for a moment.

Hugh buried his face in her hair. "I've seen violence, Ryanne. In Vietnam you couldn't escape it, so you detached yourself from it in order to survive. I see violence in my work, too, sometimes. But this—" he caressed her shoulder "—this shouldn't have happened to *you*. This kind of...ugliness should never have been allowed to touch you."

"But it did, Hugh. And I survived," she told him softly.

"I know. I guess until now all I've been seeing is the way you live with the aftermath of what happened in that warehouse. I've never let myself imagine what you must have suffered. The pain..." Gently, almost reverently, he traced the surgical incision. "It shattered your shoulder, didn't it?"

"It took some reconstruction, yes," she answered, trying not to remember the hours of excruciatingly painful therapy she'd undergone to regain the use of her arm.

"The blindness, the plastic surgery on your face, this..." He kissed the scar tenderly and Ryanne's eyes filled with tears. "I can't bear the thought of the torment you must have gone through."

Ryanne raised her face to his. "I don't want to think about the past, Hugh. Please..." She found his lips and together they focused completely on the present.

RYANNE AWOKE ABRUPTLY, startled from her deep sleep by a noise she didn't recognize. The room seemed strange to her as well, but it wasn't until she tried to move and felt the stiffness that pervaded every muscle in her body that she realized it wasn't *her* room, it was Hugh's.

The memory of the hours they had spent locked in each other's arms brought a flood of heat to Ryanne's cheeks. She had said things last night, done things that she'd never imagined herself capable of. At the time they had seemed right and natural; facing Hugh in the light of morning was a different story altogether. And, too, Ryanne had to wonder which Hugh would greet her this morning: the gentle, kind one, or the other Hugh she'd been introduced to last night—the one with the voice as cold as steel. It frightened her a little to realize she'd made love with both men. After Hugh had seen her ugly scar and learned the whole story of her brush with death, his lovemaking had become fierce, demanding, and almost overpowering in its intensity.

Instinctively she knew she was alone in the big bed, but she reached out to make certain. As she'd suspected, Hugh was gone. In a way, she was glad, because his absence gave her a chance to compose herself, and yet it also posed a distinct problem. Last night Hugh had taken her clothes off slowly, savoring the removal of each layer, but Ryanne had no idea what had become of it all. Was it scattered around on the floor? Had he tossed the lot into a chair last night, or hung everything in a closet when he got up this morning? Was there even a chair in the room, for that matter? Ryanne had absolutely no concept of what the bedroom was like.

The noise that had awakened her started again and she recognized it as a blender, or possibly an electric mixer. Evidently Hugh was making breakfast for them. Moving toward the sound, Ryanne scooted off the left side of the bed, wrapping the sheet around her. Carefully she reached for the nightstand, found her glasses, then with one arm bent in front of her and the other clutching the sheet, she moved slowly toward the sound.

The blender stopped abruptly, but she kept moving slowly in the same direction, listening to the walls now that the door was no longer helping her. The sheet, too voluminous and unstable to ever catch on as a fashion trend, slipped, causing Ryanne to stumble. She righted herself without crashing into anything, but by that time she had lost her bearings completely. Moving forward gingerly, her shin finally came in contact with something solid and she realized that there was a chair in the room, after all. And there were clothes on it, as well. Dropping the sheet, she investigated and found a shirt. The one Hugh had discarded last night, she guessed. Since her own clothes were nowhere within reach, she slipped into it, welcoming the masculine scent that clung to the soft cotton.

She started off again in search of the door, but found a wall first and moved along it past a louvered closet door and finally came to an opening. She stepped through and knew instantly from the acoustics and the lack of carpeting that she had found a bathroom. Though it was large, she located everything with relative ease, availed herself of the facilities, and splashed cold water on her face to take away the remnants of sleep that still clung to her.

Retracing her footsteps, she made it back to the bedroom and finally found the hall that led to the enormous sunken living room. She could feel the difference in air currents immediately when she stepped through the arched opening, but from there she dared go no further. She could hear Hugh in the kitchen now, but following the noise he was making would be a big mistake. If her mental image of the room was correct, the stairs down to the living room were somewhere in front of her, but if she tried to go down, cross the obstacle course of sofas, chairs, tables and lamps, then go back up, she would probably get totally lost—and break something in the process. Going around the squared-off horseshoe-shaped room was equally implausible, since she had no idea how far it extended toward the entryway to her left.

The thought of calling out to Hugh for assistance was humiliating, but she obviously had no choice.

"Hugh?" The blender started again just as she spoke, drowning out her voice, and she waited. Impatient with her own helplessness, she took a step to the right and unexpectedly came into contact with a tall table. An object—something that sounded ceramic and breakable—tottered back and forth from the impact and she reached for it instinctively. Her arm connected unfavorably with the shade of a tottering lamp and it crashed to the parquet floor just as Hugh's blender stopped.

"Damn!" Ryanne swore, but resisted the impulse to bend and inspect the damage she'd done. Glass had shattered everywhere and she was barefooted. She waited, furious with herself, as Hugh charged out of the kitchen.

"Ryanne? Are you all right?" He bounded down the stairs and across the room. A tall bank of plants at the edge of the sunken room obscured his view temporarily, and when he reached the landing, he froze. "Don't move, sweetheart. There's glass everywhere."

"I know. I'm so sorry. I'm such a klutz!"

"It was just an accident, Ryanne."

"But it was a *stupid* accident!" she snapped back. Glass crunched as Hugh moved toward her. "Be careful!"

"Don't worry. I'm not *that* chivalrous. I've got on tennis shoes. Are you hurt anywhere?"

"No. Only my pride."

"It'll heal," he assured her, sweeping her into his arms and carrying her toward the kitchen. His gallant gesture startled Ryanne and she threw her arms around his neck, discovering that though he might have had shoes on, a shirt was conspicuously absent. Her hands automatically ran across the smooth, hard lines of his shoulders.

"This must be a record for you—getting to do your Rhett Butler impersonation three times in only two days."

"Wait till you see what I do for an encore," he said suggestively.

"I thought I already had," Ryanne whispered as Hugh's lips closed over hers. A flare of remembered passion ignited their kiss and Hugh lowered her to the floor, then used both arms to pull her tightly against him.

Ryanne's bare legs rubbed against the soft fabric of Hugh's pants and the shirt she wore provided little protection against the smooth hardness of his bare chest. She arched into him as their kiss deepened by mutual consent, and when it ended they were both a little breathless.

"Good morning," he murmured, his voice a little deeper than normal.

Ryanne smiled and snuggled her head against his shoulder so that he couldn't see her blush. "Good morning. I'm sorry about the lamp."

"Don't be. All that broken glass gave me the perfect excuse to get you in my arms again. It saved a lot of awkward maneuvering and planning out a morning-after strategy."

"Does the morning after require a strategy?"

"Definitely. Feeling awkward is inevitable, and I never want you to be uncomfortable with me." He took her arm and guided her to a chair at the table. "Breakfast is almost ready. Why don't you have a seat while I clean up the lamp, then we can eat."

"Fine." Hugh tapped the back of the chair for her and Ryanne sat. "I'd offer to help, but as I just demonstrated, I'm useless in an unfamiliar environment."

There was a long pause that puzzled Ryanne until Hugh reached out and stroked her cheek lovingly. "I'm sorry I left you alone, Ryanne. I thought I could put together a quick breakfast before you woke up. The next time you're here we'll go over the house inch by inch until you know your way around."

"I'd like that," she told him with a smile. She also liked his assumption that there would be a next time.

Hugh gave her a quick kiss, then collected a broom and dustpan from the pantry. The chore took only a few minutes, and before long they were both seated at the table, laughing over the chewy little golf balls that were supposed to have been blueberry muffins. That disaster notwithstanding, it was an excellent breakfast, complete with an omelet and fresh orange juice squeezed from an electric juicer Ryanne had mistaken for a blender.

"You're going to be late for work, aren't you?" Ryanne asked as she sipped her second cup of coffee.

"Only a little. I called Mo and told him I'd meet him at the plant. He can handle things until I get there." Hugh had already explained that MacKenna and Associates were setting up a security system out in Canoga Park. The job had been contracted months ago or Hugh would have changed his schedule in order to stay with Ryanne. This was going to be a rough day for her. "Your appointment is at eleven, isn't it?" he asked.

Ryanne nodded. For days she'd been trying not to think about her impending visit with the country's leading neurologist. "Yes. It's strange...I feel as though I've waited a lifetime to see Dr. Kazlovski, and now that the time has arrived I'd just as soon call and cancel."

"You can't do that, Ryanne. It's important that you find the cause of those headaches."

"If there is a cause. My Aunt Rose used to have severe migraines and no one could ever find out why. Maybe that's why I haven't been too worried about them." She fell silent and toyed with the handle of her coffee cup. Late in the night as she'd lain awake, listening to Hugh's deep, steady breathing, Ryanne had realized something that disturbed her greatly. If she were right, it meant that Hugh had been lying to her since the day they met. She dreaded confronting the implications of her suspicions.

"Hugh...that first day you came to the house... You knew about me, didn't you? Douglas had told you more than just the fact that I had been a reporter and was blind. He told you everything, didn't he?"

Hugh closed his eyes, cursing himself for ever having agreed to Doug's request that he not tell Ryanne he knew how she'd been blinded. "Yes, I knew. Most of it, anyway. I'm sorry, Ryanne. I shouldn't have pretended not to know."

"Why did you?"

"Doug asked me not to tell you. He wanted someone in L.A. to know your history, but he was afraid you'd be angry with him for telling me. He explained the bare facts and sent me a few newspaper clippings." He reached across the table and took her hand. "This doesn't have anything to do with us, Ryanne, with what happened last night and what's been happening for weeks."

Ryanne wanted desperately to believe that was true, and yet all the time they'd been seeing each other Hugh hadn't tried to take her to bed until she'd practically forced him into it. Had his restraint really come out of a desire to let their friendship solidify before they complicated it, or had Hugh been reluctant to bed her because he didn't want to take advantage of a situation Douglas Sutherland had forced him into?

No, Ryanne thought. That's not the way it was. Her instincts when it came to romance were not well developed, but her instincts about people were acute. Hugh hadn't been pretending with her. He'd met with her that first time as a favor to an old friend, and even if he'd agreed to keep an eye on her after that, there was no need for the elaborate subterfuge of dating. She could understand his reasons for not telling her everything Douglas had passed along to him, as well. At first she'd been a stranger and his loyalties had been to his friend Douglas. And after that first meeting, the subject of her accident had not come up. Somehow she knew that if she hadn't figured out the truth Hugh would have told her eventually.

"Ryanne?" Hugh said tentatively when she remained silent for so long. "Are you angry with me? I wouldn't hurt you for anything in the world. You have to know that."

Ryanne managed a smile. "Yes."

"What made you realize that I knew?"

"You mentioned my plastic surgery last night, but I knew I'd never brought it up. Someone else had to have told you and Judith isn't exactly a chatterbox. That left Douglas Sutherland."

"And you're not angry?"

"No. I know how persuasive Douglas can be—and how overprotective. Somehow I don't think he anticipated that we'd complicate his scheme by becoming a little more than casual acquaintances."

"A *lot* more," Hugh corrected her, bringing her hand to his lips. "And whether he anticipated it or not, I will always be grateful that he brought us together."

"So will I," Ryanne agreed, then grinned impishly. "Why don't you help me pick out a suitable token of appreciation that I can take to him when I go back to Chicago?"

Hugh's hand tightened on Ryanne's and then he released it as though burned by the contact. "Fine. We'll think of something appropriate," he said tightly as he stood. "You'd better get dressed so I can get you home."

He touched her arm and Ryanne stood, puzzled by the sudden chill that had settled between them. "Hugh, did I say something wrong?"

"No, of course not," he reassured her. "I just need to get to work, that's all."

But that wasn't all, and Ryanne knew it. She'd mentioned going back to Chicago, and Hugh had turned as cold as ice. But why? He'd made it clear from the beginning that he didn't believe in long-term relationships. Had something changed his mind, Ryanne wondered, or was she just grasping at straws because letting Hugh go was going to be the hardest thing she'd ever done?

CHAPTER TWELVE

"I'M AFRAID YOU'RE NOT going to think this is good news, Ms. Kirkland," Dr. Kazlovski said as he settled into the chair behind his desk. Ryanne had been at the clinic for what seemed like hours and even after a battery of tests she knew no more now than when she'd entered. Judith was waiting for her in the reception room with Aggie, and Ryanne was anxious to hear what the doctor had to say so that she could leave. She'd spent so much time in hospitals that even after five years the antiseptic smell that pervaded the private clinic made her feel ill.

"You mean you can't find a reason why I'm having headaches?"

"No *physiological* reason," he corrected.

"Then there's no relationship between the headaches and the fall that caused my blindness?"

Kazlovski was silent for a long moment before answering. "I'm not qualified to make that diagnosis, Ms. Kirkland—may I call you Ryanne?"

"Of course." She frowned. "What do you mean you're not qualified? You're the best neurology man in medicine. If you're not qualified, who is?"

"I'm going to ask you to see another doctor, Ryanne. His name is Whitehorn. He's on staff here at the clinic, and I've already spoken with him. He's clearing his calendar so that he can see you today as soon as you and I finish here."

Ryanne's head was spinning. None of this made any sense. What possible tests could Whitehorn run that Kazlovski couldn't? "You're talking in circles, doctor. Would you please tell me what you suspect is wrong with me!"

"Ryanne..." She heard Kazlovski stand and move to the front of the desk where he sat in a chair beside her. "Physically there is nothing wrong with you. Things like this happen sometimes. Your doctor in Chicago sent me all your medical records and I've been able to do a thorough comparison of the X-rays and other tests that were taken right after your accident. Given the state of medical technology that existed five years ago, I probably would have made the same diagnosis as your own physician did. You had massive trauma to your head—there was a blood clot that did eventually dissolve, but I'm sure that was a contributing factor. I can understand—"

"What are you talking about?" Ryanne almost shouted, resisting the impulse to fly to her feet.

"Ryanne, I know this isn't going to be easy to accept—"

"Just say it, damn it! Tell me what's wrong!"

Kazlovski stood. "Nothing is wrong, Ryanne. That's what I'm trying to tell you. There is no physiological reason for your headaches, just as there are no physical indications to explain your blindness."

Ryanne felt as though she'd been hit in the stomach with a two-by-four. It was a moment before she could challenge his ridiculous diagnosis. "I'm blind, doctor," she ground out, throwing one hand up between them. "I can't see my hand in front of my face! I'd say that was a pretty strong *physical indication*!"

"I'm not denying the fact that you're blind," he told her, keeping his voice gentle, regretting the ordeal that was to come. He knew enough about situations like this one to know that accepting her blindness five years earlier had been a piece of cake compared to what accepting the truth was going to be for her now.

"Are you trying to tell me that it's all in my head? That I'm not really blind?" A shudder rippled through Ryanne's body and she suppressed it, trying to think rationally in a world that had suddenly tilted on its axis.

"No, Ryanne, your blindness is real. For some reason your subconscious mind has turned off the switch that allows what your eyes see to register in your brain. That's as real as a detached retina or an atrophied optic nerve. The only difference is that there's no physical damage. It may take a long time to find that switch, but if you can turn it back on you *will* see again."

Ryanne felt too numb to think or move. The full implications were only beginning to sink in. "And the headaches?"

"Headaches can originate from a multitude of sources, but I suspect that yours are only a signal. Almost as though some part of your mind was crying out against the injustice of your blindness. At the same time your subconscious is keeping you from seeing, it's also trying to let you know that you have the capability to restore your sight. Frankly I think that's a very encouraging sign."

"Oh, you do?" she asked, unable to keep the sarcasm from her voice.

"Yes. It may mean that your subconscious is ready to confront the trauma that caused this problem in the first place. As long as you were under the impression that your blindness was irrevocable there was little chance for you to find the source and regain your sight. Perhaps now you can."

Still in a state of shock, Ryanne asked questions by rote, recording the answers in her mind to be taken out and reviewed later. She wanted to know what made him so sure of his diagnosis; she asked how such a mistake could have been made. He lapsed into a technical explanation of the revolutionary improvements in the CAT scan apparatus that provided clear, almost three-dimensional images of the brain, but Ryanne understood little of what he was saying. She wanted to be overjoyed that she might one day see again, but there was one clear, obvious fact that eliminated the desire to rejoice.

Dr. Kazlovski might not know what had caused her subconscious mind to throw the switch that had blinded her, but Ryanne did. It was all so very simple. Five years ago she saw a man commit murder. That same man had tried to kill her, and if she hadn't gone blind, he would have kept on trying until he succeeded. In short, being blind was the only thing that was keeping Ryanne alive.

If her options were darkness and death, Ryanne was quite comfortable with the choice her subconscious had already made for her.

"WHAT IS IT, Judith? What did the doctor say? What's wrong?" Hugh bombarded Judith the instant she opened the door to him. His office had relayed her terse message to the Canoga Park site, and he'd immediately jumped into his car and broken every speed law between the factory and Malibu. He'd tried to reach her from the phone in his car, but the line had been tied up and he was nearly frantic. Seeing Judith's drawn, ashen face didn't help the terrified ache in his heart.

"Please keep your voice down," Judith requested without her usual tartness. "She doesn't know I called you."

Unable to stop himself, Hugh grabbed her shoulders. "What's wrong with her?"

"I don't know!" Judith snapped, wrenching out of his grasp. "She was with the doctor for hours, and when she came out she said there was absolutely nothing wrong with her. When I got her home she shut herself in her room and she's been there ever since. I took a tray in to her a few minutes ago, but she hasn't touched it. She's just sitting there, facing the ocean..." Tears welled in the older woman's eyes and she covered her face with both hands, whispering brokenly, "Something is terribly wrong, Hugh. She's..."

Hugh reached out and pulled her into his arms. He held her while she quickly regained control. "It's all right," he crooned softly, trying to convince himself as much as Judith. "She'll be fine. She has to be."

Judith pulled away from him and dried her eyes. "When she wouldn't talk to me I didn't know what else to do but call you."

"I'm glad you did. I'll go see if I can get us some answers, and if she won't talk to me, either, then we'll get in touch with her doctor."

"I've already done that. He insists that he can't discuss Ryanne's condition without her consent."

"Then I'll just have to get the answers from Ryanne, won't I?" Hugh started down the hall. He knocked softly on her door, calling her name, and when she didn't respond, he turned the knob and stepped inside. "Ryanne?"

She was sitting exactly as Judith had described, in a chair facing the ocean, her eyes fixed and sightless. Her legs were drawn up to her chest with her arms wrapped around them. She looked so forlorn and vulnerable that Hugh's heart broke into a dozen pieces. "Ryanne?"

"Go away, Hugh," she said emotionlessly. Her voice was like something cold and dead.

"I can't go away, Ryanne. Judith is terrified," he told her, closing the distance between them. "So am I," he added softly.

"I told her nothing was wrong."

"Ryanne, if nothing was wrong you wouldn't be sitting here like this." He knelt beside her, steeling himself to ask the question he hadn't wanted to ever have to face. For weeks now he'd been trying not to think about the fact that Ryanne's mother had died of cancer. "Did they find a tumor?" he asked softly.

"I just told you! He didn't find anything!" she shouted. "Nothing! Not one blessed thing! I'm as healthy as a horse. Of course, I'm also crazy as a loon," she added with an ugly, half laugh as she came to her feet. Unable to bear being close to Hugh, she hurried across the room, but there was no place for her to go to escape him and she knew it.

Hugh stood and watched her agitated pacing. He hated seeing her like this, but it was preferable to the emotionless cocoon she'd been wrapped in when he'd entered. "I don't understand, Ryanne."

"Of course you don't," she said bitterly. "It took me a while to comprehend it, too. Dr. Kazlovski told me I need a psychiatrist, not a neurologist."

"Ryanne—"

"I'm not blind, Hugh! There's nothing wrong with my eyes and there never has been! It's called hysterical blindness, and it happens when crazy people like me can't handle reality." In a venomous voice filled with self-loathing, Ryanne repeated everything the doctor had said.

"Then you'll see again someday," Hugh said quickly when she finished. He was enormously relieved to know she wasn't seriously ill, and it was nothing less than miraculous that she might regain her sight. Seeing her so distraught negated his joy, though. She was in shock now, with too many emotions crowding in on her, not the least of which had to be fear, he realized.

"There are no guarantees of that," she answered in a brittle tone. "Dr. Whitehorn explained that the subconscious mind doesn't work that way. Facing the fear that caused my blindness won't necessarily unlock the mechanism that's keeping me from seeing."

"But you said Dr. Kazlovski thinks your headaches were...what? A plea for help? Isn't that a good sign? Something inside you wants to see again, Ryanne."

"Why? So I can watch my own death unfold? That'll be a real pleasure, won't it?"

"Ryanne—" Hugh reached for her but the moment he touched her arm she shrank away.

"Don't. Don't touch me. I don't want to be coddled and comforted. I don't want to hear your platitudes. 'Everything will be all right, Ryanne,'" she mimicked viciously. "Or better yet, 'I won't let anyone hurt you.'"

"You may not want to hear it, Ryanne, but it's very true. I *won't* let anyone hurt you," he told her in a voice that was quiet, but fierce in its conviction.

"That's a lie, Hugh, and you know it," she retorted. "You know as well as I do that if someone wants me dead there's not a power on earth that can keep me alive—not you, not the police, not God, not anybody! If I wake up tomorrow morning and see the sunrise, you can bet your sweet life I won't be alive to see it set!"

Hugh wanted to argue with her, to convince her she was wrong, but he knew she wasn't. There were witness protection programs that sometimes worked—provided the witness was willing to go into hiding and give up friends, family and careers. They also had to be willing to live in constant fear that they would be discovered. Under those circumstances, a normal life was virtually impossible. Certainly it was better than death, but Hugh didn't care for either of those alternatives. If Ryanne did regain her sight and go into a witness protection program he would lose her forever.

The ramifications of the double bind Ryanne was now in hit Hugh like a freight train, and like Ryanne, he had no idea what to wish for. To hope that she would never regain her sight was too cruel for words, and yet to pray for it to return was like sentencing her to death.

"What? No protests? Aren't you going to tell me I'm wrong? Aren't you going to tell me about witness protection programs or something equally encouraging?" she asked sarcastically. Obviously her mind had already traveled the same torturous route as Hugh's.

"No, Ryanne, I'm not."

"Well, tell me something!" she shouted as her fierce anger began to evaporate leaving nothing but cold terror in its wake. "Tell me . . . tell . . ." A wrenching sob shattered her voice and the tears she'd needed to shed finally broke free. "Oh, God, Hugh . . . I'm so scared."

Hugh had her in his arms in an instant, and this time she did not try to pull away. He held her close, stroking her hair and murmuring wordlessly while she cried. He rocked her gently until the storm subsided.

When she was calmer he encouraged her to talk to Judith, who was half out of her mind with worry. He called Ryanne's friend into the room and the two women embraced, holding on to each other as Hugh began the explanation that he wasn't sure she would find reassuring. Ryanne told her about the tests she had taken and the hour she had spent with the psychiatrist.

Judith accepted the results stoically, and when everything had been told, her response was succinct.

"You're a survivor, Ryanne. You'll survive this, too." She glanced at Hugh sharply, giving him a look that charged him with making sure that she did.

He nodded to her, wordlessly accepting the responsibility of keeping Ryanne alive, then he took her back into his arms and held her as the night fell around them.

CHAPTER THIRTEEN

It was 2:00 A.M. in Chicago, and a light, misty rain turned the city streets a shiny black. On the glistening surfaces the street lights were reflected, like diamonds against black velvet. Every so often, a car sped through the intersection, taking advantage of the deserted street, but Arlen Beck paid no attention. He was focused totally, impatiently, on the phone in the booth that sheltered him from the drizzling rain. He checked his watch again and calculated the time difference. In Los Angeles it was two minutes after midnight. If all had gone as planned, Keegan would be calling any second. Beck waited, his heart thundering, ready to grab the receiver, but the phone refused to ring. Five minutes melted into ten; ten melted into twenty.

At two-thirty, Beck began cursing. He swore at the tardy Ace Keegan for keeping him in suspense, and he cursed the rain and the cramped phone booth. Most of all, he cursed Ryanne Kirkland for not having died five years ago as she should have. If not for her stubborn will to live, Beck's life would have been nearly perfect.

He fancied himself an important man in the syndicate, well on his way to the kind of power Del Michelon wielded. He'd started with nothing and now he was on the verge of having it all. At least, he had been until Ryanne Kirkland made an appointment with a hotshot specialist in Los Angeles. As he waited in the phone booth, Beck could almost feel his carefully constructed world tumbling down around his ears.

The later the hour grew, the more that feeling intensified. He simply couldn't afford mistakes. That was why he was out on the street at this absurd hour, miles from his home in the suburbs. After all the planning he'd done, after all the expense he'd put out to keep Keegan in Los Angeles, discreetly watching Ryanne Kirkland for nearly two months, Beck wasn't about to let a little thing like a traceable phone call mess things up. All of Keegan's calls to Beck were supposed to be made from Los Angeles pay phones, and all were received in the same phone booth on Kruger Street in Chicago. Nice, neat, and completely untraceable. Five years ago, Beck had made a grave mistake by not making sure that a busybody reporter was dead. If it became necessary to try to eliminate her again, he was going to be damned sure there would be no need for a third attempt. Del Michelon didn't like inefficiency, and the last thing Arlen Beck wanted was to displease his boss. Others who had done so had, on occasion, paid for their errors with their lives.

At two forty-three the wait finally ended and Beck had the phone's receiver to his ear before the echo of the first aborted ring had faded into the night.

"Keegan?"

"Yeah. It's me."

"Where the hell have you been? What went wrong?"

"Chill out, man," Keegan advised in a negligent voice that infuriated Beck. "Everything's cool. I just ran into a little delay, that's all."

Beck checked his watch unnecessarily. "Yeah, a forty-five-minute delay. What happened? Did you get her records out of the clinic?"

"Nope. That's the delay I meant. It's gonna take a couple of days longer."

A small spike of fear ran down Beck's spine. Michelon was expecting a report first thing tomorrow morning and keeping the boss waiting wasn't a healthy thing to do. "No way, Keegan! I told you I wanted answers tonight, and you promised you could deliver!"

"Yeah, well that was before I knew Simpson was gonna pick tonight to come down with the flu."

"Who the hell is Simpson?"

Keegan sighed audibly. "He's the night watchman at the clinic. For a hefty fee, Mr. Simpson gave me the layout of the joint and agreed to look the other way when I break in."

"Damn you, Keegan—"

"Hey look, man, it's not my fault there's a major bug goin' around. Simpson's sick as a dog—I checked it out for myself. That's why I was late making this call." It was a convenient lie, but Ace Keegan had had a lot of experience making lies sound like the truth. The night watchman really was sick in bed, and Keegan *had* verified it—earlier in the evening. He'd followed the lovely Ms. Kirkland from the clinic to her ritzy Malibu beach house, then he'd gone to arrange a few last minute details with Simpson. He'd found the man in bed, and Ace hadn't spent much time loitering around to offer his sympathies. The last thing he needed was to get bitten by a bug.

Once Keegan had found out there was no way he could get into the clinic tonight, he'd gone to a little bar up in Santa Monica where a couple of local rubes had obligingly lost a few hundred dollars to Ace at the pool table. It didn't bother him in the least that his last game had kept his employer waiting in a damp Chicago phone booth. Nor was he particularly disturbed that Simpson was going to be out of commission for a couple of days. After nearly two months, Hollywood was beginning to feel like home to Ace. He was going to be sorry when this cushy little job was over. Malibu Beach was a great place to get a tan—and the women weren't bad to look at, either.

Beck was fuming. Tomorrow morning, Michelon would expect him to have the results of Kirkland's visit to the doctor, and the syndicate boss wouldn't be happy if Arlen couldn't deliver. A flu virus wouldn't mean a whole lot to Del Michelon. For a moment, Beck considered ordering Keegan to go ahead with the break-in despite the absence of a friendly night watchman, but he knew that wouldn't be a smart move. The risk of getting caught would be multiplied a hundredfold, and if Keegan went to jail they might not find out if Kirkland was going to see or not until it was too late. No, the only option was to wait until Simpson got well and returned to work. Surely a day or two wouldn't make that much difference.

"All right, Keegan. We'll wait—for now," Beck decided. "But I want you to look for another way to get into that clinic, and I want a report on every move Kirkland makes until you get hold of her records. You got that?"

"Yeah, yeah. I got it."

"Good. I'll be waiting at this number for a report tomorrow night. And don't keep me waiting again!" Beck slammed down the phone and realized that his hand was trembling.

"Damn," he muttered, turning up the collar of his jacket as he stepped into the drizzling Chicago rain. Meanwhile, in Los Angeles, Ace Keegan sauntered through the balmy Southern California night back toward the bar he'd reluctantly left just a few minutes ago. It was about one in the morning, but the streets were still buzzing with traffic, and Keegan enjoyed the rhythm of the street.

Yes, indeed, he was going to miss this place. But if it turned out that Beck decided it was necessary to kill Ryanne Kirkland, there was no way Keegan would be able to stay.

He'd have to do the job, then head back to Chicago. The thought of reneging on his contract with Beck never occurred to Ace. The old saying about "honor among thieves" applied to hired killers, too. No matter how much he might like to hang around Los Angeles, he wouldn't back out on the job.

But he didn't have to be in any big hurry, either. Not for the first time that day, Ace hoped that Simpson took his time recovering from the flu.

IT WAS WELL after midnight before Hugh could finally persuade Ryanne to take one of the sedatives her doctor had prescribed. The next few days were going to take quite a toll on her and she needed all the rest she could get. Dr. Whitehorn had scheduled daily sessions with her for the next week to help her deal with the intense conflict she was experiencing. He was also going to be searching for that switch in her subconscious Dr. Kazlovski had referred to. Hugh wondered if Ryanne would allow the psychiatrist to poke around in her head until he found it.

Of course, Hugh realized that Ryanne was the only one who could actually flip that switch, and he also knew that even a conscious decision to confront her fear of "Worsted" did not mean her sight would miraculously return. Her subconscious had blinded her and it would be her subconscious that allowed her to see again.

Standing alone on Ryanne's deck with the quiet house behind him, Hugh began to review everything he knew about the attempt on Ryanne's life five years earlier. He wished he had the information Doug had sent him so that he could study it more thoroughly, but the papers were back in his office. Calling upon his memory, his mind floated back to the first conversation he and Doug had had about Ryanne, and almost instantly something he'd forgotten came back to him with terrifying clarity. For weeks now he had been so involved with Ryanne, so consumed with his growing feelings for her that he had completely forgotten the reason Doug Sutherland had contacted him in the first place. It hadn't just been that he'd wanted her security system checked out, or that he'd been playing matchmaker. Doug was convinced that Worsted knew every move Ryanne Kirkland had made in the past five years, and if that were true, the murderer had to have known about her appointment with Dr. Kazlovski. He had to be worried, wondering if perhaps the doctor could restore her sight.... He would make every attempt to learn the results of Ryanne's tests, and eventually he would learn that the woman who could put him in the electric chair might miraculously regain her sight at any moment.

Naturally Hugh was only speculating. He couldn't know for certain that Worsted was aware Ryanne was in Los Angeles, let alone that she had planned to see Dr. Kazlovski. But he didn't dare assume less than the worst, because there was a danger here that no one had yet perceived. Whether or not Ryanne regained her sight might be completely irrelevant. Just knowing that she had the capability could be enough to push Worsted into action. He wouldn't dare wait, because the moment she regained her sight she would be placed under police protection and spirited away into a witness protection program where he might never be able to get at her. He would strike now, while she was blind and vulnerable.

The threat of immediate danger galvanized Hugh into action. With a muffled curse at his own stupidity, he hurried into the house. Turning on the kitchen light, he grabbed for the phone and began making calls.

The first was to Ben Rosenthal, with a terse order to get out to the Burbank hangar and prepare the company jet for an immediate flight. The second roused a groggy Mo Johnson from a sound sleep—possibly the last he would see for days. Without bothering to explain, Hugh told Mo to get to Ryanne's house at once, and before Hugh had even completed dialing his next number, Johnson was half dressed and almost out the door.

Methodically Hugh took the necessary steps to ensure that Ryanne would be protected while he flew to Chicago and back. He had to get to Doug Sutherland and the Chicago police in order to find out everything there was to know about Worsted. Ryanne could tell him the man's real name, of course, but she didn't know where he was or what he had been doing for the past five years. For all he knew, Worsted could have been hit by a crosstown bus or drowned in Lake Michigan. Hugh had to know if the threat to Ryanne was as real as he suspected, and he had to learn all he could about her enemy. Five years ago, Worsted had been a small-time hood, according to Ryanne. Did he have an arm long enough to reach her in Los Angeles?

Ryanne wouldn't be truly safe until Hugh knew exactly what he was up against, and as much as he hated to leave, all the answers were in Chicago.

"Judith?" Hugh knocked softly on the door of her upstairs room. "Judith, wake up."

"What is it?" she asked, opening the door as she wrapped a robe around herself. "Is Ryanne all right?"

"For the time being, yes." Without garnishing the facts, he explained the situation. Judith took it all in calmly, just as he'd expected her to. "My jet is being prepared for take-off and Mo Johnson will be here any minute with a couple of freelance bodyguards I use from time to time. They're trustworthy, and they're good at what they do. All three of them will stay outside the house—I don't want Ryanne to know what's going on."

Judith nodded. "You're right. She doesn't need this added to everything else. What about her appointment tomorrow at the clinic?"

"Mo will take care of everything. No one will get close to her with him standing guard, I promise. I should be back by tomorrow night. If she should ask about me in the morning, tell her I had to leave early to finish the Canoga Park job, but that I'll drop by later."

Judith returned downstairs with Hugh, making a pot of coffee while they waited impatiently for Mo to arrive. When he got there, Hugh explained the situation to him in a terse, shorthand language that had developed naturally from the years they had worked together.

Once he was satisfied that Mo had the facts he needed, Hugh headed for the airport. The jet was kept fueled and ready for takeoff at all times, and Ben, an experienced pilot, had already filed their flight plan. When Hugh arrived, the jet was on the landing field and within minutes they were in the air.

"HUGH MACKENNA, this is Lieutenant Rube Lilenthal," Doug Sutherland said. "Rube was the investigating officer on the Vinnie Perigrino murder."

The rotund police officer wiped the raspberry filling of his jelly doughnut off his hand before he extended it to Hugh.

"Sorry about that, MacKenna," he said apologetically, referring to the sticky handshake. "Dougie here—" he cocked his head toward Douglas "—got me out of bed a little early. I usually eat breakfast at home, but when he phoned to say an illustrious PI from Hollywood was on his way to the station, I figured I'd better dash right over."

Lilenthal's sarcasm was as thick as molasses and the best Hugh could manage was a tight smile. "It's a real thrill to meet you, too, lieutenant."

"Could we cut the crap and get down to business?" Doug interjected, taking a chair opposite Lilenthal's. Hugh's phone call last night had been like a nightmare come true, and today Doug was in no mood to listen to a police officer and a private investigator try to one-up each other. Cops and PIs, everybody knew, were natural rivals. Doug had known Ryanne since she was a baby; her father had been Doug's best friend. Her safety was more than a matter of mild concern to him. "Hugh needs to see everything you've got on Arlen Beck."

Lilenthal gave Hugh a thorough once-over, noting the expensive suit he was wearing and the even suntan that virtually screamed California. He'd also arrived in Chicago an hour ago via his own personal jet, which in itself told Lilenthal a lot. MacKenna obviously made a better-than-average living in movieland, and that thought galled the police officer who had spent twenty-four years on the force and could barely pay the rent on his mediocre apartment four blocks from the station house.

Nevertheless, there was something about MacKenna that did command the lieutenant's grudging respect. His tan may have been as pretty as his face, but there was a hard edge around his eyes that suggested he could be as tough as he was civilized if the situation called for it.

Putting his personal bias aside, Lilenthal nodded for Hugh to take a chair, and both men sat. "Doug told me there's a chance we may have an eyewitness to the Perigrino murder, after all," he said, getting down to business.

"There's no way of knowing that for sure," Hugh replied, not happy with the detective's cavalier attitude. He made a supreme effort to keep his tone professional. "There now exists a possibility that Ryanne Kirkland may someday regain her sight, but that possibility alone may place her in a great deal of danger."

"I'd say so, yes," Lilenthal agreed. "As long as she's in California she's out of our jurisdiction, of course. There's not a damned thing we can do to protect her."

"I'm taking responsibility for Ryanne's safety while she's in L.A., lieutenant. What I need from you is information. I have to know what I'm up against. I'd appreciate anything you could tell me about the man you suspect of killing Vinnie Perigrino and attempting to murder Ryanne Kirkland."

Lilenthal nodded and reached for the file under his half-eaten jelly doughnut. He extracted a photograph from the file and tossed it to Hugh. "Arlen Beck, age forty-nine, born and raised on the South Side of Chicago. He started out as a punk, but managed to elevate his status by marrying the daughter of a moderately well-to-do banker who ran a small, legitimate savings-and-loan company uptown. Beck polished up his act just enough to convince his wife's old man to leave him control of the S and L when he died. Seven years ago the father-in-law keeled over from a coronary and suddenly the S and L wasn't so legit anymore. Beck organized a gambling syndicate with some of his old friends from the neighborhood and presto-chango, dirty gambling money went through Beck's S and L washing machine and came out smelling rosy clean."

"Was Vinnie Perigrino one of Beck's bag men?" Hugh asked.

"Yeah. He carried money to Beck. A couple of weeks before he died we busted him on an unrelated drug trafficking charge and he rolled over like a boulder in a landslide. He told us he'd give us Beck if we'd be lenient on the trafficking charge. The district attorney bought it and Perigrino was supposed to set up a time and a place for us to catch Beck in the act of receiving a chunk of the syndicate's cash."

Hugh frowned. "Then why weren't your men in that warehouse when Ryanne was shot?"

It was clear from Lilenthal's expression that he objected to Hugh's accusatory tone, but he answered the question anyway. "We're not quite sure what happened, but we think Perigrino was trying to double-cross us and warn his boss."

"But Beck killed him anyway."

"My guess is that Beck got wind of Perigrino's arrest and the deal he'd made and thought it would be smart to rid himself on one distinct liability. Someone in the D.A.'s office leaked the deal to ace reporter Ryanne Kirkland and she became another of Beck's liabilities."

"So where's Beck now?" Hugh asked.

"Sitting very pretty," Lilenthal said disgustedly. "Two years ago this man—" he extracted another photograph from the file "—Del Michelon, brought Beck's operation under his protective influence. Beck is in the big leagues now."

"Damn," Douglas swore softly. He hadn't known about this.

Hugh looked at his old friend sharply. "You know Michelon?"

"I know about him," Doug confirmed. "He's one of the two most powerful crime bosses in the state of Illinois. If Beck is heavily into Michelon's organization, Ryanne is in real trouble."

"That's right," Lilenthal agreed. "Michelon can't afford to have Beck brought in on a murder rap. Del had nothing to do with Perigrino's death because he wasn't associated with Beck at the time, but he can't afford the possibility that Beck might cop a plea to a lesser charge in exchange for information about Michelon. Believe me, that's a deal the D.A. would snap up in an instant. We want Michelon bad." He paused for a moment. "Of course, it depends on how much Beck knows, and on how much damage he could do the syndicate. But you can bet your life Michelon's not going to sit still and watch us haul Beck in."

"In other words, history is repeating itself," Hugh commented, drawing the correlation between Beck and Perigrino five years earlier, and Michelon and Beck now. But in this situation, the easiest way to minimize losses would be to dispose of Ryanne.

"You grasp the situation perfectly, Mr. MacKenna," Lilenthal told him. "Right now I wouldn't want to be in Ryanne Kirkland's shoes for all the money in Fort Knox."

Hugh stiffened but made no comment. He continued asking questions, garnering every fact he could. Lilenthal was abrasive but cooperative, and Hugh soaked up the information like a sponge.

"You realize, of course, that Beck's not going to come after her himself this time," the cop said as he rose and moved to the door of his office. He flagged down a uniformed officer in the busy squad room and requested a file, then returned to his seat.

"Any ideas on who he might hire?" Doug asked.

"Not really. I'm gonna let you look at our hit file, though, just in case." The young officer rapped once on the door, stepped in and handed Lilenthal a thick file folder, then retreated without a word. "We try to keep this current, but you know how a bureaucracy works. In a perfect world, there would be a photograph, rap sheet and current status report on every known hit man who operates out of Chicago. But this ain't a perfect world. And, of course, nothing's to say that Beck's going to send local heat. He could hire independent muscle in L.A. I imagine you got one or two pretty boys out there who would be willing to take a few minutes away from working on their tans to take the job, right?"

Hugh was already so absorbed in the file that he barely heard Lilenthal's jibe. When he didn't comment, the lieutenant shrugged, picked up the remainder of his jelly doughnut and washed it down with his cold coffee.

The silence lengthened and finally Lilenthal said, "Look, MacKenna, why don't I get you a desk outside so you can peruse that at your leisure. I got work—"

"Are these statistics current?" Hugh interrupted him.

"More or less. Like I said, this is not a perfect world. Why? You find something interesting?"

Hugh looked closer at one particular photograph, then glanced at the list of previous crimes attributed to one Asa "Ace" Keegan. In addition to a basic physical description and a list of previous arrests and convictions, there was also a notation of the man's suspected connection with the Michelon syndicate. By far the most interesting bit of information, though, was a recently added, handwritten memo that stated the alleged hit man had dropped out of sight two months ago—right about the time Ryanne came to Los Angeles.

He handed the papers to Lilenthal, who looked them over dispassionately. "Could be." He shrugged his shoulders and handed the papers back to Hugh.

"Can I get a copy of this to show my men back in L.A.?"

"Technically, no," Lilenthal answered. "However, we do cooperate with law enforcement agencies in other states from time to time. Have you got a friend on the force in L.A.? Someone who might be willing to slip you a copy of a photo that got wired from here to there? After all, it would only be the polite thing for us to let the L.A.P.D. know that they may have a suspected felon in their midst."

"If you can get it to L.A., I can get my hands on it. Send it to Detective Victor Coffin. And while you're at it, why don't you send through a copy of Arlen Beck's photo?"

"I was going to suggest that myself," Lilenthal answered. "If Miss Kirkland should get her sight back unexpectedly, shove that picture in front of her face and get a positive ID, would you? If she fingers him, we'll have him in custody by the time she gets to Chicago."

"What about security?" Douglas asked. "No offense to the department, lieutenant, but members of the force have been known to let things slip from time to time. What steps are you prepared to take to ensure Ryanne's safety if someone tips off Michelon and Beck about an imminent arrest?"

Lilenthal threw Douglas a withering look, then turned the same expression on Hugh. "You get her to Chicago and I guarantee we'll get her to court. Here." He scribbled something on a slip of paper and handed it to Hugh. "This is my home number in case you gotta get hold of me at night. If Ms. Kirkland gets her sight back, I want to be the first person who knows about it. You got that?"

Lilenthal's look was so commanding that it was easy for Hugh to see how he had earned his lieutenant's stripes, but Hugh wasn't one of Lilenthal's officers and he had no intention of pretending that he was. He returned Lilenthal's long look as he stood. "Lieutenant, I appreciate your time and your help. And if Ryanne regains her sight, I guarantee you that you'll be *one of the first* to know. If you learn of anything that might be helpful, you can reach me at this number." He extracted a business card from his jacket and handed it to Lilenthal. "Thanks again for your help."

"Don't mention it," Lilenthal murmured sarcastically, hating that this pretty-boy Californian had just told him who was the boss.

"Do you think there's any chance that Keegan will be the one to go after Ryanne?" Douglas asked a few minutes later as he drove Hugh back to the airport. Hugh noticed that like himself, Doug was treating the threat to Ryanne as fact, not a remote possibility.

"I'd say the chances are roughly equivalent to my being elected Pope by Christmas. More than likely Keegan's disappearance means he'll eventually turn up floating in Lake Michigan."

"So what are you going to do now?"

Hugh shrugged. "Get back to Ryanne as quickly as possible and do what will probably be the hardest thing I've ever had to do in my life."

"What's that?"

"Tell her what we suspect. I can't imagine that this little bit of news will help her cope any better."

With one hand on the wheel, Douglas ran the other through the thin patch of graying hair on top of his head. "I don't know about that, Hugh. Think about it for a minute. From what you've told me, Ryanne's subconscious blinded her to keep her from getting killed. It doesn't take a Rhodes scholar to see the warped logic of that defense mechanism. But once her subconscious realizes that the blindness is no longer keeping her safe, maybe it'll flip that switch you told me about. I mean, at this point, Ryanne could protect herself a whole lot better if she could see, right?"

"That's true," Hugh agreed. "But I don't know if her subconscious is going to see it that way. She just has so much garbage to sort through that I'm afraid she's going to overload. She took the news pretty hard yesterday."

"What else would you expect?" Doug shook his head. "Damn, this is all so eerie. What was it you said earlier about history repeating itself? Truer words were never spoken."

Hugh had the feeling he'd missed part of their conversation. "What? You mean Perigrino and Beck?"

"No. I was referring to Ryanne and her father, Martin Kirkland."

Hugh turned sideways on the seat. "What's Ryanne's father got to do with this? He was killed in a hit-and-run accident when she was a little girl."

Doug's answering smile was grimly ironic. "Is that what she told you?"

"You mean it's not true?"

"Well, yeah...in a manner of speaking. What Ryanne neglected to tell you was that the accident took place two days before her father, Martin Kirkland, was to give testimony before the grand jury that was trying to indict Spence Leroy."

Hugh frowned, trying to remember why that name sounded familiar. "The mobster?"

"The very same."

Gradually the details of the sensational case came back to Hugh. He'd only been a kid at the time, in his senior year of high school, but the trial of Spencer Leroy had been nationwide news. Even a self-absorbed teenager couldn't avoid hearing about it. His current events class had followed the sensational case for weeks, but until this moment, Hugh had forgotten about the reporter who'd gone undercover to get the goods on one of the biggest gangland bosses in the Midwest. Vaguely Hugh recalled that the reporter had been betrayed by a friend who had lured him out of hiding and into a parking garage where he was killed by a car that ran over his body repeatedly just to make certain he was good and dead.

No wonder Ryanne hadn't wanted to discuss her father's death.

"Did Kirkland work for the *Examiner*?" Hugh asked.

"Yeah. And he even won a Pulitzer for the mob story—posthumously," Doug said with disgust. "That wasn't a helluva lot of comfort to Ryanne and her mother at the time. It was all so damned senseless! Martin had already turned over to the police everything his investigation had uncovered and he'd written an entire series of articles we were already in the process of publishing. His testimony would have made Leroy a lot easier to convict, but by the time they killed him, Martin wasn't really vital to the D.A.'s case. They murdered him out of revenge, or maybe as a lesson to others.''

"Didn't they have him under protective custody?" Hugh asked, trying to remember details that had been forgotten long ago.

"Sort of. He took Beverly and Ryanne into hiding, but it was for their benefit more than his own.''

Poor Ryanne, Hugh thought, trying to imagine the fear, uncertainty and ultimately the grief she must have suffered all those years ago. The cause of her blindness was clearer than ever, now. The foundation for it had been laid nearly twenty years ago by her father's death, and when she had been confronted with an uncannily similar situation, her subconscious mind had offered what seemed to be the perfect solution.

The men were silent for the remainder of the drive, each lost in his own thoughts. They reached the airport and Hugh thanked Doug for his help, but the newspaper editor stopped him before he could leave the car.

"Hugh…this isn't just a job to you, is it?" he asked, even though he already knew the answer. "I mean, this has gone a lot farther than you keeping an eye on Ryanne because I asked you to, right?"

"Yes."

"Are you in love with her?"

Hugh took a deep breath and released it slowly. Love wasn't a word he'd allowed himself to use when thinking of Ryanne. She saw their relationship as a pleasant, short-term affair; Hugh saw it as more. To protect himself he'd refused to name the emotion he felt for her, but Doug was forcing him to confront it head-on and Hugh wasn't ready for that.

"I'm not going to let anything happen to her, Doug. I promise you."

"I know that, but you didn't answer my question."

"Ryanne considers what we have is a summer fling," he said tightly.

"Hmm. That doesn't sound much like the Ryanne I know," Doug observed. "How do you feel about it?"

Hugh frowned. He wasn't accustomed to being pressed. "I care about her, Doug. All right? I'll do whatever is necessary to get her out of this mess alive and worry about the future later."

A wry smile crept across Doug's craggy face. "In other words, you love her so much that you can't see straight."

Hugh glanced out the window at a DC-10 that had just taken off. The jet thundered overhead, almost obscuring his quiet answer. "That's about the size of it. You happy now?"

"When I dance with the bride at your wedding, *then* I'll be happy. Right now I'm just very relieved and grateful that she has you to protect her."

"Let's hope it's enough." Hugh opened the door and stepped out. "Thanks again, Doug. I'll keep you posted."

They said a hasty goodbye and Doug sat quietly, watching his young friend hurry across the parking lot toward the small terminal that provided a clearing house for the private planes that came and went out of the busy airport. Hugh's sense of urgency was apparent even in his retreating back, and though the situation was grim, Douglas Sutherland couldn't hold back a small, self-satisfied smile.

"The bigger they are, the harder they fall," he mumbled. "Keep her safe, boy. I love her, too."

CHAPTER FOURTEEN

THE INTERIOR OF Hugh's BMW was as silent as a tomb. Midafternoon traffic on the San Diego Freeway was light, but Ryanne had no way of knowing that. She sat quietly, running over in her mind her session with Dr. Whitehorn— a session that had included Hugh MacKenna. Yesterday when he had dropped by the house after work, he'd made no mention of his trip to Chicago. He had insisted on being allowed to drive Ryanne to her next therapy session, though, and now she knew why. Late yesterday Hugh had made his own appointment with Dr. Whitehorn to discuss how his suspicions regarding Arlen Beck should be presented to her. The psychiatrist had suggested that they tell her together during this afternoon's session. She presumed the doctor had wanted to be around in case she fell apart.

But she hadn't. She was too numb; not surprised, shocked, or even particularly frightened, just...numb. Ryanne supposed that given time she would have come to the same realization about Beck that Hugh had, but he had spared her that personal revelation. She wanted to feel grateful not only for his concern for her welfare, but also for the protection she now knew he was providing for her. Unfortunately feeling anything at all was beyond her. She just wanted to be home and safe, but the knowledge that there was nowhere she could truly consider safe made even the desire to be home seem a wasted effort.

The car stopped and when Hugh shut off the engine Ryanne reached for the door handle. Hugh stopped her with his voice. "Just wait, Ryanne. I'll come around and get the door."

She started to protest that such chivalry wasn't necessary, then realized that Hugh wasn't being polite. He didn't want her stepping out of the car alone, making her an easier target. A shudder of apprehension trickled down her spine and she sat patiently, waiting.

He walked beside her as Aggie led the way to the house, and though he didn't speak, Ryanne could feel the coil of alertness that emanated from him. This Hugh was different from the one she was familiar with. His every word and movement now reminded her of the hard, cold stranger she'd been introduced to in Hugh's bedroom three days ago—the one she'd realized was capable of killing if the need arose. As a woman who needed protection, Ryanne appreciated this iron-willed stranger, even as she mourned the loss of the warm, gentle man she'd been so close to falling in love with.

Close to falling in love? Some part of Ryanne's confused, clouded mind mocked the thought. There was nothing close about it. Though she'd refused to admit it, she'd fallen in love with Hugh MacKenna.

Considering my life expectancy now, it's a good thing he doesn't believe in long-term relationships, Ryanne reflected with morbid humor.

Aggie stopped at the front door and before Ryanne or Hugh could reach for the knob, Judith opened it from the inside.

"Thank you, Judith," Ryanne said. She moved into the foyer, well past the door's opening, and while she removed Aggie's harness Judith looked at Hugh as though to say, "How did she take it?"

"Will you two kindly stop exchanging worried glances," Ryanne requested, heading for the living-room sofa. "Your solicitude is so thick I could cut it with a knife."

"Sorry," Hugh said, smiling at the first thing Ryanne had said in three days that sounded like the woman whose indomitable spirit he so cherished.

Judith, too, noticed the return to normalcy and reacted accordingly. "You haven't exactly been a barrel of monkeys yourself." She turned on her heel and left with an explanation that she'd be in the office if anyone needed her.

Ryanne chuckled weakly as she sat. "Now I know everything's going to be all right. Judith's being mean to me again."

"Everything *is* going to be all right, Ryanne," Hugh promised, joining her on the sofa.

She didn't bother responding. "I assume Judith knows about your trip to Chicago yesterday."

"Yes."

"Good."

It tore at Hugh's heart to see Ryanne so quiet and still, when she was normally so animated and bursting with life. He reached for her hand, pressing it between both of his, but Ryanne only gave him a gentle squeeze to thank him for the reassuring gesture before she pulled away. She rested her head against the back of the sofa, slipped off her shoes and placed her feet on the edge of the coffee table. "Who do you have guarding the house? Mo and Ben?"

"Mo is coordinating days and Ben's doing nights."

"Coordinating?" She turned her face toward him.

"I've brought in some extra help. One man can't cover the front and back at the same time." Because she seemed to have a need to know the details, Hugh explained all the precautions he was taking for her protection. The men worked eight-hour shifts, except for Mo and Ben, who worked twelve. "The beach is my biggest concern. One of the men stays near the deck at all times, but he doesn't have much of a view up and down the coast. I have a friend who's loaning me his yacht, though. Tomorrow it will be anchored just far enough off the beach to blend in with the other boats out there and I'll have a couple of men with binoculars scanning the shoreline. If they see anything suspicious they'll report it to Mo."

Ryanne smiled. "How many times has Mo tried to convince you things should be coordinated from the yacht?"

"About a dozen," Hugh answered, chuckling. Ryanne had only met Mo once, but she had pegged the investigator perfectly. Mo had presented Hugh with a number of reasons why he should be the one to pull the cushy duty on the luxurious pleasure craft, but Hugh knew his friend had just been joking. He was certain Ryanne knew it, too.

"This is going to be an expensive operation, isn't it?" she asked. "All those extra men, the surveillance equipment, the yacht... I'll have Judith write you out a check before you leave today."

"Ryanne, I don't want your money," Hugh insisted flatly. "This isn't just another job to me, and you're not my client."

"Yes, I am," Ryanne argued. "This is *my* problem—I'm the one who needs protection. I won't let you foot the bill for something that doesn't have anything to do with you."

"Damn it, Ryanne," Hugh swore, coming to his feet. "I care about you. I'm not about to put a price tag on what I feel!"

Ryanne knew she'd wounded Hugh by bringing up the subject of money, but she couldn't let it rest. Whatever their personal relationship, it was still going to cost a fortune to protect her. She refused to let Hugh do this out of some misguided, macho sense of loyalty. Their pleasurable, no-strings-attached affair had come to a crashing halt, and any man with sense would have turned around and walked away from her at the first hint of trouble. Hugh wasn't built that way, though, and Ryanne admired and appreciated his sense of honor. He couldn't turn his back on a defenseless woman in need, but that didn't mean their relationship meant what it once had.

"Hugh, listen to me," she said, keeping her voice soft and even. "I know you haven't looked at all of this in terms of cost—that's not you. But if I didn't have you as a friend, I'd have to find someone else to help me out—at least for the time being—and I'd have to pay for that protection. If you don't want to charge me your own personal fee, fine. I'll accept that gesture with gratitude, but you have to let me pay the salaries of the men working for you as well as any extra expenses you incur."

"Ryanne—"

She leaned forward and cut him off. "Hugh, please! Let me do that much at least! I'm sitting around this house as helpless as a worm writhing on a hook, waiting for a big fish to come along and gobble me up. At least leave me the dignity of knowing I'm doing *something* to help myself!"

Hugh found he couldn't argue with that. He was going to keep Ryanne alive, but he wouldn't strip her of her pride to do it. "All right, Ryanne. I'll talk to Judith later about expenses." He returned to the sofa and took her hand. This time she did not pull away.

"Thank you."

"Ryanne, if you really want to help, there is something else you can do."

"What?"

"I want you, Judith and Aggie to move down the beach to my house. Now before you start protesting, listen to what I have to say. My place sits on a peninsula with nothing around it for a half a mile in either direction. No one could possibly approach it without one of my men being aware of it, whereas here, the houses are close, the beach is almost always crowded.... You'd be much safer there, Ryanne," he concluded, but he could tell from her closed expression that he hadn't been convincing enough.

"I can't do that, Hugh, and you know it. I can't disrupt your life that way."

"It's not a disruption, Ryanne, it's a precaution. I've got a spare bedroom Judith can use and we can set your office up in my study."

"I don't know my way around your place, Hugh. You can't imagine what an upheaval it is to have to learn something new."

"I know it wouldn't be simple, but you could learn. I want you to move in with me."

"For how long?" she asked brusquely, tugging her hand out of his firm grasp. "A week, a month? A year?"

For forever, he thought, unbidden, but didn't dare say it out loud. Ryanne had enough to handle without adding to it a declaration of love she probably didn't even want. "For as long as it takes," he said finally.

Ryanne shook her head, stood, and meandered around the room. "Hugh, do you realize how absurd this is? What if we're wrong about Worste—Beck." She forced herself to say the name she had avoided for so long. "What if he and this Michelon person don't know about my visit to the doctor? What if they never learn the results of the tests? I'm living in an armed prison camp, and for what? The flimsy chance that *maybe* Beck or someone hired by him will make an attempt on my life." She turned to him, her voice plaintive and soft. "I'm walking a tightrope wearing a blindfold, Hugh. I'm so confused and frightened and just plain damned angry with myself and the world that I don't know what to do or which way to turn. Until I figure that out, I'll take precautions and live with the guards and the boat and all the rest of it, but I have to keep some sense of order and routine in my life or I'll go nuts. Can you understand that?"

Sighing, Hugh moved to Ryanne and gathered her into his arms. "Of course I understand." His hands cupped her face and he pressed an undemanding kiss to her lips. "I'll pack a few things and move up here tonight."

"Hugh, no—"

"Yes." He cut her off forcefully. "I'm not leaving you alone. I may come and go during the day, but at night I *will* be with you. If that means giving you a bill for my services as well as my men's, so be it, but you're not getting rid of me."

Ryanne knew it was pointless to argue, particularly when the knowledge that he would be nearby made her feel much safer and far less empty. With a nod and a half smile, she told him, "I'll help Judith make up the bed in the downstairs guest room."

Hugh opened his mouth to tell her he had no intention of sleeping in any bed other than hers, then stopped himself. Ryanne was in no shape to be pushed; he had to let her define the parameters of their relationship for the moment. If she couldn't handle intimacy with him—whether it was making love or just holding her close and safe in his arms— he wouldn't force the issue when she was so vulnerable.

"There's no point in bothering Judith," he told her, pulling her close again. "I never did quite get the hang of hospital corners, but I can make a bed myself. Just point me toward the linen closet."

"In a minute," Ryanne murmured, pressing her face against Hugh's shoulder so that he wouldn't see her disappointment and hurt. She had hoped she was wrong about Hugh's motives for protecting her, that despite the turmoil she had brought into his life he still craved the intimacy they had briefly shared. But she hadn't been wrong. Hugh didn't want her anymore, or he would have argued about their sleeping arrangements the way he'd argued about everything else.

She was a client now, nothing more. She was a responsibility, a job to do thoroughly and efficiently. The friendship they'd forged wasn't strong enough to withstand the kind of pressure Ryanne's predicament placed it under, and she knew that once Hugh was satisfied and the danger to her had passed, he would be gone from her life forever.

The thought of losing him brought a sob to her throat, but she choked it back, sliding her arms beneath his jacket to pull him closer. The movement brought her in contact with the gun holstered beneath his arm and her blood turned to ice because it reminded her that if Hugh wasn't very good at his profession he wouldn't be the one to leave her. She would be leaving him....

RYANNE HAD NEVER known a week could creep by so slowly. She was in a state of suspended animation. It was as though time had simply stopped and left her hanging in midair while the rest of the world went blithely about its business. A feeling of impending violence infused every waking hour and even haunted her sleep. She began having nightmares that left her drained and drenched with sweat, exhausted, yet too terrified to return to sleep.

More than once she had started to call out to Hugh; she'd wanted to beg him to take her into his arms until the trembling passed, but she had resisted that urge. It had become a matter of honor to make it through the night alone, and there was very little else that made her feel honorable these days. Despite Dr. Whitehorn's continued reassurance that what her subconscious mind had done to her didn't decrease her worth as a person, Ryanne couldn't shake the feeling that she was a coward of the highest order. She berated herself for having taken the easy way out of a bad situation, and nothing the psychiatrist said decreased her feelings of guilt. She thought about her father, of how he had died for something he believed in, and she couldn't escape the knowledge that she had betrayed Martin Kirkland and everything he'd stood for.

She talked about her father at length in her sessions with Dr. Whitehorn, of course. The parallels in their situations had always been obvious to her, and now she knew her father's death had contributed greatly to her blindness. Whitehorn said it had likely been the foundation of her subconscious's solution to her conundrum. Knowing that didn't help much, though. As far as Ryanne was concerned, the only thing that would redeem her now was regaining her sight and bringing Arlen Beck to justice.

Unfortunately her subconscious refused to come to the same conclusion. Even the knowledge that being blind was no longer a sure way to keep her alive didn't flip the elusive switch that lurked somewhere in the dark recesses of her mind.

Dr. Whitehorn had two theories about that particular stumbling block, and Ryanne felt both were probably correct. The first was that there was no real proof yet that she was in danger. Her subconscious was still operating on the theory that as long as she was blind, she was safe. Until it was proved otherwise, she would probably remain sightless. The second theory made sense as well; even if the danger was real, her subconscious had no reason to change the status quo as long as Ryanne had Hugh MacKenna protecting her. Her trust in him, the feeling of security and safety she achieved when she was with him made any action on the part of her subconscious unnecessary.

It was a catch-22 situation. If she sent Hugh and his guards away, she stood a better chance of regaining her sight—as well as a better chance of dying.

Ryanne found neither choice palatable. The thought of being without Hugh was as terrifying as the knowledge that Arlen Beck wanted her dead. Hugh was her rock, the only foundation she had in a world of treacherous, shifting quicksand. His presence made her feel safer, but more than that, he reminded her that there was life and hope and happiness beyond the walls of the self-inflicted prison now caging her in. For a few short weeks and one passionate night, Hugh had filled her life with joy. Inch by inch, he had wedged open a door Ryanne had kept sealed; and even if she emerged from this nightmare alive, that door would swing shut with Hugh on one side and Ryanne, alone, on the other.

"Ryanne?" Hugh poked his head into the office where she had been sitting motionless in front of her typewriter for almost an hour. All week long, she'd been making an effort to work on her screenplay, but Hugh knew she had accomplished next to nothing. Considering everything she was trying to cope with, it amazed him that she even bothered.

"Yes, Hugh?" She swiveled toward him.

"It's getting late," he reminded her gently. "Are you going to stay in here all night?"

Ryanne shrugged. "One dark room looks pretty much like any other." She ducked her head the moment the words were out of her mouth. "Sorry. That was supposed to be a joke, but it didn't come out that way, did it?"

"It's all right, Ryanne. No one expects you to be the life of the party."

"That's fortunate." She managed a smile. "Is Judith still on the phone with Webb?"

Hugh leaned against the door frame and shook his head. "No. She went upstairs about a half an hour ago. When I made my rounds checking all the doors and windows, she was in her room, curled up with a good book."

"It was nice of your father to call her. I don't think Judith expected it," Ryanne told him. Webb's phone call had surprised everyone, especially Judith. Webb had been in for a surprise, too, when he had discovered that his son had taken up residence at Ryanne's. Hugh had explained the situation to him and Webb had insisted on talking to Ryanne. They had spoken for several minutes and Ryanne had been immensely grateful that her new friend had resisted the urge to offer meaningless platitudes of encouragement and reassurance. Just knowing that he cared helped more than anything.

After her brief conversation with Webb, Ryanne had handed the phone over to Judith, then left her alone to talk in private. This ordeal was taking its toll on Judith as well, Ryanne knew, and she was grateful that her friend had someone to talk to. She only hoped that Judith would take advantage of the sympathetic, supportive ear Webb would be only too happy to lend her.

Hugh moved to Ryanne's desk and sat on the edge. "Frankly when Dad arrived I don't think he expected to be quite so...taken with your secretary. I certainly wouldn't have guessed it, that's for sure. Dad hasn't been a monk since he and Mother divorced, but he hasn't gone out of his way to develop a social life, either. He's kept his world centered almost totally around his business."

"Then you wouldn't mind it if a little romance blossomed between them?"

"Dad deserves only the best, and as far as I'm concerned Judith Tremain fits very nicely into that category. She's a wonderful woman."

Ryanne smiled, pleased that Hugh realized how special her friend was. "She doesn't let many people close enough to see that."

"So I noticed. Ryanne..." There was a slight, uncomfortable pause as Hugh sought a gentle way of telling Ryanne he had some special precautions he wanted to take tomorrow when she visited the doctor. Ryanne sensed his hesitation and the sudden tension in him, though.

"You didn't come in here just to chat, did you, Hugh?" she asked.

"Actually, no," he replied, grateful that the ice was broken. All week long he'd tried hard to be supportive of Ryanne when she needed support, and to stay out of her way when she didn't. There was a strain in their relationship that had never been there before, however, and no matter how often Hugh told himself that it was simply a result of the incredible pressures on Ryanne, he knew it went deeper than that. Until Ryanne's world had come crashing down, they had never had trouble talking. Now everything they said seemed stilted, as though words had to be censored or sifted through a filter before being spoken aloud. Maybe it was because he was no longer her lover; instead, he had become her protector—or her jailer, it sometimes seemed. And it could have a lot to do with requests like the one he was about to make.

"I wanted to discuss the clothes you're going to wear to the clinic tomorrow," he told her.

Ryanne frowned. Hugh had never expressed an interest in her wardrobe before. "Why? Are you afraid I'll mismatch the colors again?" she asked, remembering the day before yesterday when she'd accidentally donned her lime-green camp shirt instead of the lilac one that matched her cotton trousers.

Hugh laughed lightly, remembering the incident. "No, that's not it. I just want to pick out a jacket—"

"A jacket? Hugh, tomorrow is the third of July and the weatherman is predicting a temperature of one hundred. I don't think a jacket is really necessary."

"It is if you're wearing a bulletproof vest," he told her softly. Ryanne's face turned chalk-white and Hugh cursed himself for having caused the resurgence of panic in her already haunted blue eyes. He would have given anything to spare her this, but it was necessary. Tomorrow was Friday, and he had a gnawing feeling in his gut that all hell was going to break loose. He knew better than to ignore his own premonitions.

Ryanne tried vainly to keep her voice calm. "Have you heard something? Has one of the men seen—"

"No, Ryanne, nothing like that," he reassured her quickly. He saw no reason to tell her that Mo had been fairly certain he'd spotted a car following them to the clinic earlier in the day—probably the same one that had been seen cruising the neighborhood the day before. They had no proof, just suspicions, and Hugh couldn't bring himself to enlighten Ryanne without evidence. "Nothing has changed. I just want to take this extra precaution."

Ryanne nodded, understanding his concern. Here at the house she was well guarded, with Hugh inside and the others outside, not to mention the boat that sat just offshore during the day. Breaking in would be nearly impossible, so it would be logical for someone to go after her while she was out of the house—en route to the clinic, for example, or while she was there. If her therapy sessions hadn't been so important, she was sure Hugh would have insisted she remain in the house at all times.

Hugh moved toward the door, and Ryanne stood. Aggie, who'd been napping under the desk, raised her head sleepily. Ryanne heard the jingle of her choke chain and ordered the dog to stay, then accompanied Hugh down the hall. "I've never worn a suit of armor before. This should be an adventure," she commented dryly.

In Ryanne's bedroom, Hugh closed the door and opened the closet to search for a lightweight jacket that would camouflage the dark bulletproof vest he'd had one of his men deliver. "The vest is as hot as the dickens and weighs about a ton, but it'll make you feel more secure."

Ryanne laughed shortly. "Wanna bet?"

"Hey." Hugh stepped out of the closet and moved to her, pulling her against his chest. She wrapped her arms around him immediately, and held on fiercely, as though she could lose herself in his warmth and strength. "We're going to make it through this, Ryanne. I promise."

She nodded, her face pressed against his throat. "I know."

"No, you don't know," he murmured sadly. "You want to believe it, but you can't quite."

"When it's all over I'll be happy to hear you say I told you so," she said teasingly, desperate to lighten their dark mood. She needed to escape the grimness of the reality that even if she regained her sight and was able to testify, it might be years before Beck came to trial. Until he was convicted, Ryanne would never be safe; the most she had to look forward to was the same uncertainty and fear.

Hugh seemed to sense her thoughts and her need to escape them. "I never gloat, although I have been known to preen from time to time."

Ryanne chuckled. "That I'd like to see."

Hugh's voice became serious as he cupped her face tenderly between his hands. "You will someday, love. You will."

She was so beautiful with her face tilted up to his that Hugh couldn't resist. A week of wanting her but forcing himself to keep that desire under control had taken its toll on him, and without even thinking, he removed her glasses. As he lowered his face to hers, Ryanne sensed his intent and closed her eyes, accepting the whisper-soft pressure of the kisses he placed on each delicate eyelid.

From out of nowhere, Ryanne remembered the story of Sleeping Beauty, who had been awakened from a hundred-years' slumber by the kiss of a handsome prince. With all her heart, she prayed for that same magic to touch her now. She felt Hugh's breath warm her useless eyes, and for a fleeting moment she was filled with the certainty that when she opened them she would see Hugh's face, a face she knew only with her heart. He drew back, and Ryanne reached deep inside for the courage to raise her eyes to his.

All that greeted her was blackness.

A sob of anguish forced its way out and she arched, offering Hugh her lips. His mouth closed over hers and the desperation of their separate fears and needs merged into one consuming flame. Roughly Hugh pulled Ryanne to him, sealing their bodies as his mouth ravaged hers. His tongue plunged deep in symbolic union, and Ryanne eagerly clasped the back of his head, urging him on, begging for more. With a muffled groan, Hugh filled his hand with the weight of one of her breasts, his thumb teasing the crest to hardness.

Ryanne's breath caught in her throat and stayed there for a long moment before finally shuddering outward. Need so great it was almost a physical pain sliced through her with every stroke of Hugh's thumb across her breast. A sob of desperation welled but came out as only a breathy moan, and Ryanne felt a rush of liquid heat settle between her thighs.

Longing overwhelmed her and she reached with frantic, clumsy fingers for the buttons of Hugh's shirt. They refused to yield to her and she abandoned her quest and began tugging the tail of his shirt from his pants. She needed to touch him, needed to feel him touching her without the restricting barrier of clothes between them. His shirt came free, and Ryanne's hands dived beneath it, wildly savoring the hardness of his back and firmly muscled chest.

Hugh's hunger matched Ryanne's and when she touched him it was more than he could bear. He swept her into his arms and carried her to the bed without breaking their soul-shattering kiss. As though she were a priceless treasure, he lowered her to the bed and covered her body with his, pressing her into the mattress. He undid the buttons of her shirt with trembling fingers, and drew the fabric aside, trailing kisses down her neck and shoulders until he came to the lacy fabric of her bra.

With murmured sighs and whispers, Ryanne urged him on. She arched when his lips began caressing her breasts through the thin scrap of material, and the liquid ache intensified a hundredfold. Hugh was taking pleasure and giving it, but Ryanne wanted more. She wanted completion, and she wanted the sweet oblivion that could be found only when Hugh's body was joined to hers. She groped for the closure of his trousers, but when Hugh pulled away from her to discard them, Ryanne cried out at the loss of his warmth and weight pressing into her. She reached for him blindly and Hugh returned immediately. He dispatched her clothes quickly and their fevered need took control. He entered her swiftly, surely, in a frenzy of passion that engulfed them both. Separate needs, separate fears, merged into one brilliant moment of perfect oblivion in which the world consisted of nothing but intense pleasure and two souls became only one.

For that short time, Ryanne and Hugh existed only for each other, but when the moment had passed, the feeling of separateness that came as they returned to the real world was more than Ryanne could bear. The beauty of their union and the desolation of its lonely aftermath wrenched a storm of tears from her. Without really understanding why, she began to cry as though her heart would break.

Ryanne wept almost soundlessly, her head buried at Hugh's throat, and he held her tightly as his reason began to return. He felt Ryanne sobbing pitifully against him and self-loathing started seeping into every crevice of his mind. He had taken Ryanne in a fevered heat of animal passion, without care or consideration. And worse, he had taken advantage of her incredible vulnerability. Her need had been as great as his, but he had selfishly used her with no thought of what was best for Ryanne. Now she was weeping as though she had been stripped of what little pride this night-marish week had left her. Hating himself, Hugh waited until her tears began to subside before he pulled away.

"I'm sorry, Ryanne. I'm so sorry," he whispered against her temple, then released her and moved to the edge of the bed.

"Sorry?" Ryanne murmured, stunned. Hugh was sorry he'd made love to her. She had thrown herself at him, abandoning any vestige of pride even though he'd made it clear he no longer wanted her. She had deliberately inflamed him and Hugh had given in because he'd felt sorry for her. Now he was just sorry, period.

After a long, hard week, this was another humiliation. Ryanne wondered what she'd done to deserve it. Trying to salvage what little pride she had left, she sat up and wrapped the lightweight bedspread around her as she slid to the edge of the bed opposite Hugh. "No, I'm the one who should be sorry." She laughed mirthlessly. "I seem to have a habit of forcing you into things."

Hugh twisted toward her. "Forcing me? Ryanne, how can you think that?"

"Why else would you be sorry you'd made love with me?" she demanded, wiping the tears that refused to stop falling. "I threw myself at you and you took pity on me—"

"Took pity on you?" Hugh was across the bed in an instant, grabbing Ryanne by the shoulders to turn her toward him. "What just happened here had nothing to do with pity, Ryanne. I want you. God, I've never stopped wanting you! I've lain awake thinking of you alone in this room, and I swear, some nights I've thought I might go out of my mind with that wanting."

"Then why did you stay away?" Ryanne demanded brokenly.

"Because I thought you didn't want this . . . want me. You're the one who put me in the guest bedroom, remember?"

Ryanne raised her face to Hugh's. "I remember you didn't give me any argument."

"My God . . ." Hugh would have laughed at their folly if he hadn't been so moved by Ryanne's tears. He dried them with his lips and asked gently, "Did you think that because I agreed to separate sleeping arrangements I didn't want you anymore?"

Ryanne nodded. "No sane man would want a woman with my kind of problems."

He would if he loved you as much as I do, Hugh was on the verge of saying, but he stopped just in time. Ryanne wasn't asking for a commitment or an avowal of love, and he refused to complicate her already complicated life with one more item to worry about. Just as he had no intention of allowing anything to happen to her, he was equally adamant about not letting her go, but this wasn't the time to tell her that.

"I want you, Ryanne. Whether it's sane or not, it's a fact."

"Then why did you apologize for having made love to me?"

"Because I thought I had taken advantage of you."

Ryanne smiled at that. "I don't remember offering any resistance—in fact, I was the one who started the ball rolling."

"And we finished it together," he said, putting his arms around her and pulling her close.

"I don't want it to be finished, Hugh," she whispered, her face pressed against his throat. "Will you stay with me tonight?"

"Only if you promise to fall asleep in my arms," he told her softly, lowering her to the bed as his lips closed over hers.

CHAPTER FIFTEEN

THEY SPENT the long night making love and talking, then making love again. Their passion unlocked a floodgate of emotions in Ryanne, and as she lay nestled in Hugh's arms, drawing from his deep well of strength, she told him things she'd expressed only to Dr. Whitehorn—and a few she'd never dared say to anyone. She explained the deep, mortal shame she felt for having been unable to cope with her fear of Arlen Beck, and her sense of having betrayed everything she'd ever believed in or believed herself to be.

As she talked, Hugh realized that discovering she was hysterically blind had almost totally shattered Ryanne's entire ego structure. She no longer trusted her own judgment about anything, and she saw herself as a coward and a weakling. Her new lack of faith in herself made Hugh want to cry out because it was so unjustified, and he tried to tell her that the way she'd confronted her problem this week only proved that her strength of purpose and character had not deserted her. But nothing he said convinced her. Ryanne was going to have to come to that conclusion on her own, Hugh finally realized, and for now, all he could do to help was hold her close and assure her that she had not diminished in his eyes or anyone else's.

They talked into the night, long after Judith had turned out her lights upstairs. Ryanne had taken Aggie outside, then placed her on the bedchain beside her and Hugh.

Hugh brought up the subject of Ryanne's father, admitting that Doug had told him how Martin Kirkland had died, and Ryanne was grateful that he knew the story. It saved her from recounting the details that were still horrifyingly painful to her. She talked instead about her childhood and how devastated she'd been when her beloved father had been brutally murdered. She talked about her mother's death, too—the wastefulness of it, and the resentment she still couldn't quite overcome.

"For a long time after she died," Ryanne told Hugh, "I swore I'd never let myself fall in love. It just didn't make sense that anyone could give up on life like that."

"Do you still feel that way, Ryanne?" Hugh asked, wondering if he'd found an explanation for Ryanne's apparent reticence to become more deeply involved with him.

She shook her head. "No. Once I got older, I realized that the problem had stemmed from my mother's insecurities, not the institution of marriage. Without her husband, she didn't have the will to go on. I was there, needing her more than ever, but that just wasn't enough for her."

Hugh let a handful of Ryanne's silky hair slide through his fingers. "Were you and your mother close before your father died?"

Ryanne thought for a moment. "No, I don't think so—not the way some mothers and daughters are close. I loved her, but Daddy was the one I went to when I had a problem, and he was the one who sat by my bedside reading me stories when I was sick. He would stay with me until Mother would come in and insist he let me get some sleep."

Ryanne frowned at the memory. "Even when I wasn't sick she was like that. Every time Daddy started to spend time with me, Mother would always interrupt. Daddy would come home from work, put me on his lap and ask me what I'd done that day; and just as I'd start to tell him, Mother would send me on an errand or make me go do my home-work. Looking back on it, I really think she was jealous of me."

"They say all mothers and daughters feel some degree of rivalry, Ryanne. That doesn't mean she didn't love you," Hugh said gently.

"She didn't love me enough to believe that I was a good reason to fight for her life. Frankly I think she was relieved when they diagnosed her cancer. She really did want to die, Hugh." Ryanne turned toward him, laying her head on his shoulder and draping one arm across his chest.

"Right after Daddy was killed she sent me to stay with Aunt Rose and Uncle Charley for a while. Mother stayed at our house alone..." Her voice drifted off as she dredged up a painful memory. Hugh's lips pressing against her temple gave her the courage to continue. "I came home from school one day and there was this incredible tension in the house. Everyone was behaving almost exactly as they had just before they told me Daddy had been killed. I was already scared to death, and so miserably lonely that I could barely function, so their attitude really terrified me. Aunt Rose bustled me off to my room, pretending that nothing was wrong, but later that night when I crept back down-stairs to eavesdrop on her and Uncle Charley, I learned that mother was in the hospital. She'd tried to kill herself by taking an overdose of sedatives."

Hugh tightened his arms around her, stroking her back comfortingly, but he made no comment. Ryanne didn't need platitudes now, she simply needed to talk. He held her close and listened.

"No one ever told me directly what happened, and I never told anyone I knew because I felt so guilty. I figured it had to be my fault that she wanted to die."

"You know now that's not true, don't you?"

Ryanne nodded. "Yes. I stopped blaming myself a long time ago."

"Good." He brushed his lips across her forehead. "After your mother got out of the hospital, did she take you back home with her?"

"No, she came to stay with Aunt Rose and Uncle Charley, too. Aunt Rose was Dad's sister, but Mother didn't have any family of her own. I suspect they pressured her into coming to live with them because they were afraid that if someone didn't keep an eye on her she'd try to kill herself again. Uncle Charley took care of selling our house, Aunt Rose took care of me, and Mother just stayed in her room grieving, willing herself to die.... And she did."

"Ryanne, have you considered that maybe your mother's death was just as important a factor in your blindness as your father's death?" Hugh asked quietly.

Ryanne frowned. "No, I hadn't."

"Watching her waste away and die only strengthened your incredible will to survive. You father's death may have laid the groundwork for your subconscious's solution to a situation similar to his, but the unfairness of your mother's death may be what made you determined to live at any cost."

Ryanne considered the theory, making a mental note to discuss it with Dr. Whitehorn tomorrow. So far, her therapy had concentrated only on the attempt on her life and her father's death. Maybe it was time to move on to her relationship with her mother; perhaps that's where they'd find the key to restoring her sight.

They talked on, and as Hugh listened to Ryanne's outpouring of thoughts and fears, Hugh ached with so much love that he thought his heart might burst. What would it take, he wondered, to make her realize that she had a strength that was unbreakable? Like the willow, she could bend with the worst of storms and still remain standing when the tempest had passed.

"In all this soul-searching, Ryanne, have you taken any time to dream?" Hugh asked. It was nearing dawn and they both needed sleep, but neither was capable of letting go of the quiet night.

Ryanne pulled away from him and raised herself on one elbow. "Dream?" She said the word as though it was one she'd never heard before.

"Yes, dream," Hugh reiterated, winding a lock of her hair around his hand to draw her close again. "You once told me there were certain dreams that were luxuries you couldn't afford because of your blindness. But you can dream now, Ryanne, because someday soon your sight will return. If you woke up tomorrow morning and could see, and the threat posed by Beck miraculously went away, what would you do? What would you want?"

Hugh was right. Ryanne hadn't allowed herself to dream beautiful dreams of the future and she was afraid to do so now because shattered dreams were unbearably painful. But because it was late, because she was wrapped safely in Hugh's arms, Ryanne overcame her fear of disappointment and let an imaginary light illuminate what her heart wanted most.

"I would want..." *to see your face, to know you were mine forever, to share your life, bear our children and know that the darkness could never touch me again because you are my light....* The words were there in thoughts that burned brightly at the center of everything Ryanne was or hoped to be. But it was a futile dream, and saying it aloud would only make it hurt that much more when it didn't come true. Her future was too uncertain and she was too unworthy of such happiness.

Rather than give voice to her heart's deepest desire, then, she chose a simpler dream, one more realistic and less painful.

"I would want my old life back," she told him. Years of believing she'd never fulfill that lost dream added conviction to her words. "I'd get down on bended knees in front of Douglas Sutherland and beg for my old job. I would reestablish my old contacts and make new ones, and go back to fighting for all the things my father believed in. The things he taught me to believe in." Ryanne's eyes pooled with tears because she realized this dream was real, too. "I want to redeem myself and make Daddy proud of me...."

Her voice broke and the tears began to flow freely. Hugh sipped them, murmuring, "He would be, Ryanne. Never doubt it. He would be *so* proud of you."

Hugh held her tightly while she cried, and he prayed that her tears would be cleansing. Ruefully he wished that he could shed a few himself. Maybe tears would ease the terrible ache around his heart. He was the one who'd opened the door on Ryanne's deepest desire, secretly wishing that she would make him a part of her dreams. Now, he would have to live with the knowledge that when Ryanne imagined her future she saw no place for him in it. He couldn't bring himself to accept it yet, but somewhere in the deep recesses of his mind he realized that someday he'd have to let Ryanne go. Until then, though, he would hold her, keep her safe, and cling to the selfish knowledge that as long as she needed his protection he would be allowed to stay at her side.

"Hugh?"

"What?" He shook himself mentally and returned to the present when he realized Ryanne had been talking to him. "What did you say?"

Ryanne smiled into Hugh's shoulder. "Did you finally fall asleep on me?"

"I must have drifted off for a minute," he lied. "What did you ask me?"

"I asked what you want from life," she said, sliding her fingers through the soft blanket of hair on his chest. "You've achieved so much, but you must have dreams, too."

A painful stab of sorrow pierced Hugh's heart. "No, Ryanne...no dreams." His voice sounded hollow and far away. "I have everything I want right now."

CHAPTER SIXTEEN

"EXCUSE ME, Mr. Michelon, but Mr. Beck is here to see you. I told him you were at breakfast, but he insisted you would want to speak with him."

"Show Mr. Beck to the library, Gray," Del Michelon ordered the butler, who bowed deferentially and left as silently as he'd entered.

Michelon pushed back from the table, placed his napkin beside his half-eaten breakfast and glanced at his wife. "I'm sorry, dear. This will only take a moment."

He rose and ambled to the room that served as his study. His instinct was to keep Beck waiting, make him sweat, but Del was too concerned about the outcome of Ryanne Kirkland's medical tests to play that game. The day of her appointment had come and gone four days ago, and still the man Beck had sent to Los Angeles had not been able to obtain conclusive evidence as to whether or not she would regain her sight. Michelon didn't like to be kept waiting, nor did he like inefficiency. And most of all, he didn't like Arlen Beck, who'd put him in this uncomfortable position in the first place.

"Well, Arlen, I presume you have some news for me—finally," he said unceremoniously as he entered the massive room decorated in oak and leather.

Beck watched as Michelon assumed the chair behind a huge desk that Beck had always thought of as his employer's throne of power. Not that he'd been privileged to enter this inner sanctum very often. Michelon kept his personal life and his "business" interests well separated, maintaining the image of a genteel man of wealth and breeding that fooled very few. Del Michelon was a gangster, and the only people who didn't know it were the ones who didn't *want* to know it.

"Yes, sir. Keegan was finally able to break into the clinic late last night. The night watchman he'd bribed to look the other way while he gained entry didn't return to work until yesterday."

"Was Mr. Keegan successful?"

"Yes. He made the break-in look like a drug theft and vandalized Dr. Kazlovski's office as well as several others. It will take days to reconstruct their files and realize Kirkland's is missing."

Michelon nodded his approval. "Excellent. What exactly did the file say? I understand from what you told me yesterday that Ms. Kirkland has been surrounded by a cordon of bodyguards on what have become daily visits to the clinic. Were we correct in our assumption that she may regain her sight?"

Beck nodded and gave Michelon the details Ace Keegan had related to him on the phone just hours ago. Most of it had been medical mumbo jumbo to both men, but the final notation had made the situation clear: *Diagnosis: conversion reaction-hysterical blindness. Prognosis: favorable if patient consents to intensive therapy. Referral: Whitehorn.*

"So her sight could return at any time," Michelon concluded, leaning back in the soft leather chair.

"That's right. Should I tell Keegan to go ahead before they discover her file is missing and increase security around her?"

Michelon eyed the troublesome banker disdainfully. "Is there any other alternative?"

"No, sir."

"Then see that it's taken care of. Today."

"Yes, sir." Beck rose. "Ryanne Kirkland is as good as dead."

THE WEATHERMAN'S ESTIMATE of the temperature for the third of July had been way off. One-hundred would have been a blessing, and Mo Johnson didn't feel the least bit blessed. Standing just outside the bank of doors that led to the clinic, he kept an alert eye on the street and tried to ignore the sweat that poured down his torso. Without his jacket he might have had a chance of being comfortable, but the .32 Smith and Wesson nestled in his shoulder holster would have raised more than one curious eyebrow, so he suffered in silence. He glanced at his watch and noted with relief that Ryanne's session would soon be over and they could leave.

Like Hugh, Mo had a feeling that today was going to be the day. Tomorrow was Saturday, the fourth, the start of a three-day holiday, which meant that Ryanne wouldn't be back to the clinic until Tuesday. It only made sense that if an attempt on her life was going to be made, it would go down today. The best time would be in the few moments Ryanne was traveling between the clinic doors and the car, which meant Mo's scrutiny was focused not only on the street, but also on the two- and three-story buildings across the street.

So far, though, nothing had struck him as out of the ordinary. The only car parked on the street was Hugh's. Everyone else had heeded the No Parking signs. Thanks to Vic Coffin, Hugh's friend on the police force, a patrol car circled the block every few minutes and the uniforms always gave Mo a jaunty wave and ignored the illegally parked BMW.

A car squealed around the corner of Santa Monica and Beverly, and Mo straightened reflexively, his hand sliding to the gun. The car came to a squealing stop behind the black BMW and Mo relaxed. Detective Vic Coffin started toward him as Mo resumed his slow scan of the neighborhood.

"That kind of driving is bad for the tires, Vic." Mo shot him a quick grin.

"Yeah, but it's great for my macho image." Coffin was short but athletically built, and he made up for his small stature by projecting a tough-guy personality that most people believed was just a cover-up for an even tougher guy that lurked underneath.

"What brings you down here? You change your mind about giving us a little more police protection?" No actual threat had been made against Ryanne and the L.A.P.D.'s involvement was strictly unofficial.

Coffin shook his head. "No, but I ran across a report today that I thought you guys might want to know about. Could be nothing, but I've got a gut instinct that says different."

"There's a lot of that going around today," Mo said dryly. "What have you got?"

Vic cocked his head toward the building behind them. "This place was broken into last night." Mo's full attention was suddenly riveted on the police detective. "The investigating officers said it was a routine drug theft, but I don't buy it. The drugs were taken out of the downstairs clinic area, then the perpetrator went up to the second-floor office wing and trashed three offices."

"Including Kazlovski's?"

"Naturally. According to the report it'll take them days to get their files back together."

"Damn!" Mo swore. "The drug theft was just a cover-up to get Ryanne's file."

"That's what I figure. Which means your bad guy in Chicago knows all there is to know about Ms. Kirkland."

"And he's gotta go after her." Mo clapped the detective on the shoulder. "Thanks, Vic. I gotta run upstairs and let Hugh know about this. Can you cover the door for me?"

"You think it's going to go down today?"

"I'm positive."

Coffin pointed toward the door as he started to his unmarked police car. "You go back up Hugh and I'll get a couple of uniforms over here. Bring the girl down in the elevator and we'll be waiting!"

"Done!" Mo called back as the glass door closed behind him.

FROM HIS VANTAGE POINT in the corner next to the water fountain, Hugh had a clear view of the only two doors that led to the rabbit warren of offices where Ryanne had entered nearly fifty minutes ago. The door opposite him, to his left, opened into a comfortable waiting room and reception desk guarded by a pleasant young woman whose appearance reflected the clinic's upscale clientele. The door to the right, far down the L-shaped hallway, was the physician's unlabeled entrance.

Every time a patient or staff member rounded one of the corners that snaked out of his sight, Hugh tensed fractionally. He gave each person that passed him a nod or a friendly smile as he assessed them, looking for the telltale bulge of a weapon, but so far no one had looked suspicious.

A pretty young woman he had seen enter the reception room about thirty minutes earlier stepped through the patient's door on his left and flashed him a smile. With the aid of twin metal crutches, she hobbled toward the water fountain beside him.

"Still waiting, huh?" she asked as she began the laborious process of shifting her crutches and balancing her weight so that she could bend to the fountain.

"Here. Allow me," Hugh offered, returning her friendly smile as he stepped over to the fountain. He held down the button that activated a cold geyser, and the girl mumbled her thanks as she bent. Hugh repositioned himself so that he was facing the left branch of the hall, but the right was still visible in his peripheral line of sight.

Far down the right hall, a man in a white lab coat rounded the corner and moved purposefully toward the physician's entrance. He barely spared a glance at the man and woman facing the water fountain before moving on to the door, but that slight moment of hesitation was all it took for Hugh to recognize Ace Keegan.

Instinctively Hugh reached for his gun, then remembered the girl in front of him. If he called to Keegan there was no telling what the hit man's reaction might be, and if he opened fire the girl would very likely be hurt. Forcing himself to remain frozen, he waited until Keegan disappeared through the physician's entrance, then he dashed toward the reception room, leaving the startled young woman behind.

By the time he got to the door, his gun was drawn and his mind was working furiously, mapping out the twists and turns of the inner corridors that led from the physician's entrance to Dr. Whitehorn's office. He passed the receptionist's desk with a terse command to call the police, then turned down the hallway that would put him on a collision course with the man who had been sent to kill Ryanne Kirkland.

"IT WAS A GOOD SESSION, Ryanne," Dr. Whitehorn said as he helped her into the jacket that covered the bulletproof vest that had been one of their topics of conversation today. "I'll see you at the same time next Tuesday and we'll discuss making your visits every other day rather than every day, depending on how well you do this weekend."

Ryanne gave him a reassuring smile as she picked up Aggie's harness. "I don't think I'm going to fall apart, doctor, if that's what you're worried about. Though I can't say I'm looking forward to *Independence* Day tomorrow."

Whitehorn took her free hand. "It is an incongruous holiday, considering what you're going through."

"It's as good as any, I suppose." She shrugged. "I don't care for the implications of Memorial Day, and Thanksgiving would be totally inappropriate, don't you agree?"

The doctor squeezed her hand, amazed at how well she was coping with the extraordinary stress of her situation. "If you need anything at all, Ryanne, please don't hesitate to call my answering service. They'll contact me immediately and I'll get right back to you."

"Thank you."

He dropped her hand and opened the door. "Take care."

"I will, doctor. Thanks again." She gestured with her right hand. "Aggie, out. Hup-hup."

The retriever moved Ryanne into the doorway, then paused for directions. "Good girl! Left, le—"

"Ryanne, no! Get back!"

It happened so fast Ryanne had no time to comprehend what was going on. She heard Hugh's voice, but the thundering report of two bullets fired in swift succession transported her back five years into a darkened warehouse. The sense of déjà vu, of the inescapability of the hit, obscured the pain she knew she should be feeling as the two bullets slammed into her back and knocked her forward, into the door frame. Her legs tangled with Aggie's harness and she fell to the floor in a heap, conscious of more shots being

fired, of the distant sound of running feet, and finally, o
Hugh's voice close by, murmuring her name over and ove
again.

"Ryanne? Damn it, Ryanne, talk to me!" Hugh begged
tearing at her jacket to inspect the vest that had saved he
life.

"Hugh! Are you all right?" Terrified, Ryanne reached fo
him blindly, desperate to know he was unharmed.

"I'm fine, love." Fiercely he pulled her into his arms
rocking her back and forth until she could regain the win
that had been knocked from her lungs.

From seemingly out of nowhere, Mo Johnson appeare
at the door, but Hugh didn't pause to question why his as
sociate had abandoned his post downstairs. "It was Kee
gan!" Hugh told him, his voice once again filled with th
same cold, hard edge Ryanne had heard the night he'd dis
covered the scars on her shoulder. "He went down the bac
hall. Go!"

"Coffin's downstairs calling for back up!" Mo shoute
as he started off in pursuit of the gunman.

"Are you sure she's not hurt?" Dr. Whitehorn asked
bending over the couple on the floor, doing his best to re
main calm and professional. He'd never considered psychi
atry a dangerous profession until just a moment ago.

"I'm fine." Ryanne finally found her wits and eased ou
of Hugh's embrace, fighting the instinct to remain safe in hi
arms. She had to find the strength to cope with this on he
own. "Aggie? Where's Aggie?"

"Right here, love. She's fine." The dog, startled by th
shots, had hunkered down by her fallen mistress, an
Ryanne reached out to her, crooning words of reassurance
Hugh helped her to her feet and into a chair as the hall out
side came alive with the sound of curious, excited voices.

Taking charge, forcing the horrible image of Ryanne's brush with death from his mind, Hugh instructed the doctor to tell everyone that the police were on the way, then to close the door.

"You didn't get him, did you?" Ryanne asked.

"No," Hugh answered, keeping her hand in his. "We came around opposite ends of the corridor at about the same time, and you were standing between us. By the time I could get off a shot, he was already moving out the way he came in." Hugh glanced toward the door at the psychiatrist who was still as white as a ghost. "You look as though you could use a shrink, Dr. Whitehorn."

The pun cut through some of the tension in the room and they all laughed. Neither Hugh nor the doctor were surprised when Ryanne's laughter quickly turned to tears.

Hugh went to his knees, holding her while she sobbed, and Dr. Whitehorn patted her shoulder comfortingly. "Let it all out, Ryanne, that's it. This is only natural. Your body has to rid itself of all that fear-induced adrenaline, and crying is one of the best ways to release that tension."

Hugh couldn't have given a medical description of what Ryanne was going through, but he knew that what she needed now was reassurance that she had survived. He held her close, stroking her hair, until the storm had passed, but his mind was already at work on what had to be done next.

"Hugh?"

He glanced at the door as Mo and Vic Coffin came into the office, closing the door on the mayhem in the hall. Hugh caught a glimpse of a uniformed officer holding back a curious crowd. "Did you get him?"

Mo shook his head. "Sorry. He had a car waiting at one of the emergency exits downstairs. I got the license number, but I'll lay you even money the car is either stolen or rented."

"I've already got an APB out on Keegan and the car," Coffin added. "Is Miss Kirkland all right?"

"I'm fine," Ryanne told him, wiping her face with the tissue Dr. Whitehorn handed her. Hugh introduced her to the police detective, and they murmured strained how-do-you-dos.

"How did you get here so fast, Coffin?" Hugh finally thought to ask.

Vic explained about the burglary report that had crossed his desk. He also apologized for not having made it to the clinic in time to avert the near disaster. "Now that this has become an official police matter, we'll be taking you into protective custody, Miss Kirkland," he informed her. "I've got—"

"No." Hugh stood and squared off against his friend.

"Look, Hugh, you can't take her back to the house in Malibu."

"I have no intention of taking her there, and I'm not turning her over to you, either." He looked at Johnson. "Mo, get on the phone to Ben and tell him to get the jet ready and file a flight plan for Toronto."

Mo's eyebrows went up in surprise. "Toronto?"

"Just do it, okay? I'll explain later. And after you talk to Ben, I want you to head for Ryanne's place and pick up Judith. Have her throw a few of Ryanne's things and her own into a suitcase, then take her straight to the jet."

Confused, Ryanne reached out and found Hugh's arm. "What are you planning?"

"Please trust me, Ryanne. We've got to move quickly."

Hugh's precautions had already saved her life once today, so she fell silent and listened as he issued orders that only he seemed to understand. Mo was already on the phone as Hugh turned back to Coffin. "Vic, can you get a policewoman over here?"

"Yeah, sure, but—"

"And get the coroner down here, too."

"The coroner! Hugh—" Coffin stopped as he finally caught on to the investigator's intent. "Oh, I get it."

"Well, I don't!" Ryanne snapped, disturbed by his mention of the coroner. It was a grisly reminder that she'd come too close to needing one. "Hugh, please—"

He knelt beside her again. "Ryanne, unless Keegan got a good enough look at you to realize you were wearing that vest, he thinks you're dead. Or at the very least, that you're critically wounded. If we can convince him that he succeeded in killing you, then you'll be in the clear. Beck will have no reason to send someone else after you."

Like Coffin, Ryanne finally saw where Hugh was leading. "You're going to treat this area like a murder scene and have me switch places with a policewoman," she guessed, trying to ignore the cold shiver that ran down her spine.

"That's right." He looked at Coffin again. "Can we do it?"

"Piece of cake." The detective grinned as he moved to the phone Mo had just finished with, and started making a few calls of his own.

Ryanne sat quietly, listening intently as the charade began to unfold. Hugh moved her from the chair onto a sofa behind the door so that no one would see her when the office door was opened to admit a steady stream of policemen. Dr. Whitehorn joined her on the sofa, quietly encouraging her to talk about what she was feeling, but mostly Ryanne felt numb and there were only so many ways to express that kind of blank emptiness. With half an ear she listened to Whitehorn's attempts to reassure her, but her real comfort came from the sound of Hugh's commanding, controlled voice. Just knowing he was nearby made her feel safer.

It took almost an hour to set the stage for Ryanne's departure. Mo was already on his way to Malibu. He'd taken Aggie with him, and Ryanne had exchanged clothing with a policewoman who was about her size. The uniform fit a little snugly across her breasts, but a police-issue flak jacket similar to the vest that had saved her life effectively covered that flaw. Hugh tucked her long hair up into the officer's hat as a coroner's stretcher was brought in.

"This is spooky," the policewoman muttered to no one in particular as she slipped onto the stretcher and let the two attendants pull a sheet up over her head. "Somebody be sure to remind the coroner I don't need an autopsy, okay?" she mumbled from beneath the sheet, then went perfectly still as the door opened and she was carried out.

Coffin followed the stretcher into the hall, making sure the officers out there had the crowd cleared away. "Okay. Let's do it."

Hugh took Ryanne's hand and slipped it through the crook of his arm. "You ready?"

She nodded. "This is where five years of trying not to look blind comes in, right?"

"You just try to look as though you belong in that uniform and I'll do the rest," Hugh advised her, pressing a quick kiss to her lips, startling Ryanne. "I've never kissed a cop before," he explained with a reassuring smile in his voice.

"If we can hang on to the uniform for a while, I'll let you do more than kiss a cop."

"I like the sound of that," Hugh murmured seductively, hoping that their banter was achieving its purpose of putting Ryanne a little more at ease.

Apparently it was working, because she smiled her effervescent smile at him for the first time all day. "And I like the idea of falling asleep in your arms again tonight."

"That's a promise." Reluctantly he returned to business. "All right, let's go. Vic has cleared the hall and stairwell down to one of the side exits where his car is waiting at the door. No one will look twice at a detective and a uniformed officer escorting an eyewitness down to headquarters for questioning."

"What about the press?" Ryanne asked as Hugh moved into the hall. In the melee of the preceding hour she'd heard someone say that every news team in the city was downstairs.

"They'll all be focused on the body being loaded into the van, and the coroner is going to make a brief statement that should keep everyone occupied until we're out of the area."

Hugh and Coffin had covered all the bases, it seemed. Ryanne fell silent and concentrated on playing her role. When they reached the outer door, Hugh quietly gave her instructions so that it appeared she was escorting him to the car rather than vice versa. He opened the door and slipped into the back seat. Ryanne followed him as Coffin moved purposefully to the driver's seat and pulled away.

"Turn toward me and look down as though you dropped something, Ryanne," Hugh ordered sharply as the unmarked car passed a crowd of onlookers at the edge of the police blockade. When they were clear, Coffin picked up speed and Hugh told Ryanne she could relax.

"Next stop, Toronto?" Vic asked, grinning triumphantly in the rearview mirror.

"That's right," Hugh confirmed, returning the smile.

Like Mo, Ryanne didn't understand why Hugh would want to take her to Canada. She started to ask him to explain, but Hugh sensed her question and silenced her with a kiss.

"Trust me, Ryanne," he whispered, for her ears only.

She nodded and relaxed into the circle of Hugh's arms.

CHAPTER SEVENTEEN

WITH HER FEET PROPPED on the *Mary Ann*'s transom, Ryanne leaned back in the padded fishing chair and let the warm Gulf breeze wrap itself around her. Behind her, up on the flying bridge, Judith and Webb were engaged in a good-natured argument. Hugh was inside the main cabin radioing Mo and Ben, who were miles away back in Bay St. Louis, making sure they hadn't been followed after they rerouted from Toronto to the Gulf of Mexico.

For the first time in what seemed like years rather than just barely a week, Ryanne relaxed. She'd had her first good night's sleep since her ordeal of fear began, and though she knew this sense of peace couldn't last, she felt truly safe. Content to enjoy the respite, she let her mind float with the even rhythm of the boat.

Unavoidably her thoughts skidded back to the traumatic events of the previous day, but she refused to dwell there for long. She preferred to think about how kind and supportive Webb had been when his son and a decidedly tense entourage had arrived unexpectedly at his house the previous night. By the tone of his voice, Ryanne had known that the poor man was exhausted. He had just returned home after a long day with a boisterous fishing charter, yet he welcomed Ryanne and the others heartily.

Hugh had explained the situation and Webb understood immediately what his son intended to do. He had ushered Ryanne and Judith off to bed in his room, and while they slept, the men spent most of the night making sure Webb's forty-foot cabin cruiser, the *Mary Ann*, was ready to get under way before dawn. The five boats in his fleet had all been booked for the day, but he'd done some creative shuffling and combined two small parties into one larger one so that the *Mary Ann* was free for what Webb insisted on calling a family outing.

And now they were in the Gulf, with nothing around them but miles of ocean in every direction. Except for Douglas Sutherland, no one knew where Ryanne was, and the man who wanted her dead thought he had succeeded in eliminating the threat she posed to him. Ryanne recalled the morbid joke she'd made about Independence Day only yesterday. Ironically, today she did feel like celebrating her brief glimpse of freedom. Smiling faintly at the sun that warmed her, she slid lower in the chair and floated with the gentle rocking of the boat.

Hugh stepped out of the air-conditioned cabin and froze at the sight of Ryanne. Reclining in one of the two swivel chairs that were bolted securely to the deck, she looked like a sleek, sensuous cat sleeping in the sun. Her hair cascaded down the back of the chair, and the sundress she'd worn the day she met him was drawn up to her thighs so that the sun could worship her long, shapely legs.

The bunched-up dress exposed far less than a bathing suit, or even a pair of shorts would have, and yet the way the dress billowed and fluttered with the breeze was far more enticing. A stab of desire so strong it was painful sliced through Hugh and he moved across the wooden deck toward her.

"Hugh?" she questioned, cocking her head to one side, presenting him with an even better view of her lovely profile.

"Right here."

"Is everything all right back at the port?"

"Just fine. Mo says to tell you he found an excellent vet-
erinarian who had facilities to board Aggie. She settled in
okay, but she misses you terribly."

Ryanne sighed. Poor Aggie. It would have been inhu-
mane to bring the animal aboard the boat, but Aggie
wouldn't realize that this was for her own good. She would
be miserable without Ryanne, but there had been no other
choice.

Hugh stepped behind her chair, gathering her silky hair
in one hand while the other gently cupped her chin. His
husky voice erased all thoughts of the golden retriever from
Ryanne's mind. "You are the perfect picture of hedonistic
sensuality," he murmured, dipping his lips to hers for an
upside-down kiss that was slow and lazy and incredibly
arousing.

"Umm..." Ryanne's hand drifted to the back of Hugh's
head and she gave herself over completely to his tender
ministrations. "You do that very well, sir," she mumbled
when he started nibbling a slow trail along her jaw and down
her throat.

"That's because I'm...inspired," he replied between
kisses. A sudden gust of wind shifted Ryanne's dress higher
up on her thigh and she snatched at it to cover herself more
modestly, but Hugh stayed her hand. "No, no, no," he
chided. "I like that just where it is." With teasing strokes,
he caressed the long line of her thigh. He moved to her side
and rested one hip on the chair's arm so that he could press
Ryanne back with a drugging kiss. She gasped against his
mouth when his hand slipped to the inside of her thigh and
slowly worked its way upward. Despite the delightfully liquid sensations he was creating, she tore her mouth away
from his to protest weakly.

"Hugh, no.... Judith and your father..."

"Are up on the bridge and can't possibly see us. However, if it's propriety you're worried about—" Without warning, he grabbed both her hands, pulled her unceremoniously to her feet, and dragged her across the deck to one of the long cushioned seats that lined the outer bulkhead of the main cabin.

"Wait a minute! I was working on my tan!" Ryanne protested halfheartedly as Hugh plopped her down on his lap in a spot that not only was shaded from the sun, but also eliminated any possibility that they could be seen from the deck above.

"Isn't that just too bad." He silenced her with a kiss that was not demanding, but was far from casual. Ryanne's arms snaked around his neck, sealing their bodies together, and all thought of play vanished. The kiss went on interminably, fueling itself on each sigh of pleasure, and when it finally ended, Ryanne and Hugh were both gasping for air.

"Well...that was certainly...masterful," Ryanne teased when she could finally draw a breath.

"No, that was certainly frustrating," Hugh corrected. "Do you think we'd be missed if we disappeared into one of the cabins below for the rest of the day?"

"Why? Are you thinking of claiming your reward for saving my life yesterday?"

Ryanne felt Hugh's entire body tense as though she'd struck him. "I'm sorry."

"I don't want to think about that, Ryanne," he said harshly, tightening his arms around her protectively. "Seeing you standing in that hall with your back to Ace Keegan's gun was a scene from my worst nightmare."

"Mine, too."

"I thought I'd lost you," he whispered fiercely. "They won't ever get that close to you again, I swear."

His words acknowledged what they both knew to be the truth: this ordeal was far from over. Ryanne nestled her head snugly against Hugh's shoulder. "How long, do you think?"

Hugh didn't bother to ask her to clarify. He knew she was asking how many days of tranquillity they had before someone figured out she wasn't dead. In Chicago, Doug Sutherland was going through the motions of preparing a funeral service, but that wouldn't fool anyone for very long. The national media had been quick to pick up the news that mystery novelist Ryan Kirk, aka Ryanne Kirkland, had been slain in a Los Angeles medical center by an unknown assailant.

With network news teams battering at the door, eventually someone would leak the news that Ryanne's death had been greatly exaggerated. There were too many people on the L.A. police force who knew the truth, from Vic Coffin down to the policewoman who'd impersonated Ryanne on the stretcher.

"Two or three days at the most," he answered finally. The thought of varnishing the truth had never occurred to him. Ryanne had proven a dozen times over this week that she was strong enough to handle virtually anything. "And, presuming anyone is looking for us, another day or two to figure out we're down here and not in Toronto. But by then we'll have moved on."

Ryanne straightened and eased off Hugh's lap, sitting beside him but still remaining in the circle of his arms. "To where? Hugh, you can't keep shuffling me around like a deck of cards."

"I'll do whatever is necessary to keep you safe, Ryanne."

With a sweep of her hand, Ryanne gestured to the ocean. "This is wonderful, Hugh. I feel safe for the first time in days, but I can only run away for just so long, and then it has to stop."

Impatient with his own lack of solutions, Hugh released Ryanne and began pacing the deck. "Damn it, what else can we do? I am not going to let that bastard get at you again!"

Ryanne heard the anguish in his voice. If ever she had any doubt that Hugh cared for her, it would have been erased by what she heard in his voice. Though she hated to broach the subject that had been on her mind for several days, she knew she had to. For both their sakes. "Then maybe we should start thinking about ways to make me disappear permanently."

Hugh scowled. "What do you mean?"

"I mean, create a new identity for me—phony birth certificate, work history, credit cards under a new name, the whole works. My own personal witness protection program. Ryanne Kirkland has to vanish."

"That's not a solution, Ryanne! You can't go into hiding alone."

"What other choice do I have, Hugh? I can't live like this, and I can't ask you or Judith to live like this, either."

"Let us be the judges of that, okay?"

"Hugh—"

"No. We're not going to discuss this anymore," he told her with finality. The thought of losing her, of exiling her to an unfamiliar city where she would be alone and vulnerable was more than Hugh could stand. If it came down to that necessity, he would do what had to be done, but he wouldn't send her off alone. He would create a new identity for the two of them and they would start a new life together.

That meant living in the shadows, always being afraid of discovery. No matter how hard he would try to make Ryanne feel safe, she would always have a cloud of fear haunting her, and Hugh refused to accept that kind of life for Ryanne. She was a creature of light and beauty, and somehow he would find a way to keep her out of the shadows.

He returned to the lounge, gathered her into his arms and softened his voice to a lover's caress. "We'll talk about it later. You're safe here for the time being, so let's just enjoy that."

Ryanne nodded and put thoughts of the future out of her head. Like Hugh, she preferred to focus on the moment. She flashed him the smile that never failed to take his breath away. "You broke your promise to me, you know."

Hugh frowned despite the quickening of his pulse. "What promise?"

Ryanne brought her hands to his chest and splayed her fingers, savoring the firmness of his body. "You promised me I'd fall asleep in your arms last night, remember? Having Judith snoring next to me wasn't quite the same thing."

Hugh chuckled at the pout that bowed her lips. "Don't worry, love. I've taken care of that little problem. Because of Mo and Ben we were short on beds at Dad's place last night. I am happy to report that no such problem exists today. The cabin known as the master suite is all ours. Dad will occupy the captain's cabin just off the main salon, and Judith has a cabin all her own right across from him."

"What did Webb say about those arrangements?"

"Oh, he approved, but he did say he thought I should make an honest woman out of you. He even offered to perform a wedding ceremony we could make legal later." The words were spoken lightly, but Hugh held his breath, watching Ryanne's face intently, trying to judge her reaction.

Ryanne's heart turned over in her chest, but she was careful not to let her face reflect the intense emotion Hugh's casual comment aroused. Something warm and tender curled inside her at the thought of belonging to this man, of spending the rest of her life being touched by his passion and cocooned in his indomitable strength. For just a moment she caught a glimpse of a life that included Hugh and children and an overpowering serenity and joy that was almost too beautiful to bear.

But Hugh was only joking. He had no idea how close he'd come to her heart's greatest, most unattainable desire. They had an agreement that said no strings, no commitments. She knew Hugh cared about her, but that wasn't the same thing as loving someone enough to want the kind of life Ryanne was foolishly envisioning. If she betrayed her emotions now, Hugh would only feel sorry for her. He wouldn't reject her immediately, of course—he was too kind to pull the rug from under her in the middle of this nightmare—but he would begin to pull away from her. Pity would replace the warm, wonderful emotions that surged between them now, and Ryanne didn't think she could live with that.

Somehow she managed an impish smile meant to show Hugh how foolish his father's suggestion had been. "Did you quickly disavow him of any such notions?"

"No," he said a little stiffly, unable to mask his hurt. Ryanne still considered their relationship a passing fancy. The danger that had disrupted their lives clouded and confused the issue, but in Ryanne's mind nothing else had changed. If this ordeal miraculously ended tomorrow, she would pick up the pieces of her life and go on without him. Hugh had the desperate, sinking feeling that keeping Ryanne alive was going to be easier than convincing her he wasn't going to spend the rest of his life without her.

"Hugh? What is it? What's wrong?" Ryanne asked. The change in his mood was dark and drastic.

For a moment, Hugh debated telling her exactly what was wrong, but his conscience stopped him. He couldn't add to the incredible weight of the burdens she already bore. Making a supreme effort, he lightened his tone and relaxed. "Nothing's wrong, sweetheart, but I think I'd better go up to the bridge and see what Dad has in mind for lunch. If we stay here like this much longer, food is going to be the last thing on my mind."

Ryanne accepted his glib lie and shooed him off on his errand, proclaiming she was starved. In her heart, though, she knew she hadn't been mistaken about his sudden change in mood. Something she had said bothered him deeply. Or perhaps he was just regretting having mentioned his father's remark. Had he read the thoughts Ryanne had tried to keep hidden from him? Had he seen in her sightless eyes that she loved him more than either of them wanted her to?

Acting on Captain MacKenna's orders, she and Hugh prepared lunch, managing to work well together despite the cramped quarters and the impediment of Ryanne's blindness. She had spent most of the morning exploring the intricate ins and outs of the boat so that she could move through the restricted space with relative confidence, but the continuous rocking motion of the drifting vessel occasionally made her lose her bearings. Fortunately there were no breakables sitting around and all the furniture was nailed solidly onto the deck. Ryanne's shins were the only things that suffered because of her lack of coordination.

After lunch, Webb offered to teach Ryanne the finer points of deep-sea fishing. He brought out the gear and harnessed Ryanne into one of the swivel chairs. A huge rod and reel were then attached to the harness, and the fishing began. Webb and Hugh both gave her endless instructions on what to do in case she got lucky, but their good advice went straight out of her head when her rod whipped forward and something very large began running out the line.

Because of the hours she'd spent with her guide dog, Ryanne's arms were strong, and she gamely fought the fish, reeling in, then adjusting her position to accommodate the devious twists and turns the fish made. In the end, though, the fish's strength won out over her own.

"It's gone!" she wailed. She turned the reel, but the slack line confirmed that her prey had escaped. The brief struggle had been great fun, though, and she turned her flushed face toward Hugh. "It was a marlin, you said? How big was it?"

"Oh, at least twenty feet," he told her, barely able to hide the smile in his voice.

"No, I'd say more like twenty-five. Maybe even twenty-eight," Webb corrected.

"Oh, for crying out loud, you two," Judith complained from the top of the ladder that led to the flying bridge. "You show me a marlin that big and I'll show you a fish that was spawned off the shore of Three Mile Island."

Ryanne, who knew very well the men had been teasing her, swiveled her chair around toward Judith. "How big was it really, Judith?"

"Nine, maybe ten feet at the most."

Ryanne harrumphed. "Well, I see who I can trust around here."

"It's not their fault, Ryanne," Judith allowed generously. "Men wouldn't know how to tell the truth about the size of a fish if their lives depended on it."

Webb took exception to the slur, and a lively battle ensued. Ryanne and Hugh laughed at their bickering, and when the good-natured storm passed, they returned to the task at hand. Ryanne tried to convince Judith to come down and take her turn with the rod and reel, but Judith preferred to remain at the controls of the boat. She trolled slowly through the Gulf, complaining all the while about how the others were passing the time. After all, she pointed out, what were they going to do with a huge game fish even if they caught it? A dead fish would hardly make a suitable companion for the next two or three days they'd be aboard the boat. Judith's grumbling notwithstanding, they kept at it.

"I had no idea Judith could handle a boat," Ryanne commented to no one in particular as Hugh checked once again to make sure her harness was secure.

"Oh, sure," Webb replied matter-of-factly. "Judith is an old salt from way back. Her late husband was an avid fisherman. They kept a thirty-two-foot cabin cruiser up on Lake Michigan and they came down to Florida every other year for deep-sea fishing."

Ryanne turned toward Webb, stunned. She'd known Judith for years, yet her friend had never imparted that information to her. Webb MacKenna, on the other hand, had known Judith for barely two weeks and obviously knew her life story. Ryanne didn't know whether to be amused or insulted. "That's amazing."

Not realizing the source of Ryanne's befuddlement, Webb told her, "Yep, your Mrs. Tremain is quite a woman. She's spent most of the day telling me how I can double my fleet's profits during the off-season."

"Really?" Hugh looked at his father with barely concealed amusement. "Is that what you two have been arguing about all day?"

"Of course. I can't let her think she knows everything, can I? A woman's got to be kept in her place."

"And where, *exactly*, is that?" Ryanne asked, bristling at the sexist remark.

"*Any*where she wants to be," Webb answered.

They all laughed and returned to the serious business of fishing. Ryanne's marlin apparently was too smart to be hooked a second time, though, and it appeared that he had warned all his friends that these were dangerous waters. Shortly before sundown they abandoned their efforts, and while Hugh and his father fixed supper, Judith affixed braille markings to a deck of playing cards she'd found. After they had eaten, Webb brought out a set of poker chips and over the next few hours, Judith proceeded to take them all to the cleaners.

"It's a damned good thing we're not playing for cash," Webb grumbled as he tossed one of his last three chips into the kitty while Judith shoveled out cards like a Vegas hustler. "That woman would own the *Mary Ann* by now—and the rest of my fleet, too."

Ryanne smiled at him as she read the raised dots on the cards. "By the way, Webb, I've been meaning to ask you how this lovely boat got her name. Who is the *Mary Ann* named after? A long lost sweetheart?"

"Well, actually—" Webb began, but Hugh cut him off hurriedly.

"You don't want to know, Ryanne. It's a very boring story."

Hugh's reticence told Ryanne that the story wasn't boring at all. Embarrassing, maybe, but hardly boring. She was barely able to suppress a giggle of anticipation. "Oh, I wouldn't be bored, I'm sure. Would you, Judith?"

"Not a bit," Judith answered evenly, deliberately laying the cards down and staring at Hugh. "I'd give anything to know what's got Hugh squirming."

Webb chuckled. "Like he said, it's no big deal. You see—"

"Dad..." Hugh sent him a quiet warning, which his father proceeded to ignore.

"You see, I didn't name her, Hugh did. He was down here with me on his summer vacation when I got the boat, and he insisted on calling her the *Mary Ann*."

"Aha!" Ryanne leaned toward Hugh and pounced. "As I asked earlier, who was Mary Ann? Some teenage femme fatale?"

"No, she was one of the cazamas n gilginlm," he said swiftly, putting his hand over his mouth to blur the words.

"What?"

"She was one of the castaways on *Gilligan's Island*!" he practically shouted. "There, are you happy now?"

Even the hand Ryanne clapped over her mouth couldn't muffle her shriek of laughter. Judith and Webb joined in and the raucous laughter went on and on, rolling through the cabin, feeding on itself like an infectious disease until everyone but Hugh was wiping away tears and fighting the hiccups.

"I'm glad you find this so amusing," Hugh said irritably, staring at them as though they'd lost their collective minds. His disgruntlement only fueled the dying mirth and they started up again.

Slapping his thighs in disgust, Hugh threw in his poker hand and stalked to the galley where he snatched a beer from the refrigerator. "Can I get anyone anything while I'm here? MacKenna Charters is having a special on hemlock today. I recommend it highly."

Ryanne shrieked again, enjoying the best laugh she'd had in longer than she could remember, and Hugh decided he'd had enough. "Okay, that's it!" he said to no one in particular as he started for the door. "If anyone wants me for something other than a good laugh, I'll be outside—alone."

Without Hugh to heckle them, Judith and Webb brought their hilarity under control quickly. Ryanne took a little longer, but she eventually got herself down to tiny giggles spaced intermittently between gasps for air. "Do you think I should go after him?"

"Only if you're ready to humble yourself and soothe his wounded ego," Judith warned her.

"I could probably handle that. Webb, did Hugh really have a crush on the girl on *Gilligan's Island?*"

Webb lowered his voice confidentially. "My son would never speak to me again if I told you that he actually wrote her a fan letter and kept her autographed picture pinned up in his room all that summer."

"Well, I wouldn't tell me that, then, if I were you," Ryanne advised him, rising.

"Never crossed my mind. I wouldn't dream of embarrassing the boy like that."

Ryanne laughed and made her way slowly to the cabin door, leaving Judith and Webb behind to play a ruthless game of blackjack. She stepped into the night air and let the subtle sounds of the wind and the ocean wash over her.

"Hugh?" she called softly.

"I'm here in the chair, Ryanne. Wallowing in my humiliation."

"Oh, you poor thing," Ryanne cooed as she moved to him. "Did we hurt your feelings?"

"I am devastated," he told her in a tragic tone that would have been exaggerated even in Shakespeare's time. "I have been cut to the quick, wounded to the very marrow of my existence, flayed open by—"

"A simple yes or no would have sufficed," she cut him off dryly. "Is there anything I can do to make it up to you?"

"As a matter of fact—" he reached out and pulled her onto his lap "—there is. A kiss from a gorgeous redhead has been known to do wonders for a man's flagging ego."

Ryanne snuggled closer. "I thought you went for pig-tailed brunettes," she said teasingly, bringing her face close to his but withholding the suggested remedy.

Hugh lowered his voice until it was nothing more than a husky, seductive whisper. "Hey, I'm flexible."

In answer, Ryanne wiggled her bottom seductively against him. "I think I'd have to argue about that, Mr. Mac-Kenna."

Hugh moved his lips a little closer to Ryanne's and ran his hand down the long line of her leg, then back up again, pushing up her dress on the return trip. "Believe me, Ryanne, that's a purely involuntary reaction. I was sitting out here in the scented night air, remembering past de-lights, and this unslakable passion consumed me." Ryanne gasped when his roving hand moved higher and her breath-ing became sharp and erratic.

"I saw that beloved face," he continued sensuously. "I could almost feel those beautiful breasts beneath my hands..." Matching words to deed, Hugh unfastened the ornamental buttons on the bodice of her dress and lowered his head to the slope of her breasts, fanning her skin with kisses and soft words. "Even on this dark, moonless night, I could imagine moonlight illuminating that tiny waist and gently flaring hips—" He peeled back the bodice and closed his lips over the crest that had already hardened and blos-somed beneath his touch. Ryanne's breath caught in her throat and she clasped her hands to his head, twining her fingers in his hair, pressing him closer.

Hugh's own breathing became labored as well, but he continued with his erotic story, slowly working his way back up Ryanne's throat until his lips were at her ear. "And then the phantom moonlight faded, my vision disappeared, and I was left alone...aching...and I called out...Mary Ann! Mary Ann, come back!"

Hugh chuckled devilishly at his own joke and Ryanne instantly snapped out of the wonderful lethargy he had induced. "You snake!" she hissed, playfully slamming her clenched fist against his shoulder. "I'll make you think, 'Mary Ann, come back!'" she mimicked wickedly, grabbing a handful of hair at the back of his head and dragging his mouth to hers. As a retaliatory measure she teased him by undulating her hips and stroking and tempting his tongue with her own, in the same rhythm her body was moving to.

Hugh responded immediately, giving back measure for measure the pleasure Ryanne was giving him. Starved for the taste and feel of each other, their kiss deepened and their bodies strained to get closer, until finally Ryanne pulled her lips away from Hugh's.

"Do you think we would be missed if we disappeared into our cabin for the rest of the night?" she asked, paraphrasing the tempting suggestion Hugh had made earlier today.

"I couldn't care less." He kissed her tenderly. "I am going to make love with you tonight, Ryanne, and God help

CHAPTER EIGHTEEN

WRAPPED IN HUGH'S arms, Ryanne closed her eyes and willed sleep to come, but her mind was racing too quickly to allow that peaceful oblivion. She stirred restlessly, remembering the words Hugh had whispered over and over again during their lovemaking.

"I love you, Ryanne...I love you...I love you..." He had chanted the words tenderly as he had taken possession of her body but with each passionate thrust that pushed Ryanne to the edge of sanity, the words had become fierce and intense. Still, they had been uttered so quietly that they had barely registered at the time. Now, though, she could hear nothing else.

Restless and confused, Ryanne slowly eased out of Hugh's embrace. He stirred back, his brea... froze until he settled back, his brea... even cadence. Quietly, so as not to distu... and she ...anne her robe hanging on the back of the door and she into it. Walking carefully, she made her way to the deck sat in the swivel chair with her feet on the transom. The breeze was cool but still comforting, and she let it wrap around her while she tried to make some sense of what she was feeling.

"I love you, Ryanne...I love you..."

The words wouldn't go away, and Ryanne didn't want them to. Selfishly she wanted to believe they weren't just meaningless phrases spoken in the heat of passion, only to be forgotten in the morning. She had fallen in love with Hugh, and it wasn't the kind of love that could be ignored or forgotten. It was the kind that made a woman want to entwine her life with that of a man she knew would love, cherish and protect her.

But Ryanne knew she didn't have the right to hope that Hugh felt that kind of love, too, that he might want to share a future with her. She didn't have a future. Whether or not she regained her sight, she was going to have to go into hiding. She would have to live with the constant fear of discovery and the ever-present sense of danger. Love couldn't flourish in that kind of environment.

Though it was painful, Ryanne forced herself to face the terrible injustice she had done Hugh. She'd always prided herself on her independence, and yet this past week she had depended on him totally. She had used his strength when her own had failed. Worst of all, she had let the man she loved risk his life to save hers.

But no more. She couldn't go on drawing her courage from Hugh; she couldn't continue to put his life in jeopardy. She would never be able to live with herself if something happened to him while he was trying to protect her. Ryanne had to face her grim future and allow Hugh to get on with his life.

Today, Hugh had refused to talk about helping her disappear, but tomorrow Ryanne knew she had to make him talk about it. And if he wouldn't help with the necessary arrangements, then she would find someone who would. The sooner she was out of his life, the better.

The thought of losing Hugh was almost more than Ryanne could bear, and yet she knew her decision was the right one. The fear she had managed to keep at bay for most of the day crowded in on her, and she wrestled with it, trying to imagine how the incredible mired mess her life had

become could possibly turn out all right. She lost all track
of time, but when a gust of wind grabbed her robe she came
back to the present. The *Mary Ann* was riding waves that
were no longer gentle, and the air had the taste of an ap-
proaching storm. Ryanne knew that the sea anchor—a
sievelike affair that slowed the boat's motion and kept its
bow turned into the waves—would prevent them from cap-
sizing if a storm did arise, but in that eventuality the last
place she wanted to be was the deck.

Shivering slightly from a sudden chill in the wind, Ryanne
slid her feet to the deck and stood. The rocking of the boat
seemed far more violent than it had when she'd been sitting, and she grabbed on to the arm of the chair to steady
herself. It gave way beneath her weight, swiveling out of
reach, and the trust she had placed in its solidity was her
undoing. The *Mary Ann* slid abruptly up to the crest of a
large wave and Ryanne flailed wildly as she tumbled backward onto the transom. Her hip collided with the narrow
ledge, and her cry of pain quickly turned into a short-lived
shriek of panic as the momentum of her fall carried her over
the edge.

She landed with a sickening thud on the iron grating of a
swim platform that was partially submerged. A backlash of
water hit her in the face, and she struggled for breath and for
a handhold that would keep her from sliding into the black
ocean. Again the boat swayed with the waves, though, and
Ryanne was tossed mercilessly into the sea.

What had happened in an instant felt like a lifetime to
Ryanne. She struggled to the surface, gasping for air and
reaching frantically in every direction, searching for the
platform. A wave that took on monstrous proportions in her
terrified mind grabbed her, swept her up and dropped her
again, and Ryanne realized that if she didn't force herself to
remain calm she would drown in a matter of minutes.

Keeping her head tilted back as she began treading water, she took several deep, calming breaths of air, then began calling for help. Each time she opened her mouth, saltwater slapped her face, but she continued screaming, shouting for help, calling Hugh's name or Judith's or Webb's until her throat was raw from the effort.

Trapped in the world of her own blindness, surrounded by an even blacker sea, Ryanne shoved aside thoughts of sharks and other creatures of the deep whose domain she had unwillingly invaded. Instead she focused all her powers of concentration on listening for some sign of the *Mary Ann*—water lapping against its hull, or a faint echo of her weakening shouts. All she heard, though, was the eerie silence of the sea.

Time passed, but she couldn't have guessed how much. Bobbing like a cork, she forced herself to face the grim reality that she was probably going to die. She was strong and healthy, and if she conserved her strength, she could last for several more hours—possibly even until dawn—but by then she would be miles away from the boat. She could picture Hugh awakening in the morning, finding her gone and searching the ship to no avail. She imagined the search they would initiate. They would notify the Coast Guard and other boats would be brought in, but by then she would have grown too tired to maintain the struggle of keeping her head above water. Tomorrow night the evening news would report that renowned mystery writer, Ryan Kirk, aka Ryanne Kirkland, had died for the second time in one week.

The thought of Dan Rather trying to explain that one to twenty million viewers struck Ryanne as immensely funny. Her spontaneous, hysterical laughter was silenced by a mouthful of water, and she sputtered and choked, trying vainly to conquer the laughter that was more symptomatic of terror than amusement.

Alone and frightened, all sense of time deserted Ryanne. Hours passed and each minute was filled with nothing but thoughts of remaining afloat...staying alive. She found a rhythm in the waves and flowed with them, rather than against them, sometimes treading water, sometimes floating on her back to conserve energy. A sense of unreality overcame her. Images from the past began playing in her head like an old movie, and she became completely disconnected from what was happening to her. She saw vivid pictures of her mother and father, her Aunt Rose and Uncle Charley. She saw distant relatives and high-school acquaintances she hadn't thought of in years. A kaleidoscope of colorful scenes danced before her eyes. Some logical part of her mind suggested that she was becoming delirious from exhaustion and sensory deprivation, but when she saw lights blinking wildly in the distance, she knew she must have gone mad.

Too tired to mourn the loss of her sanity, Ryanne moved instinctively. A voice spoke to her—her father's voice—telling her to swim, and she obeyed without question. One stroke followed another, then she rested a moment, but her father's soft, quiet tones soon told her to move, and she did. Every muscle in her body cried out in pain, but she continued toward the mirage that flickered and winked at her. Saltwater stung her eyes and she closed them, pausing to rest, treading water, being lifted by the waves, then plummeted into the troughs....

The wind that stirred the water set up a ferocious roar, and Ryanne waited for the lights to reappear. She opened her eyes, expecting them to return, but they did not; her treacherous mind had taken the mirage away as easily as it had created it.

Frustrated by the disappearance that had stolen her sense of purpose, Ryanne screamed at the wind. She screamed in rage and frustration and fear until there was nothing left of her voice. Her screams turned to voiceless sobs that robbed her of what little strength she had left. The blackness of her blind existence was slowly absorbed into the void of unconsciousness, and though she fought briefly with the last ounce of her incredible will to survive, the effort was wasted.

Her last clear thought as she slipped into death was that the storm must have missed her, because the stars were twinkling overhead like a million brilliant diamonds.

"DAMN IT, cut the engine! Listen!" Hugh shouted above the roar of the *Mary Ann*'s powerful motor. Webb pulled back on the throttle and everything was silent. Manning the powerful searchlight on the bridge, Judith skimmed the beacon across the surface in a slow moving arc. They all listened. They all prayed.

"There!" Hugh shouted again, pointing to starboard. "Do you hear it?"

"I don't hear anything!" Judith hollered, unable to keep from her voice the desperate fear that had gripped her the moment Hugh had awakened her with the news that Ryanne was nowhere on the boat. For nearly an hour now they had watched and waited, trolling the water slowly in the desperate hope that they might possibly be headed toward Ryanne rather than away from her. No one had dared voice the possibility that she was already dead.

Adjusting the searchlight to the direction Hugh indicated, Judith narrowed the scope of her search, praying Hugh wasn't just hearing something he wanted to hear. But there it was again, a hoarse cry that could have been the wind; somehow they all knew it wasn't.

"She's out there!" Judith yelled.

"But where, damn it? Where!" Hugh shouted in frustration, never taking his eyes off the narrow beam of Judith's light.

"*There*! Go back! Take the light back!" Webb commanded and Judith complied. Thirty yards away a patch of scarlet spread out on the water like a trail of blood.

The boat sprang to life and Judith kept the light fixed on the object until they were close enough to see Ryanne, face down, floating still and lifeless, her robe fanned around her like a crimson cloud.

"*Nooooo!*" Hugh's agonized cry reverberated in the dark long after he sliced into the water. With strong, sure strokes, he reached her in seconds, shoved her face out of the water, and turned her in his arms like a limp rag doll. Webb brought the boat alongside them, and moments later Ryanne was sprawled on deck with Hugh feverishly repeating resuscitation techniques.

Fighting back tears, he poured his life's breath into her lungs, then flipped her over and straddled her hips, pressing against her back with hard, even strokes.

"Breathe, Ryanne, breathe," he commanded, his voice broken by the tears he couldn't hold back. They ran down his face, mingling with the saltwater that spilled in rivulets from his hair. "Please, baby, breathe...breathe...breathe... God, please...let her breathe...breathe," he chanted, never breaking the rhythm of his strokes. Frantic, he switched techniques, rolling her over again to give mouth-to-mouth while Webb applied repeated pressure to her rib cage until, finally, Ryanne coughed and began fighting her own battle. Choking and sputtering, she expelled the seawater from her lungs and stomach while Hugh held her from behind until she finally drew a ragged breath and sagged against him, spent but alive.

"Thank God," Judith whispered.

"Amen. Here, son." Webb extracted two blankets from one of the lockers and handed one to Hugh, who wrapped Ryanne snugly and helped her onto a bench. Kneeling in front of her, he rubbed her vigorously with the blanket, talking to her softly until the shock of her ordeal could pass.

Numb with exhaustion and relief, Ryanne sat motionless, trying to absorb the wonder of being alive. Every light on the boat seemed to be shining right in her eyes, and she blinked against the slicing pain. Strong, gentle hands pushed her sopping hair back and dried her face, and a deep voice filled with emotion spoke softly to her as the numbness gradually went away. The lights pierced the fuzziness of her mind, and her entire being suddenly focused on the voice—Hugh's voice. And hands... Hugh's hands. Slowly, forgetting the pain, Ryanne raised her eyes to a masculine torso with corded, rippling muscles, covered with a dark matt of fine, damp hair. It was a beautiful body, strong and perfectly proportioned, exactly as she'd always imagined it. But she wasn't imagining this.

Terrified that she was living a dream that might be cruelly snatched away from her, Ryanne reached out and touched the smooth skin of Hugh's shoulder, matching the sight of it to the feel she had already memorized. Her hand looked small and delicate against the broad planes of his chest. Gingerly she moved upward, touching him, following the movement with her eyes, across his shoulders, up his throat, until finally his jaw was cupped in her palm. It was a strong jaw, she realized distractedly... and his lips were full. She brushed them with her thumb before moving upward past his long, not-quite-perfect nose, to his deep-set eyes, which were filled with a mixture of puzzlement, relief and unmistakable love.

"Ryanne? Are you all right?" Hugh questioned her softly, growing worried. Her eyes met his in that mysterious way she had of making him believe she was looking straight at him, and the look on her face was almost rapturous. Her agile fingers flitted to the deep cleft between his brows that he knew gave him a look of perpetual arrogance. "Ryanne? Say something, love. Are you—"

"You are so...beautiful..." she whispered, her eyes filling with tears. "I never imagined..."

"Oh, dear God," Hugh murmured as he realized what had happened. A smile started somewhere deep in his heart and battered its way outward until it reached his lips and lit up his eyes. "Can you see me?" he asked in a voice that broke with emotion.

Ryanne nodded, smiled, too, and impatiently wiped the tears that blurred the most important sight she would ever see. "I see you." Her voice was hoarse and ragged, but strong enough to carry the depth of her joy. "*I can see you!*" she croaked as Hugh gathered her into his arms, lifted her up and swung her around in a jubilant circle. Her tears turned to a sob of happiness when Hugh kissed her long and deep, holding her as though he would never let go. And then Judith was there, hugging her and laughing, and then Webb had her in his arms. Ryanne returned his hearty embrace, then pulled back to satisfy her curiosity. As she had suspected, his strong, sun-weathered face was an older, more mature version of his son's. She looked back and forth between the two men, smiling through renewed tears, then went into Hugh's arms again.

"How did you find me? How did you even know I was gone?" she asked hoarsely, unable to take her eyes off the handsome face her heart had imagined a million times.

"You were supposed to spend the night in my arms, remember?" he reminded her, becoming vividly aware that

Ryanne's silk robe was plastered to her body like a second skin, and the only thing he was wearing was a pair of sodden jeans. "When I woke up and you weren't beside me or on deck, we started searching."

He didn't describe the horrible panic he had felt as he'd awakened the others. They'd torn the ship apart hoping against hope that what they all suspected couldn't be true. "When we realized you'd gone overboard, Dad calculated the drift of the boat as opposed to that of a single object being swept along by the current."

"In other words," Judith chimed in, "he spit into the wind and took a damned good guess."

"That's about the size of it," Webb agreed, wrapping a fresh blanket around Ryanne's shoulders.

She smiled at him from the circle of Hugh's arms. "I'm glad you're a good guesser. Thank you." She blinked against the brightness of the searchlight that was focused on the deck, but the pain that darted behind her eyes was a welcome one. She thought back to the last memories she had of her ordeal in the ocean. "I suppose my subconscious realized that the only thing that would save me was being able to see again. When I saw the lights in the distance, I thought I'd gone crazy. I swam toward them, but they disappeared."

"You probably got turned around and were just looking away from the boat," Judith suggested.

"If we hadn't heard you scream we might have passed you by," Webb told her.

Ryanne rubbed her raw throat. "I was so angry that the lights had vanished, and I was so tired I could hardly move. And then I saw the stars . . . and after that, nothing—" she looked at Hugh, unable to resist the overwhelming impulse to touch his face again "—until I saw you."

Their eyes met and held as emotions too powerful for words passed between them. They froze in that tableau, savoring the sight of each other even above the feel of their bodies pressing so close together.

Judith watched the tender emotions that played across both their faces and sent up another prayer of thanksgiving that Ryanne was safe and that she had Hugh's arms to lean on. No one deserved the love of a strong, courageous, giving man more than Ryanne. A sob welled in her throat and she choked it back with a no-nonsense bark of exasperation.

"Oh, for crying out loud, you two. Stop mooning around like a couple of moonstruck calves and get below. Ryanne, you take a shower and get into some dry clothes, and Hugh—"

"I'll take care of her, Judith," Hugh said with a laugh. "Why don't you make us some coffee and open a can of soup. Ryanne's going to need something to eat."

Ryanne groaned at the thought of food on top of all the seawater she had swallowed, but a hot shower and dry clothes sounded like heaven. Weak and light-headed, she let Hugh guide her inside.

Judith watched them go, her jaw set stubbornly against the tears that just wouldn't seem to go away. Webb moved to her, instinctively understanding what she was feeling. "That girl's like a daughter to you, isn't she?" he asked quietly.

The dam holding back her emotions gave way, and Judith nodded mutely, going into Webb's arms without question. He rocked her gently while the horror of the last hours was cleansed away by her tears.

"There, there, Judy honey. It's all right now. It's all right," he crooned until the sobs subsided. Her arms were wrapped around him and he pressed a kiss to her forehead, enjoying the way their bodies fit together in all the right places. He felt almost bereft when she finally pulled away.

"Better now?" he asked, smiling despite the sharp ache that had unexpectedly centered itself in his loins.

"I'm fine," she replied brusquely, as though to deny the vulnerability she had just shown.

"You know, you don't have to pretend with me," he told her a trifle sadly. "I figured out a long time ago that there was a very loving, giving woman under that crusty exterior."

"Of course you did." She said it as though she'd never thought otherwise.

"Then you don't have any reason to pull away from me, do you?"

Judith lifted her chin proudly. "No, I guess I don't." She closed the scant distance between them, put her arms around him again, and pressed a long, slow, stunning kiss to Webb's mouth—a kiss he returned with equal intensity until they were both a little breathless.

They broke apart as suddenly as they had come together, and while Webb was trying to gather his addled senses, Judith smiled at him sweetly. "Webb?"

"Uh . . . what?" he asked, unable to take his eyes off her.

"If you ever call me 'Judy honey' again, I'll break both your legs," she promised, then disappeared into the cabin with a saucy little sashay that left Webb alone on deck, roaring with laughter.

CHAPTER NINETEEN

RYANNE STEPPED OUT of the shower and dried off, barely able to believe that she could actually see the steam that clouded the room and condensed on the mirror above the lavatory. She wrapped the damp white towel around her, tucking in the edges just above her breasts, then reached for the extra one Hugh had left. Unfolding it slowly, she studied the floral print, savoring the riot of colors that assaulted her senses. Soon she would be seeing real flowers again, not just smelling them and trying to remember their beauty as she had for the past five years. For now, though, the roses stamped onto the terry cloth would do just fine. She could see now, and that was what mattered.

Smiling at her sentimentality, she bent over and wrapped the towel turban fashion around her head. When she straightened she saw her own vague outline in the steamy mirror and her heart began throbbing in her ears. Transported back in time, she remembered the months her face had been swathed in bandages. She recalled the pain of operation after operation, and she remembered her doctor's voice, calm and reassuring, praising his own handiwork.

If she wiped the steam from the mirror she would finally be able to see the face he had created, but something held her back. This night had already been a roller coaster of overwhelming emotions, and she didn't think she was ready to deal with her new face just yet. Instead she unwrapped her makeshift turban, towel dried her hair vigorously, then began brushing out the tangles. She extracted a blow dryer from the large cosmetic bag placed on the small vanity, plugged it in, then began drying her hair. The hot air dried the steam from the mirror much more quickly than it did her hair, but Ryanne kept her face carefully averted from the glass.

Her heartbeat accelerated with every second she avoided the inevitable, and she fervently wished Hugh hadn't spirited her straight into the shower when he'd brought her into the tiny bathroom off the bedroom they shared. It would have been a comfort to have his moral support when she saw her new face for the first time. But Ryanne had been swathed in a blanket from head to foot when she'd passed this mirror the first time, and now Hugh was down the hall showering in the other—tiny—stall. He couldn't help her confront this.

Exasperated with her own lack of courage, Ryanne finally stopped fussing with her hair. Mustering all her courage, she put the dryer down, turned and looked in the mirror. What she saw had her heart thundering all over again.

Intellectually Ryanne had known that she wouldn't recognize her surgically altered face, but seeing another woman's features where her own should have been was completely confusing and a little frightening. For a moment, she felt disconnected from her body, and she studied the mirror impassively.

It was a beautiful face. There was no denying that. It had a symmetry that was almost too perfect. The sharp angles she had lived with until her accident were all gone. Someone else's pert nose had taken the place of her own longer, upturned one. The square jaw she'd inherited from her father was gone now, too. It was a lovely face, but it wasn't hers.

A sudden, deep emptiness came over her as all sense of identity was swept away. *Where is Ryanne?* she wondered, reaching out to the mirror, tracing the unfamiliar lines. *Is that really me?*

"Ryanne?" Hugh rapped twice on the door before poking his head inside. "Are you feeling better?"

The door was to her left, and Ryanne could see him in the mirror, sharing space with her own strange reflection. Her bleak, puzzled stare alarmed him and he stepped inside. "What's wrong?"

Ryanne looked at herself again, gesturing vaguely at the mirror. "I don't know that woman," she said plaintively.

"Oh, sweetheart..." Until that moment it hadn't dawned on Hugh that Ryanne had never seen her new face, but he realized instantly how traumatic the sight of it had to be for her. Without hesitation he moved behind her and pulled her securely against his chest. Her eyes met his in the mirror and he smiled. It was the most beautiful smile Ryanne had ever seen. "I know that woman, Ryanne. I know her very, very well."

She gestured to her reflection again. "But that isn't... *me*."

"Oh, but it is, love. Because everything that makes Ryanne Kirkland magnificent is right *here*." Instead of pointing at the mirror, Hugh placed one hand over Ryanne's heart as he pressed a kiss to her temple. "Your face is beautiful, but what makes it so very special is that warm, wonderful smile that comes straight from your soul and makes a man go weak in the knees. Your spirit and your courage are *inside*, Ryanne. They shine in your eyes, and without them that surgically perfect face would be nothing but a pretty shell."

A mist of tears clouded Ryanne's vision. Hugh was exaggerating what he thought were her special qualities, and yet he was right. That face in the mirror didn't change who and what she was. "Thank you," she whispered.

"For what? It's the truth."

She touched his hand, which was still nestled between her breasts. She was fascinated by the sight of it next to her body. "Thank you for being here...for always knowing just the right thing to say... for saving my life. Again."

"Don't thank me for that, Ryanne," he told her gravely, his arm tightening around her waist. "Saving you was just self-preservation. I don't know what I'd do if I lost you."

Ryanne met his gaze in the mirror and wondered if the intense, possessive look in his eyes was the same one that had been there when they had made love. She remembered the heat of his passion and the pleasure they had shared, but she also recalled the words he had repeated over and over— the words that Ryanne's heart had wanted to hear, but couldn't accept.

"Hugh—"

"Hush." He silenced what he knew instinctively was meant to be a protest. He'd come too close to losing her to pull away now. Turning her in his arms, he murmured softly, "Let me love you, Ryanne." His mouth closed gently over hers and pried her lips.

A part of Ryanne accepted Hugh's kiss eagerly. For an instant, she allowed herself the pleasure of arching, opening to him and taking everything he was offering her. But there was an even stronger part of her that protested her surrender. Hugh wasn't asking her to make love with him, he was telling her he loved her and asking her to love him— to acknowledge his love, accept it... and return it.

More than anything in the world, Ryanne wanted to do just that, but she couldn't. Everything had changed the moment her sight had returned; there was no longer any question of what her future held. She had to go back to

Chicago and identify the man who had tried to kill her. The path her life would take after that was painfully predictable. To protect his star witness, the district attorney would put her in a witness protection program. Ryanne would be given a new identity. She would go into hiding and leave every remnant of her old life behind, knowing that with the incredible backlog in the judicial system and the delaying tactics of Beck's lawyers, it could take years to bring him to trial. And all that time, he would be turning heaven and earth trying to find Ryanne so that she would never be able to testify against him. It was a bleak, frightening future, and Ryanne knew that if she accepted Hugh's love she would automatically make him a part of it.

Hating herself because what she had to do would hurt both of them, she pushed at Hugh's shoulders until he broke the kiss and released her. "I can't, Hugh. I'm sorry, but I can't." Her voice faltered under the weight of her confused emotions and she twisted away from him, hurrying into the cabin next door.

"Ryanne?" He chased after her, grabbing her arm and turning her to him before she could reach the outer door. Her eyes were liquid with unshed tears, yet he could see that she had locked the most valuable part of herself—her heart—away from him. He didn't bother pretending that he misunderstood her rejection, and he couldn't hide his own heart any longer. "I love you, Ryanne."

The agony of hearing the words and not being able to return them tore Ryanne's heart in half. Every intense emotion she'd experienced these past few days crashed in on her—the fear, the frustration, the terror, the brief glimpses of joy and love and passion, the shattering experience of almost drowning, the relief over the return of her vision—everything was right there on the surface, exposed like a fresh, bleeding wound. "Don't, Hugh. Please," she begged.

"Don't what?" he demanded, unable to believe this was happening. The tortured expression that filled Ryanne's eyes sliced a searing dagger into his heart. "Don't tell you I love you? Or just don't love you, period?"

"Don't love me."

"Well, I'm sorry, but it's a little too late for that!" Hugh heard his hateful tone and stopped. He'd never said I love you to any woman before. Until Ryanne, he'd never even imagined saying it. But even with that lack of experience he knew that this wasn't the way to go about it.

Desperately trying to convince himself that Ryanne was just overwrought from her ordeal in the ocean, he gentled his voice and placed his hands lightly on her arms. "Ryanne, I love you. I'm not going to let you slip away from me—not now, not ever. I know you have to be frightened about what's ahead of you, but we'll see it through together, whatever it takes."

He meant it. Ryanne could hear it in his voice and see it in his warm, amber eyes. Hugh loved her and would do anything for her, but she wondered if he really understood that loving her meant giving up everything: his career, his company, his home, his life-style—and possibly even his life. He was offering to make an unbelievable sacrifice for her and Ryanne loved him far too much to allow him to do it. Mustering all her courage, she tried to blank all emotion from her face.

"I am really so sorry, Hugh. I didn't mean for this to happen. I thought you understood that what we had was only temporary."

Hugh stiffened as though she'd slapped him. "You're telling me you don't love me, is that it?"

Ryanne had to turn away to answer. If he saw her eyes he would know she was lying. "That's right."

"I don't believe that, Ryanne!" Hugh almost shouted, grabbing her arm to whirl her toward him. "When you looked at me before, up on deck, what I saw in your eyes was love!"

"That was gratitude!" She jerked her arm from his grasp. "That was the wonder of being alive and being able to see again! I was grateful to you for saving me, and I'm grateful to you for everything you've done to protect me."

"But you don't love me?"

"*No!*" She shouted the word because it was the only way she could force the lie out.

Hugh backed away, unable to believe how much it hurt. "Well, I guess that puts me in my place, doesn't it? Good old Hugh was great for a roll in the hay or a little protection from the bad guys, but that's all. What we had was great as long as it was light and meaningless! Too bad one of us had to go and spoil it by falling in love, right?"

"It wasn't meaningless, Hugh...not to me." Ryanne clenched her fists to hold in the pain. "But you were the one who made the rules, remember?"

"Ah, yes, the rules. Well, I got hoisted on my own petard with that one, didn't I? Tell me, Ryanne, just what is it about loving me that you find so unthinkable?"

She looked at his face, so new to her and yet so dear. In his deep, expressive voice, Ryanne had heard dozens of emotions and had imagined them all playing across the face she'd only been told was handsome. She'd visualized his teasing humor, his intense passion, his warm, seductive smile, and had mourned her inability to see them. Now her sight had returned, and all she could see were dark eyes filled with pain that she was putting there. The knowledge that she was doing it for his own good didn't help any. "Oh, Hugh... Loving you is not unthinkable. And having you love me is a beautiful gift I don't deserve—and can't accept.''

"Damn it, Ryanne, why not?'' he asked harshly, grabbing her arms, but she pulled away sharply.

"Because I don't believe in happily ever after, Hugh! And you don't, either. You told me so yourself. I don't believe in vine-covered cottages with pretty white picket fences! I don't want you to love me because I refuse to start thinking about knitting baby booties and hearing the pitter-patter of tiny MacKenna feet around the house—a boy who looks like you and a girl who looks like me! I don't want that, Hugh!''

"Then what the hell do you want?''

"I told you that the night before we left L.A.! I want my life back!'' she answered, trying to find some conviction in the words so that she could convince both of them she was telling the truth. "I can see again, which means eventually I can have back the life I lost in that warehouse five years ago. I can have my career and my freedom. I have to go to Chicago and identify the man who tried to kill me, and then I'll go into hiding until the trial is over. And when it's done, I'm going to take back everything Arlen Beck stole from me. I'm going to try to forget that these past five years ever happened and get on with my life!''

Ryanne wanted to cry out as she watched Hugh's face close against her, becoming cold and hard and emotionless. Whatever love he might have felt for her died in that instant; she had killed it.

"And there's no place for me in that life,'' he stated flatly, not bothering to phrase it as a question. He'd known the truth two nights ago, but he hadn't wanted to believe it. Now he had no choice.

"No.''

Hugh's answering laugh was harsh and cynical. "I guess there's no way I can argue with that, is there? 'So long,

Hugh, it's been swell.''' He turned and started for the door, then stopped, keeping his back to her. "I'll have Dad plot a course back to port, and I'll see that you get to Chicago safely so that you can get your life back as soon as possible." He stalked out, never looking back.

"Oh, God," Ryanne whispered, wrapping her arms around herself. She sank onto the edge of the bed she had shared with Hugh a lifetime ago, rocking back and forth, waiting for the pain to go away.

But it didn't.

CHAPTER TWENTY

AT SUNRISE Ryanne was standing on the *Mary Ann*'s deck, wishing she could find some joy in being able to see the dawn for the first time in five years. The exhilaration she should have been experiencing escaped her, though. Hugh was on the bridge, guiding the boat back toward Bay St. Louis just as he had promised. They hadn't spoken since he'd left the cabin just a few hours ago, but she knew he intended to fulfill what he saw as his responsibility to get her to Chicago. After that, he would be gone from her life forever.

"You want to talk about it?" Judith asked as she came on deck and handed Ryanne a mug of coffee.

"Talk about what?"

Judith laughed shortly and sat in one of the fishing chairs. She looked tired, as though she hadn't slept all night, either. "Ryanne, honey, this is a very small boat. If you think your quarrel with Hugh was private, think again."

Too tired and dispirited to even blush, Ryanne sat in the chair that had betrayed her the previous night and sent her tumbling into the ocean. Her movements were stiff, as though she believed she could lessen her heartache if she kept her body under the same rigid control as her emotions. "What did you hear?"

"Enough to know that some pretty ugly things were said."

"Mostly by me." Ryanne finished the thought for her.

Judith shrugged. "I did hear you tell Hugh you didn't love him. You know, Ryanne, I think that's the first time I ever caught you in an out-and-out lie."

"It's the truth," she said lifelessly.

"Honey, I don't believe that for an instant, and if Hugh's smart, he won't either, once he's had a chance to think about it."

The thought of going through another scene like the one she'd barely survived was more than Ryanne could take. She looked at Judith fiercely. "He has to believe it."

The older woman turned and looked out to sea. "Well, who knows. Maybe he will buy it. Falling in love with you took him completely by surprise, and you did trounce his heart pretty hard. It may take a while for him to get far enough past the pain and humiliation to realize that you're only trying to protect him."

Ryanne looked at Judith in amazement. "How did you know that?"

She laughed lightly. "Honey, I know you like a book. You think you're saving him from having to go through whatever ordeal you've got to face, right?"

"Yes."

"Ryanne..." Judith's voice demanded that the other woman look at her. "Don't you think that should be his choice?"

"No, I don't. He's put himself in enough danger because of me. I couldn't live with myself if something happened to him. And I can't let him sacrifice everything he's achieved in his life out of some misguided sense of loyalty or pity."

"Pity?" Judith scoffed. "Where did that come from? Hugh hasn't felt a drop of pity for you since the day you met."

"Don't you understand? I'm a damsel in distress. Hugh thinks he has to play knight errant and save me from the fire-breathing dragons."

"Oh, for crying out loud. You don't really believe that, do you? Ryanne, there were no dragons breathing down your neck until you found out the truth about your blindness. Hugh was in love with you long before that."

Ryanne covered her face with her hands and shook her head. "Judith, please... I did what I had to do. Just accept it and don't interfere. I've hurt Hugh enough already—I don't want to make it any worse than it already is."

Fighting her disgust, Judith stood and looked down at her young friend. "Honey, I've got news for you. It's not possible for a man to hurt any more than Hugh did last night when he realized you'd gone overboard. He thought he'd lost you then, and he's convinced he's lost you now. It's the same pain he'd have felt if you'd died, only you've managed to take away whatever illusion of comfort he might have gained from thinking that you loved him."

With that parting salvo, Judith retreated into the cabin, leaving Ryanne alone to wrestle with the decision she'd made. She knew how much she'd hurt him—it had all been right there in his eyes—but she couldn't change her mind. Eventually Hugh would forget about her and the pain would go away. And more importantly, because he wasn't sharing Ryanne's danger, he would live to see that day. Ryanne knew that she would go to her grave loving Hugh. What she didn't know was when that might be....

The sun was a little more established in the sky by the time they arrived in Bay St. Louis. The bright light hurt Ryanne's sensitive eyes and Judith loaned her a pair of sunglasses. Neither woman commented on the effective way they also masked the dark circles that were the result of stress, exhaustion and too much crying.

Despite the deep, aching sorrow Ryanne felt about the way things had worked out with Hugh, there was something exciting about returning to the real world and being able to see all the things she had only remembered or imagined these past years. She watched the bustling port avidly, enjoying the color and movement. Even the aged gray wood of the pier looked beautiful to her as they docked.

She caught sight of Hugh as he tossed a line to a man waiting on the dock, and she marveled at the strength and symmetry of his body. He had a lithe, catlike grace that was beautiful to watch. Following his every movement she stored the sight of him in her memory. Once they reached Chicago, memories were all she would have left.

The man on the pier tied off the *Mary Ann*'s bow as Hugh moved toward the stern to secure that line as well. He moved surefootedly along the narrow ledge beside the main cabin, grabbed hold of the ladder that led up to the bridge and swung down to the deck in one graceful, athletic motion. The movement put him face-to-face with Ryanne, but she could have been a stranger for all the notice he gave her.

No, not a stranger, Ryanne reflected, fighting the urge to cry. Hugh would have smiled at a stranger, but there was no smile on his face when he looked at her; just a cold, hard glare that bespoke utter contempt. He brushed past her without a word, finished securing the boat, then returned to Ryanne and snatched up the small suitcase at her feet.

"Let's go," he said brusquely, grabbing her arm none too gently and propelling her onto the deck. He handed the suitcase to the man who had tied off the boat, and Ryanne realized he had to be Mo Johnson.

"Where's Ben?" Hugh asked sharply, scanning the busy dock area.

Ryanne watched the puzzlement that played over Mo's face. He was a big, beefy man, but she could tell there wasn't an ounce of fat on his massive body. Despite his size, though, he had a kind, expressive face that at the moment was filled with questions. Ryanne knew that Hugh had radioed his men early this morning that the *Mary Ann* was coming in, but she assumed that no explanation had been provided.

"Ben's making a call," Mo answered, making a gesture that indicated he needed to speak with Hugh alone. Ryanne almost smiled at his pantomime efforts that were obviously meant to keep her from knowing that something was up.

"You're wasting your time, Mo," she advised him, taking off her dark glasses so that she could look him square in the eye. "If you have something to say, you can say it in front of me."

Mo's mouth dropped open as he looked at her and realized what had happened. A wide grin split his face. "You can see."

Ryanne nodded. "Yes."

"That's great!" His smile faded as he realized it wasn't quite that simple. "Or is it?"

Ryanne's subdued smile reassured him. "Yes, Mo. It's great."

"Could we cut the celebration short?" Hugh asked impatiently. "Just tell me what's going on."

Mo cast an uncomfortable glance at Ryanne before answering. "After you radioed this morning, Ben and I heard on the news that Asa Keegan was arrested at the airport in L.A. last night. Ben's calling Vic Coffin now to get some details."

"Is there a problem, Hugh?" Webb asked as he and Judith joined them on the dock.

Hugh repeated Mo's news, then looked back at his friend. Though he suspected he knew the answer, he asked, "What else?"

Mo sighed. ''The broadcast we heard said that he was being charged with the *attempted* murder of Ryanne Kirkland.''

''You mean the media knows I'm alive,'' Ryanne interpreted.

''Yep.''

''And if the media knows, then Arlen Beck and Del Michelon know,'' Hugh completed the thought on everyone's mind. Taking hold of Ryanne's arm, he began dragging her down the dock unceremoniously. ''Come on. We'll go back to Dad's place while I make some calls. Mo, you go find Ben and meet us at Dad's.''

Ryanne fought the urge to wrench her arm out of Hugh's painful grasp and tell him she didn't appreciate being treated like a piece of rotted meat that needed to be disposed of as quickly as possible. She held her tongue, though, and allowed him to pull her along, with Judith and Webb in their wake. Mo hurried off to the harbormaster's office to look for Ben, and fifteen minutes later they were all ensconced in Webb's attractive little beach cottage that sat just around the point from the harbor.

From the chair on which Hugh had all but tossed her with an admonition to sit down and stay out of the way, Ryanne watched as he made phone calls and issued orders like a drill sergeant. He ignored her assiduously and talked about her as though she weren't present. Had he not been doing it all for her sake, Ryanne would have exploded after the first five minutes. She saw the confused looks Mo and Ben exchanged as they tried to figure out what had put their boss in this foul mood, but when their speculative looks moved to her, Ryanne glanced away. She felt too much guilt already; she couldn't let anyone add to it.

She was relieved when the two men finally left for the small airport about thirty miles away where Hugh's jet was awaiting them. It spared her the constant reminder that she was responsible for the harsh tone Hugh was using with them.

From the conversations she heard, Ryanne knew that Ben hadn't been able to reach Vic Coffin in Los Angeles, and Hugh hadn't had any better luck. He was reluctant to speak to anyone but Vic, so he switched his attentions to reaching Rube Lilenthal in Chicago. Ryanne remembered the police lieutenant from the times he had questioned her while she was swathed in bandages, lying near death in the hospital. Even his name brought on a flood of painful memories. Quietly she slipped out of the cozy living room and into the kitchen, where Judith and Webb were quietly drinking coffee, trying to stay out of Hugh's way.

"What's the latest?" Judith asked as Ryanne poured herself a cup of coffee and joined them.

"Mo and Ben just left to get the jet ready for takeoff." She looked at Webb. "I think Hugh expects you to drive us to the airport to meet them."

"No problem." It had already been agreed that for the time being Judith would remain behind with Webb for her own protection. Hugh didn't want to take the chance that Beck might think he could get to Ryanne through her friend.

"Judith, after we're gone, will you look in on that vet who has Aggie? Make sure she's all right?"

"Of course. Do you want me to keep her with me?"

"I'll leave that up to you. I know Webb will want to get back to his business, and if you intend to go out on the *Mary Ann* with him, it would probably be best to leave her where she is. As soon as I know what's going to happen in Chicago, I'll send for her." She smiled wanly. "I wonder how Aggie will like being just a pet rather than a working guide dog?"

Judith made a scoffing sound. "She'll love it, trust me. She'll be fat and lazier than ever inside of a month."

Judith's feigned animosity for Aggie reminded Ryanne of all the lighthearted skirmishes that had filled her life these past few years. She was going to miss Judith's caustic wit and unflagging friendship. It hit her like a lead weight that this might be the last time she would see Judith in a very long time, and a lump of painful emotion formed in her throat. She reached for Judith's hand as her eyes misted with tears. "I could never have asked for a friend—"

"Nope." Judith stood quickly and moved to the coffee-pot. "Not yet," she said, trying to mask the sudden quiver in her voice.

"All right." Ryanne looked at Webb. She knew she had to thank him for everything he'd done, but there was a questioning sadness in his eyes that stopped her. If Judith had heard the argument she'd had with Hugh, so had Webb, she realized. It was hard to believe that he didn't hate her for the pain she was causing his son, and yet she saw no re-criminations in his sad gaze.

He reached out and took her hand. "You'll always be welcome here. You know that, don't you?"

Tears brimmed in Ryanne's eyes and her jaw quivered. "I didn't mean to hurt him, Webb."

He patted her hand tenderly. "I know you didn't, Ryanne. I think someday when Hugh's wounded pride stops smarting, he'll realize it, too."

Ryanne looked from Webb to Judith, then back, wondering if her friend had told Webb why she had denied her love for Hugh, or if Webb had just figured it out on his own. "I hope not. For his sake."

"All right, let's go," Hugh ordered tersely as he came in from the other room. "Dad, would you mind driving us to the airstrip?"

"Glad to."

Ryanne took a deep breath and turned to Hugh. "What did Lilenthal have to say?"

Hugh didn't bother looking at her when he answered. "He'll have a tight security force waiting for us at the station house at three this afternoon."

"Why not at the airport?" Webb asked.

"Because I didn't tell him where we are now or where we'd be arriving. Ben's laying in a flight plan to take us into one of the small suburban airports outside Chicago. It'll be a lot safer if we rent a car and drive in, just in case Michelon has someone in the police force on his payroll."

"That's an encouraging thought," Judith snapped.

Hugh shrugged indifferently. "Those are just the facts of life." He stabbed a cold glance at Ryanne. "Get your things so we can go," he ordered, then turned on his heel and stalked out.

"Hugh!" Webb took exception to his son's hateful tone and started to upbraid him, but Ryanne put out a hand, stopping him.

"Please, don't. I couldn't stand it if you two had words because of me."

Out of deference to Ryanne, Webb restrained his temper, but the ride to the airport was decidedly tense. No one spoke until they reached the small terminal where Mo was waiting. Hugh said a hasty goodbye to his father and left Mo with Ryanne while she said her tearful goodbyes to Judith and Webb.

It was hard for Ryanne to look at her old friend. She hadn't changed at all in five years, and Ryanne wondered if the next five would be as good to her. She glanced at Webb and the look they exchanged told her that Judith's future was secure. Fighting back tears, she reached for Webb's hand.

"You take care of her."

"Don't worry, Ryanne. I will. You take care of yourself." He gave her a big bear hug, then stepped away quickly, leaving Ryanne alone with Judith, who had abandoned all pretense of emotional stability. Tears streamed unashamedly down her face, and when she held out her arms, Ryanne went into them.

"I love you, Judith," she whispered.

Judith patted her back comfortingly. "If I'd ever had a daughter, Ryanne, I couldn't have loved her any more than I love you."

Ryanne pulled away, taking Judith's hands and squeezing them together. "Thank you . . . for everything. I'll be in touch."

They embraced again clumsily, then Ryanne tore herself away and let Mo lead her onto the plane.

She boarded, keenly aware of how different the plush interior looked compared to the way she'd visualized it on her first flight. She belted herself into a comfortable leather chair by a window and tried to relax. Thoughts of what lay ahead crowded her mind, but she pushed them away, focusing instead on the wonder of being able to see the ground slide quickly by as they took off. She watched the patchwork of the landscape below them as they flew north. Hugh was in the cockpit with Ben, and he left the copilot's station only once.

Without acknowledging Ryanne's presence, he moved through the main cabin, disappeared into a room near the back of the plane and emerged a few minutes later. He had changed out of his jeans and sweatshirt into a lightweight, pale blue suit. Ryanne realized that he probably kept several changes of clothes on the aircraft, since he hadn't had time to pack anything before they'd left Los Angeles, yet he'd had a change of clothes with him on the *Mary Ann*. Obviously they had come from his wardrobe on the plane.

On his way back to the cockpit, he stopped for a moment to inform Mo they would be arriving in about forty minutes, but still he refused to look at Ryanne. She sat frozen like a statue until he had gone, then quietly turned toward the window so that Mo wouldn't see the tears that steamed down her face.

By the time they reached their destination on the outskirts of Chicago, Ryanne had conquered her tears, but the trip to the main precinct house was a test of her already thin control. Sandwiched between Hugh and Ben in the back seat of the rental car, with Mo at the wheel, Ryanne thought she might go crazy. Each time Hugh leaned forward to speak to Mo, the gun strapped beneath his arm brushed against her, reminding her of the danger she was walking into. Far worse than that, though, was the coldness that radiated from Hugh each time their eyes met. Logically Ryanne knew that he was only protecting himself from the pain she had caused him, yet she caught him looking at her several times with something so akin to hatred that she thought she might actually die from the agony that was congealed around her heart.

With Ben consulting a city map, they made their way into Chicago. Gradually Ryanne began to recognize the familiar sights of her hometown and took over the job of navigator.

"Take a right at the next corner," she instructed Mo. "The station house is just a couple of blocks up."

It had been more than twenty-five years since Hugh had lived in Chicago, so his memory was certainly not to be trusted, but he did remember the neighborhood from his trip to the station with Doug. Ryanne's directions were accurate, so he let her guide Mo while he kept his attention focused on the busy street and sidewalks.

Part of his mind was alert to the potential danger of their situation, yet he knew he wasn't as alert as he should be, not with Ryanne so close beside him. He could smell her distinctly feminine scent that he knew so well, could hear the growing animation in her voice. He could tell that despite the circumstances of her return home, she was excited about being able to see the places she had only visualized for so long. This was where her life was—the life she had so clearly wanted to return to, the life that didn't include him.

Choking back the pain of her rejection, keeping the barriers he'd erected in place, he focused on getting her to Lilenthal in one piece. After that she would no longer be his responsibility. He could go home, pick up the pieces of his own life and forget he'd ever heard the name Ryanne Kirkland.

Their arrival at the police station had been timed almost perfectly. It was nine minutes after three, yet the cordon of police protection Lilenthal had promised was nowhere to be seen. Hugh cursed violently at the negligent lieutenant.

"You want me to drive around the block?" Mo asked.

"No, just park right in front and we'll get her up the steps fast. Get ready to move, Ryanne," Hugh ordered without looking at her.

The car rolled to a stop and in an instant Hugh had the door open and was pulling Ryanne out. Before she even had time to realize what was happening, she was sandwiched between Hugh and Ben, with Mo bringing up the rear. They spirited her across the sidewalk and up the steps into the main lobby. The front desk was a madhouse, and Hugh bypassed the beleaguered desk sergeant altogether, pulling Ryanne toward a flight of stairs.

Ryanne's depth perception was still out of kilter, and she misjudged the height of the steps. She stumbled, and Hugh barely gave her the chance to regain her balance before he virtually dragged her toward the squad room and finally Ryanne decided she'd taken all she could.

"Damn it, let go of me! We're in the station. We're safe. You can cut the strong-arm tactics!" She wrenched out of his grasp, but Hugh recaptured her quickly and pulled her close.

"When Rube Lilenthal surrounds you with half a dozen hand-picked bodyguards, *then* you'll be safe. And you'll be *his* responsibility, not mine. Until then, you stay with me and you stay close, you got that?"

"I got it!" Ryanne snapped back, letting anger override the desire to crumple into tears.

Furious at Ryanne, Lilenthal and the world in general, Hugh stormed through the swinging double doors into the busy squad room. He moved toward the lieutenant's office just as Lilenthal came lumbering out in the midst of a phalanx of plainclothes cops.

"Damn it, Lilenthal, where the hell were you?" Hugh demanded, not bothering to wait until the officer was free before assaulting him. "You were supposed to have your men outside at three!"

"Calm down, MacKenna—"

"I'll calm down when you prove you can provide Ryanne with the protection you promised!"

As the other officers dispersed, Lilenthal looked at the three men surrounding Ryanne. "I'd say Ms. Kirkland already has about three times as much protection as she needs."

"Will you all stop talking about me as though I'm invisible!" Ryanne demanded, angry at the whole lot of them.

"Sorry, ma'am," Lilenthal apologized. "I was real glad to hear you got your sight back."

Ryanne started to thank him, but Hugh was in no mood for niceties. "What did you mean about—"

Lilenthal pointed toward his office. "Miss Kirkland, if you and your suntanned friends would step into my office, I'll explain what's been happening around here today."

"Thank you, lieutenant." Ryanne emphatically snapped her arm from Hugh's grasp and stalked into the office with Hugh and the others right behind her. Lilenthal settled in behind his desk; Ryanne, in a chair opposite him. Mo and Ben remained at the door like sentries while Hugh took a position right behind Ryanne.

He glared at the lieutenant. "Well?"

Lilenthal ignored the well-dressed Californian, extracted a photograph from a file on his desk, and handed it to Ryanne. "Miss Kirkland, is this the man who tried to kill you? The one you saw murder Vincent Perigrino?"

Ryanne's hand trembled as she reached for the photograph. It had obviously been taken without the suspect's knowledge or permission, while he was eating dinner in a restaurant. The picture was grainy and the pose not particularly flattering, but Ryanne would have recognized him anywhere. She fought back her instinctive fear and tried to keep her voice steady. "Yes. Is that Arlen Beck?"

"It is. I'll have someone take a formal statement from you in a minute, but first—" Lilenthal handed her a second photograph "—is this the man who made an attempt on your life two days ago in Los Angeles?"

Ryanne accepted the photo, but all she could do was shrug helplessly. "I don't know. My sight hadn't returned—"

"That's him," Hugh stated flatly. "Asa Keegan. But I told you on the phone this morning that he'd been captured."

"Yes, you did," Lilenthal agreed. "And right after I talked to you, that detective friend of yours, Vic Coffin, called me to request that we pick up Arlen Beck. It seems Keegan folded like a house of cards when they questioned him. He knew there was an eyewitness—you—" he indicated Hugh "—but he didn't know that you and the L.A.P.D. knew his identity and even had that photo I wired to Coffin. Once they had him in custody he decided he wasn't going to take the fall alone."

Ryanne leaned forward in her chair. "You mean he confessed to conspiracy to commit murder and named Beck as his coconspirator?"

"That's right. L.A. put out a warrant for Beck's arrest and I sent a couple of men to pick him up."

"Then you've got him in custody?" Hugh asked. "Lieutenant, that still doesn't eliminate the threat to Ryanne. Beck's lawyers will have him out on bail—"

"No, they won't, Mr. MacKenna, because we don't have him—exactly."

"What do you mean, *exactly*?" Ryanne demanded. Like Hugh, she was growing impatient with the lieutenant's cavalier attitude.

"Well, you see, the coroner's having a little trouble finding all the . . . pieces."

Ryanne paled. "Pieces?"

Lilenthal gave her an ironic smile. "Arlen Beck was killed this morning by a fire bomb under the seat of his car."

"Oh, my God," Ryanne murmured, absorbing only the gruesome fact, not its implications.

"Michelon?" Hugh asked.

"Undoubtedly." Lilenthal leaned back in his chair. "Of course, we'll probably never be able to prove it. Just one more unsolved, mob-related killing."

"What makes you certain Beck was in the car?"

"Two of his neighbors saw him get in just seconds before it exploded. They were positive it was Beck."

"But why? Why would Michelon want to kill one of his own men?" Ryanne asked, then realized what must have happened. She answered her own question. "Of course. Once Keegan had fingered Beck, my testimony on the Perigrino murder became irrelevant. Michelon was afraid that if you brought Beck in on conspiracy, he might plea-bargain for a lesser charge in exchange for information about Michelon's syndicate."

"That's the way I figure it." Lilenthal nodded in appreciation of her grasp of the situation. It was obvious she hadn't lost her reporter's instincts.

Hugh still saw a few flaws in the story, though. "How did Michelon know that Keegan had been picked up in L.A.? I mean, you don't listen to the seven o'clock news and find someone who can whip up a fire bomb on ten minutes' notice."

Lilenthal laughed. "Keegan told him. Well, not directly, of course. The idiot used his phone call last night to contact a lawyer here in Chicago who is well-known for handling Michelon's legal problems. The lawyer advised Keegan to find an attorney in L.A., then undoubtedly turned around and called Michelon. That gave Michelon most of the night to figure out the most expedient way of dealing with a messy problem. And if I know Del Michelon as well as I think I do, he probably had the fire bomb as a contingency plan, anyway. My guess is that Keegan is so low level that Michelon doesn't see him as a threat."

"In other words, it's over," Hugh interpreted.

"So far as Miss Kirkland is concerned, yes. She's got nothing on Michelon." He looked at Ryanne. "We need a statement from you so that we can officially close the books on the Perigrino murder, and after that, I'd say you're free to go. The D.A.'s not happy about losing a chance to get Del Michelon, but I imagine you're ecstatic, right?"

Without waiting for an answer, Lilenthal rose and started for the door. "If you'll just hang on a minute I'll set up a stenographer and an officer in an interrogation room so we can get your official statement. Oh, and MacKenna—Coffin says he needs you back in L.A. as soon as you can get there."

Lilenthal left and the room became as silent as a tomb. Ryanne was still in a state of shock. *It's over.* The words echoed in her head, but they were just barely sinking in. A broad, happy smile lit up her face and she rose, turning to Hugh. "It's over!"

Hugh watched her smile bloom—the smile that had captured his heart the first moment he saw her...the smile that would haunt his dreams for as long as he lived. A tight fist of pain squeezed his heart, but he refused to let the wall he'd built crumble now. "Congratulations, Ryanne," he said coldly. He watched her beautiful smile fade, but he refused to regret that he'd erased it. "I guess that means you'll be getting your life back a little sooner than you expected."

He was looking at her with so much venom that Ryanne was struck speechless. She was free now, with no shadows haunting her life. She was free to tell Hugh that she had lied to him, that she loved him desperately; but his forbidding expression made the words clog in her throat. The decision she'd made the previous night for his own good now seemed like a horrible mistake.

"We need to talk, Hugh, please—"

"Please what? Please don't make a scene? Don't worry, Ryanne, I won't. I had enough of that last night." Neither Ryanne nor Hugh noticed when Mo and Ben slipped quietly out the door; Hugh was too consumed with pain, and Ryanne was too preoccupied with finding a way to bridge the incredible chasm she had created between them.

"You really hate me now, don't you?" she asked softly, unable to believe she had gone from one horrible nightmare straight into another.

Hugh gave a short, ugly laugh. "I expect I'll get over that in a few years."

"Oh, God... Hugh, listen to me, I—"

"Okay, Miss Kirkland. Detective Clinton is waiting for you." Oblivious to the tension in his office, Lilenthal took hold of Ryanne's arm. "If you'll come with me, we'll get this over with so you can go."

"Lieutenant, please wait," Ryanne begged, pulling away from him, unable to tear her eyes from Hugh's forbidding face. "Can I have just a minute—"

"I'm sorry but we're kinda busy today," Lilenthal told her brusquely. "Let's get your statement out of the way, and then you can thank the diligent Mr. MacKenna in any way you see fit."

"No thanks are necessary, *Ms. Kirkland*," Hugh said with biting sarcasm. "Just doing my job. I'll send my bill to your L.A. address with a notice to forward it to your *permanent* address here in Chicago."

It was such a cold, blatant slap in the face that Ryanne had to bite her lip to keep from crying out. It was a moment before she could speak. "Hugh, we have to talk. I'll be back as soon as I give my statement."

Lilenthal started out and Ryanne followed. Giving a simple statement was a small price to pay for her deliverance from the dark future she had anticipated, and yet she couldn't help cursing the lieutenant, Detective Clinton, and the entire Chicago police force because they were keeping her from clearing up this agonizing mess with Hugh. But she went into the small interrogation room as directed, officially identified Arlen Beck as the man who'd tried to kill her five years ago and answered endless questions. She finally emerged over an hour later, physically exhausted and emotionally drained, with no thought on her mind except seeing Hugh.

"Miss Kirkland?"

Ryanne was so busy surveying the busy squad room that she barely noticed the fresh-faced policeman who addressed her. "Yes?" she answered distractedly.

"Lieutenant Lilenthal said I should take you home—or wherever you want to go."

"Thank you, but I have someone waiting for me. Hugh MacKenna is—"

"'Scuse me, ma'am, but he's gone."

"Gone?" Ryanne turned to the officer, finally giving him her undivided attention. "Gone where?"

The officer shrugged. "He and the other gentlemen left right after you went into the interrogation room."

Ryanne closed her eyes to fight back a sudden rush of tears. She could barely muster enough strength to ask, "Did he . . . leave any message for me?"

"No, ma'am," the officer replied, wishing he could do something to ease the obvious distress of his lovely assignment. "He just said something about having a plane to catch, and left."

The news was one emotional blow more than Ryanne could bear. Her ability to think and reason left her just as suddenly as Hugh had, and the pain of his desertion crashed down on her. With a wrenching sob, she crumpled under the weight of the pain, oblivious to the sympathetic officer who grabbed her in time to keep her from hitting the floor.

CHAPTER TWENTY-ONE

HUGH STOOD on his deck staring at the horizon, wondering how long it would be before he could watch a beautiful sunset without trying to imagine how he would describe the clouds and the colors to Ryanne—for that matter, before he stopped looking at everything that same way. It had only been a week since he'd left her in that Chicago police station, but already Hugh had realized it was pointless to wonder how long it would be before he forgot her completely and the pain of losing her went away. Right now he couldn't believe it would ever happen, but he kept hoping that at least memories of the little things like the sunsets they'd shared would eventually fade.

The persistent ringing of his doorbell drew Hugh's attention, but he seriously considered ignoring it. The moment he'd returned to Los Angeles the previous week the media had pounced on him like a pack of hungry wolves, and the only way he'd been able to avoid them was to take off for the small cabin he owned in the mountains near Lake Tahoe. With no phones and no television there, he'd been able to escape the press, but not himself, and certainly not Ryanne.

Since she'd never been to his cabin, Hugh had thought it might be easier to think there, but memories of her had followed him, haunted him, until he'd finally given up the effort to outrun the pain. He'd returned to Los Angeles only a few hours ago, hoping that returning to work would be better therapy for his aching heart.

Whoever was at his door refused to give up, and finally Hugh relented and went to answer it. Mo Johnson was standing there, and Hugh stepped back to admit him.

Mo gave Hugh a quick once-over, noting the dark circles under his eyes and the growth of a week-old, untended beard. He noted, too, the faded jeans and cropped football jersey that had seen better days. "Are you trying to set a new fashion trend, or is this a costume for undercover work on skid row?"

Hugh shut the door and ignored the jibe. "How did you know I was home?"

"I saw the Jeep in the driveway."

"With detecting skills like that, I may have to give you a raise." He moved to the bar. "You want a drink?"

Mo pointed to the glass already in Hugh's hand. "What are you having?"

"Soda water. I tried staying drunk for a few days, but it didn't help."

"That seems obvious."

"There you go detecting again."

"Just give me a beer," Mo instructed and Hugh complied.

"How are things at the office?" Hugh started out to the deck again and Mo followed.

"Not great. We're being sued."

Hugh barely raised an eyebrow. "By whom?"

"Miller. He's unhappy that we brought in a subcontractor to finish the job in Canoga Park while we were...busy elsewhere."

Hugh heard the slight hesitation and almost smiled. "You mean while we were protecting Ryanne. It's okay to say her name, Mo. I've just about stopped flinching every time I hear it."

Hugh was at the edge of the deck, facing the sunset, and Mo joined him. He leaned against the rail and gave his friend a sidelong look. "She's back in L.A., you know."

Hugh schooled his face to show no emotion. He'd just bragged that hearing about her didn't make him flinch and he refused to make a liar out of himself so soon. "No, I didn't know, but I guess it's not surprising. She's got that screenplay to finish."

"I don't think so. The report of her death apparently shook up the producer and director pretty bad. *Entertainment Hollywood* is reporting that they grieved for about ten minutes, then hired another writer. No one seems to know if Ryanne is going to let it pass or sue."

"She won't sue," Hugh said flatly. "She's too anxious to get back to Chicago. By now I'm sure Doug Sutherland has offered her back her old job."

"Maybe." Mo fell silent for a moment before dropping the next bombshell. "She called the office asking for you every day you were gone."

Hugh gave a half laugh. "She probably wanted to complain about the bill I sent her."

"Don't you think you should at least call her to make sure?"

"No."

"You're being pretty thickheaded about this, aren't you?" He held up one hand to stop Hugh's reply. "Look, I don't know what happened to change things between the two of you, but—"

Hugh turned to Mo impatiently. "I told her I loved her, and she handed my heart back to me on a platter."

Mo nodded sadly. "That's kinda what I thought. I always figured that when you fell, you'd fall hard. But I thought Ryanne had fallen pretty hard, too. It doesn't make sense."

Hugh stiffened, remembering Ryanne's flat rejection of him. "She wanted to go back to her old life."

"That's understandable. After all, she's been pretty restricted for the past few years, being blind and all. Maybe if you gave her some time—"

Hugh turned to his friend. "Look, Mo, she made it perfectly clear that there was no room in her life for me. How much am I expected to take from her?"

Mo shrugged. "As much as she's worth."

Hugh turned back to the ocean without a word, but Mo refused to be dismissed. "Tell me, Hugh. This declaration of love you made to her—was that before or after she spent a couple of hours in the ocean wondering if she was going to die before or after the sharks got her?"

Mo wouldn't have thought it was possible for his friend to get any more tense, but Hugh did. "After."

"And after she got her sight back, too—which was all after she'd been shot in the back by a hired hit man."

"Look, is this leading anywhere?" Hugh demanded harshly.

Mo raised his hands as though to ward off Hugh's belligerence. "No, no. I was just getting ready to applaud your timing. Most guys declare their love over an elegant candlelight dinner. I gotta hand it to you, Hugh. You've got style. Ryanne had just gone through some of the most traumatic experiences any human could. That's good timing, buddy. I imagine she was really emotionally equipped for your confession."

"Believe me, Mo, she wasn't at all confused about her feelings for me. I know she'd been through a lot, and on top of it all, she was still terrified about whether or not she was going to escape from Beck. But I told her I would see her through it, no matter what happened, even if she had to go into hiding."

"Oh, great!" Mo declared expansively. "I'm sure she really needed to feel responsible for your life as well as her own!"

"That's not the way it happened!"

"Are you sure?"

"Hell! I'm not sure of anything!" Hugh shouted, fighting the urge to hurl the glass in his hand onto the rocks below him.

Mo placed his hand on his friends shoulder and softened his voice. "Talk to her, Hugh. She couldn't possibly say anything that would make you hurt worse than you do now. And who knows—you might feel better." He moved his hand and started toward the house. "I'll let myself out. Will you be in the office tomorrow?"

Hugh nodded without turning. "Yeah."

"Okay. See you there."

Mo left and Hugh stared at the colorful horizon. Had Ryanne really called him every day? he wondered. He hadn't yet checked the message service that handled his home number, and suddenly it became important that he did so. He hurried inside and dialed his service. The woman on the switchboard sounded overjoyed to hear from him and began reading the dozens of messages that had stacked up while he'd been gone, but he cut her off, asking for only the ones from Ryanne Kirkland.

There were ten of them, and they all said the same thing. *Please call as soon as you return. Ryanne.* Simple and to the point, but without a hint of why she wanted to speak to him.

Taking the cordless phone with him, Hugh returned to the deck, dialed four digits of her number, then hung up. If he was going to put himself through the torture of speaking to her, it might as well be in person, he decided. It was hard to admit he'd have grabbed any excuse to see her again.

He tossed the phone into a chair and started for the stairs that led to the beach, then stopped abruptly. Ryanne was there below him, standing on the rocks, staring up at the house—and at him. He froze, waiting, his heart beating so hard he thought it might burst out of his chest.

Finally, Ryanne thought, praying that the gaunt, forbidding man staring down at her wasn't just a figment of her imagination. He looked different with a beard, but it was Hugh, she was certain. Her agonizing week of waiting was finally over.

After he'd left her in Chicago, Ryanne had collapsed from emotional and physical exhaustion. Lieutenant Lilenthal had wanted to call an ambulance, but Ryanne had insisted that he notify Doug Sutherland instead. Doug had taken her back to her condominium and stood guard, keeping the media at bay, while Ryanne slept for nearly thirty hours straight. When she'd awakened, her only desire had been to talk to Hugh, but by then he had disappeared, and his loyal staff at MacKenna and Associates had refused to tell her where he could be reached.

Ryanne had spent the next few days in a sickening state of suspended animation that was remarkably similar to the frightening hours she'd spent alone and adrift in the ocean. Being without Hugh, knowing how much she'd hurt him, and not knowing if he would ever forgive her, had nearly driven her insane. Meanwhile she was besieged by reporters, all clamoring for details of her brush with death and the miraculous return of her sight. When Judith brought Aggie home, they all returned to the beach house to wait...and wait...and wait.

She called Hugh's home and office every day, and she spent a lot of time on the beach, walking up to this house, which she knew in her heart had to be Hugh's. Until she saw him standing there on the deck, though, she hadn't been certain. Now she was. Hugh was home, and one way or another for good or ill, this torture was going to end.

Picking her way carefully across the rocks, her heart thundering in her chest, Ryanne continued climbing until she was standing on the deck with Hugh. The distance between them was only a dozen feet, but four yards had never seemed more uncrossable.

"Hello, Hugh."

"Ryanne."

Despite the forbidding scowl on his face, Ryanne managed a small smile. She'd been through a week of hell, waiting for him to return home, and she wasn't about to be frightened off now that she finally had his attention. It terrified her to think that she might have hurt him so badly that he would never forgive her, but she owed him the truth. After that, it would be up to him to decide what to do with it.

"I almost didn't recognize you—" she touched her own jaw "—with the beard and all."

"How did you know I would be here?" he asked, turning back to the sunset so that he wouldn't have to look at her magnificent face. The desire to gather her into his arms despite whatever protests she might make was overpowering, so he gripped the rail until his knuckles turned white from the strain.

Ryanne followed him to the seaward edge of the deck, but kept her distance. "I didn't know. I've been walking up here every day since I got back last Tuesday. I wasn't even positive this was your house. I'm finding that nothing I see looks the way I had visualized it."

"That must be hard for you," he said without turning to her.

Not as hard as this, she wanted to say, but didn't. "I'm coping. Judith is a big help, but she won't be with me much longer. She's taken a new job, you know."

"No, I didn't know. But I suppose it makes sense. Not many reporters have private secretaries, do they?"

"No, they don't." Ryanne fought to keep her voice even despite Hugh's bitter tone. She didn't have the right to wish that he would make this easier for her. She wanted to just blurt out what she came to say, but those words wouldn't come, so she kept up her inane chatter to fill what would otherwise have been intolerable silence. "I guess you haven't talked to your dad."

"Should I have?"

"I suppose not. But you see, Judith's going to work for him as his new business manager."

That bit of news forced Hugh to look at her. "I didn't know he needed one."

Ryanne smiled. "Neither did he until Judith convinced him he did." There had also been some mention of marriage, but Judith had refused to speculate on whether anything would come of it, and Ryanne felt that Hugh should hear that particular development from his father, not from her.

Hugh nodded and looked away from Ryanne again. "I hope it works out. They'll make a good team."

"Yes."

A long silence stretched between them. Hugh wanted to demand that Ryanne say what she had come to say, and then leave. But she'd be gone forever, and as torturous as being with her like this was, being without her was going to be even worse. "Mo was just here," he told her, making conversation to fill the uncomfortable silence. "He told me Ted Braxton signed someone else to finish your screenplay."

"That's right."

"Are you going to sue?"

Ryanne shrugged. "I don't know. I haven't really been able to think about the future yet."

"Didn't Doug offer you your old job back?"

"As a matter of fact, he did."

Hugh laughed humorlessly. "And you didn't snap it up?"

"No." Ryanne looked out at the sunset. "The *Chicago Daily Examiner* isn't the only newspaper in the country. And I still have several Cameron Lawe books under contract. I thought I might write one a year and still be able to work in journalism . . . maybe even here in L.A."

Hugh's breath hissed as though she'd struck him and he turned to her with his eyes narrowed sharply. Living without Ryanne was going to be hard enough, but having her in the same city might very well be impossible. The temptation to see her would always be there, tantalizing him. "Why in hell would you want to stay here?" he demanded harshly.

Ryanne turned then and poured all her heart into one simple phrase. "To be near you."

The look Hugh saw in her brilliant blue eyes nearly took his breath away. He saw warmth there, and a touch of fear, but most of all, he saw love. Or, at least, what he wanted to believe was love. "Damn it, Ryanne, what are you trying to do to me?"

Ryanne reached up and touched his face as tears pooled in her eyes. "I'm trying to tell you what I wanted to say a week ago in Chicago—what I *couldn't* say that night on the boat. I love you."

Hugh would have sold his soul to believe it, but her abrupt change of heart didn't make sense. "Look, Ryanne, if you think you owe me something—"

Ryanne's heart sank. She'd told him how she felt and he didn't believe her—or he didn't want her. Ryanne wasn't sure which was worse. "I do owe you something, Hugh—"

"No, you don't! If you want to thank me for protecting you, fine! Paying your bill will be thanks enough. But don't feed me your pity, lady, because I don't want it!"

"Pity?" Ryanne could hardly believe what she was hearing. "You pigheaded oaf! I don't pity you, I love you!"

"Since when?"

"Since...since..." Confused and upset, she tried to remember when she'd first realized she loved Hugh, but it seemed that she'd loved him forever. "Since...I don't know when! June first, maybe. Possibly the second, but certainly no later than the third!"

The tight fist of pain in Hugh's gut began to uncoil as laughter bubbled in his chest. Ryanne loved him, and nothing else mattered. "June third, huh?" he asked, chuckling at Ryanne's belligerent pose.

"About then, yes," she answered, her own smile growing. It was going to be all right. The pain was slowly disappearing from Hugh's wonderful golden eyes.

"So you're telling me that you lied to me on the boat," he said softly.

"Yes."

"But why, Ryanne? Why?" Hugh wanted to draw her into his arms, but he couldn't, not just yet. He had to understand first.

Ryanne's eyes filled with tears. "*Because* I love you."

Suddenly it all became clear. She had lied to protect him, to keep him from sharing the dangerous, uncertain future she had been expecting. She had loved him enough to give him up. Overcome with emotion, Hugh could bear the distance between them no longer. He reached for her and she went to him.

"Damn you, Ryanne. Damn you," he murmured, his arms locked around her, his face buried in her silky hair. "You were trying to protect me, but you had no right to make that decision."

"Yes, I did!" Ryanne insisted. "It was the only way I could be certain you'd never be hurt. I couldn't let you go on risking your life for me!"

Hugh grabbed Ryanne's shoulders and held her away from him, fighting the urge to shake her. "Don't you realize I have no life without you?"

Ryanne's jaw quivered as she tried to hold back tears of joy. "Does that mean you might eventually forgive me for lying to you?"

"Eventually," he said grudgingly, though he held nothing back in the look he gave her.

"Do you think you might someday... marry me?"

"Even if I have to carry you kicking and screaming to the altar." He drew her toward him again, intent on sealing their strangely worded proposal with a kiss, but Ryanne pulled away. Taking hold of Hugh's hand, she led him into the house, through the living room, into the bedroom.

There she released his hand, and Hugh watched, puzzled, as she moved through the room, opening the drapes to let in the fading sunset, turning on every lamp until the room was ablaze.

When she had finished, she knelt on the bed, and held her arms out, her eyes brimming with tears and love. "Share the *light* with me?"

Hugh thought his heart might burst. He moved to her, taking her into his arms as he murmured, "Oh, yes. The light, the dark, the twilight, the dawn, and everything in between."

"Forever?"

"And ever... And ever after."

He was determined to release his bride
from her vows. Ever since the accident,
he knew he'd have to go it alone.

BLIND TO LOVE

Rebecca Winters

CHAPTER ONE

"DR. STILLMAN—are you saying that my husband's blindness is irreversible?" Libby Anson fought for composure. Throughout the long nighttime flight from London to Nairobi, she'd held on to the hope that his condition was temporary, that an operation would restore his sight.

"I'm afraid it is," the doctor answered quietly, extinguishing the little spark of hope that had refused to be quenched until now. He leaned forward in his chair. "When the roof of the mine collapsed, the force caused a tiny fragment of ore to penetrate your husband's skull," he explained. "I'm convinced the nerves in the optic tract were severed, because he can't discern light at all. I'm very sorry."

"I can't believe it." She shook her head, causing the glistening black hair to settle loosely about her shoulders. "Does Vance know his blindness is permanent?"

"Yes. He demanded the truth as soon as he regained consciousness."

"But it's been over two weeks since the accident. I don't understand why someone didn't call me. I'd have come on the next plane. When I think that he's been lying in a hospital bed all this time, and I knew nothing..." Her voice trailed off.

"I assumed he'd been in touch with his family. But the night before last, I learned that he had no visitors or phone calls except from some employees at Anson Mining. So I took the liberty of calling his office to get the phone number of a relative. A Mr. Dean told me that Mr. Anson's next

of kin was his father in London, and I phoned him immediately."

Libby frowned. "Hasn't Vance mentioned me at all? I
don't understand."

The doctor regarded her fine-boned, oval face, obviously concerned by the troubled expression in her eyes.
"Until you appeared on the ward moments ago, I didn't
even know Mr. Anson was married. Let alone that he had
such a lovely wife," he said in an aside. "Your marriage is
a well-kept secret. No one in his company has the slightest
idea. How long have you been married?"

Libby sucked in her breath. "Three weeks. Vance had to
fly back here right after our wedding ceremony to take care
of an emergency at one of the mines. Since he didn't expect
to be gone for more than a few days, we decided that I'd stay
in London until he could join me, and we could leave on our
honeymoon. I've had no word from him since." Her voice
trembled as she spoke. "He said he'd be in an inaccessible
area of the highlands and that he'd call me as soon as he
could." She paused. "Your phone call to his father was the
only contact any of us has had." A new wave of pain as-
sailed her. By not acknowledging to anyone that he was
married, Vance had wounded her deeply.

"Under the circumstances, you can't know how pleased
I am that you're here." The doctor smiled kindly. "I think
you've provided me with a missing piece of the puzzle."

Libby uncrossed her long, slender legs and leaned forward. "What puzzle, Dr. Stillman?"

"Your husband is a proud man, but his fierce desire to
remain independent in the face of his loss had me worried.
Now that I see you, I'm beginning to understand."

"What do you mean?" Libby asked urgently, eyes fastened on his.

He linked both hands behind his head. "If I had a beautiful new bride waiting for me and then suddenly lost my

sight, frankly speaking, my first thoughts would probably be suicidal.''

"You're not saying Vance doesn't want to live?" she cried out. "Is that why he didn't call me as soon as it happened?''

"Not at all," he hastened to assure her. "But what he *has* done is turn within himself because he can't bear the thought of being dependent—on anyone, but especially on you. He's a brilliant, successful man who's used to being in complete charge. He's built up an enviable mining career here in Kenya. A large corporate staff waits on his decisions. More important, he's acquired a wife and he wants to be all things to her. To *you*. Suddenly his blindness has struck at his very sense of self, his manhood. He's lost faith in his ability to be your protector, breadwinner, lover...."

"Vance is all those things to me, blind or not." Her voice cracked with emotion. "I—I thought you'd phoned Vance's father because you'd been unable to reach me. I didn't know Vance hadn't.... Do most people react like this in his situation? Do they turn away from the people who love them most?''

He averted his eyes and rubbed the pad of his thumb along the edge of the folder in front of him. "A certain amount of depression always accompanies a loss like this, but each case is different, naturally. Like most men, he wants to be the perfect husband, but being blind is an unknown factor—something beyond his control. He's afraid.''

Tears filled her eyes. "I can't imagine Vance being afraid of anything.''

His brows quirked. "Neither can he...."

Libby blinked as the meaning of his words penetrated her mind. It was always night for Vance now. She couldn't fathom what that would be like. Her heart ached for him, compounding her sorrow. With an effort, she lifted her head. "Is he in pain?''

"Except for an occasional headache, he's in excellent physical shape. I am concerned, however, about the fact that he blames himself for the accident, which took two lives."

Libby gasped softly. She hadn't known, she hadn't thought beyond her husband's own loss.

"I didn't want to discharge him without knowing if he had a close friend or family who'd watch out for him. So far, he's rejected all offers of help. Except for a handful of men from his company, he's refused any visitors. As I explained, I phoned his father to find out what arrangements had been made, if any.

"I have to tell you I'm relieved you've come. Particularly since he insists on leaving the hospital today. He'll put up a fight, but I believe he needs you desperately. Are you up to it?" He eyed her anxiously.

Libby took a deep breath and lifted her chin a fraction. "I need Vance much more than he needs me. I'm his wife and I intend to have a life with him in every sense of the word."

A smile of relief broke out on the doctor's face. "Bravo— he's a lucky man to have a woman like you, and I hope that one day soon he realizes it."

The doctor's words hit upon a growing fear in Libby's heart. Vance had had two weeks to start erecting barriers. The first had been his failure to phone her. "I'd like to go in and see him now," she said decisively, rising to her feet. "Thank you for your time, Dr. Stillman. I'm grateful you've been here for Vance."

He stood up and shook her hand. "Good luck to you, Mrs. Anson. I'll be in to see your husband shortly and answer any questions you may have. Why don't you take him his lunch tray? His appetite isn't quite what it should be, which isn't unusual, of course. But maybe you can succeed where others have failed."

Libby's fears worsened. "I'll try."

"May I ask you a personal question?"

"Of course." She stared at him, wondering why he seemed so intent.

"How long have you known your husband?"

"Almost three years. I met him when my stepfather bought the stud farm next door to his family's property. Why?"

His eyes narrowed on her profile as she turned to leave. "I'm relieved to know your marriage wasn't the result of a whirlwind courtship. At least you know what you're up against."

Libby left his office and shut the door, leaning heavily against it. *Did she really know Vance as well as the doctor assumed?* They might not have had a whirlwind courtship, but with him in Kenya and her away at the International School in Geneva, they'd spent precious little time together. She'd treasured those rare occasions when Vance was able to fly home to see her. When she thought she couldn't bear to say goodbye to him one more time, he'd asked her to marry him, promising her that marriage would solve all their problems.

A shiver rippled over her body as she remembered what Vance had whispered to her at the airport after their wedding. "Now that we have the ceremony out of the way, we can get on with the courtship, Mrs. Anson." His searing kiss with its promise of rapture had been all that sustained Libby for the past few weeks.

She moved away from the door, mentally preparing herself for the first sight of her husband, the conversation that would follow. Somehow she'd find a way to convince him that they would have a wonderful, fulfilling marriage in spite of his blindness. After all, they loved each other. She'd be his eyes! Their physical love would bind them even more closely together. Maybe they'd start a family right away.

They both wanted children...unless Vance had changed his mind.

Libby paused beneath the overhead light to examine the rings on her left hand—tangible evidence that their marriage had taken place. A wide band of hammered gold set off the teardrop amethyst. Both the gold and the stone were from the Anson mines, and she remembered how Vance had told her that the color of amethyst always reminded him of her eyes. Suddenly, the desire to be held in his arms had her running down the corridor to the nursing station.

CARRYING VANCE'S LUNCH TRAY, Libby entered the private hospital room.

"You can take that tray back where it came from," Vance's deep voice rang out with all its familiar force. "I'm leaving in a few minutes, and it will only go to waste. Take it to the poor devil next door. He's the one on the bland diet."

After that outburst, Libby hesitated to identify herself. She walked slowly across the room, passing close to him out of necessity.

"I told you I wasn't hungry! For the—" He suddenly broke off talking, and his chin lifted, instantly alert. "That perfume—I thought for a minute..." His voice trailed off and he turned away, running a distracted hand through his dark hair.

Libby's hands shook, causing the teacup to rattle and the covering over the plate to slip. Carefully, she put the tray on the bedside table, then turned to drink her fill of the beloved figure. He was dressed in silk pajamas and a robe, both in a coffee shade. Had a friend or employee brought them from the farmhouse? Were they his taste, or had one of his secretaries purchased them?

Again Libby's confidence was shaken because she hardly knew the Vance who inhabited this part of the world. The bits and pieces of information in his letters and phone calls didn't cover everyday personal habits.

She was stunned by how little his features had changed. The lines around his mouth were deeper, the mold of his lips more cynical, but his masculine beauty was as dominant and devastating as ever. He'd obviously insisted on shaving himself; normally a fastidious person, he'd missed several places. His hair was longer, and he'd lost weight, making him look all of his thirty-one years, but he was still perfect to Libby.

She watched in fascination as he attempted to pack. Items were tossed into the wrong section of the suitcase in haphazard fashion. He swore violently when some of the cassettes slid off the bed and fell to the floor. Cold fingers squeezed Libby's heart as she watched him feel his way around the end of the bed and get down on his hands and knees to search for them.

Without conscious thought, she made a motion to help him find the elusive tapes. Vance's dark head reared back abruptly, like a finely mettled stallion's. Libby gasped involuntarily, unable to help herself. His eyes stared straight ahead, velvety brown and beautiful. But angry! She couldn't believe he wasn't able to see her.

"What in hell do you *want*? You couldn't possibly be Mrs. Grady. She knows better than to try to force me to eat," he remarked in acid tones, making her shudder.

Libby's eyes played over him. No signs of his wound were visible. Dr. Stillman said the tiny shard had entered the skull well past the hairline—an infinitesimal perforation produced by the force of falling debris.

The deep mahogany tan he maintained year-round gave him a deceptively healthy look, though she knew he had to be in a state of shock.

"Have you seen enough, whoever you are?" he snarled at her, making her jump. "Don't you know it's impolite to stare at a blind man?"

Libby was horrified. She didn't recognize the man who inhabited Vance's body. She felt the moisture gather along her brows and chided herself. This would never do. She was reacting in exactly the way she'd sworn she wouldn't.

"Vance?" Her voice trembled with need.

The gasp that finally came out of him sounded like ripping silk. "Dear lord, it *is* you," he whispered, his voice hoarse with shock and with something else as yet undefinable. A whiteness appeared around his taut mouth as he got to his feet. "Libby." It was almost a groan, as if her name had been called forth from some dark, hidden place. But there was an intimate quality in the sound of her name. His voice betrayed intense emotion, and that was something to cherish.

"Yes, Vance." She flew across the hospital room. "You were supposed to come back to London, but under the circumstances, I'll forgive you," she whispered against his lips before locking her arms around his neck and kissing him with an ardor born of all the emotions she'd experienced in the past two days. His body remained rigid, but she hadn't imagined that first brief moment when she'd felt an answering response. Then he was pushing her away and backing around the end of the bed, banging into the handle that raised and lowered it. He cursed again, and his chest heaved as if he were out of breath.

"What are you doing here, Libby?" The cold hostility of his tone alarmed her.

She swallowed hard. "What kind of question is that to ask your wife?"

He thrust his fists into his robe pockets and stood half-turned away from her, his features like stone. "You *know* I don't want you here. I said it all in the letter."

Her heart hammered and she drew closer. "What letter?"

"The letter I dictated to a secretary here at the hospital. She assured me she posted it."

"Vance—I didn't receive your letter. I swear it."

A long silence followed as he assessed the sincerity of her words. "Provided you're telling me the truth, then I don't understand why you're here at all. The plan was that I would get in touch with *you*."

She moistened her lips. "Dr. Stillman called your father yesterday morning and told him about the accident. He phoned me immediately, and as soon as I could make arrangements, I flew out on the next available plane." He paled, and gripped the footboard until his knuckles shone white. "Vance, why didn't you tell me what happened? Why didn't you share something that important? You know I'd have been here in an instant."

She reached over to grasp the hand closest to her. As she pressed his fingers gently, he shook her hand off and backed farther away. She'd never known physical rejection from Vance, and it hurt.

"You shouldn't have come," he muttered grimly. His hand hovered over the things in his suitcase, as if he wanted something to throw. "That letter was sent special delivery. Obviously Dr. Stillman's meddling, however well intended, brought you here before you could receive it. It explained why I don't want you here and why our marriage won't work."

She took a deep breath, trying desperately to remain calm. "Well, now that I'm here, you can tell me in person."

She watched as his other hand felt for the handle of the suitcase. A pulse throbbed at his temples and the whiteness around his lips intensified. "Go home, Libby. There's nothing for you here." He closed the lid but couldn't fasten it because the cord of his shaving kit was in the way.

She'd tried to prepare herself for changes in his behavior, but this harsh cruelty had never been part of him before. He'd turned into a forbidding, implacable stranger. She had an idea that if she made any more physical overtures, he'd push her away bodily. "I am home," she whispered. "We were married three weeks ago and I have the rings to prove it. I believe part of the vows went, 'for better, for worse, in sickness and in health, so long as we both shall live.'"

"I'm blind, Libby. Something far different."

"You're alive!" she flung back on a rush of emotion. "When I heard you'd been in an accident, all I cared about was that you hadn't died. As awful as your blindness must be, it's something we can deal with. I'll help you. I'd do anything for you."

"Wrong, Libby!" She heard him curse beneath his breath. He stood rigidly by the bed, hands clenched. Anyone else would have heeded all the warnings and fled his presence by now. "There's no *we* about it. I told Dr. Stillman. *No visitors.*"

"A wife hardly fits in the same category." She stood her ground. "Why didn't you tell Dr. Stillman you were married? Have you so little faith in me that you thought I might embarrass you in front of your friends and associates here?"

"That's not the reason and you know it." He ran both hands through his dark brown hair in an attitude of abject frustration. "You couldn't possibly understand, Libby."

"Then help me! I love you, Vance. Let me be a wife to you. Please hold me," she begged, starting around the bed toward him.

Vance's eyes narrowed. "Stop it, Libby. The accident changed everything."

"Including your love for me?"

A shadow of pain came and went on his face so quickly that she almost missed it. "I'm not the same man you married. Being blind alters a person's perspective in every conceivable way. It's like being reborn. I have to go my own way. Alone. I'm sorry the letter didn't reach you in time to avoid this unnecessary trip."

"Unnecessary?" A rush of anger swamped her. "You can't alter the fact that we're married, Vance. Since I'm here, the letter is no longer relevant. I refuse to give up on a marriage that hasn't even begun!"

"And it's not going to!" The authoritative tone brooked no argument. "I'm leaving the hospital for the flat this afternoon. I'll arrange for a taxi to run you to the airport. You can be on the next flight back to London."

"You're not serious."

He straightened to his full height, his jaw tensed with anger. "I've never been more serious in my life." His harsh tone convinced her that he meant what he said.

"There are no more flights back to London till morning." She said the first thing that came into her mind, stalling for time. "But if you're that anxious to get rid of me, I'll take a taxi to a hotel."

"No, Libby," came the unexpected comment. "I won't allow you to stay in a hotel alone. You're not familiar with Nairobi. Besides that, you're far too beautiful to be here on your own." He rubbed the back of his bronzed neck in frustration, and mumbled something unintelligible. "I suppose there's nothing for it but to take you back to the flat with me. We can get a taxi to take you to the airport first thing in the morning."

"Vance, I'm a twenty-three-year-old woman—not a child you can order around!" The words slipped out before she could prevent them.

A dark brow lifted dangerously. "And the man you married no longer exists." He stalked to the bathroom and slammed the door.

"Stop feeling sorry for yourself!" she shouted at him angrily.

"Mrs. Anson?"

Libby whirled around, her cheeks hot and the adrenaline pumping through her body. "Dr. Stillman—"

"Why don't you step out into the hall for a minute? I'd like to talk to you."

Libby followed him into the corridor, leaning against the wall for support. The confrontation with Vance had drained her and she felt ill. "You could probably hear us quarreling," she murmured with her head in her hands. "I'm so ashamed for losing my temper like that. But he refuses to let me get close to him, and for a moment, I forgot about his blindness. All I could think of was that he's not going to give us a chance."

"I thought something like this might happen. You have to realize he hasn't accepted his blindness yet. He can't believe he won't see again. That, plus the shock of your being here, is why he's reacting this way."

Libby lifted her head. "But for how much longer? I'm his wife. I love him so much."

He nodded. "I wish I had a pat answer for you, but I don't. You're going to have to give this some time."

"I'm running out of time, doctor. He expects me to fly back to London in the morning."

"The day isn't over yet," he reasoned. "What are your immediate plans?"

Libby blinked to stem the threat of tears. "He says we're going to his flat. Naturally I'd hoped he would want to take me to the farm. When I think of the plans we made..." Her voice faded away.

"Don't give up on your plans. This is only the first day. And please remember that I'm here. You can call me day or night. I've left numbers where I can be reached, along with his discharge papers and pain medication. Keep in mind that the head matron, Mrs. Grady, is experienced in working with the visually handicapped. She can assist you in helping your husband adjust to a daily routine when the time comes. Call her and make an appointment to come in.''

Libby smoothed back a strand of hair. She couldn't think past tomorrow morning when Vance intended for her to be on that plane back to England, but she didn't speak her thoughts.

''Thank you again, Dr. Stillman. I've appreciated the talk.''

He patted her arm. ''Good luck.''

Libby stared at his retreating back before slipping into the room once more. While she'd been talking to Dr. Stillman, an orderly had helped Vance change into hip-hugging Levi's and a safari shirt—an outfit he'd often worn when they went riding together. The slight weight loss enhanced his dark, handsome looks, making him appear even taller. Despite the austere expression on his face, he looked wonderful.

''Vance?''

''Where have you been?''

Perhaps she was grasping at straws, but she thought she detected a trace of anxiety mixed with the gruffness of his tone.

''Dr. Stillman wanted to say goodbye and wish us well.'' His mouth thinned, but he said nothing. ''What about your lunch?'' she went on. ''Aren't you going to eat before we go?''

''What does it take to convince you I'd choke on food right now?''

''Then do you mind if I eat it? I—I haven't had a meal since yesterday afternoon. I know it's silly, but I don't feel well.'' The light-headedness she'd experienced out in the hall grew worse, and she subsided into one of the chairs near the closet. Waves of nausea washed over her, bathing her in perspiration.

''Libby?''

She didn't imagine the alarm in his voice this time, but she felt too ill to respond.

He felt his way over to her and slid a warm hand beneath her hair to her nape. "Your skin is clammy. Put your head between your legs."

Libby followed his advice, too weak to do anything else. When the buzzing in her ears finally receded, she lifted her head, relishing the feel of his hand against her skin. His fingers worked their way into her hair, massaging her scalp with gentle insistence.

"Better?" With his face this close, she could see the trace of laughter lines around his mouth. She nodded, then realized he couldn't see her. For a moment, she'd forgotten.

"Yes. Much better, thank you."

"Don't move." Her heart filled with love as she watched him try to find his way to the table and search for something for her to eat. After a few mishaps, he managed to come back with a glass of juice.

Libby took it from his hand and drained the contents. The orange juice was lukewarm, but she didn't mind. In a few minutes her strength started to return. "That tasted good."

"Why in the name of heaven didn't you eat on the plane?" he asked, crouching down beside her. His hand found her arm and slid to her wrist, absently feeling for her pulse. The action caused her to tremble.

"Probably for the same reason you didn't eat your lunch." She stifled the urge to draw his dark head to her chest. "I'm all right now, Vance."

She heard him sigh deeply. "You need to eat. I'll call for another tray."

"No. I'll finish yours. Let's not bother anyone." She stood up on still-weak legs and reluctantly pulled out of his grasp. Walking unsteadily over to the table, she began to eat the roll and chicken.

Vance straightened, but with uncharacteristic hesitancy started and stopped several times before reaching the wall phone. He swore as the receiver dropped to the floor, but eventually managed to reach the hospital switchboard and put through a call for a taxi. After that, he made another call. When he didn't speak English, Libby assumed it was Swahili, which he seemed to speak like a native. He replaced the receiver just as the orderly she'd seen earlier appeared in the doorway.

"We're ready for you, Mr. Anson. The wheelchair is directly behind you."

Libby noted the way Vance's hands clenched into fists at his side. "I can walk out of here on my own two legs."

"I know how you feel, sir, but it's hospital policy."

"Vance—" Libby interjected before more arguments could ensue. "Since I came here directly from the airport, I left my luggage down in the reception area. I'll go see about it and meet you at the main doors."

"How much did you bring?"

Her eyes closed. "Everything I own except my horse, King, and Daddy is making arrangements to have him shipped to Mombasa within the week. I thought it would be fun to drive there and pick him up after he's out of quarantine."

His eyes smoldered. He started to say something, but she slipped out of the room beyond earshot. All the way to the foyer, she kept recalling her stepfather's words. "Vance has been blessed with a greater gift than his eyesight, and that's your love, honey." It was easy enough for her stepfather to say. After the death of Libby's natural father, her mother had married a widower who'd never had children of his own. Libby filled the void in his life and he doted on her. They'd been a happy family, open in their affection. But Libby knew it would take a lot more than love to help Vance now.

CHAPTER TWO

"IS YOUR NAME ANSON?" The man addressing Libby climbed out of a taxi.

"Yes. My husband will be ready any minute."

The man scratched his head as he surveyed the amount of luggage surrounding her. "Is this everything?"

"No. My husband has a suitcase."

The driver muttered something in his native tongue and started loading bags into the rack on top of the vintage Peugeot. What he couldn't fit there he piled next to the driver's seat. "You get in back and I'll put one of the cases at your feet."

Libby did as he suggested, realizing it would be a tight squeeze. Moments later, she caught sight of Vance being wheeled out the front doors of the hospital. The afternoon sun glinted in his hair, highlighting the chestnut tones blended with the brown. In sunglasses, he looked perfectly normal, but she could sense from his taut features the kind of tension that gripped him. It took a rare sort of courage to leave the hospital and the security it offered. Libby recognized this was a moment Vance had to struggle through alone, but she still felt excluded.

The consequences of his loss were beginning to make their impact. She felt angry all over again that his blindness had the power to rob their relationship of its former intimacy. The closeness, the sharing—that all seemed to have fled. He lived in his own world now, and she didn't have the faintest idea how it felt, or how to gain entrance.

"Here's your cane, Mr. Anson. Compliments of the hospital floor!" The orderly put it on Vance's lap, but he immediately pushed it away.

"I have no use for this. If I have to resort to a cane, I might as well walk around with a microphone telling everyone I'm blind."

Libby was aghast at Vance's rudeness, but the orderly appeared unperturbed as he steadied the wheelchair. Vance put a hand on the frame of the open door and started to climb in back. Inadvertently, his other hand brushed against the curve of her hip. She felt its heat through the thin fabric of her cotton shirtwaist. Her body quickened when his hand trailed to her thigh; it was as if he needed to touch her and couldn't help himself. The intimacy of the moment forced a soft gasp from her that he must have heard. He immediately withdrew his hand and sat back as the door closed, careful not to have any contact with her in spite of his long legs.

Libby couldn't take her eyes off him. His dark good looks filled her vision to the exclusion of anything else and increased her longing to hold him close. Her body was still reacting to the touch of his hand and her heart thrilled at the undeniable proof that he desired her, however much he might want her out of his blind world.

The driver started the engine and drove out into the stream of traffic. He maneuvered the battered taxi with death-defying skill through the crowds of honking cars and noisy people. She listened to the volatile exchanges coming through the open window. "Vance," she ventured, stretching her hand to his bronzed forearm without thinking. He flinched as if the warm touch of her fingers scalded him. She quickly removed them. "Everyone sounds angry."

Vance sat rigidly staring straight ahead. "Swahili is an animated language. The natives shout it quite naturally. You get used to it," he muttered, sounding far away from her just then. He remained silent throughout the rest of their journey to his flat.

The driver drove like a maniac, but so did everyone else. It was another thing she'd have to get used to. Because, despite Vance's edict that she return to London, she had no intention of leaving him.

In a few minutes, the taxi came to a stop in front of a modern, five-story apartment building in the heart of the city. Vance had once explained that his corporate office was within walking distance of the flat for easy access. In a way, she was thankful for the flat; it would allow her, finally, to be alone with him—away from everyone else. Maybe then she could try to reason with him, secure in the knowledge that no one would interrupt them.

"The driver will take the bags to the lobby, and the concierge will let you inside the flat," Vance explained, causing her spirits to plummet to a new low.

"Where are you going?" She tried to sound interested rather than devastated by the unexpected arrangements. Everything in her wanted to cry out at this injustice that prevented him from loving her. Until the accident, Vance could hardly bear to have her out of his arms for any reason. Now he couldn't wait to be rid of her.

"I have things to do at the office, Libby, and I have no idea what time I'll get back tonight so don't wait up for me. I've asked the concierge to put groceries in the kitchen, so you'll be able to eat when you want. Don't go outside if you get restless. You can watch TV if you're bored, but under no circumstances do I want you wandering around downtown Nairobi unescorted. Do you understand?"

He'd always been protective of her, but right now his concern seemed obsessive. Still, she had no desire to add to his anxieties. "I'm going to bed. Jet lag has caught up with me. I did promise to phone the parents and let them know

I'd arrived safely. Do you mind if I call your father and tell him you're all right? Naturally, he's worried."

He gave an exasperated sigh. "I don't see the necessity since you'll be back home tomorrow night. But I suppose it would be a good idea to let them know so they can make arrangements to meet your plane."

That hateful, patronizing arrogance aroused her anger again. She whirled around and reached for her train case. The driver transported the rest of her luggage to the door of the apartment building. Another man who appeared on the porch indicated he was the concierge and that Libby should follow him.

She glanced over her shoulder, anxious for Vance in spite of her churning emotions. She had to suppress the urge to warn him to be careful, to remind him that it was his first day out of the hospital. His stern profile daunted her. This was the side of him presented to the business and professional world. A man in command—strong, shrewd. Without such leadership qualities he could never have carved out an empire for himself in this still-primitive land. But Libby knew a tender, softer side of Vance. An ache passed through her body as she wondered if she would ever see that side of him again.

She shielded her eyes from the blazing sun. "I'll give Winslow your love. See you later," she called after him. But Vance made no acknowledgment. The driver returned to the taxi and they sped off into the afternoon traffic.

A searing pain racked her body as her eyes followed the path of the taxi until it was out of sight. Afraid she'd break down in front of the concierge, she hurriedly followed him into the building and accompanied him to the third floor. "The building has security, Mrs. Anson. No one can come in through the door without a special key. You'll be safe here."

Libby whispered a quick thank-you and closed the door, falling against it as deep, choking sobs welled up inside her. Huddled there, next to the door, she gave way to her despair. Pressing her knuckles to her mouth, Libby sobbed out the anger at the unfairness of it all, her grief at Vance's resistance to her overtures of love. Mingled with her sorrow over his blindness was this devastating ache she couldn't assuage. The loss of his sight seemed to have robbed him of the ability to reach out to anyone. Particularly his wife.

Unaware of the passage of time, Libby relived those first moments in the hospital room when she'd thrown her arms around him and kissed him. Caught off guard, he'd responded with all the old hunger and passion—until he remembered his blindness. Then he'd pulled away and retreated behind his barriers. It occurred to Libby that the Vance she'd fallen in love with was still there, buried beneath layers of pain and bitterness. But how to find that man again? She *had* to if she ever hoped to experience happiness again. Raging against the fates that had brought them to this point would accomplish nothing.

On a sniff of determination, Libby wiped her eyes and moved away from the door, suddenly aware of her surroundings. She made a cursory inspection. The serviceable, two bedroom flat, which came furnished in pseudo-Mediterranean decor, was obviously not a place that reflected Vance's personality but one that simply met his needs when he worked in Nairobi.

Kicking off her sandals, she padded into the kitchen and warmed a tin of soup so she wouldn't feel faint again. But halfway through the meal she lost her appetite completely and headed for the bathroom to take a shower. A while later, after making the phone calls to reassure the families, she prepared for bed.

Though her French lace nightgown would be wasted on Vance, she had a need to pretend she was a bride as she slipped beneath the covers. He'd shattered her dreams of what their honeymoon was going to be like. Libby couldn't forget that she should have been lying in his arms right then, loving him and being loved. His determination to send her out of his life tormented her, but her body begged for sleep.

She finally succumbed, burrowing her face in the pillow where the faint trace of Vance's cologne still lingered. Hot tears trickled out of the corners of her eyes as she fell into a troubled sleep.

The flat was pitch-black when she awoke hours later. A noise disturbed her and she sat up in bed with a start. Had Vance come home?

Her ears strained to listen as she heard him bumping into something and swearing softly under his breath. He hadn't yet had a chance to feel his way around the flat. She threw off the covers and slid out of bed, hurrying into the hall to turn on a light.

Out of the corner of her eye, she caught a glimpse of movement. Vance had just settled down for the night in the guest bedroom. His dark tousled head moved restlessly on the pillow as he attempted to get into a comfortable position. His bronzed shoulders were visible above the covers.

Libby's heart melted with love for him. Full of resolve, she moved over to the bed and put a hand on his leg. "Vance?"

He jackknifed into a sitting position, taking part of the covers with him. "What do you think you're doing?"

Libby recoiled instantly. His furious outburst reopened the wound inflicted earlier. "I came to tell you you got into the wrong bed." She moistened her dry lips. "You promised me that when we were together again, we'd go someplace private, and you'd never let me out of your arms. I've been living for that, Vance. I've ached for you...."

In a lightning move, he flung himself from the bed, and shrugged into the same brown robe he'd worn at the hospital. "Since you're awake, we might as well have a talk, Libby. Come into the other room."

No matter how hard she tried to brace herself against his continual rejection of her, she couldn't get used to the searing pain that accompanied it. As she followed him into the living room, she had to force herself to keep from helping him. He bumped into several pieces of furniture before he reached his destination. He looked haggard—tortured even—and raked a suntanned hand through his dark hair. Libby caught glints of the rich mahogany color as he disheveled it with his fingers.

Concern for his well-being took precedence over her own pain. "Are you hungry, Vance?"

His chest rose and fell. "Food's the last thing on my mind."

"I'm sure it's been a horrendous day, but you still need something to eat," she said softly. "I'll make supper." Not waiting for a response, she hurried through the dining area to the kitchen. In a matter of minutes, she had water boiling and sandwiches made.

"I told you. I'm not hungry." She hadn't heard him come to the doorway.

"Perhaps not, but I am." She put a plate of ham and tomato sandwiches on the table, then followed with the instant coffee, which she preferred to tea. Vance was still standing at the kitchen entrance as she sat down and took a bite of sandwich. She fastened her attention on him. Despite his dark tan, he looked like a man who bore the weight of the world on his shoulders. Dr. Stillman's observation about Vance's depressed state worried her, as well. "Won't you at least sit down while I eat? You look exhausted."

He rubbed the back of his neck, something she'd occasionally seen him do when he felt frustrated or preoccupied. "Did anyone call the flat while I was out?"

"Not that I'm aware of. I fell asleep shortly after the concierge let me in. Were you expecting an important call?"

He dismissed her question with a vague gesture, putting his hands in his robe pockets. "Have you had any recurrence of the nausea you experienced this morning?"

In the face of everything, his protective instincts still prevailed, making her love him all the more. "No. None. I'm convinced it was simply low blood sugar and no sleep. The person I'm worried about is you." She couldn't keep her concerns bottled up any longer. "You're barely out of the hospital. I'm sure Dr. Stillman would agree with me that—"

"Don't say another word!" he cut in on her almost brutally. "You sound suspiciously like a wife, and I have enough to deal with already." His face darkened. "How can I make you understand that I'm not the same man you knew in England? You seem to be treating this as a temporary setback. I assure you it isn't."

Her chin went up. "I can remember telling you the same thing a couple of years ago, when you forced me to get back on King after I fell off. I broke two ribs and felt like death, but once my injuries had healed, *you* made me go down to the stable and climb back in the saddle. When everyone else was ready to coddle me, you ignored my misgivings and persisted until I found the courage to face my fear. I was so terrified, I didn't think I'd ever be able to get close to King again, but the Vance I knew wouldn't let me give up!"

His face closed as he advanced slowly into the kitchen, feeling for the nearest chair. "I'm blind, Libby. Blind!" he said with such emotion the cords stood out in his neck. "You could have no possible conception of what that means. We're not talking about a few broken bones. I'll never be able to read another blueprint...survey a site—let alone drive to one—never take another step without a damn cane to keep me from crashing into walls. How does it feel to know your husband can't see to protect one hair on your head?''

In a fierce, sweeping gesture to drive home his point, his hand accidentally knocked over the coffee mug nearest him and it pitched to the floor. Libby jumped up from the table in surprise and dashed to the sink for a cloth.

''Dear lord—did I burn you?'' He felt his way over to the sink, his hand brushing against her forearm.

''No. It's nothing,'' Libby hastened to reassure him, hearing the torment in his voice. ''The coffee wasn't that hot.'' She felt a curious languor as his hands ran up and down her bare arms. They stood so close, the scent of her perfume and the male tang of his skin combined to form a heady stimulant. His breath on her lips sent a voluptuous warmth through her body. ''Only a few drops spilled on my nightgown.'' Unable to do otherwise, she melted against him.

For a split second, his dark face descended and she lifted her mouth expectantly for his kiss, aching for him with every heartbeat. Then she heard his sharp intake of breath before he pushed her away from him.

A moan sounded low in her throat as he wheeled around and felt for the nearest chair back. The unexpected moment of closeness and intimacy had passed, leaving her totally bereft. He stood rigidly by the chair while she cleaned up the liquid on the floor. Fortunately the mug hadn't shattered.

''I'm not only helpless, I'm dangerous.'' The self-loathing in his voice shocked her.

''Don't talk like that, Vance.'' She gave in to the impulse to press herself against his back, sliding her hands up his arms. But he moved away abruptly with none of his earlier gentleness, forcing her arms to fall to her sides. ''You've always made me feel safe. Your blindness has nothing to do with it. You must know that.''

He swore violently as he turned around in her direction. His handsome features were distorted by lines of rage. "I can't even find you!"

"The accident barely happened. Give it more time. Give us more time," she begged.

"Time?" A harsh laugh ripped out of him. "You don't seem to understand, Libby. My blindness isn't going to get better. Your husband isn't whole. When are you going to face that fact?"

"You're feeling sorry for yourself again." It killed her to say it when her instincts told her to wrap her arms around him and absorb his pain. His head reared back in fury, but she forced herself to go on. "All right, you've lost your sight, and I can't imagine how it must feel, but you seem to have lost your nerve as well as your charm along with it."

A dark, ruddy color stained his cheeks. "Who taught you how to hit a man below the belt? I would never have suspected it of you."

Libby hugged her arms to her chest, shaking at her own temerity. "There's a lot you don't know about me. Unfortunately, this accident has revealed something about you that I never knew before. I just hope you don't treat your employees like you're treating me. You have an enviable reputation, according to Dr. Stillman. He told me how successful and brilliant you are—a man in charge of your own destiny. It might be to your advantage if everyone goes on believing that! Don't worry, I won't let on to anyone that you're giving up so soon."

"That's right, because you won't be here!" he rasped, slamming his fist on the table so hard the sandwich plate jumped.

Libby shrank from his anger. "I can see there's no getting through to you right now. I'd hoped we'd be able to work things out, but it seems I was wrong."

"Libby!" he shouted as she fled past him and ran to the bedroom, slamming the door. He wasn't far behind. Before she could catch her breath, the door flew open. "Don't ever run out on me like that again." His voice contained a veiled threat. "I'm not through with you."

She spun around on her heels. "I thought you were. What I don't understand is why you married me in the first place. We took vows before God. Didn't they mean anything to you?"

"There was no altar, Libby."

In shocked silence, she took a step toward him. The blood drained from her face. "You mean, because we weren't married in a church you don't consider the ceremony binding? How dare you say that?" A blackness swept over her. "Here." She pulled off her wedding rings and dropped them in his robe pocket. With their bodies almost touching, she could detect the sudden pallor of his face.

"Stay here alone, my beloved husband. Wallow in your dark world and enjoy your misery. Don't ever take risks. Don't ever let anybody get close to you. Least of all your *wife*." She closed the door in his face, already regretting her impulsive actions.

Those rings had been part of her. The night he'd flown to Switzerland to surprise her with the engagement ring was the most thrilling night of her life. Until then, she hadn't known the depth of his love; now, she'd thrown the rings back at him. It hadn't even been twelve hours since they left the hospital. Vance was still just as intent on forcing her to give up, and once again, she'd let him get to her. *Would she never learn?*

Throughout the rest of the night, Libby went over their bitter exchange in her mind. They'd both said things that were calculated to injure beyond the ability to heal. Like water bursting over a dam, words had tumbled out of her mouth—words she couldn't take back. In the heat of the moment, she'd forgotten his suffering because she'd been so overwhelmed by her own needs.

His tortured attempt to explain what blindness was like began to make inroads on her mind. Guilt consumed her as she absorbed the full impact of what he'd been trying to tell her—to impress upon her. How had she dared say those things to him? If their positions were reversed, wouldn't she have done everything in her power to break off with Vance? To free him from a bondage not of his own choosing? And yet...*wouldn't she have wanted him to fight for her anyway? Wouldn't she be devastated if he gave up so easily?*

Not having closed her eyes all night, Libby was grateful for morning. She felt an overpowering need to talk to Vance one more time. If they could start over again... If there could be a new beginning...

She'd never been prone to headaches, but when she got out of bed, the pain at the back of her skull made her slightly ill. Her eyes burned. Had Vance lain awake all night, too—waiting for morning to come so he could send her back to England? She hadn't heard a sound since awakening.

After making the bed, she dressed in aqua-colored cotton pants and top, securing her hair with a chiffon scarf in a lighter shade of the same hue. A minimum of makeup and she was ready to go in search of her husband. In spite of everything that had happened, in spite of everything that had been said, she was determined to make their marriage work.

The moment she stepped into the hallway she heard voices coming from the living room. They were too low for her to distinguish individual words, but their visitor was male.

Like an incoming tide, rage churned inside her again. Vance had done this to prevent a scene. He'd taken every precaution to ensure that she didn't miss her plane, cutting off their last hope of communication. *What could she do? Pretend to be too ill to leave the flat?* Vance would never believe her. He was prepared for every conceivable argument. The only thing to do was let him have his way. She'd go to the airport. But it didn't mean she'd get on the plane. What Vance didn't understand was that for her, a life without him couldn't be any worse than being blind.

"Mrs. Anson." A man with a build like a rugby player and a shock of white-blond hair stood up as Libby entered the room. She estimated him to be in his late forties. His glance was sharply appraising, which didn't surprise her since Vance had told no one of her existence. "I'm Martin Dean, filling in until the boss is back in the office. It's a pleasure." He extended his callused hand in greeting.

"How do you do." Libby shook his hand, looking from him to her husband. Her pulse quickened as she gazed at Vance. He stood in the middle of the room with his strong legs astride, dressed in blue jeans and a dark green pullover. He looked relaxed and at ease, and certainly nothing like the implacable man he'd been last night.

"I'm so sorry about barging in on your honeymoon. Vance is a deep one. May I congratulate you on your marriage? I had no idea until moments ago that Vance had a wife to come home to." His glance flicked to the taller man. It gave Libby a chance to study Vance's second in command. Trusted enough to be put in charge during Vance's absence, he'd nevertheless been kept in the dark about their marriage. "Your taste is impeccable, old chap." He grinned at her as he spoke. "No wonder you kept flying to Switzerland."

"Well, she's here now, thank God," Vance murmured with such emotion Libby was stunned. "Sweetheart?" He held out a beckoning hand. Libby couldn't believe this was happening, but she needed no prodding to lessen the distance that separated them. His hand closed possessively over hers as soon as she reached him. "Did we waken you?" he whispered, brushing his mouth against her cheek the way he used to.

Libby could hardly breathe. "No. In fact, the flat seemed so quiet, I thought you'd gone out."

His arm went around her slender shoulders and he pulled her close. "Not a chance, Mrs. Anson." Then he lowered his mouth to hers in a hard, lingering kiss. The contact made Libby reel. Caught off guard, she swayed and felt his other arm go around her for support.

Martin started to chuckle. "Maybe I'd better wait outside in the Land Rover. Or better yet, why don't I go to work and pick you two up this afternoon? I shouldn't have intruded."

Vance took his time about lifting his head. "Don't apologize, Martin. You had no way of knowing I was keeping Libby to myself. Fortunately, my beautiful wife and I will have all the time alone we want when we get to the farm." Her astonished gasp was stifled once more by the pressure of his mouth as he sought a more satisfying response from her. For some unknown reason, Vance wanted the other man to witness this display of husbandly affection. He demanded her cooperation with the matchless mastery of the old Vance.

He drank deeply, pulling her into a whirlpool of desire. She forgot everything. The pain, the cruelty, the rejection. Obviously reluctant, he let her go. "Maybe you'd better grab a bite to eat before we embarrass Martin further," he whispered after lifting his head. "He's offered to drive us to the farm. If your case is packed, he'll take it out to the car."

Without his arm around her shoulder, Libby would have fallen. She averted her eyes from Martin's interested gaze. "I'll hurry." She headed for the kitchen in a weakened state, full of unanswered questions. But whatever Vance's motives, he didn't plan to send her away after all.

She made toast and poured milk, but her thoughts centered on her husband's sudden about-face. Her fingers went to her lips, which still tingled from the pressure of his kiss. Had he, too, regretted their words of last night? Did he waken wanting to start all over again? She hadn't imagined the hunger in his kiss. At some point, he'd forgotten the other man's presence, just as she had. Surely this meant that Vance wanted to make their marriage a real one, that he'd realized how cruel, how unnecessary, it would be to go on denying them what they both craved. The farmhouse represented home and a fresh start.

When Libby finished eating and she'd tidied the kitchen, all the bags had been taken out of the flat. Martin assisted Vance to the Land Rover. This time, Vance climbed into the back seat ahead of Libby. When it was her turn, he grasped her wrist and pulled her onto the seat beside him, pressing a kiss to the side of her neck.

"You can put the rest of her things in front with you, Martin," he called out the open window. "I intend to enjoy my wife's company during the drive."

"I understand completely." His man-to-man laugh floated through the open window as he arranged the luggage to his satisfaction. Occasionally, Libby caught him glancing inside at the two of them. Their marriage had clearly come as a shock to him. Perhaps he felt slighted because Vance had chosen to keep it a secret. After all, the two men worked closely together.

While Martin was busy, Vance took advantage of their brief privacy. He reached for Libby's hand and held it fast. But his tone was reserved, even formal. "The discussion I wanted to have with you last night got out of hand. There are things we need to talk over in a rational manner—as you so succinctly pointed out to me—so we're going to the farm where the atmosphere is more conducive to the kind of conversation I have in mind. I'd appreciate it if you'd hold your questions until we're alone. I prefer to keep our private life private." He whispered the last as Martin opened the door and swung his compact body into the driver's seat to start the motor.

Vance's words dashed her hopes once more. His amorous performance had been solely for Martin's benefit. An ache passed through her body as Vance lifted her hand to his mouth and kissed the palm—a calculated cruelty under the circumstances.

Unwilling to suffer through this alone, Libby nestled closer to Vance and brushed her mouth against his. "How far is the farm?"

His chest rose and fell noticeably. "An hour from Nairobi."

"How lovely." She spoke the words at the corner of his taut mouth and had the satisfaction of feeling his body tense.

"Martin...as long as you've offered your services, will you drive us by the Bantu pharmacopoeia on our way out of the city? Libby shouldn't miss it."

Vance had once written her about the native bazaar, which sold everything from monkey skulls to fried porcupine. She derived immense pleasure from the fact that her nearness forced him to rely on counteractive measures to combat it.

She settled against him, her hand still in his. If nothing else, a sight-seeing jaunt would give her more time like this, sitting quietly close to Vance. More time to feel like the hopeful young bride she was pretending to be.

CHAPTER THREE

THE MAU ESCARPMENT rose nine thousand feet. The farm was located near the six-thousand-foot level where the air was thinner. A few tufts of white cloud passed overhead, but it was a beautiful June morning, warm and fresh.

As the Land Rover drew closer to its destination, Libby noticed the absence of villages. In their place were patches of evergreen forest separated by wide expanses of grassland. An occasional native tending a flock of impala would wave to them as they drove farther into the highlands.

Libby lifted her head from Vance's broad shoulder and studied his aquiline features. He'd fallen asleep, head resting against the back of the seat. The dark shadows beneath his eyes led her to believe he'd tossed and turned all night, as she had. He looked vulnerable, with his compelling mouth softened in repose, and with tendrils of dark brown hair spilling over his tanned forehead.

She relished the feel of his ripcord-strong leg brushing against hers. Her glance rested on their hands entwined on his hard thigh. In sleep, Vance hadn't let go of her. All the bitterness of the night before seemed to have faded away, but she knew this respite was only temporary.

Vance awakened when Martin drove the Land Rover around a sharp corner and geared down to a dirt road. Tightening her grip on his hand, Libby gazed out her window. Cultivated fields with row after row of blossoming fruit trees greeted her vision. In the far distance she noticed a copse of oak trees. The car drew closer and she saw a snowy-white Dutch farmhouse glittering in the sunlight. The oaks formed lacelike shadows against the exterior.

The house reminded her of the charming Hampshire barns she'd seen in England. Vance explained that a transplanted Dutchman had come to Kenya in the late 1800s, and had incorporated the local one-story farmhouse with the Amsterdam gable—the important gable placed over the front door to contain the attic. The effect was exquisite. Farther on she could see a group of outbuildings surrounded by wildflowers of every hue and description.

"How incredibly beautiful it is," she cried as Martin stopped the Land Rover. Vance relinquished his hold on her, and Libby climbed out of the seat to survey her kingdom. She sucked in her breath. "Oh, Vance...I had no idea." She gazed heavenward. At this elevation, the sky was an intense blue, and the temperature that of a delightful spring day. There would be plenty of light for a herb garden.

Her gaze was drawn to the window facing west with its leaded panes. Frothy lace curtains peeked through. Vance had accomplished more than she'd realized since they made their wedding plans. A fresh wave of love and longing swept over her. Her eyes sought her husband, but he was busy helping Martin with their bags.

Libby remained motionless, worshiping this tall, darkly tanned man who had such inherent authority and power, yet could display infinite tenderness. Her eyes played over him, admiring the fit of his clothes, the lean tautness of his muscles.

"I can't wait to see inside, Vance," she called out and started to pick up some of the supplies stowed in the back of the car. Though she wanted to put her arm through his, she didn't dare. His efforts to do as much as possible without Martin's assistance pleased her. She didn't want to interfere or impede his progress, particularly in front of the other man. If her eyes didn't deceive her, he seemed to move with a determination that had been missing yesterday. Perhaps he'd put on this air of confidence for Martin's benefit, but the results were gratifying. Surely Vance could see that he functioned beautifully when he gave himself half a chance.

"Libby?" Vance paused on the porch while Martin went inside the house with more luggage. "Will you forgive me if I talk to Martin before he goes back to Nairobi? I promise it won't take long."

She walked up to him and pressed another kiss to his firm chin. "Don't worry about me. I'm dying to explore the house."

Vance stood there with his hands on his hips, an expression of barely controlled patience on his face. Martin reappeared in the doorway, then, but fortunately, Vance was facing Libby.

She smiled at the other man. "Thank you for driving us out here, Mr. Dean. You can't possibly know how excited I am to be home. And now I'll leave the two of you alone so you can talk business." She raised up on tiptoe and kissed her husband lightly on the lips, aware of the other man's scrutiny.

"Please call me Martin, Mrs. Anson. We don't stand on ceremony here. My wife and I will be extending an invitation to dinner one day soon. That is, when Vance here is willing to share you. Or should I say if?" he amended with a grin.

Libby's gaze flicked back to her husband. "We'll look forward to it, won't we, Vance?"

"Marj is an excellent cook." It was an answer of sorts. Libby squeezed Vance's hand and proceeded into the farmhouse.

Her first impression was one of airiness and light-white walls with splashes of vivid color from native African fabrics and dark-toned woods indigenous to the area—exactly as she and Vance had planned. The reality far surpassed her wildest expectations.

The central hallway was flanked on one side by a living room and library. To the right was the dining room and beyond it, the kitchen. The bedrooms were located at the rear.

Libby mused that Vance must have moved heaven and earth to have the walls treated and ready for paint this fast. The only rooms ready for occupancy were their bedroom, the kitchen, bathroom and library. Everything else required paint, floor coverings and window treatment—projects she and Vance could carry out together. She experienced a great thrill as she imagined the finished interior with colorful native area rugs and furniture, interspersed with treasured family heirlooms. Her eyes grew misty. How she'd longed for this moment...

Excitement gripped her as she carried her train case to the master bedroom—the room with the Swiss lace curtains showing through the window. From a brief comment she'd once made about that particular fabric, he'd created a room of great beauty. It meant that he'd planned to marry her long before they'd even become officially engaged; something she hadn't really known before this moment. This knowledge took her breath away. She sank down on the double bed and gazed about her, taking in the armoire, built-in dresser and fabulous area rug of African origin. Vance had chosen an apple-green motif with native accents. She couldn't fault his taste.

A photograph propped on the dresser drew her attention. Vance must have had it enlarged from pictures he'd taken when he visited her in Lausanne. She stood beneath a Gothic arch at the Château de Chillon with the battlements in the background. She'd worn her black hair even longer then. The fact that he'd gone to the trouble of preserving this particular picture touched her deeply. He'd proposed to her on that trip. Libby had a dozen favorite photographs of Vance she intended to add to the dresser. She refused to entertain any ideas of leaving Kenya, and certainly not on this glorious day.

On her way to the kitchen, she peeked inside the other two bedrooms. The one on the north would make a perfect nursery. She dreamed about having Vance's baby, perhaps in a year or two. Already, her mind was filled with ideas for decorating the empty room.

The other bedroom came as something of a surprise because the walls needed to be repaired. There was evidence of a fire, though she couldn't tell how recent. Vance had purchased the farm when he first came to Kenya, but he hadn't started major renovations until he asked Libby to marry him, and it had stood vacant for several years.

She knew the kitchen was her favorite room in the farmhouse as soon as she entered it. A huge, ceramic-glazed fireplace with authentic blue Delft tiles dominated one wall. It dated back to the building's origins, and the scene was as quaint as the old quarter of Amsterdam. She understood why Vance had been charmed by its beauty. From the previous owner, he'd inherited an antique oak table—rectangular in shape—with four intricately hand-carved chairs. Obviously he intended to keep and restore as much of the original farmhouse as possible. The whole idea enchanted Libby.

Sitting at the table, she could look out the mullioned windows to a glorious vista of blossoming fruit trees that stretched as far as the eye could see. The delightful view captured her attention for a long time. Vance had found paradise here. Resolving to share it with him, she took a deep breath and looked about her to see what should be done first. Martin had brought in the boxes containing food stores. She'd be able to acquaint herself with the kitchen's layout as she put things away.

A double sink and new plumbing had been installed. The old oak floors had been sanded and stained to a gleaming amber color. She reflected that in everything he did, Vance was a perfectionist. He'd created an efficient, fully functional room, yet he'd retained all the warmth and charm intended by the first owner. What an irony that anyone so artistic, so aware of beauty, should have his sight taken away...

By the time Libby had emptied the boxes it was noon, and she found that she was hungry. Hoping Vance's appetite had returned, she proceeded to fix lunch, then walked through the house to the library in search of both men. Martin would probably need a meal before he returned to Nairobi, she thought. But when she reached the front hall, she heard the sound of the Land Rover. Vance was in the act of shutting the door.

"Vance, I was just coming to tell both of you that lunch was ready."

He stiffened at the sound of her voice. "He had to get back in a hurry. We're alone, Libby."

Something in his tone sent an apprehensive chill down her spine. Gone was the attentive lover of the morning.

"I'm afraid our lunch isn't terribly interesting. Soup and sandwiches. But I promise to do justice to our evening meal." When he didn't respond, she turned and walked back toward the kitchen. He followed with some difficulty, feeling the walls until he entered the kitchen and found a chair. To her surprise he sat down and began touching everything carefully. She moved a plate of food in front of him. "I used the ham from last night, but maybe it doesn't appeal."

"I couldn't care less what I eat. However, I happen to know you're an excellent cook, so stop hovering." Libby swallowed a retort as she saw him actually pick up a sandwich and begin to eat. Not only that, but he seemed to enjoy it and ate with apparent appetite. She'd begun to wonder how long he could go without sustenance. He ate everything on his plate and drained his glass of milk with few accidents.

"Did you and Martin get some work done?" she asked conversationally. Vance was being too quiet, and she feared that his silence portended more depression. Right now she didn't want anything to mar the magic of their first meal together in their new house. For a little while she wanted to pretend that everything was normal.

"Unfortunately not. He found your presence to be a more interesting topic."

Libby took a deep breath. "Why didn't you tell him about our marriage? It put him in an awkward position."

He lay down his fork. "If you recall, the wedding was so quickly planned, it would have been difficult to let anyone know. Besides, I'd intended to introduce you to my staff at a formal reception, here at the farm. But I don't want to discuss that right now."

Libby eyed her husband, unable to gauge his mood. "The farmhouse—the orchards—everything is so beautiful, I can't believe it, Vance."

His features hardened perceptibly. "Save it, Libby. Now that we have all the preliminaries out of the way, I want to talk to you, but I want your promise that you won't interrupt until I'm finished."

She blinked. "You have it."

"I hope you mean that," he said in a sober voice, "because when you hear what I have to say, you're not going to like it." His words struck a chord of fear in Libby's heart.

"When you appeared in my hospital room yesterday—unannounced *and* uninvited, I might add—I could have strangled you with my bare hands."

The venom in his tone made Libby quail. She looked down at her empty plate. How could he change from loving husband so quickly?

"I believe you when you tell me you didn't get my letter. Knowing you as I do, you wouldn't have left a stone unturned to talk to me on the phone, if it *had* arrived. Unfortunately, if you'd waited in London another twelve hours after hearing about the accident, you would have received it. In your haste to fly to my side," he began in that hateful, mocking tone, "you made your presence known to everyone in sight. By playing your wifely role to the hilt in front of Dr. Stillman, you've caused a series of consequences that have put you, me and my company in more jeopardy."

"What?" she gasped aloud, lifting her head.

His beautiful mouth curved into a cruel line. "You promised."

At this point, Libby started to shake and couldn't stop.

Vance pushed himself away from the table and stretched his long legs to the side, his arms folded across his chest. "I have an enemy, Libby. Someone within my company is out to ruin me, and maybe they've succeeded. The mine collapse was deliberate sabotage with devastating results—two murders, and my sight gone."

Libby didn't move a muscle, but the shocking revelation had turned her eyes an inky purple color.

"Your arrival on my doorstep has complicated things because you could be used as a target, as well. It's truly unfortunate that Martin called Dr. Stillman to check on my status this morning and found out my wife had arrived on the scene. The news is all over Nairobi by now. The damage is done. If I know you, you've already seen the back bedroom. Someone set fire to the farmhouse the night before our wedding—one of the reasons I had to cancel our honeymoon so abruptly.

"At first, I attributed the fire to a disgruntled orchard worker on a drunken spree—something of that nature—but I didn't want to take any chances of it happening again when I brought you here to live. I'd hoped to have the room completely repaired and the culprit caught. But for some time, we'd been having problems at the mine and that week, they got worse. The rest, you know."

Everything he said made a horrible kind of sense to Libby.

"Whenever there's a mine disaster, a board of inquiry meets to investigate. If they can prove negligence, then my company will be dissolved and I'll be barred from ever practicing in Kenya again. News of this sort travels fast. I seriously doubt I'd be given a license to work anywhere on the African continent, especially if I'm blamed for the death of two men."

She heard the deep sigh that emanated from him, and in it, the pathos.

"Waking up blind made me see more clearly than ever that I'm a target. The person responsible must be elated that my sight was taken during that cave-in. But what he—or the group of them—doesn't know, is that I intend to fight them. I have a large company with a big payroll. Hundreds of families are looking to me for their livelihood and I'm not going to let them down if I can help it. This kind of tragedy gives the mining and engineering industry a bad name, particularly in Kenya where mining is at the embryo stage."

Libby studied her husband, spellbound by everything she heard. She'd had no idea . . . no idea at all. . . .

He stared in her direction, almost as if he could actually see her. "I wish I hadn't married you," he said, and his voice was too hard, too uncompromising for pretense. "I want an annulment as soon as possible. Unfortunately, I need to ask a favor of you first."

Silence pervaded the room for a long moment. His desperate situation shattered all her hopes that they could have a future together. She was too numb to speak.

"Libby?" A tiny nerve leaped at the corner of his mouth.

She sucked in her breath. "You told me not to interrupt." She had the satisfaction of watching his hand tighten into a fist against the wall.

"I phoned Charles Rankin from the hospital as soon as I could think rationally. He's agreed to put his affairs in order and fly down here to represent me."

"Thank God!" Libby blurted out, unable to stop herself. If anyone could help Vance, Charles would be that person. Almost twenty years his senior, Charles made a formidable Queen's Counsel and had served as best man at their small garden wedding.

"Hiring Charles is no guarantee, Libby, but he's the only man I trust to make sense of this nightmare. We've talked constantly on the phone, planning our strategy. But your arrival has changed things considerably." He paused as if searching for the right words. "No one knew of our marriage before the accident, and as I told you, I'd planned to have a formal reception announcing it after we returned from our honeymoon. The accident put an end to that. I didn't want a soul to know I had a wife. Whoever is out to destroy me might use you as a means of getting to me. A wife makes a man vulnerable in a dangerous situation like this. Under the circumstances, I didn't want you anywhere near me, for your own sake and mine."

Libby understood so much now—so much. Unable to remain in a seated position any longer, she rose to her feet. "Did you explain all this in the letter?"

"In essence, yes."

"In other words, my coming has put another whip in their hand." Her voice caught. She needed time to sort everything out, to look at the situation from this new perspective.

He rubbed his neck. "Exactly. And after you went to sleep last night, I phoned Charles to let him know you'd come. He agrees with me that the proverbial cat is out of the bag. He feels we have to change tactics."

What was he saying? Libby held her breath.

"If you go back to London now, you might make matters worse. A wife who would run at the first sign of trouble could harm my image with the officials investigating the disaster. Not only that, a united front would instill confidence in the families who rely on me for their living. A wife has a softening influence—a subtle form of power—but it works." His lips twisted almost menacingly.

"I didn't mean to compound your problems."

He shifted in his chair and sat forward. "What's done is done. However, we do have a slight edge. No one knows I suspect foul play except for Charles. If the enemy can be kept in the dark a little longer while Charles does some snooping on his own, it might work to my advantage." His fingers curled around the knife handle. "It would mean pretending to settle down to wedded bliss. I'm to act the part of the besotted bridegroom in public. Everyone will believe that I haven't a care in the world...not with a beautiful new wife in my arms to keep me fully occupied."

When we both know the idea is abhorrent to you. His behavior in front of Martin Dean was no longer a mystery.

"We would have a marriage in name only, Libby. But no one in the world would know that, except for us. And Charles, of course."

"Of course." The bitterness rose in her throat like gall.

His dark eyes narrowed pensively. "I wouldn't ask this of you, but other lives are involved. I can't even give you a timetable. Charles will be flying in some time next week. He'll be our houseguest both here at the farm and at the flat."

"I see." Libby stared straight ahead, seeing nothing.

"More than a few eyebrows would lift if I put in an appearance at the office this week with you living here at the farm. Martin knows we're alone, and by the tone of his voice, I could tell what an impact you made on him. He's not usually so quiet. He told me that if I had any brains at all, I'd just hibernate here with you. In about an hour, everyone at the office will have heard that I'm enjoying my honeymoon. But the decision is yours." He inhaled sharply. "Is it too much to ask, Libby?"

Yes! she wanted to shout at the top of her lungs. Vance sat there within touching distance—the gift without the giving. How could she bear it? Did she love him enough to sacrifice her own needs? To put his above all other considerations? Her lips trembled as she attempted to find the words. Hadn't she wanted to be his wife under any and all circumstances? Were the fates mocking her now?

Libby looked over at the man who held her heart in the palm of his hand. Emotion swelled within her breast at his dark, brooding expression. Wasn't it possible that in time, living together as husband and wife would break down his resistance? He'd loved her enough to marry her. She knew that beyond any doubt.

Libby moistened her lips nervously. "I realize you have an entire company to consider. Now that you've explained everything, of course I want to help."

"Thank you, Libby." His chest heaved with what she felt to be relief. "I'll take every conceivable precaution to protect you. As soon as you're free to return to London, I'll make this up to you.''

It was on the tip of her tongue to tell him there was only one way he could do that. ''If it's all right with you, I'd like to shower and change. It'll take me the rest of the day to unpack.''

He stood up. ''This is your home for the time you're here. Do whatever you please. It's not necessary to ask my permission. There's only one more thing I'll ask of you.''

Libby's head came up as he reached into his shirt pocket. ''It's vital that we make our marriage look as real as possible. I'll have to ask you to wear these rings for a while longer.'' He put them on the table. ''If you need me, I'll be in the library on the phone.'' He left the kitchen, feeling along the wall as he went.

The amethyst caught the sun and acted as a prism, throwing tiny rainbows onto the ceiling. Now she understood why Vance had held her left hand during the ride to the farm. He didn't dare let on to Martin the true state of affairs between them.

Libby stretched out her hand and slid the rings back in place. She'd bitterly regretted her thoughtless action of the night before. If she had her way, they'd never leave her finger again.

After doing the dishes, she hurried to the bathroom off their bedroom and took a quick shower. The fixtures were new and gleamed a spotless white. It occurred to her again that her husband had performed a minor miracle here in the remote highlands.

She dried herself with a fluffy towel in her favorite periwinkle color and slipped into jeans and a cotton sweater. To keep the hair out of her eyes, she brushed it to one side and braided it with deft fingers, tossing it over her shoulder. She spent part of the afternoon emptying suitcases, hanging clothes in the closet and putting her toiletries in the bath-room.

With her personal unpacking taken care of, Libby headed for the kitchen to prepare a special dinner. There was a cer-tain comfort in knowing that Vance was just a few rooms away instead of thousands of miles away on another conti-nent. What Vance had told her made her want to be within touching distance every second.

In her opinion, Charles couldn't get here fast enough. Vance needed help desperately. She was glad he had the support of Martin Dean, but it crossed her mind to wonder why he'd made no mention of Peter Fromms, another company executive. Their friendship went back to their university days. Once, in London, Libby had met Peter at a party given at the Anson home. She had the impression, then, that the two men were close. And yet, Vance had asked Charles to be his best man. When Libby questioned his choice, she'd been told that Peter couldn't get away. The vague answer hadn't satisfied her, but she'd been too busy to worry about it. Perhaps now that they were settled in at the farm, she could find the appropriate moment to ask Vance about Peter.

Deciding that their first dinner alone warranted some-thing special, she put on a lightweight yellow linen dress, and wore her hair flowing over one shoulder. For an added touch, she put on the gold earrings Vance had given her the year before. Though he couldn't see her, she felt better get-ting dressed up, and dabbed on some Madame Rochas as a finishing touch.

"Vance? Dinner's ready."

He sat in a swivel chair at a large desk, speaking into a Dictaphone. He switched it off at the sound of her voice and turned in her direction. "I'm not up to much where food is concerned. You go ahead without me."

"It's a light quiche and salad. You need a break," she persisted.

He rubbed his eyes with the palms of his hands. He looked drained. "I'm waiting for an important call."

"You can take it in the kitchen. The quiche is coming out of the oven now, so don't be too long." She turned on her heel and walked through the living room, listening for his footsteps as she entered the kitchen.

A tossed green salad with vinaigrette dressing stood ready in the refrigerator. She'd found a bottle of imported Riesling on one of the shelves and put it on ice for the occasion. After taking the quiche from the oven, she stepped outside to gather a mass of wildflowers. She arranged them with unconscious artistry in a blue and white porcelain bowl— part of a collection Vance had purchased with the farm.

Minutes went by. The lightheartedness she'd felt earlier while preparing their dinner dissipated as she began eating her salad, still alone at the table.

Vance's sudden appearance in the kitchen caused her heart to race out of rhythm. He'd decided to join her, and it was all she could do not to jump up and throw herself in his arms.

"You've put flowers on the table. I detect salvia," he said, sitting down in the same chair he'd used at lunch. His hair looked disheveled, as if he'd run his hands through it many times.

"Mmm. And dahlias, petunias, stocks and sweet canna. Oh, Vance, there's a perfect place to grow herbs outside the kitchen window. It's delightful."

"You sound happy, Libby," he murmured, picking up his fork. A troubled look marred his intelligent face.

"Why wouldn't I be? You've made the farm breathtaking. No wonder you never wanted to come back to England. The fragrance from the blossoms is heavenly. I can't wait to explore the property. Let's go riding first thing in the morning.''

"That's impossible." He swallowed his first bite of quiche.

"I don't see why. Dr. Stillman said you were totally fit and that you could take up your usual activities. Besides, Diablo must have missed you these past few weeks, and I'm sure he needs the exercise.''

His mouth tightened into a thin line. "My farm manager takes care of the livestock, Libby." That shuttered look was back. "If you're so anxious to get out in the open, take the Jeep and drive along the access roads through the orange groves. You can see a great deal that way.''

"I'd prefer to ride. If it's all right with you, I'll saddle Diablo.''

"Diablo is too spirited, even for you.''

"Then ride double with me. We've done it dozens of times. Just a slow walk around the property. Surely that's not too much to ask.''

There was a sustained silence before he reached for his wineglass and sniffed the bouquet. "I didn't know I had any wine in stock," he commented, ignoring her plea about riding.

"I found it while I was putting away the groceries. I wanted this to be a kind of celebration. Our first dinner alone in our new home.''

A dark flush stained his hard cheekbones. "As I told you earlier, you have a talent for cooking. Everything is delicious, as usual.''

"Thank you." She pushed away her half-empty plate. "Would you like to listen to some music after dinner? I brought a new recording of the Brahms First Piano Concerto with me. I think you'll like Graffman's interpretation.''

"Not tonight, Libby."

She excused herself from the table. "What would you like for dessert?" she countered on a lighter tone. "A fig? Or a mango?"

"Nothing for me."

Her eyes went to his empty coffee cup. She reached for the pot and went over to his place to refill it. Inadvertently, her leg brushed against his arm at the same moment that her hair trailed across his cheek. She heard his quick intake of breath before he unexpectedly got to his feet, throwing his napkin on the table. It took the empty wineglass with it.

"Good night," he muttered. In his haste to get away from her, his shoulder bumped against the doorjamb. Several well-chosen epithets escaped before he disappeared from view.

Later, after the dishes were done, Libby walked past the library. As she feared, the sofa bed that stood opposite his desk had been made up; perhaps the farm manager had helped him with it. Vance was already huddled under the blankets and if he wasn't asleep, he pretended to be. She tiptoed down the hall to their bedroom and prepared for bed. Would he ever relent and let her help him relax . . . let her give him the comfort she craved to shower on him? Hot tears drenched the pillow. What irony that after waiting almost three years to become his wife, she now lay alone in his bed, feeling more empty, more lost, than she'd ever felt in her life. . . .

CHAPTER FOUR

A KNOCK ON THE BEDROOM DOOR awakened Libby from a sound sleep. A glance at her bedside clock said it was after 10 a.m. She couldn't believe she'd slept so late and sat up in the bed, pushing her hair out of her eyes. "Vance? Do you need something?"

"I'm sorry to disturb you," he said through the partially open door, "but since I'm leaving in a few minutes for the rest of the day, I didn't want you waking up, wondering where I'd gone."

Libby shot out of bed and hurried over to the door, opening it wider. "I thought you didn't want to be seen at the office."

"I'm not going to Nairobi."

"Where then?"

"If you must know, I'm going to pay a visit to the families of the two men who were killed during the mine collapse. I couldn't go to their funerals. They live in a Bantu village farther up the escarpment."

"How will you get there?"

"By car, naturally." His mocking voice hinted at a sense of humor that had been buried since the accident.

"I mean, who's driving?"

"James, my farm manager."

"Let me drive you there instead."

"No, Libby. I told you before. I want you to keep a low profile until an arrest is made."

"Surely there can't be any harm in going with you? Mightn't it look better if we were together while you visit the bereaved families? You told me a wife gives you more credibility. And if people in your company already know that I'm here, it might seem odd if I didn't go with you. Please, Vance. I want to get out and see something of the country while I'm here," she added on a sudden burst of inspiration. "What could it hurt?"

He had the harassed look of a man who'd reached the end of his patience. "I need to go right away. Rain is forecast for later in the day, and once it starts, the track into the village becomes a swamp."

"I can be ready in five minutes."

He raked a bronzed hand through his hair. "Better bring a sweater. The air gets cooler the higher we go, particularly when mist accompanies the rain."

She closed her eyes, inordinately pleased that Vance had agreed to take her with him. She resolved not to keep him waiting any longer than necessary. "I'll hurry."

"I've made coffee and toast. Better eat something, first. While you're doing that, I'll have James bring the Jeep around the front."

Her eyes rested on his retreating back. In khaki shirt and trousers, his lean, bronzed body looked more appealing than ever. She assumed the farm manager had assisted him in getting dressed. Libby wondered how long Vance could go before he'd be forced to ask her for help, but she'd worry about that another day.

After a quick shower, she put on jeans and a pale blue blouse with collar and cuffs. Her Scandinavian-knit sweater would do as a wrap. With so little time to get ready, Libby left her hair loose, only brushing it until it fell about her shoulders. She'd apply lipstick after breakfast.

The same kind of fluffy white clouds she'd seen yesterday dotted the blue sky as she maneuvered the Jeep along the farm road to the paved highway twenty minutes later. She was used to driving Land Rovers and trucks with trailers on the stud farm, and the Jeep held no mysteries for her. Fortunately, Vance didn't seem to be nervous, and this in turn made her relax. She imagined he had much weightier matters on his mind.

"Do we turn left now, Vance?"

He nodded. "Follow the road for approximately nineteen miles, until you come to a three-way stop. At that point I'll give you further directions. How's the fuel?"

"It says full."

"Good. Let's go."

She saw more of the same scenery they'd passed yesterday, miles of evergreen forests, interspersed by patches of grass, stretching in every direction. So far, there were no humans in sight. Libby felt a sense of isolation that made her thankful to be enclosed in the car with her husband. She had a healthy regard for adventure, but she was in Africa, and it wasn't like driving from London to Hammersmith. Vance would know what to do if she came up against a problem—like a mother lion searching the bush for her lost cubs. She'd heard of things like that happening to tourists out in the high country. But with Vance, she could face anything. The fact that he was blind didn't change that. If only he understood...

They'd traveled about ten miles along the highway when Libby became aware of a noise that sounded like thunder. Vance must have guessed her thoughts, because he turned his head toward her. "Don't be alarmed. A herd of gazelles grazes along this side of the forest. Besides zebras, they're the animals you're most likely to see on this trip."

Libby expelled a sigh. "Anything else I need to know about?"

The ghost of a smile hovered on his well-formed lips. "I doubt we'll run into any lions or cheetahs in this neck of the woods. They prefer the dry thornbush country. If you want to see that sort of wildlife, you can visit the Masai-Amboseli Game Preserve. It's only a few hours from Nairobi in the opposite direction."

His comments put her at ease, as she knew they were intended to. If she'd obeyed her impulses right then, she'd have stopped the car to make love to him. But she also knew that if she initiated anything, it would backfire on her and she didn't want to ruin this outing.

By the time they reached the spot Vance had told her about, Libby could see a little higher up the escarpment. The forest thinned out to a stand of bamboo and beyond that, moorland. She noticed a distinct drop in the temperature, not only from the thinner air, but because the clouds were clustering in preparation for a storm.

"If you look carefully, Libby, you'll see a track running between the road we're on and the road turning left. Follow it straight into the forest. It winds for about five miles and comes into a clearing filled with huts."

Libby hadn't noticed the track until Vance pointed it out to her. "Should we put the Jeep in four-wheel drive?"

"Not necessary at this point."

Libby started the Jeep again and crossed the highway onto the grassy track, which was little more than a trail, barely discernible through the dense evergreens. With the sun hidden behind clouds, the forest was so dark, it felt like evening.

"Tell me about the men who were killed."

Vance shifted his weight on the seat. "They were hardworking family men who were originally herdsmen from the

Bantu tribe. When I opened up the Naivasha mine, they came to work for me. Kenya often experiences seasons of drought, and this forces the men to look for other jobs.

"These two decided to learn the mining business and stayed with it because it meant a steady income and medical care for their families, plus a pension plan. The reason I'm visiting their wives today is to express my condolences, and also to explain that the company will fully support them."

Libby eyed Vance thoughtfully. He would be generous; she knew that about him. The fact that someone apparently harbored jealousy over Vance's success was still incredible to her. She prayed that whoever was responsible for the cave-in would soon be caught.

As Vance had indicated, the track ended in a clearing with about two dozen huts. A group of children dressed in bright cotton shorts and dresses caught sight of the Jeep and ran toward it.

"*Jambo!*" Vance called to them from the open window and they conversed back and forth with him in Swahili.

"What are you saying to them?"

"I've told the children why I've come and asked them to tell the women. They're shy. It's better to let them make the first move."

Libby watched in fascination as the children ran off and talked among themselves. It didn't take long before they were back, the oldest boy, about twelve years of age, acting as spokesman. Another long conversation followed. Vance frowned and Libby could tell immediately that something was wrong.

"What is it, Vance?"

He rubbed his chin. "They say I'm not welcome here. The women won't talk to a . . . murderer. I was afraid this might happen. As far as they're concerned, anything to do with me or my company brings death.''

"Do they speak English?"

Vance nodded.

"Then maybe the women would talk to me. Do they know you lost your sight in that accident? It could make all the difference in how they feel."

"Forget that tack, Libby."

"Vance, don't you see? They're grieving, and they would understand that I, too, am in pain. We share a common bond. Perhaps if they realized that, they'd listen to you. It's worth a try."

"I shouldn't have brought you with me." He slapped his leg in exasperation. "You're my wife. So as far as they're concerned, you bring bad luck, too."

"Not if I have anything to say about it. Vance, you came here to try to comfort these people. Let's not leave until we've exhausted every possibility."

In a lightning move, he reached out his hand and grasped her wrist. "Look, Libby. These women are feeling hostile at the moment. You have no knowledge of their ways and beliefs. I refuse to put you in a potentially explosive situation."

His grip tightened, and she put her other hand on top of his. "At least ask the children if the women would be willing to talk to me. All they can say is no."

Tension filled the silence as he let go of her wrist and pulled away from the hand that had been caressing his. After a few seconds, he said something else to the children and they ran off. Neither he nor Libby spoke while they waited.

It wasn't long before the children all came back one more time. The spokesman pointed to Libby. "You can go. But not him."

"I don't like this, Libby. I'd rather you didn't do it."

Her heart pounded hard. "I want to. I admit I'm nervous, but I have an idea how those women feel."

His face wore a haunted expression. "At the first sign of trouble, you start screaming and don't stop."

"I promise." She slid out of the Jeep before he could change his mind and followed the children to a hut near the edge of the forest.

As she walked around to the entrance, a woman in a flowered dress stepped out, holding a baby, with a toddler clutching her skirt. Another woman stood in the doorway. Their dark eyes stared at her without the slightest glimmer of welcome. Libby felt no fear, only sorrow that they'd lost their husbands. Vance, after all, was still alive....

"I'm Libby Anson," she began, putting her hands in her back pockets.

They said nothing. She cleared her throat.

"I know your men are gone, and nothing can bring them back, but my husband wants you to know that the company will pay your support for as long as you live."

The women simply stood there. She had no idea if she was getting through to them.

"It's true that my husband is still alive, but the accident hurt him, too. He can't see anymore, and because he can't see, he doesn't think he's a man. And because he doesn't think he's a man, he wants to send me away. I want to stay because I love him the way you loved your husbands."

The women in the doorway took a step closer.

Libby took a deep breath and went on. "My husband's suffering, and if you would let him help you, it would help him. He couldn't come to see you before now because he just left the hospital yesterday. First thing this morning, he told me he wanted to come here to see you, to make sure you were all right—to tell you not to worry about money."

"Some people say the accident happened because of him," the woman nearest Libby said in a slow, measured voice.

"Does it make sense he would cause an accident that would leave him blind?" Libby reasoned, staring at the woman until she averted her eyes. "He's trying to find out who caused the accident, and when he does, that person will be punished."

"Where are your babies?" the other woman asked shyly.

Libby swallowed hard. "As long as my husband is worried about you and his company, there will be no babies."

The two women looked at each other, then back at Libby. "You want babies?"

"Very much," came her heartfelt reply. "I want sons and daughters as fine as yours."

"Your husband cannot see your eyes?"

"No. Everything is like night."

"You don't need to see to make babies." The other woman smiled as she spoke.

"You're right, but Mr. Anson is a proud man. Do you know what that means?"

Both women nodded. One of them said, "When my husband did not come back with meat from the hunt, he ran off for three days. I could not find him anyplace."

The three women gazed at one another with understanding.

"Mr. Anson is out in the car. He'd like to tell you these things himself, if you would follow me." Without waiting to see whether they did, Libby walked back to the Jeep. Vance stood in front of the hood, his arms folded across his chest, waiting.... A reassuring sight.

"It's all right, Vance," she murmured, wrapping her hand around his upper arm. Some of the rigidity left his body when she touched him. He unexpectedly put an arm around her shoulders.

The two women weren't far behind. They spoke to him in Swahili, sounding reserved at first, but he answered them warmly and a long conversation took place. Libby needed no translator. Everything Vance felt was expressed in his eyes and his gestures. He pulled two envelopes out of his breast pocket and urged them to take the money. After a slight hesitation, they accepted his offering, then grew more animated.

Vance's hand tightened on Libby's shoulder. "They seem very taken with you, and they've invited us to stay for a meal. We can't refuse," he muttered beneath his breath so only Libby could hear. "Taste everything offered."

Something in his manner told her she was in for a few surprises and that he found the situation amusing. She slid her arm around his waist. "I'll eat everything you eat."

Together they walked to a cleared space outside the huts, which appeared to be the communal dining area. Long poles were crisscrossed over an open fire, and a baglike holder hung suspended above the flame.

Vance planted himself on the hard-packed earth and pulled Libby down beside him. Wooden plates and implements were soon placed in front of them, the plates filled with various foods that Libby found totally unrecognizable but quite edible. On her first try, she thought the meal tasted something like cornmeal, sweet potatoes and rubbery chicken. Best of all, everything was hot, and the fire felt good. The sky looked ever more threatening as giant thunderheads moved swiftly overhead, ushering in a cold wind. The children seemed impervious to the chill.

"We've got to get out of here, Libby. I can smell rain in the air." She and Vance finished their food and as politely as they could explained that they needed to leave before the storm hit. They thanked their hostesses profusely, then hurried back to the Jeep.

The first drops of rain spattered the windshield as Libby started the motor. The downpour began in earnest before she'd gone a mile. Vance hadn't exaggerated. Beneath the sparse grass oozed thick, slippery mud, several inches deep. To Libby it felt like driving on a skating rink, particularly since they were on a decline all the way to the main road. It was all she could do to keep the Jeep from veering sideways off the track.

"I can't seem to control the car." Libby could hear the panic in her voice.

"In that case, slowly pull over to the side and turn off the motor. We'll wait for the cloudburst to pass."

"I'll try," she said unsteadily, but when she started to do as he suggested, the Jeep turned a half circle. In her effort to right the car, she overcorrected, sending them over the side of the track.

"Vance! We're going to crash!" A split second before the impact, Libby felt his arms enfold her shoulders, shielding her face. She waited for the splintering of glass and crunch of metal, but all she heard was the soft brush of pine needles against the body of the car. The rain came down harder.

"We're all right, Libby," he murmured in husky tones, pressing feverish kisses on the side of her neck, crushing her close to him until her shivering stopped. "Just well and truly wedged in a copse of pines."

A shudder racked her body and she clung to him. "I've never been so frightened in my life. The wheel spun right out of my hand."

"Shh." He lowered his mouth to hers. "It's over. Don't think about it." And then he was kissing her with such hunger it was impossible not to respond. The accident had set their emotions at a pitch. Libby couldn't get enough of him as one kiss became another. The ecstasy of being in his arms like this surpassed her daydreams and even her memories.

Hardly conscious of what she was doing, Libby's hand slipped inside his shirt, seeking the warmth of hair-roughened skin. "I love you," she whispered, covering his face and eyelids with kisses.

Suddenly he expelled a long breath and sat back in the bucket seat, putting her gently but firmly away from him. "You seem to be fully recovered from our little mishap. I'm going to get out—try to tell how far down we're mired."

Libby needed the few minutes that he was outside to pull herself together. Being so rudely transported back to reality was more shocking than the accident had been. Perhaps he'd only intended to comfort her, but the raw passion of his kisses set her aflame. The strong physical attraction had always been there, from the moment they met, but now it was like a conflagration. If he touched her one more time, she felt as if she'd go up in smoke.

THE RAIN STILL CAME DOWN steadily as Vance climbed into the Jeep. He shrugged out of his parka and tossed it in the rear, then wiped his muddy hands on the paper tissues Libby gave him. "We're stuck here until the rain stops. When you can see to back out, I'll push. I think we'll be able to get ourselves up to the road without too much trouble. As far as I can tell, nothing is broken or even badly damaged."

"How long do you think it will rain?"

"Not much longer, but while we're waiting, we might as well get comfortable. Turn on the ignition and I'll switch on the heater."

It wasn't long before the interior of the Jeep was warm and cozy. Vance reached around the back of her seat and rummaged for a satchel on the floor. He opened it and pulled out a bottle of brandy.

"Behold—my first-aid kit, but this is one of the rare times I've had to use it." He felt for the glove compartment and lifted out a thermos, unscrewing the cup. "Would you like a drink?" He carefully poured the brandy, spilling only a few drops, and offered her the first sip.

It was on the tip of her tongue to refuse, but she changed her mind. She had to do something to counteract his nearness. "Thank you." The fiery spirits burned their way down her throat and she coughed.

When she handed him the cup, he quickly finished off what he'd poured. Then, far too soon for her liking, he poured himself another drink. Vance was normally a temperate man, and it surprised her to see that he intended to get drunk. There was no other explanation.

Some time later, she realized that the rain had stopped. She'd been so busy observing her husband's behavior, she hadn't noticed. "Vance?"

"Mmm?"

"Shall we try to get ourselves out now? It's not raining anymore."

"In a minute."

"But it's getting late. It'll be dark soon."

"It's always dark," his voice slurred. "Don't be afraid."

She took a deep breath. "I'm never afraid with you."

"Then you sure as hell should be." On that note, he made himself more comfortable and fell asleep with his head against the window.

Not knowing whether to laugh or cry, Libby rested her head on the back of the seat. Today's experience had shown her yet another side of her husband. If loving him meant spending the night in a muddy bog in the highlands of Kenya, so be it. He couldn't ignore her presence indefinitely. There had to come a time when he'd lower his defenses, and she planned to be there, waiting. She turned her head to look at him. Little by little, her eyelids drooped.

The next thing she knew, Vance was shaking her awake. "Libby?"

She lifted her head, surprised to discover she'd been asleep against his shoulder. A huge white moon had appeared over the top of the escarpment. No trace of clouds remained.

"What time does my watch say?"

She rubbed her eyes and sat up. "Ten forty-five."

He muttered something unintelligible beneath his breath. "I apologize for passing out on you like that."

"It's all right."

"No, it isn't," he snapped, his voice sharp with self-loathing. "I should be getting down on my knees to you for smoothing the way with those women today. That took courage." He reached behind him for his parka and opened the door. "Put it in reverse, and when I say go, press the accelerator. The mud's a little firmer now, and we just might be able to perform the required miracle." After a dozen tries, Vance managed to shove the Jeep over the lip of the track. He jumped inside, almost insultingly enthusiastic to be free of their predicament. "Let's go home."

Home. Whether it was a slip of the tongue or not, Libby obeyed his edict with the greatest of pleasure.

CHAPTER FIVE

THE FIRST WEEK PASSED swiftly as Libby settled into a routine at the farm. By tacit agreement, Vance didn't go into the Nairobi office. He ate breakfast with Libby and they listened to the news over the radio. Then Vance spent the rest of the day with his farm manager, coming home only for lunch. Libby, in turn, did the laundry, cleaned the house and made preparations for dinner. She treasured her evenings with Vance the most.

Vance would come in, shower and change. They'd enjoy a sherry on the *stoep*, then eat dinner together. Sometimes they spent the evening quietly, listening to classical music; other nights the conversation was intellectual and stimulating... and impersonal. They talked about everything except themselves, their feelings, their future. But it was a start; Libby knew that. And anyone seeing them would have assumed they'd settled down to wedded bliss. No one could guess that intimacy between them—the intimacy afforded by marriage—was nonexistent.

Since that night in the forest, Vance had made every effort to keep physical as well as emotional distance between them. And Libby knew that as soon as he started putting in full days at the office, the nature of their time together would change once again. Not only would he be burdened with worry over the board of inquiry findings, but once Charles arrived, Libby doubted she and Vance would have any time alone at all.